Marked by Destiny Duology

ASSASSIN'S DESTINY and ELFAEN SWORD

What readers are saying...

"It is a real page-turner—I didn't want to stop reading until I found out what was going to happen next. I will definitely be looking out for other books in this series!"

"This is a great read. Good wins over evil! I look forward to more from Suzann Fortunato!"

"Fortunato has a great ear for dialogue, and her youthful protagonist, who finds herself unexpectedly burdened with vampire-kllling powers a la Buffy, rings true."

"An excellent debut novel by this up-and-coming new author! Had a hard time putting this one down to do things like work and laundry!"

"Kept me reading till the very end. Written very well and will keep so I can read again. Can't wait for the second story to come out... I hope there is one! :)"

"Little twists and turns kept the reading exciting, fresh and interesting... I couldn't put the book down and cannot wait for the sequel! AWESOME!"

"A great series for teens and tweens that reminds the reader of the Shadowhunter chronicles.…. If you're looking for something with heroic heroines, lots of action, magic, mystery, and a truly awesome world-building plot, come to this series. You'll find assassins, elves, vampires, demons, and more."

A YA URBAN FANTASY
DUOLOGY SET

MARKED
BY
DESTINY

INCLUDES
ASSASSIN'S DESTINY
AND
ELFAEN SWORD

SUZANN FORTUNATO

STAKES & SWORDS
PUBLICATIONS

Design and distribution by Bublish

ISBN: 978-1-647047-73-3 (paperback)
ISBN: 978-1-647047-72-6 (eBook)

ASSASSIN'S DESTINY

Marked by Destiny Book 1

PROLOGUE

H E STRODE THE STREETS AS ONE OF THEM, though he was anything but. Those around him were human, frail helpless mortals who thought they were strong. Some even thought they were invincible, with their guns, knives, poisons, and black belts in karate. But they were all weak, susceptible to disease, and easily killed by lack of food, water, or air. He found them all quite laughable.

No matter where he chose to live, the pimps, gang- bangers, serial killers, and drug dealers caused him no more fear than any of the other humans. He could move faster, hit harder, and leap higher than any of them. He could recover from gunshot or knife wound, or drowning. Drugs and poisons didn't keep him down for long, and in fact, alcohol only made him a bit tired. Falls from even the greatest of heights merely dazed him. Bones straightened and repaired themselves, muscle and sinew knitted together, skin mended itself, vision returned, hearing restored. Unless his heart was pierced through the middle or his head severed from his body, he would always heal completely. Sunlight didn't even cause him trouble, as long as he wore his dark glasses. Neither did garlic or holy objects. And, Blood-Hunters were born, not created from a bite like those movie creatures called, vampires. Those myths were mere nonsense.

Aidan didn't feel the heat any more than he felt the cold. He favored wearing black leather and didn't care if he stood out among the crowds of men in short sleeved shirts and women in tank tops and shorts. What did it matter? He'd be here for a while and then move on. Just like always. Nobody would know him beyond the superficial pleasantries of business deals; not the occasional Shifter, Elfae, or Blood-Hunter who crossed his path, let alone any human. He hadn't even seen an Elfae in months or, an Assassin in decades, which was fine with him. Elfae were born with magic abilities, making them tricky to deal with, and the Assassins of course wanted to kill him. The Shifters were all right, for the most part, as were the other Blood-Hunters. Shifters had that animal thing going on, which at times made them rather touchy, and the majority of Blood-Hunters were devious and lacked self-control which made them dangerous to be around. His kind usually either stayed in the Coven they'd been born into, or became a loner. Aidan was a loner. He preferred it that way.

At the moment, he was a Blood-Hunter on a mission, and with any luck the box would be in his possession before the week was out. Nothing else mattered.

CHAPTER ONE

SKYE WALKED THROUGH THE MAIN DOORS OF Cardiff High School, her mind still half on the strange dreams she had the night before, dreams she'd been having most nights lately. They had become more and more intense, but also confusing. They were like watching bits and pieces of horror movies with vampires and werewolves and demons. Where was her mind getting this stuff, anyway? Certainly not from her day-to-day life and she almost never watched scary movies.

Rachael, Skye's best friend, fell into step with her as they headed down the hallway to their lockers.

"Cute shoes!" Rachael gasped. "Where did you get them?"

"I'm not telling. You'll only run out and buy the very same ones."

Rachael made a face. "Imitation is the sincerest form of flattery." Her brow furrowed. "Or something like that."

They arrived at their lockers, which were side by side, and Skye fiddled with the padlock. "I wish I could just wave a magic wand and this thing would open," she muttered.

"Did you let Todd know if you'll be his date at the graduation party yet?" Rachael asked, as she pulled books from her locker.

She applied some extra pink lipstick and peered into the mirror on her locker door, then ran a brush through her silky blonde hair and adjusted her bangs. She gave Skye a sidelong look, but Skye pretended like she hadn't heard, while she silenced her phone for class.

"Well, did you?" Rachael demanded. She'd put her lipstick and brush away, closed her locker and stood at rapt attention, waiting for Skye's reply.

Skye tucked a dark auburn strand of hair behind her ear. She straightened her peach-colored skirt and cream lace blouse, stalling just to tease Rachael.

"Well?" Rachael prompted.

Skye grinned. "Yes, I did. I told him I'd meet up with him there."

"I knew you would! He really likes you. You two are going to be great together!"

Skye lifted one shoulder and gave a half-hearted shrug. "For all the good it will do. You and I are leaving for San Diego a week after graduation and Todd is going to be going to college in another state. I'll probably never see him again."

They started walking to their first class, amid the throng of students. "You never know what could happen. Maybe he'll miss you so much he'll transfer back here."

Skye rolled her eyes. "I doubt that seriously, Rachael."

"Well, you never—"

The bell started to ring. Skye and Rachael dashed down the hall, dodging kids who'd been hanging out in the hallway. They tried to go through the door at the same time, and finally squeezed through. The bell stopped ringing just as Skye slipped into her seat.

"What are you going to wear to the party?" she asked. "Do you know yet?"

Rachael sat in front of Skye but turned to face her, just as the teacher walked into the room. "I'll figure it out at the last minute, like I always do."

Skye looked up as the teacher began to discuss the day's lesson, but her mind was elsewhere. How wrong was it that Todd had just realized he liked her one week before they graduated from high school? What was the point of being with him at the graduation party, anyway? A couple of weeks from now, she and Rachael would be leaving Coronado Island for San Diego, a short ferry ride from pier to pier. Their parents would help them get settled in, buy them some furnishings and supplies and all that, but then their folks would head for home and the two of them would start fixing up their two-bedroom apartment. Todd Fairbanks was blessed with a chiseled jaw, wavy blond hair, and a goofy sense of humor she liked a lot, but there would be no future with him. The truth was she liked him, but not *that* much. Not enough to try and have a long-distance relationship.

"Skye? Hello, earth to Skye."

She jerked at the sound of the teacher's voice. "Um, yes, sir?"

"We're waiting for you to read from page 132 of the text. You *do* have your text book with you?"

"Ah, yes," Skye fumbled through the pages and while she did, the teacher used the time to speak to the class.

"Just because graduation is only a week away, doesn't mean we don't have to finish up with our assignments. You may be finished with all your homework and tests for other classes by now, but you still have one more test in this class, on Wednesday, and you had better be ready for it." The teacher turned back to Skye. "Are you ready Ms. Falco?"

"Yes, sir. From the second paragraph?"

The teacher nodded, and Skye began to read aloud.

At lunch break, Skye joined Rachael at their table, along with a couple of their friends.

"I'm so glad we're almost done with this," Sarah announced as she plunked her cafeteria tray onto the table. She adjusted her round, Harry Potter-like glasses as she sat down.

Angela echoed her sentiments. "Me too. What is this food, anyway?" Her blonde brows folded into a frown.

"Meatloaf, duh!" Sarah said and dug in. "The mashed potatoes are kinda runny, but they taste pretty good."

"Of course, it's good!" Rachael said after taking a bite. "Our parents pay like a zillion dollars a year for us to go to this place. The food better be good."

"Skye, you haven't said anything about Todd and the graduation party. You *are* going to be his date, right? Aren't you excited?" Angela asked.

Skye looked up to see all eyes on her. "Um, yeah, of course."

"You don't sound like it," Sarah pointed out. "What's wrong?"

Skye stalled by taking a huge bite of her meatloaf. She really didn't want to explain to her friends that she really wasn't as into Todd as they thought she should be, because Sarah, Rachael and Angela all thought Todd was fantastic. Any one of them would've been thrilled to be his date for the party.

Rachael answered for her. "She thinks there's no point in them getting together because we're going to be going to college here in California and he'll be going to school out of state."

7

"So what? The two of you can still have fun at the party," Sarah replied.

"Time's up people. Lunch is pretty much over. Back to the grind." Angela stood and the others did the same, taking along their trays of empty plates.

Skye made it through the rest of the day and tried not to dwell on those ridiculous dreams. Still, she found her thoughts wandering back to her most recent dream as she sat in Spanish class, and again while she was in Biology. Only during P.E. was she able to forget for a while, but even that was short lived. Somehow, she seemed faster and stronger, but surely that was impossible. Or so she thought until at one point she kicked a ball clear off the field. Kids jumped out of the way as the ball rocketed by, and then stared at her in amazement. Skye shrugged, not knowing what to say. It was probably just some weird fluke, but there was too much weird going on lately and she didn't know how to sort it all out.

After school, as she walked to her car, a brand new, red Chrysler 200 convertible, a graduation present from her parents, she looked up and noticed a man leaning on the trunk. He was impeccably dressed in dove grey slacks, soft leather shoes of the same hue, and a grey silk shirt with narrow black stripes running vertically. His hair was dark brown, on the longish side, and Skye thought she saw flecks of grey in it. His arms were crossed over his chest and he studied her, just as she studied him. She frowned. Who the heck was this guy? And why was he touching her car?

"Skye Falco, I'm John Preston." He reached into a pocket and pulled out a business card. He held it out to her.

Skye's frown deepened. "How do you know my name?"

"It was given to me."

"By whom?" Wouldn't her English teacher be proud? She finally remembered when to use 'whom' in a sentence.

"Take the card and you'll see."

Skye stepped forward and snatched the card from his hand, then stepped back to read it.

Bureau of the Extraordinary
American Division
John Preston
Handler

Beneath the word 'Handler' was a phone number. She looked at him. "I've never heard of the Bureau of the Extraordinary, and I still don't know how you got my name. What's this about?"

"You're having some dreams. Dreams you don't understand. Am I right?"

Skye was amazed and a little frightened that he knew so much. How could this man, a total stranger, know about her dreams? She hadn't told anyone about them, not even Rachael. She felt her heart pounding in her chest, but told herself to get a grip and answer the man. He was, after all, leaning on her car, so it wasn't like she could just ignore him, jump in and drive away. Well, maybe she could, but then she'd probably run him over and get arrested for murder.

"Ah, yeah, sort of," she mumbled.

"You are a gifted girl, Skye. Soon you will be able to see things others can't. You'll have knowledge of things most extraordinary, and you'll be able to do things even you will hardly believe. The Bureau knows this. You have a destiny, a career, if you will, which is probably going to be very different than whatever you had planned for yourself. Call me when you're ready." He walked away from her convertible and got into the grey Corvette parked next to her car.

Skye watched as he pulled away. How very odd. And intriguing. Not to mention, creepy. How could he know? How could this Bureau know? Who gave him her name? No one knew what she'd been going through lately. No one! What was this all about, anyway?

She watched as the man, John Preston, drove off, then slid his card into her purse and got into her car. She had a test to study for, and then she was done with high school, a thought that made her so happy it pushed away any other concerns. Weird guys in fancy sports cars, even ones who knew about her dreams, would just have to wait. She had to get home and study for that last test of her high school career, which would take place the day after tomorrow. Skye started her car and joined a few other stragglers leaving the parking lot, and headed for home.

She studied that night, her focus surprisingly good given her lack of quality sleep recently. Between the strange dreams and the excitement of the upcoming graduation, sleep seemed more of a luxury than a necessity.

As she got ready for bed, however, thoughts of Mr. Preston, his business card and his mysterious words crept into her mind. What in the world had he been talking about? Cryptic much? She drifted off to sleep, but it wasn't restful. Information about weapons floated through her mind: guns, knives, crossbows, and swords. Glowing eyes stared out at her from otherwise normal faces. She fought unseen foes, her entire concentration on punching, kicking, leaping and grappling at the wind, at the darkness. And all the while, John Preston's voice spoke to her, saying, *"Call me at the Bureau of the Extraordinary. You have a destiny."*

Skye woke up with a gasp, perspiring, with the sheets tangled around her legs. Light seeped into the room. She looked at the clock on her nightstand. Soon she would have to get ready for school, but not yet. She lay in bed and watched the sun light up the dim room. Soon the shadows faded and the muted gray of her surroundings become more distinct: the pale green of her walls, her dresser with her walnut jewelry box, the picture of horses running in a field that she'd painted as a child. As the sun rose higher, Skye could make out the detail in the design of her cherry wood four-poster bed, the lamp on her nightstand and the texture of the beige carpeting. Her quilt was a blend of cream, pale green, blue and soft yellow.

While her eyes saw her room revealed in the dawn of a new day, her mind tried to sort through her bizarre dream, but nothing made any sense. She was exhausted. That much was certain. The memory of John Preston was front and center in her thoughts. Maybe she should call him. Maybe he'd be able to explain to her about these crazy dreams. She didn't like that he knew so much about her when she didn't know him at all. And what *was* the Bureau of the Extraordinary? She untangled herself from the sheets and grabbed her iPad to Google it. Why hadn't she thought of that before? But her search was futile. Absolutely nothing came up. With a sigh of frustration, Skye set her iPad aside and wondered what sort of new weirdness today would bring.

School was pretty uneventful. Just the usual crush of humanity, except the hallways seemed extra loud with the voices of students excited by the coming summer vacation.

"I know what I'm going to wear to Todd's party," Rachael announced, as she and Skye retrieved their books for their afternoon classes. "It's a cute little dress and it's pink. Wait until you see it. You'll love it."

Skye smiled. "Naturally it would be pink." Pink was Rachael's favorite color.

"I'm going to wear my silver heeled sandals, and I'm going to look fabulous. You're coming to my house after school, right? To study for tomorrow's test?"

"Right." Skye was happy for Rachael that she'd found such a great dress, but her mind was on other things. She'd cut her leg shaving this morning, and although her leg had bled, it stopped even before she could reach for a tissue to soak up the blood. Strange. Usually, if she cut herself shaving, it would take two tissues to soak up all the blood.

And then, when she'd cut too close to her locker door, and the corner had scraped her arm; the scratch disappeared almost before she could say, "ouch." Double strange.

"Skye?" Rachael gave her a little shake. "Hey, you're off in some far distant land again. What's going on with you lately?"

Skye gently pulled away from Rachael's grasp. "It's nothing. I've just got some stuff on my mind, that's all. Come on. We have to get to class."

Rachael smiled. "Like Todd?" she asked, as they headed down the hall.

"No, I—"

"You're not worried about the test tomorrow, are you? Because there's no way you're not going to do well on it."

"No, it's not that."

"Then what?"

They ducked into the classroom and Skye slid into her seat. The teacher strolled in, and class started. "It's nothing really," Skye muttered and turned toward the front. Right, like she'd tell Rachael she'd had dreams about fighting fangy men with solid black eyes and others who changed back and forth from animal to human. Like she'd tell her how lately she was faster and stronger. How she could probably kick a ball to New York and back if she wanted to, and had recently beaten one of the track and field guys in an impromptu race at the park. And then there was the rapid healing, too. And like she'd tell her that some forty-year-old guy had known her name and given her his business card and that he worked for some weird and mysterious company that she knew nothing about. Right.

Skye followed Rachael home after school but once they were inside, she stopped dead, right in front of Rachael's dad's office. Had that glass case with the knives always been there? How had she not noticed that before?

"Rachael, I didn't know your dad had a knife collection."

Rachael turned to glance at the display case in her dad's office, just off the entryway. "Um…you didn't? It's been there for the last five years. I'm surprised you hadn't noticed it before." She shrugged. "But then again, it's not like we ever go in there."

Skye felt drawn to take a closer look. "Do you think your dad would mind if I…" Her words drifted off as she started to walk into the office.

"Uh, sure, go ahead." Rachael followed Skye into the room.

Skye stood in front of the wall display. She had no idea why these knives were so intriguing to her, but they were. Her palm itched to hold one, to feel its weight in her hand.

"May I?" She looked over at Rachael as she reached toward the cabinet door.

"It's locked."

"Oh." Skye drew back her hand, disappointed.

"Skye? What's going on with you? You usually look at shoes this way. Or maybe even eye shadow colors, but knives?"

Skye gave herself a mental shake. What in the world was she thinking? She smiled at Rachael, turned away from the knives and tried to laugh it off.

"Yeah, I'm being a dweeb. Sorry." Skye tried her best to sound normal, but those knives were beautiful! Even without reading the labels, she'd recognized some of them, knew their names. How weird. She tore herself away from the gleaming blades.

"I could use a snack, then let's get to studying for this test. I want to ace it and then it's party time this weekend!" Skye brushed past Rachael and headed for the kitchen. She'd been to Rachael's house so often that she treated it as if it were her own. Rachael trailed along after her and they put together a snack of apples smeared with peanut butter before hitting the books. Thankfully, Rachael didn't ask any more questions, and their study time passed uneventfully.

Skye stayed over at Rachael's house for a dinner of lasagna and garlic bread. Rachael's parents were there and her younger sisters, Emma and Cara, who were twins, made the meal interesting with their junior high school stories of their teachers, classes and their friends. Skye always liked having dinner at Rachael's house because of the twins, although Rachael often complained that the younger girls could really get on her nerves sometimes.

After dinner, Skye and Rachael went out for ice cream at Scoops, before Skye went home. While they were waiting to order, Skye felt an arm go around her throat. Without even giving it a second thought, Skye slammed her elbow into the gut of whoever was behind her, reached back, grabbed his shirt, thrust her hip back and flung him over her shoulder and onto the floor. And then, to her utter horror, Skye saw that the person behind her had been Todd.

The customers and employees of Scoops, stood gawking, but Skye dropped beside Todd and apologized.

"Oh no! I'm so sorry. I didn't realize it was you! Todd, Todd, can you hear me? Are you okay?"

Todd sat up and frowned at Skye. "What was that all about? A little extreme reaction, don't you think?"

"I know, I know, I'm so sorry!" Skye was shocked. She'd reacted instinctively, not fearfully, but how did she know how to do that? Plus, she was so embarrassed. She'd just dropped the guy who'd asked her to the graduation party! She offered Todd a hand up. He scowled and got up on his own.

"Skye!" Rachael gasped. "When did you start taking self-defense classes? You were awesome!"

"You were, actually." Todd grumbled. "I never would've figured you for it though."

Skye looked around at the customers and the employees. Some were smiling, others simply looked shocked. Some even started to clap. She was so relieved no one was calling the cops, and Todd seemed to be okay, but where had that burst of knowledge and strength come from? There was no time to dwell on it, however, because they were next in line. She gave her ice cream order and moments later she, Rachael, and Todd were sitting outside eating their ice cream.

"That was embarrassing. So, when *did* you start taking self-defense classes?" Todd asked. He seemed to have regained his sunny nature and smiled at her.

"And where?" Rachael added. She laughed. "It's all so un-ladylike that I'm surprised your parents had you take them."

"Ah, it was my idea actually," Skye stammered. Now why had she said that? "I thought it might come in handy now that we're going to be away from home and going to college and all that."

Rachael nodded. "Yeah, you're right."

Todd nodded. "Not a bad idea, really. But next time make sure who it is before you give them the old heave ho into the gutter."

Skye laughed, but then she saw something that made her nearly choke on her own laughter. The man who'd given her his business card, John Preston, stood not ten feet away. He wore light brown trousers and a milk chocolate shirt. He smiled knowingly at her. "I can explain everything. Call me." He nodded to Rachael and Todd, then walked away.

"Who was that?" Rachael asked.

"Someone I met the other day."

Todd frowned. "What was he talking about?"

"Oh, nothing. Nothing important." Skye forced a smile. "I guess I should be getting home."

Todd gave her a funny look. "Well, I'm going too then. See you at school."

Rachael gave Skye a confused look as they headed toward the parking lot as well. "Are you sure you don't want to tell me what that was all about back there?"

Skye felt her face grow hot. She didn't want to talk about her dreams, not even to her best friend. Not now anyway. "Which part? The man or the martial arts display?" Skye tried for a light tone.

"Both!"

"Not really. Maybe some other time." Skye got into her car. "I'll see you at school tomorrow." She drove off, leaving Rachael with a puzzled expression on her face. Oh well, Skye couldn't explain something she didn't understand herself, now could she?

CHAPTER TWO

THAT NIGHT, WHILE SHE SLEPT, SKYE FOUGHT men with scary black eyes and long pointy fangs. The fact that they had sharp, mammoth incisors and weird eyes didn't seem to faze her while she dreamed, but when she woke up, she was shaky and confused. Why couldn't she dream about something fun? But no, instead she dreamed about slugging it out with some freak-o monster guys. And what the heck was the Bureau of the Extraordinary? An American Division... meant what? That they had people all over the world?

Skye showered and readied herself for school. Once downstairs, she ate a bowl of granola and yogurt while reading the note her mom had left her about Sunday night's charity event. The event was one her mom helped plan to benefit the local animal shelter. Every year the shelter held an auction to raise money, which took place after a $100 a head dinner at the Hilton Hotel, on the huge patio along the side of the main dining room. It was the last big event Skye was expected to attend before leaving for San Diego, and to tell the truth, she didn't mind going to this particular function. Some were incredibly boring, but this event would feature at least a dozen dogs serving as co-hosts, wearing bow-ties or bows on their collars or ribbons in their fur. Skye loved dogs, but had never had one, due to her father's allergies. That's why he wouldn't be at this event, though he always accompanied her mom to every other charitable event she attended.

Skye rinsed her dishes, quickly ran upstairs to brush her teeth and put on some perfume and lipstick, and then grabbed her books, purse and keys. As she drove to school, she thought about what to wear for the charity event, which led her to thinking about what to wear to Todd's party. Maybe her blue chiffon dress for the charity dinner and the emerald green sheath dress for the graduation party. Skye smiled. Yes, that would be perfect. It was just the right thing for her last party with her friends.

After parking her convertible, Skye gathered her things and headed for the school's main entry. There weren't many students left milling around, and Skye looked up at the clock in the steeple above the doorway. She was running late. How had that happened? She didn't want to miss her test, so she bounded up the remaining steps to the entry, and then the next thing she knew the world turned upside down and she was laying on the ground. She sat up, and immediately felt the sharp pain in her ankle. She looked around her at her books and purse strewn on the pavement, and heard the bell for first period begin to ring. She'd worn heeled sandals with her jeans today, and they had been her downfall, literally, when it came to running upstairs. Her jeans were scuffed, her palms raw and scratched, and one sleeve of her red silk blouse was torn at the elbow. There was blood on her elbow as well and it throbbed. Great!

And then suddenly two hands slipped under her arms and lifted her to her feet. Skye turned her head to see none other than John Preston standing there. This time he wore olive green slacks and a caramel gold shirt with a tie that was a swirl of both colors and a little cream and black as well. The man dressed well, that was for sure.

Skye was shaken, both by the fall and by seeing him here. "Are you following me?"

"Here, let me get your things for you." He let go of her to retrieve her purse and books, and she teetered a bit on her heels. She couldn't put any weight on her one foot at all.

"I think I have a sprain, or maybe it's fractured," Skye said, while Mr. Preston gathered her things. "And my elbow is bleeding."

He smiled at her. "I think if you check again, you'll find that your elbow and ankle are not as badly wounded as you at first thought. Nor are your hands."

Skye frowned, but took another look at her hand and elbow. The skin was perfect, without blemish, without even a slight scratch. She blinked in surprise.

"But—"

"Check your ankle. Put some weight on it," Preston encouraged.

She did, and was stunned to find she could put her full weight on her foot, without even the slightest bit of pain. Skye slowly rotated her ankle, then looked up at Mr. Preston.

He gave her a crooked smile and handed over her things. "You're going to be late for your test. You'd better get going."

"But how—?"

"Go. And don't forget to call me when you're ready. I promise you, I'll explain everything." He turned and walked away without a second glance.

Skye didn't know what else to do but follow his instructions. She dashed the last few steps to the door and raced to her classroom. The test was in progress and the teacher frowned at her but handed her a copy of the exam anyway. Mr. Shepherd was cool that way.

Skye tried to concentrate on the test instead of all the other things that crowded her mind, and in the end, she was pretty sure she'd gotten at least a low B. She didn't even care, really. She had other things on her mind.

Skye somehow managed to get through Wednesday without further mishap. She'd created quite a stir when she'd appeared late to class with her sleeve torn, and looking disheveled. Rachael and her other friends quizzed her about her fall. Sarah offered to loan her a shirt to wear for the rest of the day, since she had an extra one on a hanger in her locker. Skye declined and simply rolled up her sleeves. As much as she loved Sarah, the girl's taste in clothing was nothing like Skye's and Skye could guess what sort of top Sarah probably had stashed in her locker.

She fielded their questions, but left out the part about John Preston and her miraculous healing. After everyone had a good laugh about her clumsiness, Angela asked if anyone had heard about how Mike McClure had fallen right in front of the cafeteria yesterday, and Skye was no longer the center of attention.

"So," Rachael began as they walked to their cars at the end of the day, "I think we should go over to Crate and Barrel and maybe Williams Sonoma to get some ideas for stocking our new place. Oh, and Pottery Barn! That place is fantastic, don't you think so?" She didn't wait for Skye's response before continuing. "Hey, how do you think you did on that test? I'm pretty sure I got a B, but it's hard to tell sometimes, you know?"

But Skye wasn't really listening. Bizarro dreams, miracle healing, and the mysterious John Preston. She couldn't seem to stop thinking about him and the Bureau of the Extraordinary. Not only was she dying to know what was happening to her, but she was also a little annoyed that he didn't just come right out and tell her instead of making cryptic comments and mysteriously showing up here and there. She'd had enough. She stopped walking and started fishing through the contents of her purse.

"Skye?" Rachael had taken several steps past Skye, then turned and walked back to her side. "What's going on? Did you even hear anything I said to you?"

Skye continued to look through her purse. She intended to give Mr. Preston a piece of her mind. "Yeah, but right now I'm looking for something."

"Okaaay, you know you're acting weird, right? You sure that fall didn't rattle something in your head?"

"Argh! Where is it?"

"What? What are you looking for?" Rachael's tone held both annoyance and worry.

Skye found the business card, and let out a sigh of relief. She straightened and smiled at Rachael. "Yeah, sorry. I'm fine. It's just been a long day. Oh, and I think I probably got a B on the test, and all the stores you mentioned are great. Let's go soon and check them out."

Rachael nodded. "Okay. I'll see you tomorrow." She climbed into her blue Murano, gave Skye a wave, and drove out of the parking lot.

Once Rachael was gone, Skye pulled John Preston's business card from her purse. She stared at it, as though it might reveal the answers to all her questions. She'd have to call him. Was that healing thing just a coincidence? And what about the speed and strength she'd noticed lately in P.E. and at the park when she'd challenged Bart Kelly to that race? And the spontaneous self-defense skills. A fluke? Oh, and her fascination with Mr. Perry's knife collection? What about that? She hadn't wanted to let on to Rachael, or even admit to herself, how much those knives had interested her. In fact, she'd had to bite her tongue over dinner so she wouldn't ask Mr. Perry a bunch of questions about them.

"Argh!" Skye shoved the card back into her purse. She was being ridiculous. There were only two more days of school, then no more tests or papers due. Graduation was this weekend, and the party was right after. On Sunday there was the Pause for Paws event for the Dog Pack Shelter, and somewhere in there she and Rachael would browse for ideas at three very upscale stores and plan their futures. Everything was going to be great!

She started the drive home, and got caught up in traffic. She knew the streets were busy this time of day, but there was an accident at Eagle Ave. and Bayside which slowed things down even more. She stopped at a red light and started to reach for a CD to play, when a strange sensation overcame her. She felt as though every hair on her body stood at attention, and her skin prickled. It wasn't an uncomfortable sensation, but it certainly was strange. She looked up and her eyes immediately fell on the man crossing the street in front of her. There was something about him that was odd, but she couldn't put her finger on it. Well, except for the obvious. He wore a long black leather coat, black leather jeans with black boots and a black shirt. In this weather? Was he crazy? His hair was shoulder length, dark chocolate brown, and he wore very dark wrap-around sunglasses.

Once he'd crossed the street and sauntered down the sidewalk a short distance, the prickly sensation went away. The light changed and Skye continued on her way, having completely forgotten about the CD she'd been searching for. Why in the world had her attention been so riveted by that guy? El Creepo Goth Guy dressed all in black. Ugh! And what about the strange sensation she'd felt? What was that all about? Well, shake it off, right? She was almost home. A shower and a tasty dinner would be waiting for her, followed by painting her nails and choosing what to wear for her last two days of high school. Her red shirt, the one she'd worn today, would be put into the trash. Tomorrow maybe she would wear her pale-yellow capris and matching top, with her gold sandals. She smiled. Yeah, that would look great.

Skye slept fitfully that night. Her dreams once again filled with strange images: ferocious animal faces attached to half-human bodies; people with pointed ears, who created fire, wind and waves of water with their hands, and their words, and their force of will and El Creepo Goth Guy was there, too. He looked at her and his eyes slowly bled to solid black. He smiled at her, and she saw fangs emerge from his gum line. He reached for her.

Skye bolted awake. She stared at the ceiling, unseeing, as words she'd never heard or seen before flashed through her mind: Shifter, Elfae, Blood-Hunter. What did they mean? Did they have something to do with her dream? Was she going mad? She looked at the clock. It was nine o'clock already? Why hadn't her alarm gone off? Great. Now she was not only late for school. She already missed her first class and was in the process of missing the second one as well. Skye sat up and rubbed her eyes. Maybe she'd skip the whole day. Half the student body was probably absent anyway.

When she got downstairs, there was a note from her mom next to the bagels on the counter. The note let Skye know that both of her parents had to leave the house early this morning; her dad had an emergency surgery to perform, and Skye's mom was helping with some final arrangements for the Pause for Paws event. That explained why nobody came and woke her up when her alarm failed.

Skye nibbled on a bagel with cream cheese as she went back upstairs and got dressed. She put on the yellow capris and top she had planned to wear to school, then slipped on her gold sandals. Thirty minutes later, the bagel was consumed, her makeup was on and her hair was brushed and pulled back into a high ponytail. Skye grabbed her purse and sunglasses and headed for her car, and then to her favorite place for coffee.

Java Joe's was crowded, but she was able to find a little table for two in the back corner. She'd planned to get a mocha to go, but then changed her mind and decided to stay. Why not? It's not like she had anywhere to rush off to.

There were magazines in the rack on the wall, and Skye snatched a few at random and settled in for a relaxing morning browsing through celebrity gossip, clothing styles, and make-up tips.

She'd finished with one magazine and had moved on to the second, when she started having the same odd sensations she'd had yesterday. Her hair on her arms and back of her neck, lifted, and her skin prickled. Skye looked up in time to see Creepy Goth Guy from the day before as he strode across the room to the counter. She watched while he ordered a coffee, and then stood looking for a place to sit. His eyes fell on the empty chair across from her, and Skye looked away. Seconds later the prickly sensation was gone. Skye looked around. Creepy Goth Guy was nowhere to be seen. Thankfully. She sighed in relief and went back to her magazine and her mocha.

Later that afternoon, back at home, Skye had just finished repainting her toe nails when Rachael called.

"Why weren't you in class today? Are you sick?"

"No, just overslept, but I didn't think it would make much difference if I skipped. It's not like we're doing anything anyway."

"True. Half the class wasn't there."

"I figured."

"Come over and hang by the pool with me. We need to talk about decorating our apartment and we might as well catch some rays while we're at it. There are still a couple of hours of sunshine left in the day."

"Sure. Just give me a few minutes to let this polish dry and I'll be over."

She waited until she could safely put her sandals back on, then headed to Rachael's house. Along the way, Skye stopped to put gas in her car, and thought she was hallucinating when she looked over at a guy already at the pump and saw a haze around him. The haze was in the shape of a wolf or maybe a large dog. She blinked, and the wolf/dog shape was gone.

At the intersection where she turned onto Rachael's street, Skye stopped at the stoplight. A man and woman crossed the street in front of her. Both of them were quite tall, like basketball player tall, which is what had first caught her attention. The woman looked incredibly striking in a short black dress, high heels and huge dark glasses. The man wore a dark navy business suit. They looked like they'd either just come from a business meeting, or were perhaps on their way to an early dinner or late lunch at the Bamboo Club, which was right across the street. Skye did a double-take, however, when beneath their average exteriors, she thought she saw a flicker of something else. She leaned forward and squinted, and all at once the 'something else' became clear. The man and woman had long pointed ears, extending a good two inches toward the tops of their heads.

The light changed, and someone behind her honked. Skye turned into Rachael's neighborhood, but couldn't stop thinking about what she'd just seen. Her hands trembled on the steering wheel. Could anyone else see what she'd seen? What was happening to her? Hadn't Mr. Preston said something about her soon being able to see things others couldn't? Or something like that? She really, really, had to call him, and soon!

Skye slammed on her brakes, and just narrowly missed hitting a black Escalade. She'd run a stop sign she'd been stopping at for the last four years! What was wrong with her? She had to get it together! The driver of the other car, a middle-aged man, graying at the temples, glared at her, then kept going. Skye continued on to her friend's house, then parked and headed for Rachael's front door. After a few steps, she noticed the front door stood wide open. Skye stopped and looked around. Now what? Every horror movie she'd ever seen should've been enough to warn her away. She was already shaken by what she'd seen at the crosswalk, and didn't know if she could take any more. Part of her wanted to get right back into her car and drive away. On the other hand, what if something had happened to Rachael, her sisters, or her parents? Should she call 911 right now? Should she investigate first?

Skye bit her lower lip and took a tentative step forward and then another. Ever so slowly she walked to the doorway.

"Rachael?" she called out when she reached the entry, but no one answered. "Mrs. Perry? Mr. Perry?" Still no answer. Skye had thought things couldn't get any weirder than they already were, but when she reached the living room, she found out she was wrong.

"Surprise!"

People jumped out from left, right, and in front of her, and for a moment a scream caught in Skye's throat. She jumped back before she realized it was her family and Rachael's, and they had shouted birthday greetings.

"But it's not my birthday," she gasped.

Rachael grabbed her arm. "I know, I know. Its next month, but you and I will be in San Diego by then so we decided to throw you a surprise party now. Besides, one of your presents came early." She gripped Skye's shoulders and turned her to face the hallway.

"Derek!" Skye rushed over to her older brother and gave him a hug. "You're home! When did you get here? How long can you stay?" Her brother was in the Marines, and she hadn't seen him in over a year.

"Isn't it wonderful?" Skye's mom asked. Skye's dad stood beside her, grinning. So, they weren't working or off planning a charity event. They were here!

"I've got a few weeks. Enough time to eat some home cooking and see my little sister graduate," Derek said.

Skye hugged him again. Now she was almost sorry that she and Rachael would be moving away in less than ten days. She wanted more time with her brother. He looked good. Clean cut, dark hair and whiskey eyes, just like hers. In spite of his Marine haircut, she thought he looked like any other guy his age in his blue jeans and long-sleeved T.

"Hey there birthday girl!"

Skye turned to see Rachael's parents.

"Happy surprise birthday, Skye," Rachael's mom said.

"Thank you. This really is quite a surprise!"

Emma and Cara lunged at Skye and wrapped her in twin hugs.

"We really scared you!" Cara said.

"Yeah, sorry," Emma added. "But now you're happy, right?"

Skye nodded. "Oh yeah, very happy."

Rachael laid a hand on each of her sister's shoulders. "Okay, let's give the girl some room, huh?"

Everyone moved out of the narrow hallway, Rachael's dad went to close the still open front door, and the party really got started. There was plenty of food, arranged buffet style on the dining room table and drinks were in the kitchen.

Rachael turned on some music and Skye talked with her brother, ate, and tried to forget the strange things she'd seen on the way over until she happened to look up and see a faint shimmer around Rachael's parents. It looked as if their ears were more pointed than they should be.

Skye's eyes flicked around the room until she spied Emma and Cara. They were goofing around, dancing to the music. Their ears looked pointier too! Skye frowned. It was happening again. Was she hallucinating?

"Skye? Are you okay?"

She turned to see Derek watching her, a look of concern on his face. Luckily his ears looked normal.

"Oh, yeah, sure." Skye forced a smile. "I just need to go talk to Rachael about something. Be right back."

She found Rachael in the kitchen. Skye paused in the archway and looked at her friend. Her ears also looked more pointed than they had previously. Skye once again looked behind her, around the living room. Only the Perry's had funny ears. Not her mom and dad, and not Derek.

"Skye, get out of here! I'm putting candles on your cake." Rachael moved to shield what Skye already knew was a chocolate cake, and for the first time ever, Skye saw that Rachael's eyes weren't just green. They were three shades of absolutely not normal shades of green! Skye gasped. She couldn't help it. She ducked back into the living room.

To say Skye was freaked out would be an understatement. She kept looking sidelong at Rachael and her family. She was on the verge of a panic attack. There had been just too many weird things going on in her life this past week. She now knew she would *definitely* be calling John Preston the first chance she got. He seemed to be the only person who might be able to shed some light on things.

CHAPTER THREE

"**S**KYE!"

She jumped at the sound of Rachael's voice. "What?"

"Come on, don't just stand there. Grab some cake!" They'd all finished singing to her and Skye was supposed to have the first piece. She pasted a smile on her face as she ate cake, opened her presents and gave the appropriate comments of thanks for each gift. A year ago, she wouldn't have been pretending. Today, however, all she wanted was go home and call John Preston and pummel him with questions.

As the evening wore on, Skye had noticed Rachael's mom's eyes were tri-purple, her dad's were tri-blue, and her sister's each had tri-colored yellow/orange/gold eyes. They were all beautiful and eerie at the same time. Skye also noticed her own parents and brother showed no reaction, so most likely she was the only one who saw the unusual ears and eyes. What the heck was going on?

She tried not to stare, especially when she and her family said goodbye. Once home, Skye stayed up for a little while longer, just to see if by chance anyone mentioned seeing anything strange at the Perry's house, but no one said a thing. She finally went up to her room to bed, but she couldn't sleep. She kept turning everything around in her head, but it made no difference. There was nothing within her point of reference to explain any of it.

Finally, she fell asleep and dreamed. Her dream was a slide show of people with pointy ears and multi-hued eyes. A name came to her, and then she knew as surely as if someone had whispered the term in her ear:

Elfae. The name was as clear to her as a first grader's schoolbook, and so was the knowledge that came along with it.

Elfae: an ancient race of people with the ability to disguise their true nature with a bit of magic used to make someone appear to be something they are not. The name of this type of magic was 'glamour'. Skye knew Elfae were able to do another form of magic as well, which was creating or moving air, water or fire.

Next, were images of people who had a shadow form, which looked like a wolf or large dog. The people's images blurred, and within seconds they had changed forms and turned into wolves. Again, the information seemed to download into her mind.

Shape-Shifter or Shifter: a race of people who have the ability to change forms, mostly into wolves, but occasionally some take other forms. Magic transforms them, but it is their only form of magic. They generally don't harm humans, but have been known to kill livestock or wildlife while in animal form and—

"Skye! Wake up." Someone gently shook her.

"What? What's going on?" Skye sat up and blinked. Her brother, Derek, sat on her bed. He grinned at her.

"Come on, wake up. Aren't you going to school today? It's your last day."

Skye closed her eyes and flopped back down onto the mattress. "Ugh! No. I'm not going. It doesn't matter. There's nothing going on anyway and I'll see everyone at graduation tomorrow."

"Then get up. I'm taking you to breakfast."

"What time is it?"

"Past time for breakfast. At least if you're a Marine it is."

"So that means, what? That it's 5am?"

Derek stood. "Come on, sleepy-head, just get up. We'll go to Amy's Pancake House. That place is still open, I hope."

Skye sighed and sat up again. She swung her legs over the side of the bed and looked up at him. "Yeah, it's open, and still my favorite breakfast place." She rubbed her face, still trying to wake up. "Go down stairs. Give me an hour and I'll be down."

"No, not an hour. Thirty minutes. I'm hungry, I'm buying, and I'm driving, so get a move on or I'll leave you behind."

"Right." Skye gave him a salute, rose to her feet and headed for the shower.

Even while she showered, dressed in her green and blue sundress and put on make-up, earrings and her favorite bracelet, she kept going over recent events in light of her dream. It was almost as if she'd been connected to a mainframe and had information downloaded into her mind. So, if she were to believe it, Rachael and her entire family weren't human, they were Elfae. And so were the people she'd seen at the intersection. On top of that, the guy she'd seen at the gas station was a Shape-Shifter, or just Shifter for short. But what about that tingly sensation she'd gotten twice lately, and all the other stuff? Would she have learned about that too if Derek hadn't come in and roused her? She felt exhausted just thinking about all of it.

"Tick, tock, Skye!" Derek shouted from downstairs.

"Coming!" Skye snatched her silver purse from the door knob, then dashed down the stairs. "All right, let's go, what are you waiting for?" She grinned at her brother and headed for the garage.

At the restaurant, Skye ordered her favorite omelet and tried to pay attention to Derek's stories about his life as a Marine. She was only half listening though. Her eyes darted around the room, as she tested her newfound strange ability. There were three Shifters in the booth across the room; a father, mother and little boy. She could see the outline of their animal form surrounding them. At a table near the door was a young couple. Both had pointed ears, but Skye was too far away, and at the wrong angle, to see what colors their eyes were.

She felt the hair rise at the back of her neck and on her arms. That tingly, prickly feeling came over her, and she glanced around, expecting to see Creepy Goth Guy. The only times she'd had that sensation, he was around, and Skye was smart enough to put two and two together, but he wasn't in the restaurant.

"Skye? Have you heard anything I've said?" Derek turned to follow her gaze around the room. "Something wrong?"

"No, I——"

The waitress chose that moment to bring their food. After she left, Skye tried to pay attention to what Derek said. She even told stories of her own about school and her friends, many of whom Derek knew. She scanned the room with her eyes. The odd sensation was still there, but what could be causing it?

The woman with a cascade of gorgeous red hair, sitting at the counter, looked perfectly normal. No pointy ears. No shadow outline of a wolf. But Skye knew she was different somehow.

"Skye, I'm losing you again."

Her eyes slid back to Derek. "Sorry." She gave him a smile of apology. "Guess I'm just excited about graduation, the party afterwards, and getting the apartment, decorating it, and—"

"And starting college in the fall. I get it." He settled back in his seat and sipped his coffee. "So, who's hosting the party? Where's it going to be?"

"Todd Fairbanks. And it's going to be at the club, in the private room out near the pool."

He nodded. "Yeah, I remember my grad party there. Nice. Well, don't get into too much trouble."

"Not to worry, big brother. I still don't drink, or do drugs or smoke. I'm about as pristine as a cool girl can be and still be cool." The prickly sensation had vanished. Her eyes darted to the counter. The woman was gone.

"Of course, you're cool. You're my sister!"

She brought her eyes back to Derek and made a face. They both laughed.

Rachael had decided to skip classes too, so they went window-shopping to get ideas for their apartment that day, instead of waiting until Monday. Skye found she could see through Rachael's glamour quite easily, just as she had the night before, but this time it didn't bother her. Today her eyes simply glided over the differences in Rachael's eyes and ears and she saw her only as her friend, not some freaky girl from another race. But why? How could she accept this weirdness so easily now? And why hadn't Rachael ever told her she and her family were Elfae? Surely Rachael knew. Maybe Rachael never mentioned it for the same reason Skye hadn't mentioned her dreams. Rachael probably assumed Skye wouldn't believe her. Maybe it was time she talked to Rachael about all this.

While Rachael directed their journey from place to place and pointed things out, Skye nodded or shook her head and made suggestions. All the while she was aware of the Shifters and Elfae around her. As the day had worn on it became easier and easier to spot them without staring, and Rachael no longer seemed to notice anything odd about her friend's behavior.

After Skye returned home, alone in her bedroom at last, she pulled John Preston's business card from her purse, then grabbed her cell phone and punched in the number. He answered on the fourth ring.

"Preston."

Skye didn't know what to say, so she blurted out the first thing that came to her mind. "I know about the Elfae and the Shifters."

There was a pause on the other end of the line. "Skye Falco, I presume."

"Uh, yeah. It's me. I've been having these weird dreams for the last week or so."

"I'm aware of that."

"Oh, that's right." Skye took a deep breath to steady herself. "But, how could you know that? And how did you know I'd heal like that, that day at the school? And how did you know I'd be at the ice cream parlor that night?"

"All in good time, Ms. Falco."

"But I have so many more questions! Why can't you answer them? What about when I went all Jet Li on Todd? How did that even happen? And how about those dreams? What does it all mean?"

He ignored her questions and asked one of his own. "Anything else besides the Shifters and the Elfae?"

"Anything else?" Skye parroted back. "Ah, I don't know what—oh, you mean like that tingly sensation I get sometimes, and the hair sort of goes up on the back of my neck?"

"Yes, exactly."

"Well, that's it. I mean, I don't know anything else about it. I—'

"Call me on Sunday, Ms. Falco."

"But what about all this other stuff? What about the men with black eyes and fangs from my dreams? What is the Bureau of the Extraordinary? And on your card it says you're a Handler. What's a 'Handler'?" Skye paused, but there was no reply. "Hello? Mr. Preston?" It was then she realized John Preston had hung up. "Argh! Of all the nerve! He wanted me to call him and then when I finally do it, he hangs up on me. What a jerk." She threw her phone on the bed and flopped down on her back. Well, she'd just call him again on Sunday. She didn't know what else might happen between now and then, but next time Mr. Preston would either answer all her questions or he'd better leave her alone for good.

That night she dreamed again; of people with black eyes and razor-sharp fangs. Creepy Goth Guy was in her dream, and so was the woman at the breakfast counter at Amy's Pancake House. Then quite abruptly, just like in last night's dream, she had a word for what they were; Blood-Hunter.

Blood-Hunter: a species that needs to ingest blood once a week in order to survive. The Blood-Hunter's eyes are sensitive to sunlight. They can be killed only by decapitation or something driven straight through their heart. They don't have to kill humans to survive, but over ninety percent of the time, that's exactly what they do. And, Blood-Hunters were born, not created from a bite like those vampires on TV.

And then, as if a veil had been abruptly lifted from her mind, Skye knew what she was and what her purpose in all this was to be. She was an Assassin, a killer of Blood-Hunters, and although she still dreamed, she could see, as though in a slide show, the history of the Assassins, as it flashed across her mind's eye. Assassins were born, not chosen by some board of directors. Some Assassins were male and some were female. Sometime during their teen years, these new Assassins would begin to have dreams that would awaken them to their new capabilities and responsibilities. It was the Assassin's duty and destiny to protect humanity from the non-human bloodthirsty, the deranged, and the megalomaniacs waiting eagerly for an opportunity to emerge and destroy humanity.

Skye awakened with a gasp, and stared up at the ceiling. She was in her room, not in the midst of some dream, but the panic that had seized her, refused to abate. The room was mostly dark, with only a few streaks of moonlight shining through the curtains. She lay there, trying to sort through the deluge of knowledge given to her in her dreams. This data was in her head now, as if it had always been there, and although the information was incredibly strange, she'd seen many weird things recently and the dream information seemed to finally make sense of it all.

First there were the strange sightings of Elfae and Shape-Shifters. They were real. Not fictional creatures from books, movies or her dreams. And now Skye knew what that tingly sensation meant; that a Blood-Hunter was nearby. She still had questions, but at least now she understood why she had the ability to see and sense beings that were not entirely human, had been intrigued by Mr. Perry's knife collection, and knew how to lay Todd out without giving it a second thought. She was an Assassin.

Skye sat up in bed, her eyes wide and her breath coming in short pants. This was ridiculous! She couldn't possibly do this. The very idea of it was insane. Just because she could fight monsters in her dreams, didn't mean she could fight them in real life! Why her? How could she possibly have been born to this? Surely there were other people out there who were more suited for this sort of thing. She had to talk to Preston, get him to see she was all wrong for this. Surely, he and his organization would let her off the hook once they saw how unsuited she was for this sort of thing. How had he gotten her name anyway? How did he find her? There were so many questions.

Skye closed her eyes and tried to go back to sleep. She counted sheep, but they turned into wolves. She tried to count backwards from one hundred, but her mind wandered. She spent the rest of the night tossing and turning. She drifted off at some point though, because the next thing she knew her mom was in her room opening the curtains.

"You've slept long enough, honey. Today is a big day. Graduation! I made an appointment for you to get a manicure and pedicure, and then I thought we could have lunch at The Tavern. We both like that shrimp salad with the parmesan peppercorn dressing."

Skye was still tired, but the spa and lunch sounded like just the distraction she needed to keep from thinking about—no, stop. Not thinking about it.

Lunch was, as always, delicious. While they ate they talked about the upcoming graduation, the charity event, and Skye's move to San Diego with Rachael. At the spa, they browsed through fashion magazines while getting their pedicures, and laughed at the crazy fashions some of the celebrities wore. Sometimes being with her mom was more like having an older sister. Skye loved days like this; especially now. It made her feel so normal; like she was just a regular girl about to graduate from high school, not a would-be Assassin.

That evening, Skye walked across the stage and accepted her diploma, then cheered for the rest of her classmates. When the ceremony was finally over, she was surrounded by family and friends; everybody running around hugging each other. Once, she thought she saw John Preston among the crowd, but when she craned her neck to see better, she couldn't see him anywhere.

"Skye, come on!" Rachael shouted over the happy clamor all around them. "Everyone is heading over to the club. Our parents can drop us off, and then Todd's parents hired limos to take everyone home after the party is over."

It took another forty-five minutes before they were actually able to get out of the parking lot. By then Skye had shed her cap and gown to reveal her green sheath dress underneath. It was sleeveless, with wide straps and a scoop neck. With her hair down, held back by two diamond-like barrettes, her strappy sandals, and her newly painted finger and toenails, Skye knew she looked fabulous.

"Let's go check out the buffet table," Angela said once they arrived. Her golden blonde hair was swept up in a twist and she wore a pale green dress, which complemented her hazel eyes.

"Angela, you're always hungry!" Rachael laughed.

"I don't think it's that," Sarah replied. "Mark is over there. I think it's *him* she wants, not the food." Tonight, Sarah's brown bangs were styled to the side, her brown hair curled. Her dress was chocolate brown with copper-colored accents. She looked very elegant, and not at all like the tomboy she was every other day of the year.

"You guys go on, I'll catch up," Skye said. "I should look for Todd."

While the others journeyed to the buffet table, Skye surveyed the room. Across the gathering of laughing, talking graduates, she found him. He spied her at the same time and they waved at each other. He started toward her and seconds later stood at her side.

"I wanted to make sure not to sneak up behind you again," he said. "I wouldn't want to get beat up at my own party, by a girl in a dress." He looked Skye up and down. "And a sensational dress it is too. Or maybe it's just because you're in it." He grinned.

"Thanks! You look terrific too." Skye was truly happy for about thirty seconds, and then she started getting that hair-raising feeling, accompanied by the tingling, prickling feeling that could only mean one thing. A freaking Blood-Hunter was here somewhere.

CHAPTER FOUR

S HE SMILED AT TODD. AND WONDERED HOW SHE could get away long enough to find out who had crashed the party. Or maybe it was someone who worked here at the club, or even a fellow student! Even if she could find out, what could she possibly do about it? Could she really do in real life what she did in her dreams? Could she fight a Blood-Hunter and win? Could she drive a stake through its heart and kill it? And why was she even thinking these things? But Skye was filled with an unexpected and equally irresistible urge to find the creature that might very well be stalking one of her classmates right this very minute.

"Um, I'm going to go use the lady's room. I'll be back in a sec." Hardly waiting for Todd's reply, Skye darted away and tried to lose herself in the crowd. It wasn't too hard really. They had a pretty large class, and everyone was invited. Most people wouldn't stay the entire evening, but at the moment the rather small room was filled to capacity.

Trial and error quickly taught her that finding a Blood-Hunter was a lot like playing a childhood game. She'd go one direction and then another, getting 'warmer' or 'colder' depending on how close she was to the Blood-Hunter.

Out on the patio, just outside the French doors, was the redhead from Amy's Pancake House! She had to be the one. Getting the tingly sensation twice while in her presence was too much of coincidence to be ignored.

The redhead wore a low-cut red satin dress, showing off some pretty impressive cleavage. The dress was practically backless too, which Skye noticed when the Blood-Hunter turned around, and had only lace mesh to hold it together. The dress was also extremely short and barely covered her backside. On her feet were stiletto heeled pumps with a peek-a-boo opening at the toes. The outfit reminded Skye of one of the ridiculous celebrity getups she and her mom had laughed over at the spa. Just then, Don Jackson, one of Skye's classmates, swaggered over and began to flirt with the scantily clad redhead. Seconds later the two of them sauntered away, through the semi-shadows, headed toward the cabanas. Skye glanced around, but no one seemed to notice the two who had wandered off. A strange calmness came over her and all uncertainty was gone. The noise in the room seemed to fade and the people around her receded into the background. Her hands fisted and her mind centered on one thought. Kill the Blood-Hunter before it kills an innocent human.

Skye turned and spied Carley Rogers not three feet away. The girl wore two gleaming chopsticks in her hair. "Excuse me, Carley. Do you suppose I could borrow one of those chop-sticks?" Skye smiled sweetly at the other girl.

A look of confusion crossed Carley's face. "Ah, sure, I guess so. Here, take both of them." She slipped the black lacquered chopsticks from her shiny black hair, and it tumbled to her waist. She held them out to Skye. "But why—?"

"Thanks." Skye took the chopsticks from the other girl's hand. "I'll return them soon, or buy you new ones if they get broken. I promise."

Skye turned and headed outside through the French doors, then followed the path Don and the redhead had taken. When she caught up with them, the moonlight gave off just enough light for her to see the Blood-Hunter's blackened eyes and her exposed fangs as she lowered her mouth to Don's neck. Poor Don, he turned just at that moment and let out a shriek, stumbled backward and fell. Skye gripped one of the chop-sticks in her fist and ran forward.

Instincts she didn't know she had, took over. She blocked punches and threw some of her own. Once, fangs grazed her arm, and eyes as black as coal bored into hers. Seconds later Skye found herself on her back with the Blood-Hunter leaning over her, fangs bared. Skye wedged her knee between their bodies and rocked to the side then kicked with all the force she could muster. One of the Blood-Hunter's hands came away from Skye's shoulder and she took advantage of the moment to rocket a punch into the Blood-Hunter's jaw, and then scrambled to her feet. She buried one chopstick into the Blood-Hunter's chest, but it obviously missed the heart because the Blood-Hunter pulled it out and came after Skye once again.

She had one more chopstick left. She had to make it count or she'd be dead in seconds. Skye turned away from the Blood-Hunter. Risky, but she had a plan. When the Blood-Hunter was within arm's reach, Skye whirled around, the chopstick in her fist, and the Blood-Hunter's own momentum caused her to impale herself on the chopstick. This time Skye's aim was true. She watched, panting, as the Blood-Hunter stared down at the chopstick protruding from her chest. Her eyes flicked up to Skye's. They were still solid black. Seconds later her body crumpled into thousands of pieces, which disintegrated. They turned to vapor, and floated away on the breeze.

Skye stood there and watched, strangely fascinated at the Blood-Hunter's rapid decomposition, then stooped to pick up the chopsticks. They weren't damaged; not even a bloodstain marred their lacquered surface. She turned to find Don lying in a lounge chair with his eyes closed.

"Are you okay?" Skye called out.

"Yeah." Don opened his eyes and sat up slowly. "I must've been hallucinating. I thought that girl had black eyes and fangs, can you believe it? I tripped, and then I hit my head. I've had my eyes closed trying to keep everything from spinning."

"Maybe you should go home, Don."

"Yeah, maybe I will." He rose from the lounge chair and unsteadily headed back to the party, one hand on his sore head.

Skye watched him go, and then just as quickly as it had come, her confidence vanished. Had she really just fought with a Blood-Hunter and killed it? She'd never had a physical fight with anyone in her life! Her hands started to shake and she wrapped her arms around herself. One minute she was calm and rationalizing it all, and the next she was freaked and practically hyperventilating. She had to get a grip.

"Good job, Skye. Excellent in fact."

Skye jumped in surprise and turned to see John Preston walking toward her. He was dressed in black, and held a crossbow.

"Not many do as well on a first kill. You kept a level head. You're a bit of a risk taker, but I can help you fine tune some things."

Skye scowled at him, anger now chasing away her panic. "How do you always seem to know where I am and what I'm doing? It's creeping me out." She pointed at the crossbow. "And when were you planning on using that thing, *after* I was dead?"

He shrugged. "You didn't need my help. You did just fine on your own."

Skye's eyes narrowed. "We really need to talk. Me being an Assassin is all wrong, and—"

"Be sure and call me tomorrow. We'll get together and I'll fill in any gaps in your knowledge." He smiled at her. "Don't fret about it, Skye. You did just fine, really." And then he stepped back, blended in with the darkness and was gone.

"Don't *fret* about it?" Skye sputtered. The sounds of the party reached her ears. It was in full swing now. She looked down at her dress. It was rumpled, and her hair no doubt needed some brushing. A strap on one of her shoes had snapped, but she could still walk without much trouble. She noticed one of her nails had broken off.

"That figures," she muttered. "Right after getting them done at the spa, too."

She checked her arm where the Blood-Hunter's fang had grazed her. The wound was mostly healed. She took a deep breath and blew it out, then started back to the party. She was probably in shock. How else could she explain how she could fight for her life, then brutally kill someone, and then return to the graduation party as though nothing had happened? Shock. She was in shock.

Once inside, she found Carley and pressed the chopsticks into the other girl's hand. "Thanks."

"Where have you been?" asked Todd, when she finally found him, near the buffet table. "You've been gone a really long time."

"Well, I—"

"There you are!" Rachael appeared at her side. "Where have you been?"

"I just asked her the same question," Todd replied. "She said she was going to the bathroom, and then she was gone for half the night."

"What?" Skye was shocked. "No, I've only been gone a few minutes!"

Todd shrugged. "Well, it seemed like a pretty long time to me."

"Well, I just—"

"Skye, I need to talk to you about something. Come outside with me." Rachael pleaded, and for the first time Skye realized something was wrong with her friend. She looked on the verge of tears.

"Sure." Skye threw Todd an apologetic smile. "I'll be back."

"Yeah, right." She heard him mutter as she turned away.

Skye followed Rachael outside onto the patio. She looked beautiful in her stunning pink dress and strappy shoes. Her pale blonde hair looked lovely, her make-up was perfect, but her eyes were now spilling tears.

"Rachael, what's wrong?"

"Do you remember Joe Haynes?"

Skye frowned. "Of course, I remember him. He was your Jr. High School boyfriend and my next-door neighbor back when we were kids. Why?"

Rachael blinked furiously, fighting back tears. "I found out something about him tonight."

"What?"

"He's dead." Rachael wiped at the tears on her cheeks.

"What happened? How did you find out?"

"You know Joe's parents decided to send him to a different private school, not here at Cardiff, right?"

"Right. He went to Rockfield."

Rachael nodded. "Anyway, Veronica Parker, from our school, started going out with him sophomore year. They dated through junior year, and then broke up half way through senior year. I just talked to her. She said he was killed in some sort of accident just last week!"

Skye was stunned. She hadn't seen Joe in years, but she remembered him as a pudgy little boy who grew into a lean and lanky guy, who played tennis, was a runner, and liked to go scuba diving. "How did he die? Was it a scuba diving accident?"

Rachael shook her head. "No. He was camping with some friends. You know, blowing off the last week of school. Anyway, he went out to get firewood and was gone a really long time. The other boys went looking for him and they found him with his throat bitten or slashed or something. He was still alive but he didn't make it to the hospital."

Skye gasped in shock. How could something so horrible happen to their childhood friend? Joe had been a great kid. A really nice guy. All sorts of memories flooded Skye's mind, but then something else rammed its way into her thoughts. She had a sneaking suspicion she knew what had caused Joe's death. A Blood-Hunter. She had to find out for sure.

"Come on, Rachael. Let's go home."

Rachael again wiped at her tears and tried to make herself presentable. "No, we can't. The party isn't even half over, and what about you and Todd?"

Skye shrugged. "It doesn't matter. I've told you that before. Todd and I don't have a relationship. It was doomed before it started. Let's go. I'll call Derek. He'll come pick us up." She'd hoped to talk to Rachael about her and her family being Elfae, maybe after the party, but tonight was obviously not the best time after all. Too much had happened this evening; far too much.

That night, Skye didn't dream. Of course, she didn't sleep much either with her mind in a whirl. She kept replaying the fight with the Blood-Hunter. Then she thought about what she'd say to John Preston to convince him that she just wasn't the right person for this whole Assassin gig. So much had happened recently, her mind was filled to overflowing.

When morning finally came, Skye threw back the covers and got up. She washed her face, pulled on jeans and a pink t-shirt with little faux pearls along the neckline, and ran a brush through her hair. After swishing some mouthwash and slipping into her pale pink sandals, Skye plopped back down onto the bed and reached for her phone. She fished John Preston's card from her purse, and hoped he didn't mind an early call. She keyed in the number and listened to it ring on the other end.

"Preston."

"Mr. Preston, its Skye Falco."

"Hello, Skye. You're up early."

"We need to talk."

"Yes, we do."

"I think a Blood-Hunter might have killed one of my friends."

There was a pause, as if he hadn't expected her to say that. "Last night?"

"No, no, about a week ago."

"Tell me about it."

Skye told him everything Rachael had told her. "Is it possible, or am I jumping to conclusions?"

"There are several Blood-Hunters currently in the area. One we've been tracking is known as Nicolai. Another he's been seen with is Aidan. But I'd have to see actual evidence to be sure if it was a Blood-Hunter that killed your friend. I'll contact some people and see what I can find out."

"You know all their names?" Skye was stunned, so much so she was momentarily sidetracked. "Seriously? What was the name of the fake red-head I staked last night?"

"That was Penelope. And no, we don't know the names of all of them."

Skye gave herself a mental shake to get back on track. "So, you're a Handler, right? I know what that is now. You're someone who gives Assassins additional training and gives them information to help them find and kill Blood-Hunters and other nasty monsters."

"I also, occasionally, offer back-up."

"How did you know about me?"

"Why don't you meet me at that pancake place on Main St. in an hour?"

"Amy's?"

"Yes. I can answer your questions then, and fill you in on what will be expected of you."

"Well, that's what I wanted to talk to you about. I don't think I'd make a very good—"

"See you then, Skye."

"Wait, I—" But the connection was gone. "Argh!" Skye threw her phone back into her purse. "I am not going to do this. I'm going to college. I'm going to marry a nice guy and have a house and a couple of kids and a dog. I'm not going to be an Assassin for the Bureau of the Extraordinary."

She grabbed her purse and headed for her car. She was far too antsy to hang around the house. So, what if she was early to Amy's Pancake House? It was better than pacing around her bedroom.

She drove to the restaurant and parked, played a game on her phone, and kept checking the time. At just five minutes to go, she locked up her car and went inside. John Preston was already there. She spotted him immediately. He sat facing the door, in a corner booth. How had he gotten in here without her seeing him?

Skye cut through the crowded restaurant and joined him. This time he wore a terra cotta colored long-sleeved pullover. Skye thought it was probably made of silk knit. For the first time she noticed his eyes were hazel.

Skye barely looked at the menu, since she already knew what was on it from eating here so often. The waitress appeared and Skye ordered her usual omelet, along with orange juice. John Preston ordered steak and eggs with coffee.

"Okay, so about this Assassin business," Skye began, as soon as the waitress left.

"Yes?"

She gave him a level gaze. "I don't want to do it."

His eyebrows lifted. "You don't have a choice."

"What do you mean I don't have a choice?"

The waitress brought Preston's coffee and Skye's orange juice.

"What do you mean?" Skye repeated, once the waitress was gone.

He took a sip, then placed the cup back in its saucer. "I mean exactly what I said, Ms. Falco. Being an Assassin is something you were born to do. It isn't a matter of choice."

"So, you can't get me out of it? You mean I have to do this forever?"

"Not forever."

"You mean just for a year or something, and then I'm done with it?"

"Not exactly."

"Well, what then?"

He took another sip of his coffee. "Being an Assassin is a lifelong commitment."

"But you just said—"

"But your life may be considerably shorter than that of your high school classmates."

Skye had leaned toward him during their conversation; now she rocked back, suddenly at a loss for words. "What?"

"Well, it is a dangerous business."

"But you don't understand. I'm a girly-girl." She held up her hand so he could see her nails. "See, French manicure. Oh, and look." She plucked at her top. "See, pretty clothes." She lifted her necklace and then pointed to her earrings. "See, expensive jewelry." She leaned in again. "Don't you see, Mr. Preston, this is all wrong. I can't be an Assassin."

"You already are one, Skye."

The waitress brought their food, but Skye was no longer hungry. Preston, however, dug right in. After a few mouthfuls, he continued their conversation.

"Now, there are some things you should know, other than what you've already learned from your dreams. For instance, I have two other Assassins assigned to me besides you. Their names are Ben and Natalie. You will meet them eventually. Natalie is twenty-one and Ben is twenty. A bit older than you are, but I'm sure the three of you will get along quite well."

Skye tried again. "But seriously, I don't want to do this."

Preston ignored her and continued. "Now, just so it's all clear, you are perfectly welcome to tell your friend, Rachael, about all this, if you haven't already. Being as she and her family are Elfae—"

"You know about Rachael?"

"Yes, of course. Now, as I was saying, you are free to reveal yourself to her if you wish, or you may keep your status as an Assassin to yourself. Although I'd think that would be rather difficult since the two of you will soon be sharing an apartment in San Diego."

Skye glared at him. "You know, it's really irritating how you know so much about me but I know nothing about you."

"My personal information is not really relevant, but I can tell you this. I'm forty years old. I've been a Handler for the last fifteen years, and I'm good at what I do."

"So, what about my friend who was killed? Are you going to do something about that?"

"As I told you, I'll have to see evidence to confirm the cause of death first to determine if your friend was killed by other than human hands."

"And if it *was* a Blood-Hunter?"

"If it was a Blood-Hunter, or some deranged Shifter or Elfae, then that individual will be dealt with. Very possibly by you."

"No, no, no," Skye shook her head. "There is no way that's going to happen. I told you I don't think I'm cut out for this sort of thing, and I don't want to be. I don't want to do it."

"And I told you, you can't opt out. This is a calling. Few are called. The ones who are called are needed. There is no choice in the matter."

"But I don't want this calling. This calling is ruining my plans for my future. I don't want to be an Assassin. I don't want a Handler. I don't want my friend to be an Elfae, and I know there's nothing I can do about that, but—"

"And there is nothing you can do about the rest of it either, Ms. Falco. The die is cast, the tickets are purchased, the—"

"The guillotine is on its way toward my neck?" Skye's eyes were wide and her voice was shrill, but she couldn't help it. With some effort she lowered her voice.

"Well, I wouldn't put it that way, Ms. Falco. I have every confidence your head will remain on your shoulders. But I do think you're going to be quite good at removing the heads of many surprised Blood-Hunters."

Skye closed her eyes and buried her face in her hands. "This can't be happening to me. Please say this isn't happening. It's all just some crazy dream and I'm going to wake up now and it's going to be last week and I can start over."

"I'm sorry, Skye, but there are no do-overs. This is your new reality. You're going to have to get used to it. You've done remarkably well so far, by the way. Most times I have to assist with a first kill, but you handled yourself admirably."

Skye shook her head. "No. Please, no. I really don't want to do this. I don't want to die young. My life has barely started. Please don't make me do this." She felt her eyes tear up and she was embarrassed, but couldn't help it. Everything in her life was spiraling out of control and she hated it. She felt fear and anger like she'd never felt before, well up inside her. "I won't do it. I won't play your stupid monster-killer game. I refuse to see Shifters and Elfae. I refuse."

Preston finished his meal and settled back in the booth. "Stop acting like a child. You can't stop seeing them, and you know it. You are what you are and you know what you know. The prickling sensation you feel when a Blood-Hunter is around isn't going to magically go away either. You can try to ignore it, but you'll always know what it means and that you might've saved someone if only you had acted in their defense."

What he'd said about her was true, but she wasn't ready to completely give in just yet. "I'm still going to go to college."

"Of course, you are. Live your life, but know there will be times when you'll have to walk away from a class or a party or a dinner or a sports event, and take care of business. In addition, you will have to patrol a designated area each night, to troll for Blood-Hunters."

"Seriously? Like, use myself as bait?"

"Exactly. Oh, and you might want to consider adding some darker colors and more durable fabrics to your wardrobe. Most of what I've seen you wear so far is highly impractical for an Assassin."

Skye glared at him. "Now you're giving me wardrobe advice?"

He lifted one eyebrow.

"Aw, come on, can't we just forget about all this?" Skye pleaded.

"I'm afraid not."

Skye reached for her purse and made a move to stand up.

"You're leaving? You didn't eat your breakfast," Preston remarked.

Skye shrugged. "Yeah, I lost my appetite. Thanks anyway." She got up and turned toward the entrance.

"Good-bye, Skye. I'll see you in San Diego."

"Not if I see you first," Skye muttered to herself as she strode to the door.

CHAPTER FIVE

S KYE PEELED OUT OF THE PARKING LOT AND headed straight for Rachael's house. Along the way she activated her Bluetooth and called to make sure her friend was home.

"I have to talk to you. It's important."

"Okay, but what—?"

"I'll explain when I get there. See you in a few." She disconnected before Rachael could say good-bye, and pulled into her friend's driveway fifteen minutes later.

"What's going on?" Rachael asked as she let Skye in.

"Let's go to your room and close the door."

"Secretive much?" Rachael bounded up the stairs after Skye, who had taken the lead, even though this wasn't her house.

Rachael's room was a tribute to Laura Ashley, with floral patterns on the bed and walls, and lace on the pillow shams, curtains and even draped over the nightstand. Rachael sat on the bed, her back against the headboard and gestured for Skye to sit facing her. At that moment Skye realized that Rachael's other persona, the Elfae one, didn't bother her in the least any more. Her eyes just slid over the differences.

"What's up?" Rachael asked. "Is this about our move, about Todd or Joe?"

"No. Well, not really." Skye cleared her throat. It was harder to begin than she'd thought it would be. "Over the last week or so, I've had strange dreams. Then, things started happening to me."

"Like what?"

"Like, I've been faster and stronger than usual. Also, I heal from injuries quicker." Skye looked up at Rachael. She hadn't realized she'd been averting her eyes. Rachael didn't look skeptical, only interested, so Skye continued.

"Remember when I came to class late and my sleeve was torn?"

Rachael nodded.

"Well, I'd been running up the stairs and I fell. My hands were all scraped up and my ankle was sprained or maybe even broken, and my elbow was cut open. But then everything healed almost immediately. It was really bizarre." Skye took a breath. "Anyhow, I also know things because of the dreams. I know how to fight and how to use knives and—"

"That's why you were so interested in my dad's collection that day," Rachael interrupted. "And that night at Scoops, that's why you went all Jet Li on Todd!"

"Ah, yeah," Skye nodded. "And there's more. I get this sort of sixth sense, I guess, when certain kinds of people are around, and I also can see things about other people that..." Her words trailed off when she saw the look on Rachael's face.

Rachael lifted one delicate manicured hand to her ear. She gently ran her fingers through her hair, and flipped a few pale locks over her ear to cover it. "Can you see them?"

Skye slowly nodded her head.

"And my eyes?"

Skye nodded again. They started at each other for several seconds. Skye was nervous. This could be one of those make-or-break moments of their friendship.

"You're an Assassin." Rachael said it softly, but there was no mistaking the anticipation in her voice.

Skye released a breath she hadn't known she'd been holding. "So I'm told."

Rachael leaned forward, excitement lighting her eyes. "Have you been contacted by the Bureau of the Extraordinary yet? Who's your Handler? Have you already killed a Blood-Hunter?"

Now Skye's eyes widened. Her friend knew more about this stuff than she did! But then Rachael had apparently known what she was her entire life, whereas Skye had only learned of all these things in the last week.

"John Preston is my Handler, and yeah, on the night of the graduation party I killed a Blood-Hunter."

"Oh my gosh! Really? During Todd's party? That explains why you disappeared for a while! Why didn't you tell me that night? Why—?"

"Because you were upset about Joe. Which reminds me," she paused. "He might've been killed by a Blood-Hunter."

Rachael nodded. "I thought of that. Or maybe even a deranged Shape-Shifter. So what happens now? Does Mr. Preston know who might've done it?"

"Well, um, yeah, he mentioned a couple of names, but he also said there are a lot of Blood-Hunters around here and he has to see evidence to determine if it actually *was* a Blood-Hunter or a Shape-Shifter."

"I've heard Preston is one of the best Handlers out there, Skye. You're lucky to have him. When will you go after Joe's killer?"

Skye bit her lower lip. "Ah, well, that's just it. I really don't want to do this Assassin thing. I have a plan for my life, and fighting Blood-Hunters isn't it. I just want to live my life and be a regular college student. I want to find a nice guy who loves me, get married and—"

"And have 2.5 really nice children and one really nice dog. I know, I know. You've been saying that since we were ten, but this changes everything, Skye. Do whatever Mr. Preston says. He's your Handler. He's there to help you."

Skye rolled her eyes. "He told me to go out and buy darker clothing in more durable fabrics."

"So?"

"So that's not how we roll, Rachael! We wear colors, like pink and yellow. We wear heeled sandals and silk blouses. We get our nails done at the salon and wear diamond jewelry!"

"And again, I say, so?"

"So, what if your life had been the one that was drastically changed overnight? What if you were told you had to throw your entire future in a dumpster and face almost certain death before the age of thirty? How would you feel? Would you be so anxious to rush into it?"

Rachael tilted her head and looked at her. "And do you really have a choice?"

"No. Not really."

"Then what is there to talk about?"

"First of all, if I do this and we live together in San Diego, then we could both be in danger."

"Don't say 'if'. You *are* going to do this. You're an Assassin now. Besides, I can take care of myself." Rachael sounded so sure of herself, that Skye wondered what else her friend might've kept hidden from her all these years. Or maybe it was just bravado.

"Well, what if I just ignore all of it. I mean, blow off Preston, ignore the tingling sensation and—"

"Oh, right. You cannot stand there and tell me you're the kind of person who would ignore someone's cries for help if you could help them. In spite of our upbringing, which has made us look suspiciously like Barbie dolls with cell phones, we aren't like that. We aren't so self-absorbed that we wouldn't stand up to a bully or help an abused puppy or—"

"All right, all right!" Skye threw up her hands. "You sound just like Preston. He said practically the same thing to me. Fine I'll accept this Assassin stuff is my responsibility. At least for now." She sighed. "Let's talk about something else. So, what are you wearing to the animal shelter charity event tonight?"

"I'm wearing pink, of course. I'll show you." Rachael went to her closet and pulled out a dress. "Have you told anyone else about all this stuff?"

"No. I don't think anyone would believe me anyway. My parents would probably have me committed for psychiatric care if I started talking about all this to them. I won't tell anyone about you and your family or any of the rest of it either."

Rachael let out a deep sigh. "Good. Thank-you. So, here's the dress. What do you think?"

Skye went through the motions, gave all the proper 'oohs, and ahs' and made suggestions for what shoes Rachael should wear with it, but her mind kept cycling back to other things. Like trying to figure out how to have both the life she wanted, and do the job she'd so recently been assigned to do, in the world she'd been thrust into. Plus, how to stay alive while doing it.

Later that night, Skye strolled around the charity event in her cerulean chiffon dress. It fell to just above her knees, had short, fluttery sleeves. Her dark auburn hair was held back by a blue headband, edged with faux pearls. Her shoes matched her dress.

The patio was crowded with nearly three hundred guests, and although Rachael would sit with her parents at another table, Skye knew that as soon as the dinner was over and the silent auction started, the two of them would prowl the aisles to look at things to bid on. There were several dogs parading around on leashes with their owners who were the promoters of the event.

Each year Skye loved to crouch down to pet and talk to the dogs. It was the closest she'd ever come to having one, so it was a real treat. So far she'd already greeted a Golden Retriever, a Pit Bull, a Poodle and a Chihuahua. She spotted a Collie and a Labrador Retriever not far away and headed over to get a closer look. Each of the dogs either had on a bow or a bandana. They were all friendly and were a great representation of how wonderful an adopted dog could be.

"There you are." Derek joined her just as she stood up from greeting the black Lab. He looked great in his dress blues. "Dinner is going to be served soon, and Mom suggested we head over to our table."

"Have you seen Rachael?" Skye asked as they walked together.

"Yeah. Their table is right next to ours."

As they approached their seats, Skye spotted Rachael and waved. Both Rachael's parents waved also. Skye wondered if Rachael had already told them about her. Probably, judging by the way both Mr. and Mrs. Perry looked at her.

The dinner was delicious. Patrons had a choice of either roast chicken, roast beef, tilapia or a strictly vegetarian dish made of pasta and sautéed vegetables. Each meat entree was served with rice pilaf as well as a mixture of steamed vegetables. Desserts included lemon cake, raspberry sorbet or chocolate mousse. Skye was stuffed by the time it was over.

While she and Rachael, along with dozens of others, looked at the many items to be auctioned off, the staff cleared tables and brought coffee or tea to those who wanted it. Soon, the first of several speakers got up to talk about the shelter, the dogs and the various projects the shelter had underway. It was while Skye admired a purse and cosmetic bag set to be auctioned, that she first noticed the hair on the back of her neck lift. Immediately the hair on her arms followed suit, and then the tingly, prickly sensation came after that. She scanned the crowd to see who might've triggered the reaction, but found no one who looked suspicious. But she did see someone she knew, and she wasn't happy about it. John Preston. He said he'd see her in San Diego, so she hadn't expected to see him again so soon. The last thing she needed tonight was a repeat of the graduation party battle with the Blood-Hunter.

"Look at this necklace!"

Skye heard Rachael's voice, but barely glanced down at the pretty, hand-blown, multi-colored glass beads. Under normal circumstances she would've examined it more closely and most likely put a bid in, but right now she had more important things tugging at her attention.

"There's a Blood-Hunter here somewhere," she whispered in Rachael's ear. "Preston is here too."

"Where?" Rachael's head snapped up as soon as she'd finished writing down her bid for the necklace. "Where is he?"

"The Blood-Hunter or Preston?"

"Either! Both!"

"Preston is one row over, looking at a painting. See him? The guy with the dark hair and the grey silk shirt?"

Rachael leaned in a bit to get a better view. "Yeah, I see him. What do you suppose he's doing here?"

"Stalking me? Tracking a Blood-Hunter? Supporting homeless dogs? Who knows? But I'm going to find out."

"But, shouldn't you kill the Blood-Hunter first?"

"I don't even know where the darn thing is. I've looked around, but it's not like anyone has a sign around their neck that reads, 'Hi, I'm a Blood-Hunter'. Besides, I don't even have a weapon. I'm going to talk to Preston. Find out what he's up to." Skye walked around the corner and into the next aisle, with Rachael trailing after her.

"Is it okay if I come along? I'd like to meet him."

"Sure. I don't care."

Skye stopped next to John Preston, but before she could speak, he turned and smiled at her.

"Ah, Ms. Falco. Lovely event, isn't it?"

"Yeah, but I thought I wasn't going to see you again until I was in San Diego."

He shrugged, then glanced at Rachael. "And who is your friend? Wait, let me guess. This must be Rachael Perry, am I correct? I'm John Preston."

Rachael nodded and smiled. He held his hand out and she shook it.

Skye fought back her irritation and lost. "So, again I ask, why are you here?" She couldn't keep the annoyance from her voice.

Preston dropped Rachael's hand and turned to Skye. "I'm here to support the event. I've bid on several items. Perhaps I'll wind up with a few of them. Why else would I be here, Skye?" His eyes focused on something across the room.

She turned to see Creepy Goth Guy perusing the auction items. How bizarre. She wouldn't have guessed him to be the type to come to a charity event and bid on high dollar items. He was too much of a weirdo in his black leather from head to toe.

"That's Aidan, one of the Blood-Hunters spotted in this area recently. I mentioned him to you before."

Skye was intrigued. So that explained it. Creepy Goth Guy was indeed a Blood-Hunter, and his name was Aidan.

"Aidan what?" she asked, her anger toward Preston temporarily gone.

"Just, Aidan. That's all we know." Preston glanced at Skye. "Didn't you sense him?"

She shrugged. "Well, yeah, I sensed something, but—"

"Well, keep an eye on him. If he does anything threatening or suspicious, you know what to do."

"With what?" Skye's anger turned to dread. This *was* going to turn out to be just like graduation night after all.

"You're a clever girl. You'll figure out something. You did the last time."

"Ah, Skye? He's bidding on something," Rachael whispered. "I think it's that ornate wooden box. I thought that was a jewelry box. Why would he want that?"

"Maybe he has a girlfriend," Skye muttered. She turned to say something to Preston, but he was gone. She looked all around her, but he clearly was no longer in the auction bidding area. She whirled around, her eyes searching for Creepy Goth Guy whose real name was Aidan, but he was gone too!

"Where's Mr. Preston?" Rachael asked.

"I don't know, but Aidan is gone too. Good riddance to both of them. Is there anything else you want to bid on?"

"Um...shouldn't you...you know...?"

"No. Not now. Forget about it."

"Okay." Rachael eyed Skye with some skepticism, then looked around them at the various items for auction nearby. "Let's head down this row. Then we will have seen everything."

The two of them walked along, occasionally stopping to examine something a bit closer, but Skye's mind was only partially involved. The evening wouldn't be over for a couple more hours. Was Aidan still lurking about somewhere? She supposed not, since she didn't feel any prickling along her skin. He hadn't been at the dinner. She would've noticed. So, he just showed up to make a bid or two and then left? Very strange. Although Skye kept searching the crowd for Aidan's black, leather clad body for the rest of the evening, she didn't see him again.

CHAPTER SIX

THE FOLLOWING WEEK WAS ENTIRELY UNEVENT-
ful. Skye didn't see Aidan, didn't hear from John Preston, and she
was lulled into thinking maybe all that nonsense would simply go
away. She spent much of the time preparing for her move to the San Diego
apartment with Rachael, and on their moving day, Derek and Skye's dad
helped transport boxes and suitcases from their car into the apartment,
while Rachael's dad did the same with Rachael's things.

"My room is on the right," Rachael said. "Skye's is on the left."

The dads and Derek followed directions, and deposited the appropriate
boxes and suitcases into their proper places.

"I love this bathroom!" Rachael exclaimed. And Skye had to agree
with her.

It was a Jack and Jill set up, with one entrance from Skye's room and
another from Rachael's. The walls were white, but the tile on the floor
and half way up the walls was a combination of light-colored natural stone
with ceramic accent pieces done in various shades of blue and green. There
was a wall in the center with a mirror on either side. Each side also had
its own sink, medicine cabinet, and storage cupboards and drawers. The
counters and sinks coordinated with the rest of the color theme, in rich
hues of blue and green.

"That's the last of it," Derek said.

Rachael's dad glanced around the apartment. "You girls will have a lot
of sorting out to do."

"No problem!" Skye beamed. "We'll get it done."

Skye's dad nodded. "All right then, we'll leave you girls to it."

"Your moms should be here soon to take you girls out to look for a coffee maker and whatever else you need," Rachael's dad added.

"Okay, thanks!" Skye called out as her dad, Derek, and Rachael's dad slipped out the door. Once they were gone, she darted here and there, unpacking clothes and make-up, pictures and jewelry, books and other odds and ends. She was so excited to have her own place. Well, hers and Rachael's. It would take them the rest of the day and probably at least a couple of more to get everything situated and in its place. Thoughts of John Preston and the whole Assassin business threatened to inch into her thoughts, but she pushed them firmly away.

After numerous trips to the grocery store, drug store, mall and various other places like to the university campus, Skye was no longer intimidated by her surroundings. She felt almost as at home in San Diego as she had across the bay in Coronado. By Saturday evening, both girls flopped on the sofa in the living room, exhausted but happy, and surveyed their surroundings.

Rachael smiled. "It looks great."

"Yep, everything is perfect."

"So, you hungry?" Rachael asked.

"Yeah, how about some of that left over tortellini?"

"Sounds good. Salad?"

"Sure."

They got up and went to the kitchen. Skye put the pasta in a bowl to be microwaved, while Rachael pulled lettuce, tomatoes and other salad makings from the refrigerator and started chopping.

"You know, it's weird you haven't heard anything from Mr. Preston all week. Don't you think maybe—?"

There was a knock at the door, and Skye looked up in surprise. Who would come visit them, unannounced, at seven o'clock at night? She peaked out the window. "Speak of the devil."

"What? Seriously? At dinner time?" Rachael muttered.

What was the point in denying him entry? She opened the door and let him in.

"Ms. Perry," Preston gave a nod to Rachael after coming in, then turned to Skye.

"I brought you some supplies." He hefted the large bag he held in his fist, and deposited it on the wooden coffee table. He unzipped the bag and withdrew a surprising number of weapons: knives, stakes, even a small crossbow!

"Any of these can pierce the heart and kill a Blood-Hunter. I have swords also. Sometimes decapitation is a superior alternative."

Skye tore her gaze from the array of weapons. "Well, um…I—"

But Preston continued. "Now, both Nikolai and Aidan are still in the area, and have been seen squabbling over a rather ornately carved wooden box. The same box we saw at the charity event on Coronado Island, in fact."

"Um, excuse me, but—" Rachael began, but the timer on the stove interrupted her. Rachael ducked into the kitchen.

"We were just about to eat," Skye said. "Maybe we can talk about this some other time."

"Go right ahead. Don't let my presence here stop you."

For a split-second Skye wanted to use one of those weapons he'd delivered on him. The man was so presumptuous! She had so hoped the week of not hearing from him meant the Bureau had reconsidered having her as an Assassin after all, but apparently it was just the lull before the storm. She got a plate and sat down with Rachael to eat while John Preston explained what he knew about Nikolai, Aidan and the box.

"The box, apparently, has been passed down through more than a couple of generations of Blood-Hunters. It ended up at the charity event because it was stolen in a robbery several years ago, and thereby passed into the hands of humans. It contains an ancient evil which must never be released."

Rachael set down her fork and looked at him. "What kind of evil?"

Preston glanced over at her. "The kind that takes the form of a demon."

Skye sucked in a breath and Rachael's eyes widened.

"So how does this box work? Is it like…a cage for the demon or something?" Skye asked.

"Yes, that's it exactly. So far, none of the humans who have come in contact with the box have managed to open it, neither accidentally nor on purpose. Most probably none of them has any idea of what it truly is," Preston replied. "Besides, there is magic involved. An incantation must be spoken as the box is being opened, and the box has many drawers and compartments. The correct sequence must be used in opening the box, to release the demon spirit."

Skye pushed her plate away. A month ago, her biggest worry was what to wear to school each day, and when her next nail appointment should be, but now, however reluctantly, she was being drawn into a world of violence, mystery and magic. Surprisingly, she felt drawn to it rather than repelled by it as she would've expected. Maybe being an Assassin really was a part of her DNA after all.

"Has anyone figured out if Joe Haynes was killed by a Blood-Hunter?" Rachael asked. She seemed to have lost her appetite too.

Preston turned to her. "Yes. My sources have confirmed it."

"Who did it? Was it that Aidan guy?" Poor Rachael looked as though she might start to cry at any moment.

"We don't know. The Blood-Hunters in that area are a transient group. Penelope is no longer a problem, thanks to Skye, but Nikolai, Aidan and several others have been spotted in the area within recent weeks."

"Didn't you say there were a *lot* of Blood-Hunters here?" Skye asked.

Preston nodded. "Yes, quite a few. We don't know what the connection is between Nikolai and Aidan. Aidan is a loner, while Nikolai is affiliated with a Coven."

"A Coven is a group of Blood-Hunters with a blood connection, right?" Rachael asked.

"Correct," Preston replied. "Usually the Coven is small, six to twelve individuals within a family. They don't get any bigger than that, because it's simply not in the nature of Blood-Hunters to form larger societies."

Skye settled back in her chair and looked Preston in the eyes. "I don't suppose there's even a little teeny, weeny chance that I don't have to do this?"

He cocked his head and lifted an eyebrow.

Skye's eyes widened and she held up her hands in surrender. "Okay, okay, I had to ask. I wouldn't be me if I didn't ask." She nodded. "Okay, so, if you're *really* sure I'm capable of doing this—"

"I am."

"Then what is it I'm supposed to do?"

"I'll call you tomorrow and tell you where to patrol in the evenings. You'll need to do some reconnaissance, and then, of course, do what an Assassin is meant to do."

"What should I be looking for? How do you tell the good Blood-Hunters from the bad ones? Are you sure this Bureau of yours can—?"

"Be assured, Ms. Falco, the Bureau is far reaching, both in this country and abroad. The organization's focus is on maintaining the delicate balance between the humans and the non-humans and keeping knowledge of their existence from the public. We keep an eye out for deranged Shape-Shifters who get a taste for human flesh and go on killing sprees. We also look for the occasional demented, power hungry Elfae who wants to rule the world, and we stop them. Trust me; we're very good at what we do." Preston stood. "I'll be in touch to give you specific locations, but in essence, you'll look for Blood-Hunters and for any suspicious activity they might be involved with. Once we get started, this will be a nightly obligation until the box is recovered and the killer of Joe Haynes is terminated. And to answer your other question…determining a good Blood-Hunter from a bad one is relatively easy since most of them would just as soon kill a human as draw breath. The good ones are few and far between."

Preston showed himself out. Skye and Rachael finished what was left of their dinner in silence.

The next night, Skye waited on pins and needles for Preston to contact her. Most of the night passed without her hearing a thing from her Handler, but finally at 10pm he called.

"Aidan and Nikolai are at MacGregor's Irish Pub and Eatery. It's just three blocks from where you live, heading south. It's a restaurant, not just a bar, so you won't have any trouble getting in. Bring Rachael along. You'll look less conspicuous that way."

Skye frowned. "I don't want to put her in danger."

"Just go there and listen in on their conversation. Take note of any other Blood-Hunters who might be present as well. The more we know about the box, who has it, and what the connection between Aidan and Nikolai is, the better. You still have my number?"

"Yes, but—"

"Good. Call me with a report." He hung up.

Skye turned to Rachael. "You up for going to an Irish pub?"

Rachael shrugged. "Sure, I guess, but can we even get in? We're too young. We won't be allowed into a bar until we're twenty-one."

"Preston says it's a restaurant too, so we won't have a problem."

"Okay. That's good. You know I really can't drink alcohol. It isn't good for Elfae. Makes us lose our ability to hold the glamour that keeps humans from seeing what we really look like."

"I didn't know that."

"Yeah. Maintaining glamour is very important to our survival."

Skye nodded. "I'll find MacGregor's Pub on the Internet and see exactly where it is. Preston said three blocks from here, but I want to double check."

Thirty minutes later they were at the restaurant. Immediately Skye felt the hair prickle at the back of her neck.

She and Rachael picked a table in the middle of the room and picked up their menus.

"Blood-Hunters are here somewhere," Skye whispered to Rachael.

"What'll you have?" asked the waitress.

Skye jumped. She hadn't even seen the woman come up, so intent was she on finding the Blood-Hunter.

"I'll have a cheese burger and a Coke please," Rachael replied.

"I'll have the fish tacos and an iced tea," Skye said. Once the waitress was gone, she focused her attention on finding the Blood-Hunter. At least she knew what Aidan looked like. He looked like a creepy goth guy. But she had no idea what Nikolai looked like, or any of the other local Blood-Hunters either.

As luck would have it, she spotted Aidan when he turned away from the bar, and moved toward a table not too far from where she and Rachael sat. The problem was, it was far too noisy for her to be able to catch anything being said over at the other table. She did notice there were two other men sitting there, however. One had shaggy blond hair and a scar on his neck. The other had short black hair, a mustache and goatee, neatly trimmed, and eyes as dark as coal.

Skye leaned toward Rachael. "I found Aidan. He keeps some pretty rough company. At least from the looks of them."

Rachael followed her gaze. "Ugh. You're not kidding. Now what?"

The waitress brought their drinks, then left again.

"So, what's the plan?" Rachael asked. "There's no way we can hear their conversation from here."

Skye knew she had to do something to get closer to the other table, or their entire evening would be a waste of time. She took note of where the restrooms were located, and quickly came up with a plan. "I'll be right back. Cross your fingers that this works." She stood up.

Rachael's eyes widened. "What're you going to do?"

"Nothing I haven't threatened to do before to get a guy's attention." She smiled, but deep down, she was really nervous. Not only was this going to be a bold move on her part, but these guys weren't humans, they were Blood-Hunters!

She headed for the restroom, right by the table where Aidan and the others sat drinking and talking. When she was alongside Aidan's chair, she pretended to trip, and nearly landed in his lap. His beer sloshed over the rim of his glass, but he managed to catch her and set her back on her feet in one swift movement.

He grinned at her. "Watch where you're going, darlin'."

Skye took one look into his eyes and decided maybe he wasn't a creepy Goth guy after all. He was gorgeous! Irish accent and all. She smiled at him. "Oh, I'm so sorry. I twisted my ankle and just toppled over." She rubbed it a bit, just to look convincing. "Again, sorry."

"Well, be on your way then. We have business to discuss."

Skye turned to see who had spoken. It was the man with the black mustache and goatee. His face was hard and cruel, but Skye was close enough now to detect that he wasn't a Blood-Hunter like Aidan and the other man at the table. She didn't think he was entirely human either, however, and she looked for Elfae glamour, or the Shape-Shifter's signature wolf shadow around his features. She couldn't see either form of natural magic. So, what was he? She'd have to ask Preston about that the next time she talked to him.

"Nonsense." Aidan pulled out the fourth chair at the table for her. "Have a seat."

"I have a friend with me." Skye turned to look at Rachael who smiled. She looked nervous, but then so was Skye.

"Invite her over then. I'll find another chair." Aidan looked pointedly at the man with the mustache. "Our business is done here for tonight."

The other man stood and glared at Skye and then Aidan. "You're not helping your own cause by putting things off. This isn't over."

He disappeared through the crowd, and Skye hoped she'd seen the last of him. He made her uneasy, especially since she couldn't pin down what he was or how he fit into the situation.

"Well, go get your friend then, now there's room." Aidan indicated the chair just vacated by the man with the mustache.

"Oh, I don't know." This was exactly what Skye had been hoping for, but she had to play it cool just the same. "Our food hasn't come yet and I—"

"There's the waitress with your food now. Perfect timing."

Skye turned to look, and sure enough, the waitress had just set down their meals. "Well, I hate to—"

"Yes, yes! Come on, I don't bite. Call your lovely friend over and we'll pass some time getting to know each other."

Skye nearly choked on laughter. Did he really say, 'I don't bite'? She looked at Aidan's companion to see his reaction.

"Sure, bring her over. The night is young." His accent was slightly Russian sounding. This then, most likely was, Nikolai.

"Okay, well, if you really don't mind. It is crowded, and I'm sure some-one else would be glad to have our table." She gave Aidan a brilliant smile, then made her way back to the little table where Rachael still sat. "Come on. Pick up your plate. We're moving."

"We're doing what?" Rachael blurted, her eyes huge and round.

Skye picked up her drink and her food. "Just remember not to say their names. We're not supposed to know anything about them."

Rachael scooped up her plate and glass. "Okay, but I hope you know what you're doing."

When they returned to the other table, only Aidan was there. Skye hesitated. "Where's your friend?"

Aidan looked up at her. "Our business was done. He left. Come on, have a seat."

Skye frowned. Something wasn't right here. The other guy had sounded like he wanted to stay and now he was gone. She sat across from Aidan, in the seat recently vacated by the evil looking man with the mustache and goatee. Rachael slid into the seat next to hers.

"So," Skye began. "Your friend didn't give the impression he was leaving. Did something change?"

Aidan's eyes hardened. "You might say that. But like I said, our business was done. It was time for him to go." He took a sip of his beer. "Why? Were you interested in him?"

Skye shook her head. "No, absolutely not."

"Well, you're asking a lot of questions for someone who isn't interested." He lifted an eyebrow.

"No, trust me," Rachael piped up. "She isn't. I'm Rachael by the way, and this is Skye. And you are...?"

"Aidan. Pleased to meet you both. I haven't seen you here before."

"We just moved here," Skye replied.

"Ah, 'tis a fine place."

"San Diego, or this place?" Skye asked.

"Both!" Aidan grinned.

An hour slipped by while the three of them made small talk. Skye despaired of learning anything worthwhile. Later, when she and Rachael were back home and by themselves, something occurred to her.

"Rachael, can Elfae recognize Blood-Hunters and Shape-Shifters and visa versa?

"No." Rachael shook her head. "We know each other exists, and we can recognize each other, but not in the way you can, now that you're an Assassin. For instance, I didn't know Aidan was a Blood-Hunter, only that he was something other than pure human. That's all."

"So, what would he sense about you?"

"He would sense my magic, but Shape-Shifters have a type of magic too. He would realize I'm not human or a Blood-Hunter, but that's it."

Skye thought about that. "He didn't say anything about it tonight when we were at the restaurant."

Rachael shrugged. "He wouldn't. He would probably assume that because I was with you, and you're human, that you don't know I'm Elfae or Shape-Shifter, any more than you'd know he was a Blood-Hunter. He'd keep his mouth shut, because the one thing we all have in common is that we must remain invisible to humans."

"Why? I mean, Preston mentioned that too, but—"

Rachael gave her a look that said she was an idiot. "Because most humans would either consider us as something to lock away and study, or hunt down and kill." She shrugged. "Of course, most of the Blood-Hunters deserve to be killed."

"But that wouldn't happen!"

"Oh, yes it would. It has, and it would again, believe me. So, most of us keep a low profile; except of course for the occasional wacko. The Blood-Hunters are more inclined to have wackos among their numbers. I'm told it's the whole blood lust thing. They often lose control and kill people, or they just don't care, like Mr. Preston said."

"Hey, speaking of wackos, I don't suppose you could tell what that other guy was? You know, the guy with the mustache? He was...I don't know, different somehow."

Rachael shrugged. "I just thought he was human. He wasn't?"

"No. Maybe. I don't know. There was something...off, about him."

"Well, talk to Preston about it. Maybe he'll know something."

"I figured his main focus was Blood-Hunters."

"Maybe, but like he said, the Bureau of the Extraordinary does lots of other stuff, so he'll be able to find out who that guy is."

Skye yawned. "I'm too tired to think about this stuff anymore. I'm going to bed."

"Shouldn't you call Preston and tell him—"

"And tell him what? That we had dinner with a Blood-Hunter?" Skye went to her room and got ready for bed. She looked down at her nail polish. It was chipped. In spite of all that had been on her mind recently, the fact that her nails didn't look perfect, suddenly became a huge irritation. She decided that the first thing she would do when she got up tomorrow, was paint her nails. At least that was one thing she was reasonably sure she could have some control over. Polish might be tricky, and possibly messy, but it wasn't deadly. At least it wasn't if you didn't swallow it or get it in your eye or something. And what were the chances of that anyway?

CHAPTER SEVEN

THE NEXT MORNING. AFTER PAINTING HER NAILS A brilliant shade of red, Skye called John Preston. Twenty minutes later she had a patrol route for the daytime and another one for the night.

"Are you kidding me? I'm supposed to do this twice a day? When am I supposed to have a life?"

"You're not in school yet, Ms. Falco. You have plenty of free time."

"Why is it that half the time you call me Skye and the other half I'm Ms. Falco? I hate that whole Ms. Falco thing. It's so formal. It's...I don't know...weird. Just call me Skye, okay?"

"Fine, and you can call me, Mr. Preston or Preston. Not, John. I'm your Handler, not your buddy. Are we clear on that?"

"Wow. Okay. Yeah, crystal. You don't have to get all testy. But seriously, I'm not going to get any summer vacation at all, what with you having me make the rounds of every place Aidan or that Russian Blood-Hunter have ever been."

"His name is Nikolai. I've confirmed it in our database, using the description you gave to me as a point of reference. I have the computer results right in front of me. He got that scar on his neck from nearly being decapitated by an adversary two decades ago."

So, it *was* Nikolai. "An adversary? Does that mean an Assassin?"

"It could mean that, or possibly he angered another Blood-Hunter, or even a Shape-Shifter or an Elfae."

Skye thought of how Aidan had seemed angry with Nikolai the night before. She wondered if the two of them would come to blows and kill each other off. That would sure make her job easier. Then she could call it a day and go to the beach.

It was strange to think of killing creatures that just looked like regular people part of the time, not monsters. In fact, she didn't know if she would even be able to kill a Blood-Hunter who wasn't all fangy and black-eyed. It would be too much like killing a human. In spite of what she knew of the Blood-Hunter's 'dark side', if Aidan continued to look all handsome and sounded all sexy with his Irish brogue, she felt sure she couldn't kill him. No way. Yeah, it would be better if Nikolai and Aidan offed each other. Way better.

Skye shifted the phone to her other ear. "Does your computer tell you who killed Joe Haynes? That would be helpful."

"I still have no idea. The width of the bite marks would indicate a male attacker rather than female. Additionally, the bites themselves are proof of a Blood-Hunter rather than a Shape-Shifter, having made the kill."

Skye's stomach turned over. "He's not a 'kill', he was my childhood friend. He was a person. Joe was a person."

Preston's voice softened. "Of course, he was. My apologies, Ms... ah... Skye. In any case, we're no closer to pinpointing who killed your friend, other than to confirm it was a male Blood-Hunter."

"So, it could be someone other than Aidan or Nikolai, right?"

"Yes. It is absolutely possible. But your mission, at the moment, has to do with the box we discussed. We must find it and keep it from being opened. All hell will break loose, quite literally, if that box gets spelled and opened."

Skye's lips twisted into a wry smile. "What if Aidan or someone, just thought it was pretty and wanted to have it? Or bought it to give as a gift. Have you thought of that? Maybe you're blowing this whole thing way out of proportion. Maybe nobody is looking to open it."

There was silence on the other end of the line, and then Skye heard Preston sigh. "As a Handler I've learned that seldom is a Blood-Hunter's motive simply to buy a gift for a loved one, or to own something because it's pretty. Whoever has it, knows full well what it is and what it does. The only rub is whether or not they know how to get into it."

Skye sighed. If Aidan bid on the box at the charity event, then he was smack dab in the middle of everything.

"I wonder who donated the box to the shelter charity event in the first place."

"A woman by the name of..."

Skye heard pages rustling.

"Shannon Doyle," Preston continued. "We've looked into it. So far there is no connection between Aidan or Nikolai and this woman. She is simply a huge animal lover and supporter of the shelter and has been for several years now, so she donated the box."

"And did it bring a high bid?"

"Yes. The animal shelter made two thousand dollars off the high bidder that night."

Skye was shocked. "So, who was the high bidder?"

"We're running the name through our records. So far, nothing. It's possible whoever it was used an alias."

Skye frowned. "But they'd have to present a credit card and get it on record before the auction began. That's how silent auctions work."

"I know that, but a stolen credit card and fake name wouldn't be found out until much later. In the meantime, the shelter would've contacted the high bidder with the phone number the person left as a contact number. The person then would come retrieve their item, and that's that. It may take some time, but we'll figure it out. In the meantime, I suggest you start patrolling the routes I gave to you. Perhaps you'll run into Aidan again and get some inkling as to who currently has the box. That is the most important thing, after all. It's the first step in getting the box safely into the hands of the Bureau."

Skye's voice dripped sarcasm. "So, I'm just supposed to casually bring the box up in conversation?"

"You'll figure it out. You're a resourceful girl."

"Well, what if—?"

"Don't worry about it, Skye. You just do your job and I'll do mine. Now please, enough talk. Go patrol."

"Yeah. Okay, I'll talk to you later," she said.

"Report back to me twice a day from now on."

"Right. I will." Skye tapped the button that disconnected the call. "I'm going out!" she called to Rachael, who poked her head out of her bedroom at the sound of Skye's voice.

"I'm going out too. With a friend of mine. Her name is Starr. She's one of my Elfae friends. We're getting together for lunch. Where are you going? Do you want to come with us?"

Skye shook her head. "You two go ahead. I'll catch up with you later." She wasn't jealous of Rachael's freedom to go out and have fun. On the contrary, Skye was actually relieved. She didn't want to involve her friend in everything she was doing, especially when things might get more complicated and more dangerous.

When Skye went to change out of her pajamas and get dressed, she studied her clothes. In spite of the fact, she was loath to believe it, could Preston's admonishment for her to add darker and sturdier fabrics to her wardrobe be a good idea after all? On the practical side, dark clothes would help her blend into the shadows if she had to sneak around at night. Also, sandals looked great in the summer with dresses, capris and even jeans, but they didn't protect her feet or give her much in the way of traction if she had to climb or run. When she fought with her first Blood-Hunter, she'd probably gotten lucky it was a girl. The Blood-Hunter had worn a dress and heels, just like Skye had, but if she'd fought a guy, someone like, Nikolai, for instance, would she have been as lucky? Or would her clothing have worked against her and defeated her in the end? It was something to think about.

She reached for her white capris, pulled on a red peasant blouse that matched her newly polished nails and slipped on her gold sandals. Her little cross-body gold metallic purse finished the look, along with a thin gold headband to hold her hair back. Skye looked in the mirror. She tried to picture herself wearing black jeans and a pullover, along with utilitarian type black boots. Ugh! Maybe. Eventually. But not today. Not when the sun shone an invitation to be outdoors, and there was a cool breeze helping to make the day not too awfully warm. Today she'd wear what she liked.

She headed out, but paused by her open closet door. The duffle Preston had brought over was there. Skye bent down to retrieve a wooden stake. She opened her purse and dropped it in. Better to be safe than sorry.

The first place on the patrol route she'd gotten from Preston was the Auto Mall Sales & Repair, which was located the full length of one city block. Various high-end auto dealers sold vehicles there on either side of the street, and several repair shops also had businesses for both foreign and domestic cars. Since Preston had discovered Aidan owned a Boxter, and also loved to look at other expensive cars, this was one of the places she was told to patrol.

Skye parked her 200 in the public parking area, located dead center of the block, and proceeded to stroll up one side and down the next. Mercedes Benz, Jaguar, Volvo, BMW, Lexus, Land Rover, everywhere she looked there were cars to drool over. Though she enjoyed looking at the cars just as much as everyone else on the lots, she was soon distracted by the prickly sensation that could only mean one thing; a Blood-Hunter was nearby. She looked around, and saw Aidan looking at a Lunar Blue Metallic SLK Class Roadster. Thank goodness it was him and not Nikolai or some other Blood-Hunter. She wasn't sure what she would've done, but this was easy.

"Nice car," she called out.

He lifted his head and turned toward the sound of her voice. "Ah, it's the girl from the pub. Skye, isn't it?"

She headed over to him and smiled up into his green eyes. "Yes, Skye. And your name is Aidan, right?"

"That it is."

"So, looking to buy a new car?"

"Nah, mine's just in getting an oil change, so I'm doing a bit of window shopping. What about you?"

Skye shrugged. "The same. About the window shopping I mean."

Just then a salesman walked up. Both Aidan and Skye made their excuses and moved off the lot onto the sidewalk.

Aidan checked his watch. "Time for me to go. Nice to see you again." He turned to go.

"Wait!" Skye called out.

Aidan turned and looked at her.

Skye gave a little laugh. "I was just wondering…"

Aidan's eyes lifted in amusement. "Yes?"

"Ah, never mind." She waved at him. "Nothing. Bye."

Aidan tilted his head and gave her a puzzled look, then turned and walked away.

Skye watched him walk away. She felt like an idiot. She'd accomplished nothing. And how could this guy be a Blood-Hunter? He seemed so nice. He was even polite! Obviously, that didn't have any bearing on things. She gave herself a mental shake and went back to her car. Oh well, just so the day wasn't a total loss, she could always go to the mall. A little shopping sounded like fun.

It didn't take long and Skye was right in her element. Shops all around her! Where to begin? In every store, she was immediately drawn to her usual colors and styles, but then Preston's words came back to her. Dark colors. More sturdy fabrics. She'd only intended to window shop, but before Skye realized it, she had black jeans, draped over her arm, as well as both long and short-sleeved black tops. She tried them on, and stared at her reflection in the mirror. It all looked so drab, so boring. She supposed she could dress it all up with an ornate belt, a colorful scarf, or some big chunky jewelry. She selected a few items to buy, then continued on to look at shoes. Where did one find black boots in the middle of the summer?

Skye walked through the mall until she came across a likely store. The front of the shop gave her pause. It was painted solid black and the windows looked like they were covered in giant spider webs. Skye took a deep fortifying breath, and plunged into the store.

Loud, harsh music assailed her ears. She headed straight to the back of the store where the boots and other shoes were, glanced around, then spun and made a beeline out of the store. It was enough she'd purchased a whole shopping bag filled with black clothing. She'd just have to be satisfied with some black sneakers because there was no way she was ever going into that store again! The mere thought of putting those hideous boots on her feet was enough to make her gag.

Skye walked as quickly as she could, away from the Goth store. Did Aidan shop in stores like that? Probably not. His clothing looked expensive; all that leather. How did Blood-Hunters make money? Did they steal it? Invest it? Gamble? Pass it down to themselves from generation to generation?

When she finally left the mall, Skye had added black sneakers and socks and a pair of black capris to what she'd come to think of as her new Midnight Collection, as well as a pretty new skirt in a swirl of yellow, orange, gold and red. It made her happy just to look at it, after all that dreary black!

By the time Skye returned home, it was almost dark outside. She'd frittered most of the day away, and now she'd have to spend her evening patrolling. She hauled her shopping bags to her bedroom, and unpacked everything, then proceeded to clip off tags, put some items in the hamper to be washed, and then tried to decide what to wear for this evening's patrol.

She chose the new black capris and tossed them on the bed. Next, she retrieved her new black socks and sneakers, then tried to decide on a top to wear. Her instincts pulled her toward the array of blues, greens, pinks and sunny yellows in her drawer. Heck, half black was a start, wasn't it? She'd wear the turquoise blue tunic with the sash, and a pair of tiny flowered gold barrettes in her hair.

Skye changed clothes and looked again at herself in the mirror. Oh, how she wanted to wear her black sandals instead of the sneakers. She tugged them off along with the socks, and slipped on her sandals instead. They were a gladiator style, and wound around her ankle with multiple straps across her arches. That looked *so* much better than those clunky new sneakers! With a satisfied smile, Skye reached for her purse, then headed for her car once again. She had patrolling to do.

In spite of her original dread at the idea of being an Assassin, Skye now found herself strangely motivated. Part of it was to avenge her friend, Joe. Another part was that she really, really, didn't want that box, with the demon imprisoned inside, to be opened. If she could help stop that from happening, then she'd do what she could. Skye also realized she sort of liked knowing about things other humans didn't. Of course, that knowledge came with great responsibility, but she tried not to focus on that part. She also tried not to think about the husband and family she'd now probably never have, and her life expectancy being quite possibly much shorter than she'd originally expected. Then again, maybe it could all still work out somehow; she'd live to a ripe old age, and find true love somewhere along the line as well. She could always hope for the best.

Chapter Eight

SKYE STARTED HER EVENING PATROL. IT WASN'T until she reached the neighborhood park, that she began to get that prickly feeling at her neck again. She ducked behind some nearby bushes, then played 'warmer/colder' with her senses until she found the Blood-Hunters.

Under a canopy of trees, with the moonlight filtering through the leaves, stood Nikolai and Aidan. Skye glanced down at her shirt. It looked dark, but not dark enough for her to be entirely invisible. She thought about her gold barrettes. Was the moonlight gleaming off them this very minute, giving away her position? She yanked them from her hair and stuffed them in her pocket. Next time she'd just pull her hair into a ponytail or twist it into a braid. But then she got caught up in the conversation between the two Blood-Hunters, and forgot about clothes and accessories.

"Where's Lucius?" Aidan asked.

"He's staying away, thanks to you," Nikolai snapped. "But that's fine. He doesn't need to talk with you anyway. I have the box; he has the spell. You're out of it."

"I'm not out of it! By rights that box is mine, and I mean to have it back!"

Skye thought she could even see a flash of Aidan's fangs in the moonlight. She scrambled up onto a large rock behind some trees, so she could see better.

Nikolai's lips twisted into a cruel sneer. "Possession, as they say, is nine-tenths of the law. I have the box. I out bid you for it. It's mine."

"And if I'd won the bid?"

"I'd have stolen it, of course." Nikolai looked quite menacing. Especially since he had several inches on Aidan, who was probably around five foot ten. He jabbed Aidan in the chest with his finger. "The box is mine and there's nothing you can do about it."

Aidan drew himself up to his full height. His upper lip pulled back to reveal two long pointy fangs. "Nikolai, you don't know what you're doing!"

"Yeah, I do."

"No, you don't! Now give me the box!"

"No. You want to be the one to do it, don't you? You want to take credit for releasing Mortmal the Destroyer into the world. But that will never happen because I am going to be the one. Me! And—"

"You insane moron! I—"

And that was when Skye's sandal started to slip against the face of the rock she stood on. She willed herself still, but the sandal continued to slip until she was forced to leap off her rocky perch or fall to the ground in a heap. Her newfound strength served her well, however, and she managed to regain her feet quickly. She took off at a dead run, but her sandals slipped in the wet grass and it was all she could do to keep her balance and gain traction. She really wished she had on those sneakers after all, but it was too late to fret about it now. She had to run, and probably for her life. She didn't want to wait around to see how she'd fare in a fight with two Blood-Hunters at once. She figured it would be far more difficult than fighting one in spike heels and a tight skirt. Unfortunately, she didn't get far.

Aidan stood in front of her, so suddenly that she skidded to a halt and nearly smashed into him. She quickly backed up to put some distance between them. Nikolai was off to her left. Her heart started to pound, but then a strange calmness flowed through her. She could deal with this. She had to.

"An unanticipated snack." Nikolai sauntered forward, his eyes black, and his grin revealed gleaming fangs. "It's your little friend from the other night. That's what you get for being nice to them. Better to have had her blood and been done with it. Where's the little blonde? Hiding behind a tree, perhaps?"

Skye cast a level gaze his way. "You won't live long enough to find out."

In a blur of movement, Aidan was upon her. He stood behind her, one arm around her waist and the other in her hair, cocking her head to the side, his hot breath on her neck.

"I'll take care of it," he snarled at Nikolai. "You've got the damn box. This is mine. Now, go!"

Skye panicked for a second, but then realized her odds were better against one Blood-Hunter than two. Maybe this would work out to her advantage.

Nikolai chuckled. "I'm glad you finally see things my way." He gave Skye a lingering look up and down. "Enjoy your snack." And then he faded into the shadows.

Aidan released her, but not before she'd elbowed him in the gut and leapt back, ready to fight.

He barely reacted to her elbow, and instead put his hands on his hips and shook his head. "You're going to fight me after I just saved your life? What's wrong with you, girl? Walking alone at night. Eavesdropping on people. Picking fights. You don't look the type."

Skye started to drop her fists, but Aidan shoved her backwards into a tree trunk and hovered over her, his hands painfully tight around her upper arms.

"What do you know, girl? I think maybe you've seen too much. Too much for me to let you live."

Skye tilted her chin up and looked him in the eyes. "Seen too much? You mean like do I see fangs in your mouth and do I see your eyes like obsidian staring at me right now? Do I know you and your friend are Blood-Hunters? Oh, yeah, I'm aware of that." She thrust her arms up between them and broke his hold. "Now what have *you* seen, huh? What are you looking at, Aidan?"

The moment was almost here. The fight would soon be on. Could she win? Could she kill him? She was probably outmatched with Aidan, and the thought caused a shiver of fright to run down her back. This could be the night her young life was over. She steeled herself for the battle that was sure to come.

They stood not three feet apart and he stared at her, his eyes narrowed. Their color returned to green and his fangs receded. "I think I'm seeing something I haven't seen in quite a while. I think I'm looking at an Assassin. *Skye*."

Damn, did her name have to sound so wonderful when he said it with that Irish brogue?

"So, now what?" she asked.

"Well, that depends on you. We can fight or we can go our separate ways."

"So, you can get your hands on that box? Take it away from Nikolai?"

Aidan's eyebrows lifted slightly and he cocked his head. "What box would that be, darlin'?"

Should she reveal what she knew? Why not. "The box you bid on at the Pause for Paws event a couple of weeks ago. The box Nikolai apparently out bid you on and now has."

He sidestepped her reference to the box by changing the subject. "Your Handler has brought you up to speed, I see, about Nikolai. Very clever how you wheedled your way into sitting at my table the other night. And I suppose seeing you at the car dealers was planned as well. How long have you been an Assassin? I'm sure I would've known if there had been one here for very long."

"I've been one long enough."

"Long enough?"

"Long enough to kick your Irish backside."

Aidan started laughing, and Skye used it as an opportunity to side-kick him in the stomach. He stumbled back, but didn't fall. The smile was still on his face.

"If that's the way you want it then, darlin'. Bring it on." In three strides he was on her, and the fisticuffs began.

Bobbing and weaving, Skye was at a disadvantage in her gladiator sandals. She landed some blows but slipped on the damp grass and that was all it took for Aidan to get the upper hand. His fist connected with her jaw, snapping her head back, and down she went.

He stood over her, wiping blood from his lip. It still ran from his nose where she'd popped him. "Not bad for a girl."

She propped herself up on both elbows and glared at him. The thought occurred to her that he probably could've already killed her by now if he'd really wanted to. He was toying with her. She swept her legs around and knocked his legs out from under him. He fell hard, with a surprised look on his face. Skye leapt to her feet and he did the same.

He pointed at his face. "You don't see fangs, do you? And my eyes aren't black. I haven't even begun to fight. I'm not even angry, just amused. Stay out of my way little girl. Forget about the box. Just stay home and pray I wind up with it, not Nikolai."

There was another blur of movement, and he was gone. Skye dropped her fists and stood up from her slightly crouched position. "Note to self… Next time when patrolling wear sneakers," she muttered. She'd learned her lesson. Also, a ponytail or braids would be a good idea, to keep the hair out of her face. Another lesson learned. She adjusted the barrettes in her hair once again, then noticed the stake she'd previously tucked into her back pocket was gone. She searched the ground for it, and finally found it several feet away. Okay, she'd have to ask Preston about a way to anchor it and make it more secure. The stake wouldn't do her any good lying on the ground. It needed to be in her hand.

Skye turned and headed back to her car. She was ready for a long hot soak in the tub. She gingerly rubbed her neck, but it was already starting to feel much better. Pain seemed to come and go rather quickly these days, and for that she was grateful. If Aidan was just entertaining himself, she'd have to be much more careful in the future. He was much better at fighting than the female Blood-Hunter she'd staked, that was for sure.

As she drove home, Skye thought about Nikolai, the box, and the references to Lucius and someone called, Mortmal the Destroyer. It must be the name of the demon in the box. That didn't sound good. She'd have to ask Preston. She'd call him when she got back to the apartment; after that hot soak in the bathtub. But, as luck would have it, Preston called her before she even got the water turned on.

"You hadn't called. It's midnight. I thought I should check on you."

"I'm fine. Well, a little scuffed up, but otherwise good. I was just about to run a bath could I—?"

"What did you find out?"

Skye sighed. "Couldn't this just wait until—?"

"No. Your responsibility as an Assassin requires you—"

"All right, all right! I saw Nikolai and Aidan at the park. They were arguing over the box, and then they saw me, and Aidan told Nikolai to leave and then he and I duked it out for a while and then—"

"Wait, slow down and breathe. Now what about the box? Start there."

Skye gave up on getting off the phone quickly, and collapsed on her bed. "Aidan wants the box. Nikolai says possession is nine-tenths of the law. And then there was some mention of a guy named, Lucius, and also Mortmal the Destroyer. Oh, hey, how can I get a stake to stay in my pocket? Or is there some other way to—?"

"Mortmal the Destroyer! So, they most certainly *do* know what they're after. Did they say anything else about this Lucius character?"

Skye wracked her brain trying to remember. "Oh, yeah, he has the spell. Nikolai said that Lucius has the spell."

"This is bad. Really bad." Preston's voice sounded tight with anger and maybe even fear. "If they have the box and a Spell-Master—"

"What's a Spell-Master?"

"A Spell-Master is a human who steals magic and uses it to cast spells. It's a dark type of magic. Not at all like the natural abilities of the Elfae."

Skye sat up. Now she was really intrigued. "Stolen magic? Who do they steal it from? And how?"

"They steal it by killing Elfae. Then they—"

"What?" Now Skye was on her feet. "There are people out there who kill Elfae for their magic? But how do they even know about Elfae? I thought you said no humans could see Elfae because of their glamour!"

"I don't know how these people learned about the Elfae, but the way they locate them is easy once a person knows a little about glamour."

"What do you mean?"

"Usually, Elfae are very careful not to drink alcohol or take any sorts of medications which might cause them to lose control of their glamour. But, if a knowledgeable person were to secretly put something into an Elfae's drink, eventually the Elfae's glamour would slip, the human would know the Elfae was an Elfae, and then—"

"And then the human would kill the Elfae and take his or her magic." Skye was terrified for Rachael. Did her friend know there were people out there who could and would do something like that to her?

"Preston, I've got to go. I need to talk to Rachael." She hung up without waiting for a reply. And where was Rachael, by the way? Had her car been in the parking lot? Skye didn't remember seeing it, but she hadn't exactly been looking for the Murano, either. Instead of running the water for her bath, she knocked softly on Rachael's bedroom door. When there was no answer, she slowly turned the knob and looked in.

"Rachael? Rachael, are you in here?"

"Huh? What? Skye?"

Skye saw Rachael's form in the darkness, as she reached for the lamp by her bed. It snapped on, flooding the room with a gentle light. Rachael turned to her with a confused frown.

"What's going on? What time is it?"

"It's around one in the morning." Skye entered the room and sat at the end of her friend's bed. "I just wanted to make sure you were here. That you're okay."

"I'm fine."

"I need to talk to you."

"Now?"

"Yes, now. I just got off the phone with Preston. He told me there are people who kill Elfae and steal their magic. Do you know about that? He says they sometimes put something in your drink to—"

"Ugh, I know, I know." Rachael plopped back onto her pillow and closed her eyes. "Can't we talk about this in the morning?"

"It is morning. You really do know about this, or are you just saying that to—?"

"Yes, yes, I know about it. And I mean later in the morning. Like about eight hours from now."

"But I'm worried about you. What if—?"

"I told you I can take care of myself. I've been an Elfae my whole life, Skye. You've only been an Assassin for a few weeks. Trust me. I know about the Spell-Masters. I've known for most of my life."

Skye didn't know whether to be angry at her friend's tone of voice and condescending manner, or just chalk it up to Rachael being annoyed at being awakened.

She sighed. "Okay, okay, we'll talk about it some other time. Go back to sleep."

Skye left the room and closed the door behind her. Thoughts of a steamy hot bath beckoned, and she started to run the water. Once the tub was filled, she settled in for a good long soak, but after only a few minutes she found she could hardly keep her eyes open. Now, it was her bed that called to her, not the bath. Skye released the drain and got out. Half asleep, she pulled on blue satin pajamas, brushed her teeth and crawled into bed.

Sleep came at her fast and hard, but dreams of Aidan, the mysterious box, and Rachael being kidnapped, made for a restless night. When she awakened, it was with a gasp of fear. How could she have such utter calm come over her when she was about to fight a Blood-Hunter, yet be terrified of a dream? It was all completely ridiculous. She willed herself to calm down. She took a couple deep breaths and let them out. Her life wasn't exactly normal anymore and since that wasn't likely to change, she was going to have to get used to it. She closed her eyes and did her best to go back to sleep.

When Skye finally emerged from her bedroom, it was to find Rachael munching on a bagel with cream cheese along with some fruit salad. She sat at the kitchen table looking at her laptop, and barely said, hello.

"I'm sorry about last night. About waking you up," Skye said, while rummaging in the refrigerator. Finally, she changed her mind about making an actual meal, and settled for a small container of yogurt with granola, instead. She sat across from Rachael. "What are you doing?"

"Not much, just browsing." Rachael closed the laptop. "About last night. I know you're just worried about me, but really, I can take care of myself. I promise. Elfae do have some magic at their disposal. I'll be all right."

"Okay." Skye changed the subject. "So, I found Aidan and Nikolai last night."

"You did?" Rachael leaned in. "What happened?"

"Well," Skye began, around a mouthful of yogurt and granola, "I overheard them talking about the box, but then I screwed up and slipped off the rock I was standing on and they saw me."

"Yeah, and..."

"And I ran and they chased me. Aidan made Nikolai leave, but then he and I fought."

"Did you stake him?"

"No. He left."

"Oh." Rachael leaned back. "But you're okay?"

Skye shrugged. "Sure." Her cell phone sang a merry tune, and she dug it out of the pocket of her red capris. It was John Preston.

"No need for you to continue the daytime patrol," he said, before she could even finish saying hello.

"Good. But what about—?"

"Now that Nikolai and Aidan know you're an Assassin, word will get around. Daytime patrols will be on an 'as needed' basis from now on. As for tonight, I'd like you to get back out there and see if you can find out more about the box and this Lucius character. I've put in an inquiry, here at the Bureau, for Spell-Masters with that name, and I'll let you know as soon as I learn anything. Call me this evening with a report. I will phone you if I have information about Lucius." He disconnected the call.

Skye sighed. "Well, okay then. It would sure be nice if he'd let me get a word in now and then." She took her empty bowl to the sink and rinsed it.

CHAPTER NINE

THAT NIGHT. AFTER A DAY AT THE BEACH WITH Rachael, Skye came into the living room dressed for patrolling.

"Do you want me to come with you?" Rachael asked, then her eyes widened.

Skye grinned. "I know, right? It's a lot to take in." She flipped aside her jacket. "See the holster for my stakes! Cool huh?"

"I can't believe how different you look. We're polar opposites now." Rachael whispered.

They did look very different from each other. Rachael wore a pink skirt and top with a silver belt and sandals. Her long blonde hair was loose, a silken curtain on either side of her face, held back only by a thin silver headband. On her wrist was a delicate butterfly bracelet, and around her neck she wore a fragile butterfly pendant.

Skye, on the other hand, was dressed in black leggings, flared slightly at the bottom. She wore her black socks and sneakers, as well as a black t-shirt. Her dark auburn hair was in a French braid down her back. She wore no jewelry, no hair accessories, but she did have on something that she had discovered in the duffel Preston had previously brought over. It was a holster, which was now strapped to her thigh. It held three stakes. Skye had slipped on a long, lightweight, black linen jacket over the t-shirt. It kept the holster and stakes concealed.

"Only when I'm patrolling," she replied. "I still have an entire wardrobe of clothes in pretty colors, remember?"

Rachael's eyes met hers. "You'll always be patrolling, Skye. From this night forward, you'll always have half your mind on which direction the next attack will come."

"Well, then we'll both be the safer for it, right?"

Rachael nodded. She still looked a bit in a daze. "So, do you want me to come along?"

Skye was uncertain. On the one hand, it would be nice to have her friend's company. On the other hand, could Rachael *really* take care of herself in a dangerous situation? She studied her friend, and then made her decision. "Okay. Sure. Let's go."

"Where are we going?"

"To MacGregor's Pub again."

"I'm changing." Rachael darted past Skye. "Be right back."

Five minutes later, Rachael returned wearing a pair of black jeans and boots, along with a black and pink floral blouse. Her delicate jewelry was gone, and in their place, she wore a sturdy silver cuff bracelet and a silver necklace with what looked like a half a coin for a pendant.

"There," she exclaimed. "Now I don't look so drastically different from you. I looked silly before."

Skye laughed. "No, I look silly. You looked normal."

"No, you look like an Assassin, and I—"

"You don't have to stop being you, just because I've become an Assassin!"

"No, no, it's nothing like that, but there's a time and a place for everything, right? Tonight, I'm not going to see a movie or out to dinner, I'm going to help my friend, the Assassin, look for Blood-Hunters. It only makes sense that if I'm going on patrol with you, I should dress in... how did Mr. Preston put it? Sturdier fabrics and darker clothes." Rachael smiled. "So, come on, what're we waiting for? Let's go!"

"What's that pendant?" Skye asked as they headed out to the car. "I don't think I've seen it before."

"It's something I've always kept in my jewelry box. Joe gave it to me when were in Junior High. He wore the other half."

Skye smiled. "That's really sweet."

"What's even sweeter is that he always wore his half even though we stopped seeing each other." Rachael smiled. "I wore it for a while, but you know, it doesn't always go with my outfits or other jewelry so eventually it ended up at the bottom of my jewelry box." She fingered the pendant. "Tonight, I thought I'd wear it. Maybe someday soon we'll find out which Blood-Hunter killed him. So, what's the game plan?" Rachael asked as they headed to the parking lot and got in Skye's car.

"We're going to hope that Aidan is there so I can pressure him for information or at least eavesdrop. Nikolai would be second choice."

When they arrived at MacGregor's, Skye surveyed the room, but unfortunately, she didn't see Aidan anywhere. But she did spot the guy with the dark mustache and goatee who had left in a huff the other night. Skye knew what she had to do, and she made a beeline for him, through the crowd, with Rachael right on her heels. She came to a stop right next to his barstool.

"Well, a familiar face. You didn't stick around long enough before for introductions the other night," Skye said.

The man turned his head slightly to look at her. His eyes narrowed as he studied her, then they flicked over to Rachael. "The pretty boy isn't here tonight so there's no reason for you to be here pestering me. Go away." He turned, dismissing her.

Rachael stood shoulder to shoulder with Skye. "Don't be so rude. My friend asked you your name."

And then Skye got that prickly sensation that could only mean one thing. She looked around and hoped to see Aidan. But the voice she heard wasn't Aidan's.

"Ah, look who is here."

Skye turned at the sound of the Russian accent. Nikolai moved to stand on the other side of the man at the bar.

"I see Aidan let you go after all. You look very different tonight. No cute little outfit. No more games, eh?" Nikolai smiled at her.

Skye glared at him then looked at the other man. "You never did tell us your name."

The man gave her a wicked smile. "Lucius, my dearest. It is Lucius."

Skye stiffened. So, this was Lucius; the Spell-Master. Great. She'd been afraid for Rachael, and now she'd gone and put her friend right in danger's path.

"So, boys, what's up with this whole box business?" Skye asked, while trying to sound casual. "Care to share?"

Lucius gave her a level gaze. "You are a nosey girl. What is it you think you know of a box? What box would that be?"

Skye's eyes narrowed. "You know perfectly well what box."

"She overheard Aidan and I arguing in the park," Nikolai replied, then gave her a sly smile. "Why don't you come out back and I'll let you in on our little secret? I'm so proud, I feel like sharing. Come on." Nikolai stood and headed for the door.

"Go!" Rachael whispered. "What are you waiting for? Take him out."

Skye glanced over at Lucius, who suddenly was sporting an evil grin. He slid from his bar stool. "Come along girls, if you're so inquisitive." Then he moved to follow Nikolai.

Skye looked at Rachael. "Stay here."

"Heck no! I'm coming with you."

"But Lucius is a Spell-Master," Skye whispered into Rachael's ear. "You shouldn't be around him. What if he finds out what you are?"

Rachael's eyes widened a bit, but she didn't back down. "I'll be okay. Don't worry about it. Let's go!" Rachael gave Skye a gentle shove and they pushed through the crowd, with Skye in the lead. Skye really wanted to learn as much about the box, and their plans, as possible. Still, this was all too easy. It was obviously a trap. She was in over her head and she knew it. Where the heck was Aidan when she really needed him? She didn't trust him at all, but at least he'd be a welcome distraction.

The four of them banged out the door and around the corner into an alley. Once they were all in the semi-darkness, Lucius turned and raised his right hand, palm out. He whispered something Skye couldn't understand, and Rachael suddenly stopped moving. She was frozen in mid-stride.

Skye's eyes narrowed. "What have you done to her?"

"Don't worry. She's alive. For now." Lucius gave her a menacing grin.

Nikolai moved toward Skye so fast she barely had time to block and move. They traded blows then jumped apart.

"Ah! Looks like we've got a little Assassin here. Come on, Assassin. Did you really think I would tell you my plans? You *are* green, aren't you? A newbie."

He lunged at her and sent her flying backwards to crash into a nearby dumpster. Skye momentarily had the wind knocked out of her, but the sight of Nikolai striding toward her, along with the offensive odor of garbage, quickly had her on her feet and moving away from the dumpster.

"Is that all you got?" Nikolai laughed.

Skye stole a glance toward Rachael. She was still immobile, and Lucius' attention was trained on her. Skye ran toward Lucius and slammed into him. He stumbled, then fell, and almost instantly Rachael was able to move. Skye caught a glimpse of her friend gesturing toward Lucius, but then she was too occupied with Nikolai to pay any more attention.

"Your career as an Assassin is going to be quite short," he said in her ear.

She was about to head butt him, when Skye felt again, the sensation, which alerted her to the presence of a Blood-Hunter. A flash of black streaked out of the darkness and Nikolai was no longer behind her.

Skye turned. It was Aidan, and he looked really angry. His eyes were solid black, as were Nikolai's by this time. Both Blood-Hunters' fangs were extended as they grappled with each other. Skye took that moment as a reprieve, and looked around for Rachael. She was terrified to discover that Rachael and Lucius were both gone! Skye whirled around, searching the darkness for any sign of them.

"Skye!"

Aidan's Irish brogue, speaking her name, caused her to snap her head around. She saw Nikolai's receding form near the end of the alley. Seconds later he was gone. Her eyes went back to Aidan.

"What is wrong with you, girl? How could you fall for their ruse? Have you no sense?"

"Where's Rachael?"

"A simple 'thank-you' would do." Aidan's eyes were still black, his fangs still visible. His words were clipped. He was very angry, that much was certain.

"I wanted to find out where Nikolai kept the box. I have to get it back to the Bureau so they can figure out how to destroy it and the demon that's inside."

"Back to the Bureau?" He strode toward her, with long ground-eating strides, his finger poking his own chest. "That box is mine! Mine! Not yours, not Niko's, not the Bureau's. It is mine to keep or destroy."

82

"Why? Why is it yours?"

"Because it's been in my family for generations, that's why. I finally found it again and I mean to have it back. It's mine!"

Skye was angry, and frightened for Rachael, but she didn't want Aidan shouting at her like that. "I don't care about your little squabble with Nikolai. It's my job to find out more about Lucius and the box. It's my job to get that box to the Bureau so you can just back off and—"

"No, no, no, this is not your job."

"Well, how is it *your* job?" Skye yelled back at him.

"I already told you! Are you not listening? Are you mentally deficient?"

Skye slapped her hands against the lapel of his leather coat and shoved him. "Forget about the stupid box. I don't want some demon loosed on the world, but I don't want to lose my friend to a Spell-Master either, and right at the moment Rachael's life seems just a tad more important. Now, what happened to her? Where is she?"

"How should I know? Maybe she got scared and ran off."

Skye shook her head. "No. I don't think that's what happened. You must know something. Where would Lucius take her?"

Aidan made a face. "He's a fecking Spell-Master. Who knows? I don't, and what's more I don't care. I hate those bastards as much as I hate Assassins."

"If you hate Assassins so much, then why did you get involved just now? Why didn't you just let Nikolai—?"

"Because of the box! Girl, you are dense!" He shook his head. "If you'd staked Niko, I'd not have been able to learn where he'd hidden the box. I don't give a rat's tail about you. I only want the damn box!"

"Help me find Rachael and I'll help you find the box." Skye could hardly believe the words had come out of her mouth, but once she'd said them, she thought it might be a pretty good idea after all.

"You'll help me get the box and then what? You'll bring the whole Bureau down on my head?" he scoffed. "No thank-you. I'll find it on my own."

"I won't tell the Bureau anything. I promise."

"Yeah, right."

"Really, I won't. I have much more loyalty to Rachael and her family than I do to the Bureau! It doesn't really matter to me who destroys the box. You *would* destroy it, right? The box and the demon?"

"They need to be done away with, that much is certain."

"And do you know how to do that?"

"Maybe I do, maybe I don't."

"Argh! You are so exasperating! Would you really destroy it if you could, or are you lying to me?"

He shrugged. "I happen to like this world just the way it is. I have my reasons for wanting things to stay the like they are. That's all you need to know."

Skye thought about that. She wasn't at all sure she should trust him, but right now it seemed that it would be better to work together than separately. "If you don't know how to destroy it, then maybe the Bureau does."

"Oh, we're back to that, are we? The fecking Bureau," he muttered.

"I don't know! I just want Rachael back. Do we have a deal or don't we?"

Skye knew she had put herself in a vulnerable position. Aidan would now have the upper hand, to some extent, but she hadn't lied when she'd said she felt more loyalty to Rachael and her family than to the Bureau. How could she possibly tell Rachael's mom and dad and younger sisters that Rachael had fallen prey to a Spell-Master only days after they'd moved into their new apartment? She wouldn't be able to bear their grief along with her own sorrow and guilt. On the other hand, the whole world could be in danger if that demon got out of the box. She hoped she was making the right decision.

"Come on, Aidan. This is a win-win. I get Rachael back, you get the box, and the demon and the Spell-Master get destroyed. The Bureau is happy, I'm happy, you're happy, the world would be happy if they knew about it. Everyone's happy."

Aidan's fangs receded and his eyes were no longer solid black. "She's Elfae, isn't she? I knew there was something different about her, but for all I knew she was a Shifter. Do you know what Spell-Masters do to Elfae?"

Skye looked up into his eyes. "Yes. I know, and that's why I want your help. We have to go. We have to do something. Now. Right now."

Aidan raked a hand through his hair. He paced and studied the ground, then paced some more.

"Well?" Skye prompted.

"I'm thinking. I'm thinking." He stopped pacing and looked at her. "All right. You have a deal. But if we get the box, and the Bureau takes it and I get killed, I'll..."

Skye lifted an eyebrow. "You'll what?" Some of the control over the situation had just shifted back to Skye and she knew it.

He frowned. "Never mind. I know where Niko lives. We'll go there. It's a start."

CHAPTER TEN

THEY ARRIVED AT THE GOLDEN PAVILION APART-
ment complex, after arguing over whose car to take; Skye's Chrysler
200 or Aidan's Porsche Boxter. Skye had finally given in and
agreed to ride in his car. Going anywhere with him was a risk, especially
without her own way home, but she was willing to take that risk to help
Rachael.

"This is it?" she asked, as they crept up the stairs to Nikolai's apartment. She was well aware that this could be another trap.

"Yes." Aidan bounded up the last two steps and headed for the apartment at the end of the row. He didn't hesitate, just kicked in the door.

"What are you doing?" Skye whispered, but Aidan was already inside.
She followed him in, and found him with his hand around Nikolai's neck.
Nikolai's back was pressed against the wall, his fangs bared.

He frowned. "What the hell, Aidan?" And then he saw Skye, and his
expression changed from anger to surprise.

"Where's the girl?" Aidan asked.

"Behind you, you moron."

"Not that girl. The other one. The blonde. Where did Lucius take her?"

"Are you kidding me?" Nikolai managed to rasp, even with Aidan's
fingers digging into his throat. "The two of you are working together now?
What does she have on you Aidan?"

Skye walked over and slammed her fist into Nikolai's stomach.
"Where is she?"

Nikolai grunted, but remained silent.

Aidan dug his fingers in deeper. "The lady asked you a question, Niko."

Skye lifted her leg and aimed a solid side-kick right onto Nikolai's knee. She heard it crack, and he lurched sideways with a grunt of pain.

"Where is she?" she asked again. "Where's my friend?"

Nikolai cut her off and glanced up at Aidan. "I'll tell you where the box is, if you'll let me go. We can kill this pathetic excuse for an Assassin together, and be done with it."

"You know how the Bureau works. They'll just send another Assassin. I'll take my chances with this one. But since you brought it up, where *is* the box?"

Nikolai grinned. "If you kill me, you'll never find out."

"We don't want to kill you right now, but we're happy to hurt you; a lot." Skye emphasized her point by smashing his nose with her fist, then wrenching his wrist backwards.

Nikolai's entire body folded as he tried to relieve the pressure on his wrist. Aidan followed him to the floor and pounded his fist into Nikolai's face. Blood gushed from his already damaged nose, and now, under Aidan's blows, the skin at his eyebrow split and began to bleed as well.

"All right, all right. Stop," Nikolai shouted. Aidan stopped pummeling his face.

"Well?" Skye snapped. "We're waiting."

"I'll take you to her," Nikolai muttered.

"No thanks," Skye replied. "Just tell us where to go."

Aidan shook his head. "No, if we leave him here, he'll get the box and disappear, while he sends us on a wild goose chase. He needs to come with us."

"Okay, fine. But let's get going."

Aidan hauled Nikolai to his feet. "Where?"

"Lucius has a house on Bayside. He'll take her there. His basement is soundproofed."

"He has a basement?" Skye scoffed. "Nobody in California has a basement!"

Aidan gave her another one of his, 'are you an idiot', looks. "The man is a Spell-Master. He can do whatever he wants. Make whatever he wants."

"Oh, right." Skye felt stupid.

Aidan strong-armed Nikolai from the apartment and the three of them piled into the Boxter. It was a tight squeeze. Skye could smell Nikolai's cologne and it turned her stomach. By contrast, Aidan smelled sort of woodsy. She hadn't noticed that before. Probably because she was so worried about Rachael, she told herself. She was also quite aware she was shoulder to shoulder with Blood-Hunters she would probably have to stake in the very near future.

"You do realize that I'm not giving you that box," Nikolai warned. "You may be able to rescue the girl before Luc takes what he wants from her and kills her, but neither of us is giving you the box. We both want it opened and we need each other to do that."

"He doesn't need you. I can open the box," Aidan replied.

Skye shot Aidan a sharp look. So, he *did* know how to open it. But did he know how to destroy it?

"You may know how, but you don't want it opened, do you? That's the difference between us. Luc knows that. He won't side with you over me because the two of us want the same thing. Global destruction."

"You want to destroy the world? Why?" Skye asked. "How would that be to anyone's benefit?"

Nikolai shifted in his seat and looked at her with one good eye. The other was swollen shut, though it was already looking better than it had when they'd first gotten into the car.

"When the demon destroys the world, he'll recreate it for his followers. Humans will be nothing but food, slaves of the Blood-Hunters." Nikolai chuckled.

"And the Elfae and the Shape-Shifters?" Skye asked.

"They'll be gone, along with the Spell-Masters, because the rest of us will hunt them down and kill them."

Aidan sighed. "There are flaws in your plan. It's going to be everyone for themselves. No order. Complete chaos. The Spell-Masters and the Elfae have magic at their disposal and don't think the Shape-Shifters will be that easy to kill. They will kill as many of us as we would kill of them. And don't count the humans out either. Sure, most of them will die or become enslaved, but Assassins will continue to be born, they always have been."

Nikolai laughed. "An Assassin here and there isn't going to have any noticeable effect on my plans."

"Does Lucius know about your plans?" Skye asked. "Because I don't think he'd be too happy to know you intend to kill his kind and rule the world yourself."

Nikolai glared at her.

Aidan smiled. "I think you just found us some leverage, Skye."

"Okay, listen up, boys, here's the way it's going to go." Skye began by looking at Nikolai. "We won't tell Lucius of your plans for killing Spell-Masters. I won't tell the Bureau I'm helping Aidan. You will give the box to Aidan and he and I will find a way to destroy it. And, you will also help us rescue my friend. In exchange, I'll let you live. Just get out of San Diego. Better yet, get out of California all together, so we won't ever run into each other again."

"Yeah, whatever." Nikolai shrugged. "Okay, fine. I'll help you get your friend, but you're never getting that box from me."

"We'll see. First things first." Skye was willing to do just about anything to get Rachael back, including pretend to trust Nikolai.

"Here it is." Nikolai pointed at a house on their right.

Aidan pulled up to the curb, but Skye was the first one out of the car. "You stay with him." Skye jabbed her thumb in Nikolai's direction. "I'm going to take a look around."

"You won't be able to get in. It's spelled. I can get you in. I know how," Nikolai offered.

"Or you'll get us killed, on purpose," Aidan suggested.

Nikolai smiled. "I might. That would certainly be a bonus."

Aidan shoved Nikolai in front of him. "Walk."

They stood at the front door. Skye looked around and mulled things over. "He lives in this neighborhood. He's not going to risk putting a spell on the front door that kills some little Girl Scout selling cookies when she knocks on the door." She glanced back at the two Blood-Hunters. "I like your style, Aidan. Hope you don't mind if I copy it." She took a couple of steps for momentum, then kicked the door in. There were no explosions. In fact, the house was dark and quiet.

Aidan nodded. "Well, done. Now let's see about the next step." He shoved Nikolai through the doorway and beyond the now broken front door hanging lopsided on its hinges.

Skye heard a popping sound, and then Nikolai's entire body jerked and twitched. He fell to the floor, unmoving.

"Well, that's one booby-trap down." Aidan stepped over Nikolai's body and entered the house.

Skye studied Nikolai's unmoving form. "Is he dead?"

"No, I expect he'll be coming around in a minute." Aidan beckoned for her to enter, and she did so, as Nikolai groaned and struggled to sit up.

Aidan tugged him to his feet. "Come on. Next stop, the basement. Where is it?"

Nikolai was too dazed to speak coherently, so he pointed.

"You first." Aidan gave him a shove and Nikolai lurched forward. He hesitated with his hand hovering over the knob.

"Go ahead." Skye gave him another little push, just as Aidan had done earlier. Nikolai hit the door and again there was a pop and he jerked, then fell to the floor, twitching.

"This Lucius isn't too creative," Aidan said.

Skye shrugged. "I don't suppose he has to be. That would kill most people."

"Yeah, but the people this guy is afraid of, aren't killed so easily." He tested the door, but there was no latent charge in it. The door swung open. The room below was illuminated. Aidan put a finger to his lips and Skye nodded in understanding.

Nikolai staggered to his feet and called out, his speech a bit slurred. "Hey, Lucius, I brought a present for—" And then Aidan kicked him down the stairs. He flew forward and tumbled like a ragdoll, his arms flailing, until he lay in a heap at the bottom. He groaned and lay still.

A figure appeared at the bottom of the stairway. It was Lucius, and he had one arm around Rachael. She sagged into him, and Skye guessed she was unconscious. Hopefully, not dead.

"Aidan? No need for all the theatrics. I see you've brought me the Assassin. Wonderful. Bring her down."

Aidan grabbed Skye by the arms. "Gotcha. Don't ever trust a Blood-Hunter, darlin'. We aren't a trustworthy lot."

"You're joking, right?" Skye whispered. "This is all an act, right?"

Aidan shoved her forward and marched her down the stairs. "No. This is me, doing what I do best. Lying, double-crossing, cheating...oh, and lying. Did I say lying?"

"You are such a...argh!" Skye tried to twist out of his steely grip, but she couldn't budge. They reached the bottom of the stairs and Aidan gave Nikolai a shove with his booted foot. He didn't move.

Lucius looked down at the still unconscious, Nikolai. "Perhaps it's to be you and I after all, Aidan. I wondered when things would come to blows between you two."

Lucius had deposited Rachael on an old sofa, and Aidan gave Skye a shove so she fell on top of her friend. Skye was thankful to find that Rachael was still breathing.

"Yeah, I'm with you on this," Aidan muttered. "Now where's the box?"

"We hadn't scheduled it to be opened until tomorrow night. I'm going to enjoy passing the time gaining a power boost from this lovely and soon to be dead Elfae. If she hadn't tried to use her magic on me, I never would've known what she was." Lucius turned his wicked smile toward Rachael. "She sealed her own fate."

Skye glared at him. She felt stung by Aidan's betrayal. Of course, she'd known this might be a possibility, but she'd really hoped he could be counted on. Now she'd found Rachael but lost her only ally. She had to bide her time and wait until Rachael was mobile before she tried to find a way out of this predicament.

"Why wait? If you have the power, and know the spell, let's do it tonight," Aidan pressed, and Skye wondered how she could've been so wrong about him; so completely and utterly wrong. Why had she wanted to desperately to believe in him; just because he was handsome and she liked his Irish brogue?

Nikolai mumbled something. He'd begun to come around. Aidan dragged him over to the sofa where Skye and Rachael were.

He looked at Skye with hard, cold eyes. "Keep him quiet."

"Or what?" Skye snapped.

He grabbed her jacket and lifted her up with one hand, then gave her a shake. "Or I'll bite your pretty neck and drink all your fecking blood. Now shut up and do whatever you have to do to keep *him* quiet, too." He released her and she stumbled backwards onto the sofa.

Rachael made a sound, and Skye's attention was immediately on her friend. "Rachael? Rachael?" She gave her a gentle shake. "Can you hear me?"

Skye glanced up in time to see Lucius and Aidan walk a little further away. They were deep in discussion, but she could no longer hear their words. She was more concerned with Rachael now anyway.

Rachael sat up slowly and rubbed her head. "Skye? What happened? Where—?" Her eyes snapped open and she sat up more quickly, then winced and rubbed her head again. "Skye, I'm so sorry. I thought I could handle him, but I messed up. I've never been in real combat before, only practice games. I should've—"

"Don't worry about it now. We've got bigger problems. Aidan double crossed me. Or maybe he was never on my side in the first place. Now that you're awake, we can figure out how to get out of here."

"I don't know how much help I'll be. That creep has already drained some of my power. I guess it's lucky for me that we were wrong about how Spell-Masters steal magic. They don't kill the Elfae and *then* take the magic. They kill the Elfae *while* they're taking the magic."

"Good to know. I'll be sure to inform Preston of that fact when we get out of here," Skye whispered.

"So you have one of those necklaces too."

The sound of Nikolai's voice startled Skye. She turned to look at him, and saw that his eyes were trained on Rachael's pendant.

"What are you talking about?" Rachael asked.

He rubbed his head and groaned. "I see Aidan's acting true to form. He's double crossed you, eh? That's funny."

"What did you mean about my necklace?" Rachael asked again. She held it in her hand and lifted the pendant so he could see it. "Have you seen one of these before?"

"Yeah, sure." He moved with great care as he tried to sit up.

"Where?" Rachael pressed.

"Huh?" Nikolai squinted at her.

"Where did you see another necklace like this? Where did you see another one of these pendants?" Rachael's voice was sharp, and Skye waited on pins and needles for Nikolai's reply, knowing where Rachael was headed with her line of questioning.

"It was on some guy, some kid in the woods a couple of weeks ago." Nikolai's eyes cleared, as if a veil had been lifted and he could think again. The lights were back on and someone was home. "Aw, was he someone you knew? Did he have the other half of your coin?" A low chuckle rumbled in his throat. "Oops, I think I drank your boyfriend's life away."

Rachael released the pendant and glared at him. "You're the one. You're the Blood-Hunter who killed Joe Haynes."

Before Skye could think of what to do or what to say in this situation, Rachael responded with a flash of fire from her palms. Skye jumped back, startled by this sudden violence from her friend, and afraid she might get caught up in it by accident and burned alive.

She needn't have worried. Rachael's aim was true, and the fire missed Skye by at least a foot, but Nikolai wasn't as lucky. He screamed as he was engulfed in flames. The sofa caught fire as well, and while Skye scrambled to get clear of it, Rachael rose with perfect grace, and backed away. She kept the flames coming until Nikolai stopped screaming and had disintegrated into a pile of smoldering ash. Rachael then eased up and the fire went away, but she wobbled and would've fallen if Skye hadn't caught her and supported her.

"See, I told you I could take care of myself," she murmured.

"I see that now," Skye replied. She lifted her head and saw Aidan and Lucius heading back their way at a jog. They'd been far enough away, in this convoluted basement, not to have seen what had happened. Skye visually measured the distance to the stairs and freedom. "Run!" she shouted, and dragged Rachael with her. They clambered up the stairs and dashed out of the house. Rachael stumbled a few times, but she didn't fall.

Skye and Rachael reached the car and got in, and it was then that Skye realized she'd been a complete idiot. Aidan had his keys with him, and she knew neither she nor Rachael knew how to hotwire a car. But then Rachael surprised her once again. She lifted her hand and gave it a wave. The car started, and Rachael slumped back in the leather seat. "Drive."

Skye placed her hands on the wheel, and looked back at the house in time to see Aidan running full tilt toward the car. She'd expected him to catch up to them much sooner, and drag them back. She revved the engine and floored it.

CHAPTER ELEVEN

SKYE REACHED THEIR APARTMENT WITHIN THE
hour. She parked Aidan's car in her usual parking space and wished
for her Chrysler, but it was back at the restaurant. There was no way
she would go back there to get it tonight. She didn't want to leave Rachael
alone, and she just simply didn't want to risk running into Aidan again.
She'd drive the Boxter to get her car in the morning. Skye helped Rachael
out of the car and to the door, then threw the lock.

"Thanks," Rachael whispered, as Skye helped her to her room.

"Will you be all right?" Skye asked.

"Oh, sure. I think so. I've never had power stolen from me before, but
an Elfae can be drained of power by sickness too. With rest we regenerate.
I guess that's what will happen in this case too. I'm just glad I had enough
left to avenge Joe's murder."

"I'm glad you're going to be okay physically, but what about mentally?"

Rachael frowned. "For a second he seemed so human. You know, when
he was on fire and he screamed, but then I remembered what he'd done to
Joe and how he'd made light of it like it was nothing. He's probably killed
all sorts of people and not even cared. The world is a safer place without
him. What about you? How did you feel after you killed the Blood-Hunter
on graduation night?"

Skye thought about it. "I was okay with it. I mean, she *was* about to
bite Don Jackson's neck, so…"

Rachael nodded. "At least now that Nikolai is dead that box won't get
opened, right?"

Skye hoped Rachael was right, but she was no longer sure about Aidan's motives. She'd believed he didn't want to open it, but now she wasn't at all sure that was true. She was still angry with herself for wanting so much to believe in him. Even now, she hoped he was all right, that he'd escaped the burning building unharmed. Her thoughts regarding him were certainly confused, to say the least.

Her cell phone rang and Skye looked at the screen. "It's Preston."

"Go ahead. I'll see you in the morning. Thanks again," Rachael called out as Skye headed for her bedroom.

She answered her phone and gave Preston the rundown.

———————— ·+♦♦♦+· ————————

The next morning, when Skye finally awakened, it was nearly ten. She staggered out of her room, still in her pajamas, and found Rachael, already dressed in blue capris and a blue and white floral print peasant blouse, sitting in front of the TV.

"How long have you been up?" Skye asked.

Rachael kept her eyes glued to the screen. "About an hour. Listen to this." She pressed the button on the remote control and the volume increased.

"...and the fire which engulfed the house at 5493 E. Bayside, was thought to have started when some old furniture in the basement caught fire. The fire spread up the stairway and then to the rest of the house. It's unclear as to what actually started the blaze, but no neighboring homes were damaged. No one appeared to be at home, and no bodies have been recovered. Law enforcement officials are hoping to locate the owner of the property by the end of today. In other news..."

Rachael turned the volume down again. "This is the third time I've heard the report. I've been flipping channels, but the information is always the same. So far anyway."

Skye dropped down onto the sofa beside her friend. "No bodies found. What does *that* mean?"

"Well, Nikolai was already ash, so I don't suppose he'd be identifiable after being enflamed twice. At least not unless they do DNA testing on the ash or something. As for Lucius," She shrugged. "He might have spelled himself out of there in time."

"I saw Aidan running toward us just before we peeled out of there last night. Do you think he escaped?"

"It would seem so. He most likely just took off and went back to wherever he calls home." She studied Skye for a moment. "I can't really tell, are you worried about him, or—?"

"*No*, I'm not worried about him!" Skye got to her feet and went to the kitchen. "He's a jerk. A lying, disloyal, betraying, cheating, creep." She got some cereal and a mug of coffee and returned to the living room. "And I hope I never see him again, but what if he and Lucius decide to open the box? I still don't know where it is! I'm no closer to stopping this thing than I was twenty-four hours ago."

Rachael lifted an eyebrow. "Well, I'm glad to hear you haven't gotten attached to Aidan because you might have to stake him one of these days."

"I will if I have to." Skye slurped her coffee.

"That was his car we were in last night, right?"

"Yeah."

"We should go get yours."

"I know. I'll do it as soon as I get dressed."

"You don't have the keys, remember. I'll have to come with you and start it."

"That reminds me, what you did last night with the fire? You have some mad skills!"

"Yeah. That's what I do. Some of us use water. Some air. We don't have to say a spell like a Spell-Master because our magic comes to us as naturally as breathing."

"So how were you able to start the car?"

"Ignition sparks to life." Rachael shrugged. "It's kind of in the fire family."

Skye nodded. "Oh, I get it. I'll get dressed and we can go."

"Wait. So what did Preston say last night when you told him what happened?"

"He was mostly happy. He's glad we solved the mystery of who killed Joe, and that Nikolai is dead. He's also glad we've discovered who Lucius is, and that you're home and you're okay. He is *not* happy about the box still being out there, however."

"Maybe Lucius is dead. Maybe the box was in the house and it burned up along with everything else. Maybe—"

"You said yourself that he could've spelled himself out of there."

"Well, we won't know anything for a while, I guess." Rachael made a shooing motion with her hands. "Go get dressed. We'll go switch cars and then go to a movie or something. I think we should take a break from all this."

Skye smiled. "Sounds good to me."

Half an hour later, Skye had showered, put on make-up, and brushed her hair until it gleamed. She wore a green and white floral sundress with white sandals. When she came out, Rachael greeted her.

"I looked at the movies while you were getting dressed. If we go to the Columbia Crest Theater, near the mall, we can catch a movie and a late lunch."

"Okay."

They grabbed their purses and Skye led the way out to her parking space. Before she got there, she stopped dead in her tracks. Rachael smacked into her from behind.

"What's wrong?" Rachael asked.

"The car. The Boxter. It's gone!" Skye could hardly believe her eyes.

"Gone! You mean it was stolen?" Rachael peered around Skye. "Oh."

Skye's Chrysler 200 was parked in its usual spot, and Aidan's car was gone.

Both girls stared at the car for several seconds, in silence.

"Um," Rachael began, "Do you suppose it's unlocked?"

"Let's go find out."

They approached the car, and Skye saw right away that the car was indeed unlocked. She opened the door and looked in, searching for the keys. "Well, I only know two places to look for keys. One is under the mat, and the other is behind the visor." She lifted the driver side mat. Nothing.

Rachael was quick to check the mat on the passenger side. "Nope. Try the visors."

They both flipped their visors down and the keys fell into Rachael's hand. "Here you go." She tossed the keys to Skye. "I guess Aidan returned it."

"How did he find us? He doesn't know where we live."

"Maybe he has a GPS tracker on his car or something." Rachael slid into the passenger seat.

Skye pulled out of her parking space, and headed for the theater, but she was uneasy. Okay, so Aidan had survived, but where was the box? Where was Lucius? And what were Aidan's true motives? Skye's cell phone rang and she put it on speaker.

"Hi sweetie, it's Mom!"

Skye glanced over at Rachael. "Oh, hi Mom."

"How are you honey? Is everything okay at the apartment?"

Skye forced her voice to sound happy. "Yeah, it's great!"

"Have you met any of your neighbors yet?"

"No, not yet. How're Dad and Derek?"

"They're doing fine. We had dinner with Rachael's parents last night. We were just remembering your surprise party and how fun it was. What are you doing for your birthday tomorrow? We can drive over and take you girls out to dinner. Derek is going up to Costa Mesa to visit some friends so he won't be able to come, unfortunately."

"Oh, um, that would be great. I'm pretty sure we'll both be free." Skye had completely forgotten about her birthday. How weird was that?

"I can hardly believe you're going to be nineteen!"

"Yeah. Um, what time do you want to have dinner?"

"How about if we come to your apartment around six."

"Sure. Okay. I've got to go. Rachael and I are going to a movie."

"Okay, honey. We'll see you tomorrow!"

"Bye, Mom." Skye disconnected and looked at Rachael. "I hope that's all right with you."

"Of course! It'll be fun."

"Our birthdays are so close together. We should've had a joint surprise party. Not one just for me."

"Oh, no, it's okay. Derek was the surprise. That's why we did it."

Skye pulled into the mall parking lot and parked by the theater. "So, what are we seeing?"

Five hours later, after a movie, a meal and a little shopping, the girls returned to their apartment, exhausted.

"I never guessed I'd be so tired at four in the afternoon," Rachael muttered.

"Well, if we hadn't been up half the night…"

"Oh, you mean all the killing Blood-Hunters, fighting Spell-Masters, running from certain death? So, what do we do for an encore?"

"Go to sleep?"

"This early? Are you kidding me?"

"Yes." Skye smiled. "I'm kidding."

And that's when Preston called. "Did you have a relaxing day? I hope so, because there's work still to be done."

Skye rolled her eyes and sighed. "Just so you know, my parents are going to be here tomorrow night to take me out to dinner for my birthday. So, I can't go patrolling."

There was silence on the other end of the line.

"Preston? Are you there?"

"Yes, Skye, I'm here. Of course, you must spend time with your family on your birthday. Congratulations on turning nineteen."

"Well, thank-you."

"You're welcome. Tonight, however, I need you to circulate and look for any evidence that Lucius is either dead or still in the area."

"His house burned down."

"I'm aware of that, but being as he's a Spell-Master, he might've gotten out unscathed. We need to know for certain. It is also imperative we find out where that box is."

"Rachael thought maybe it was at his house and was burned up in the fire."

"I suppose that's a possibility, but we can't take it for granted. There is too much at stake. Besides, I've been doing this a long time now and have learned the hard way never to underestimate when it comes to these things. Go by Nikolai's apartment and take a look around. Do a careful search and see what you can find."

They disconnected and Skye looked over at Rachael. "He wants me to go over to Nikolai's apartment and look for the box."

"I'll come along if you want me to," Rachael offered.

Skye gave that a moment's thought. "No, but thanks."

Rachael seemed somewhat relieved. "Okay, but call me if you need me."

"I will." Skye turned and went to change. She figured she'd get an early start, check out Nikolai's apartment, and then maybe hit a few of Aidan's hangouts just in case Lucius might be around. Truth be told, she was apprehensive about going to Aidan's stomping ground. She really did not want to see him. At all! Ever!

Skye pulled off her sundress and sandals, replacing them with black stretch jeans, sneakers, and a black t-shirt. She strapped on her stake holster, this time adjusting it as a shoulder holster, handy bit of equipment it was, and put a denim jacket on over it. She pulled her hair back into a low ponytail, and ditched the jewelry she'd had on earlier. She grabbed her ID, her keys and her cell phone, then slipped everything into her various pockets. She was ready to go.

Skye arrived at the Golden Pavilion Apartments, forty-five minutes later, and approached Nikolai's apartment with caution. After all, Aidan had kicked in the door, and who knew how many people might've heard it or saw the three of them leaving shortly thereafter.

As she walked along, she saw a couple of people going to and from their cars. One was a lady in a blue broomstick skirt and white peasant blouse exiting her vintage 1950s Chevy sedan. Another was a twenty-something guy getting into his black Toyota Tundra. No one seemed to be anywhere around Nikolai's building.

Skye climbed the stairs and paused at the landing. She listened for footsteps, doors opening or closing, or any sounds, which might be coming from the apartment itself. There was nothing. Complete silence, except for the sounds of distant traffic and some birds twittering in the trees.

The doorway to Nikolai's apartment had been replaced by clear plastic taped to the doorframe. Skye pulled some of the tape loose and entered. The place looked the same as it had last night, as far as she could tell. She looked around and noticed the walls were bare, and there was little furniture.

Skye searched the living room, then moved on to the bedroom. She checked under the bed, in every dresser drawer, and even in the closet. Trouble was, she really didn't know what to look for. A wooden box, sure, but she only vaguely remembered it from the silent auction. She wracked her brain for more details. The box had been ornately carved, she remembered that much, but had the wood stain been dark or cherry or something else altogether?

Skye was in the process of making another sweep through the closet, when she kicked aside some shoes and saw what looked like powdered wood and some wood shavings. She crouched and saw a hole in the wall, about one foot above the floor, and one foot in diameter. A secret compartment? She got a little closer to see better, then felt around inside. Nothing. The space was empty. She crawled back out and stood. Well, this was probably where the box had been stashed, but who had gotten to it first, Lucius or Aidan? Hopefully there weren't any other players in this game. Skye didn't even want to think about it. Things were complicated enough already.

She didn't think she needed to look any further, but she made a cursory examination of the bathroom and the kitchen. Not a thing looked out of the ordinary. She made her way back to the entry, paused a moment to listen in case anyone might be around to see her leaving, and then ducked through the plastic. Her surroundings were still fairly quiet, but she could see a man and two police officers walking along the sidewalk in her direction. Time to go. She kept her face averted, eyes down, and headed for the stairs. Skye was at the bottom before the three men got there, and turned away, toward the parking lot. She didn't hurry. Didn't want to draw attention to herself, but she needn't have worried. She made it all the way to her car and out of the parking lot with no trouble at all.

She went over her patrol route in her head, planning where to start. MacGregor's Pub she'd leave for last. First, she went to the park where she'd seen Aidan and Nikolai arguing, but felt no tingling sensation which let her know a Blood-Hunter was near. Next, she walked the streets of the surrounding neighborhood, and finally drove over to the Gas Light District near the Convention Center. There were lots of people milling around, but although she noticed a few Shape-Shifters and Elfae about, there were no Blood-Hunters anywhere. Aidan was nowhere to be seen or felt. Finally, the only place left was MacGregor's.

The parking lot was peppered with a few cars here and there, but Aidan's Boxter was not among them. Well, it was early yet. Skye sat in her car and waited. She watched as people came and went and started to get bored. So much so, in fact, that she almost missed seeing the man with the short dark hair enter the restaurant. He had a neatly trimmed mustache and goatee, and even from inside her car Skye could see his sinister countenance. It was Lucius. He was still alive. Did he have the box? She'd been looking for Aidan but here was the Spell-Master instead. Should she go in and confront him or wait outside and follow him when he left? Who knew where he might lead her; to the box or to Aidan? Maybe Lucius now planned to use Aidan instead of Nikolai to open the box. Yes, she'd follow Lucius. She just hoped he wouldn't stay inside the pub too long. She wanted to get this over with.

CHAPTER TWELVE

AFTER ONLY A FEW MINUTES. SKYE WAS SUR-
prised to see Lucius leave the restaurant and walk away. Game
on. She got out of her car, quickly tugged on her indigo denim
jacket to cover her shoulder holster with her three stakes, then followed
from a distance, and silently thanked Preston for his insistence that she
buy some darker clothing.

Almost immediately doubts began to assail her. She couldn't stake
a Spell-Master and get away with it, could she? He was a human, and
there would be a body for the police to discover. She could go to prison
for murder! And what about his magic? Could she even get close enough
to fight him? Would he sense her coming like she sensed Blood-Hunters?
Would he kill her with a flick of his wrist before she even got within
striking distance?

Lucius stopped at a crosswalk, and Skye stopped too. She ducked into
the shadows and then continued to follow once he started moving again.
She crossed the street with a group of people, and even if he'd looked back,
she doubted he'd notice her.

The Spell-Master entered a multi-level parking garage, and Skye was
now worried that her footfalls would be heard in the echoey environment.
The place had intermittent lighting, and Skye had to be careful to keep to
the darkness. There wasn't much activity. Only two cars drove in and one
out of the complex. Skye hated this sort of multilevel cement structure.
She'd always felt they were dangerous places to be at night, for a girl alone.
Now more than ever, she knew that to be true.

Lucius continued to walk and Skye followed. When they reached the third level, he turned and faced her. "Ah, it *is* you. The Assassin. I figured as much. Come to finish me off, have you?"

Skye wasn't entirely surprised he'd detected her, but she'd hoped for more time to see what he was up to; especially since she wasn't too keen on him using his magical abilities against her. "Just curious, you know. Wondered if you were dead or not."

"Well, I'm not, as you can plainly see."

"So, do you have the box?" Skye figured she might as well get right to the point. "It seems to be missing from Nikolai's apartment."

Lucius grinned at her; a wicked sort of smile. "I do."

Well, that answered another one of Skye's questions. One more to go. "Who is going to open it for you now that Nikolai is gone?"

"Aidan, of course."

He lifted his hand, and Skye saw his lips move. He spoke words that sounded like they were probably part of some spell, so she ducked and ran. Something behind her, maybe an energy ball of some kind, glanced off a nearby car and sparks flew. She slowly crept between cars, trying to stay out of view, in the hope of getting far enough away to avoid being a target. Another streak of lightning came within three feet of her, and again sparks danced in the air around her. Time to go.

Skye took off at a dead run. Her heart pounded from fear and exertion. She glanced back as she dodged this way and that, trying to avoid being struck and at the same time trying to stay out of Lucius' line of vision. Where the hell was the ramp going down? Had she run in circles? How had she become so disoriented?

A car careened around a corner and came to a screeching halt right next to the spot where she hid.

"Get in!"

Skye looked at the driver. It was Aidan. "Are you kidding me?" she yelled back.

"Not really," he called and made a frantic gesture with this hand. "Now, come on!"

Something hot and burning glanced off the trunk of his car.

"Would you get the feck in, please? We don't have all day," he shouted.

"Why should I trust you? How do I know you aren't just going to drive me over to—?"

Another hot something bounced off the roof of the Boxter.

"I'm not risking more damage to this car. Now get in if you want to live!"

When another energy bolt hit the concrete right above her head, Skye made her decision. She darted out from her hiding place and yanked open the passenger door of Aidan's car. She dropped down into the seat, and he took off, even before the door was closed again.

Aidan sped around the bend and descended the ramp to the next level down. Around they went and around again. Skye thought for sure they'd crash, but Aidan handled the car with authority, and a race car driver's precision. Within seconds they were out onto the street. Other drivers honked their horns and some even gave him the finger, but they all quickly made room for the speeding vehicle. Aidan slowed the car to conform to the speed limit and the other cars around them.

He looked at her. "What were you thinking, following him like that?"

Skye sat up straighter now that her stomach wasn't lurching all over the place. "How long have you been following me?"

"Since the pub. I arrived just as you were dashing off after Lucius. I followed at a distance. Now answer my question."

"I'm an Assassin, remember? I have a job to do, and contrary to what you think, that job involves more than just staking Blood-Hunters."

"Oh, really?"

"Yes, really. And I found out quite a lot to report back to the Bureau, too."

"Like what?"

Skye looked out the window at the lights and buildings flashing by. Aidan was about to pull onto the freeway. "Where are we going?"

"Like what, Skye? What do you know?"

Her head swiveled around to face him once again. "Why should I tell you?"

"Because I just saved your life, and I asked you."

His voice was calm, relaxed even. He looked at her with those bright green eyes, and she saw no threat in them. But how could that be? Of course, there was a threat. This was his MO, wasn't it? He'd pretend to be an ally, but as soon as a better offer came along, he'd switch sides. She would never be able to trust him.

"All right. Fine. I'll tell you because you probably already know everything anyway. Lucius survived the fire, he has the box, and he's expecting you to be the one to open it for him while he chants the spell. There. That's it. Are you happy now?" She saw his jaw clench.

"No, I'm not happy. I'd hoped he didn't have the box. Where was Nikolai keeping it? Do you know?"

"It was in a hidey-hole in his closet."

"Damn." Aidan bumped the heel of his hand against the steering wheel. "I knew I should've gone straight back there when the house caught fire." He turned angry eyes on Skye. "But someone had stolen my car so I had to walk."

"I didn't steal it. I borrowed it. And you got it back! How did you find where I lived?"

"I have a GPS tracker. I took your car and followed the signal, then switched them."

"How did you start my car without the keys?"

He gave her a look. "Seriously? You're seriously going to ask me that question?"

"Oh, were you a car thief in your previous life?" Skye quipped.

"Let's just say I've picked up a lot of valuable knowledge and abilities over the years, and leave it at that, eh?" He pulled over to the right and exited the freeway.

"Where are we going?" she asked again.

"Are you hungry? I thought we might get some dinner before I take you back to your car."

"Dinner?" Skye could hardly believe she'd heard him right. "You want to go out on a date?"

"A date?" He laughed. "Hardly. I'm just hungry, and blood isn't on my menu for another couple of days yet." He drove into the parking lot of Big Bob's Burgers, and parked. "Come on." He got out and headed toward the entrance of the restaurant.

Skye sat there stunned. "What? Really? Argh!" she muttered to herself, then got out of the car and ran after him.

Without turning he lifted his hand back over his shoulder and pushed the remote lock. The car beeped. He pushed in the door of the restaurant, and Skye followed.

They slid into opposite sides of a booth and picked up the menus the hostess set on the table. Skye scanned the menu briefly, then put it down. "I don't have any money with me."

"I'll pay."

She silently stared at him.

He peered over the top of his menu. "You don't trust me? I said I'll pay and I will."

"No. I don't trust you. Of course, I don't trust you. And if I see you with your fangs in someone's neck a couple of days from now, I'll run a stake through your heart before you even know what's coming."

"Hi. My name is Sherry. I'll be your waitress. Are you ready to order?"

Skye turned to see a young girl with short brown hair and too much eye makeup, smiling down at her.

"Ah, yeah, Sherry, I'll have number five, with fries," she replied. "Medium-well."

Sherry gave Aidan an expectant look. "And for you?"

He gave her an award-winning smile. "I'll have your number three, with fries, and a chocolate shake. Make the burger medium-rare."

Sherry nodded as she wrote on her little notepad. "And what would you like to drink?" she asked Skye.

"I'll have a chocolate shake too." Skye didn't smile. She was still annoyed with Aidan.

The waitress left and Skye looked back at Aidan. "So what's your plan then? Get together with Lucius later tonight and open the box? Create chaos and hell on earth? Ruin my birthday plans for tomorrow?"

His face split into a wide grin. "Is tomorrow your birthday, then? Imagine that. I'll have to get you a present."

"Your present can be not opening that box."

Aidan cocked his head and studied her. "I have no intention of opening that box. I thought I already told you that."

"You did. But then you lied, betrayed me, sided with that maniac Spell-Master, and nearly got Rachael and me killed last night!"

"Ah, now," he shook his head. "I had nothing to do with your friend getting attacked or kidnapped, or nearly drained of her power. That was your fault for bringing her along in the first place."

Skye was so angry she could hardly get the words out. "How dare you suggest—"

"I'm not suggesting anything. I'm pointing out where you went wrong and made a poor choice last night."

"Here you go!" Sherry had arrived with their shakes. "The burgers and fries will be up in a jiffy." She smiled then whirled and left the table.

Skye was angry, but she was also hungry so she immediately went to work on the chocolate shake. "I can't believe I'm eating a meal with you," she grumbled.

"Ah, you flatter me, darlin'," he laughed and sipped at his own shake.

"That wasn't a compliment."

"I can take it as one, can't I? After all, I think you like me more than you let on."

They sat in silence for a bit, while waiting for the rest of their meal. Skye's emotions were all over the place and her mind was in a whirl trying to sort them all out. Aidan confused the heck out of her. Was he deceitful and traitorous or was he actually on her side? She was attracted to him and repelled by him at the same time.

"Here you go!" Sherry's arrival with the burgers and fries broke into her thoughts. Skye grabbed her burger and dug in. The fries were salty and hot, the burger was terrific, and Skye thought Aidan had made a good restaurant selection, but she didn't want to tell him so. They ate in silence until finally, Skye pushed back from her plate, irritated with herself for eating so much. "You're sure you're paying for this?"

"Coming from a girl with boatloads of cash at her disposal, I find that a humorous question."

"How do you know I—?"

"It's obvious to anyone who is paying attention." He pulled his wallet from his pocket and peeled off some bills. "This ought to cover it." He tossed the money on the table and got up.

Sherry immediately rushed over. "I have your check ready for you." She handed it to Aidan. He glanced over it, then looked at Skye and smiled.

"I was right." He then turned to Sherry. "It's all on the table, darlin'. Have a good night."

He walked away, and before Skye had a chance to lever herself out of the booth, she had time to notice Sherry's enraptured expression as she gazed longingly after Aidan. Skye rolled her eyes.

Once back at the car, Aidan's demeanor changed from ingratiating to nearly surly, and he didn't say a word. He drove her back to her car, then sped off into the night with only a hasty good-bye. Skye then drove home, mulling over the night's events, and was more than ready to fall into bed. Which she would have done, if Rachael hadn't met her at the door.

"Girlfriend, there's a problem."

"What?" Skye closed the door behind her and felt her heart rate kick up.

"I've been calling Starr all night. You know, my friend from around here. The Elfae girl?"

"Yeah? So?" Rachael looked panicked, but Skye couldn't see what the big deal was.

"So, I've talked with her parents and she's missing!"

"Maybe she's just out with friends or—"

"No, Skye, you're not listening to me. She is missing. She went out on a date with a new guy last night and she never came home! I think a Spell-Master got her. Maybe even that Lucius guy!"

"No, Rachael that's ridiculous. When would he have had time? He was kind of busy having a firefight, then kidnapping you, and watching his house burn to the ground. No, there's no way that—"

"But that's just it, don't you see? What if Starr was at the Spell-Master's? What if the fire I started—?"

Skye realized where Rachael's thoughts were headed. "No, no, I'm sure that didn't happen. The chance that the same thing happened to your friend is so remote. Especially that she would be taken by the same guy at be at the house the same night we were there." Skye shook her head. "No, Rachael. There's no way."

"Would you go with me to look anyway?"

"The firefighters and police have already searched the house, and they didn't find any bodies."

"I know but—"

"And you realize that any number of things could've happened to her. Not that the thought of that should make you feel any better, but I'm just pointing out that this may be a job for the police, not—"

"I know, I know. But I have to do something." Rachael gave Skye such a pleading look that she relented.

"Okay. Fine. We'll go driving around. We'll go Lucius's house, and we'll go to anyplace else you can think of that Starr might be."

Rachael smiled. "Thank you, Skye!"

Skye headed back out to her car with Rachael by her side, but she really didn't see what good it would do for them to go searching. Starr could be anywhere.

After searching for nearly thirty minutes, Rachael pointed out the window. "Over there!" She indicated a place on the beach where kids were gathered around a big bonfire.

They had already been to Lucius' house, but as Skye had suspected, there was nothing there to see except a burned-out building. Rachael had been relieved, and Skye knew the thought that a fire Rachael had caused might've claimed the life of her friend, was more than she could stand. On the other hand, Skye had felt sure that had Starr been there, Lucius would've killed her for her magic, long before Rachael had started the fire. In any case, Starr wasn't there.

"Park and let's go over to talk to them. I know some of Starr's friends. Maybe some of them will be here. Maybe they'll know something."

Skye parked the car, as Rachael had suggested, and she followed Rachael across the sand toward the group by the fire. She'd left her stakes in the car. No need to draw attention to herself.

Some of the kids turned at their approach, but most looked away again. One girl, however, kept her eyes on Rachael.

"Aren't you Starr's friend? The one from Coronado?" the girl asked.

Rachael smiled. "Yes! Karen, right?"

The other girl nodded. Rachael introduced Skye and then proceeded to talk to the other girl and ask her some questions. Skye listened to their conversation, but at the same time she studied all the kids. Most were Elfae, but a few were human. Karen, for instance, was human.

"...so I told her to wait and get to know him better. I mean, she just met the guy. But she thought he was cute and he'd asked her out and that was that. I haven't heard from her since. I guess she's probably mad at me for telling her not to go."

Rachael nodded. "So, she met him at the movie theater?"

"Yeah, he works there."

"You think he might be there tonight?" Rachael asked.

"Probably. It seems like he's always there. At least every time I've been there, and I go to the movies a lot."

"What's his name again?"

"Tommy. He's tall, shaggy red hair, you can't miss him. If he's there, you'll see him."

"Thanks, Karen." Rachael waved as she turned to go. "Have fun!"

Karen turned back to her other friends, and Rachael hastened away, pulling Skye along with her. "Okay, next stop, Columbia Crest Theater."

Chapter Thirteen

SKYE LOOKED AT THE CLOCK IN THE CAR AS THEY drove. "It's almost eleven. If this doesn't pan out then we're going home."

"Yeah, okay. That's fine. At least we got a lead."

They arrived at the theater, and Skye had to practically run to keep up with Rachael, she was in such a hurry to confront Tommy.

"Is Tommy working tonight?" Rachael asked the girl at the ticket counter. "He's tall and has red hair."

"Oh, sure, Tommy. He's here."

"We need to talk to him."

"Well, you can wait for him to get off work at eleven-thirty, or you can buy a ticket and go in."

Rachael looked at Skye.

"We'll wait," Skye answered. "What door will he come out when he leaves?"

"The side door on your right."

The two of them went around the building to wait near the door. Rachael was agitated and wouldn't stand still. She paced, and Skye soon found herself doing the same. Skye began to get that prickly sensation that told her a Blood-Hunter, was nearby. Just then the side door to the theater opened and three guys stepped out. Skye doubted all three were Blood-Hunters, but one of them certainly was.

"Tommy is there. He's the one in the middle," Rachael replied. "He's the only one with red hair." She stepped forward but Skye grabbed her arm.

"Wait. At least one of those guys is a Blood-Hunter."

Rachael looked alarmed at this information but she kept quiet and waited.

All three guys were dressed in their work attire; black trousers and white shirts. One was short and rather plump while the other two were tall and on the lean side. The three laughed at something the short guy said, then he and one of the taller guys split off and headed to the right, toward the main parking lot. The third one, who fit the description of Tommy with his shaggy red hair, went left. Skye waited to see which way the prickly sensation would pull her.

"Tommy is the Blood-Hunter," Skye whispered, and started after him. Rachael followed along.

Tommy must've sensed someone behind him, because he turned and looked back.

"Hey, Tommy," Skye said.

He stopped walking and a slight frown furrowed his brow. "Who are you?"

"We're looking for someone," Skye began. "Her name is Starr." A split second later he bolted. Skye gave chase. Rachael was pretty much left in the dust.

Skye caught up to him just as he reached for the door handle of his car. She dragged him back and shoved him up against the side of the car. "Where is she?"

"I don't know what you're talking about," Tommy sputtered.

"Oh, don't you? Then why were you dashing away in such a hurry?"

Rachael came running up. She was out of breath, but she managed to get in on the interrogation. "Where is Starr? She was last seen with you, and that was just last night."

"I don't know," Tommy insisted.

"Why don't I believe you?" Skye asked. She pulled one of the stakes from her holster and lifted it so he could see it.

His eyes widened. "Who *are* you? Why are you so strong and fast? How—?"

"Where is Starr?" Skye yelled. "I don't want to have to ask you again." She twirled the stake.

Tommy shut his eyes tightly. "She's at my apartment."

"Is she alive?" Rachael asked.

"Um, I don't know for sure," he stammered.

"What do you mean you don't know for sure?" Rachael snapped. "How can you not know that?"

Skye gave him a shake and his eyes flew open. "Where is your apartment, Tommy?"

Tommy's eyes flashed between Skye and Rachael. "2826 North Harper Blvd. Apartment number three, one, six."

"Come on." Skye dragged him along. He was so pathetic, he didn't seem worth killing, and she almost felt guilty for how she knew this most likely would end, but even as she reasoned with herself, he lunged for Rachael, with fangs bared, and Skye no longer had any misgiving about what she had to do. It was all over in a matter of seconds. She staked him and after a moment of puzzlement on his face, he disintegrated and vaporized.

Rachael stared, wide eyed, at the spot where Tommy had stood. "Well, I guess the movie theater just lost an employee."

Skye grinned. "Yeah. I guess so."

By the time they arrived at Tommy's apartment complex, Rachael was antsy again. "What if she's dead? I don't want to see her that way. I don't want to see her all bloody with her throat torn out like how they found Joe."

"I'll go find the apartment. You stay here," Skye replied.

"But you don't know what Starr looks like. You've never met her. Won't you need me to—?"

"Look, if I find *anybody* in there, injured or being held against their will, I'm bringing them out. End of story. So, stay here with the car doors locked. Scrunch down so no one can see you. If I'm not back in a half an hour, call Preston." She gave Rachael the number. "No, wait, make that fifteen minutes. If I'm not back in fifteen, call him."

Skye turned away and jogged toward the complex. She took a moment to look at the directions posted on the wall. Apartment #316 was to her left. She scanned the numbers on the doors until she found it. There was a light on inside.

Skye approached with caution, and stood just outside the door for several seconds, listening. She sensed Blood-Hunters nearby, just on the other side of the door most likely. No wonder Tommy said he wasn't sure if Starr was still alive! She heard a rustling, and then what sounded like someone crying. It was time to act, but how many of them were in there? She'd have to take her chances. Skye backed up, side-stepped, and kicked the door in. It flew back with a crash, and the first one, a big gangly guy with a nose ring and greasy black hair, came at her. She staked him almost without thought, her mind already calculating her next move. The second Blood-Hunter, a muscle-bound guy with a scar on his cheek, was slightly more cautious than the first, but it still only took two tries before he joined his cohort in death.

Skye stood still; listening. She heard the girl whimper again, and it came from what she supposed were one of the bedrooms. Skye slowly made her way toward the room, and what she saw made her heart wrench and anger twist her gut. A girl was tied by her wrists to the metal bed posts. She had bite marks on her neck, arms and legs and looked to be barely conscious. Skye went forward into the room without really thinking about it, and her carelessness was almost the end of her. A third Blood-Hunter grabbed her from behind, but she reacted instinctively, just like she did with Todd in the ice cream parlor, only this time she moved faster and hit harder. Elbow to the gut, fist to the face. She followed the move with a solid kick that sent the Blood-Hunter reeling, giving her just enough time to ram a stake into his chest. Once he'd disappeared into dust and vapor, Skye turned to the girl on the bed. Now that she was closer, she could see the girl was petite, with very short, strawberry-blonde hair. Her skin was pale, and probably made more so by lack of blood circulating through her veins.

"Are there any more of them?" Skye asked after spotting a knife on the nearby nightstand and cutting through the girl's restraints.

The girl started to cry in earnest. "Tommy. Only Tommy," she stammered.

"You don't have to worry about him anymore. He's dust. Are you Starr?"

The girl nodded.

"Can you get up?"

The girl tried, but she fainted. Too much blood loss, Skye figured. She settled Starr back onto the bed, pulled out her cell phone and called Rachael.

"I found her. There's a map showing, the layout of the apartment complex, right at the end of the walkway in front of the car. It will show you how to get to apartment three one six. Hurry."

Next she called an ambulance, and Rachael showed up just as Skye disconnected. Rachael rushed to her friend's side as she started to come around again.

"We have to come up with a story." Skye began.

Rachael looked up at her. "A story?"

"Yes. An ambulance is going to be here soon, and we have to be able to tell them something believable."

"Well, what can we tell them? She has bite marks on her. They aren't animal bites, but even if they were there aren't any animals here," Rachael gestured around the room.

"Sicko men," Starr murmured. "Kidnapped me. Thought they were vampires. Like in the movies. Fake fangs."

Skye nodded. "That'll do." She left Rachael to comfort Starr and went outside to wait for the ambulance. What would people do if they knew that movie vampires had real life counterparts called, Blood-Hunters? She stopped her musing when she heard the ambulance approach, and headed out to direct the paramedics to the right room.

———— ·+◆◆◆+· ————

The next morning, Skye was still in a deep sleep, when her phone started to chirp a little tune. She roused enough to reach for the phone and look at the name on the screen. It was Preston.

"I didn't hear from you last night."

"Nice greeting. I'm fine, thanks for asking."

"Well? Did you learn anything useful?"

Skye flopped back down onto the bed and stared at the ceiling. "I rescued an Elfae girl from four Blood-Hunters. They're all vaporized and she's in the hospital."

"The hospital? Was her glamour still intact?" Preston sounded panicked.

"Yes."

He blew out a breath. "Good. And what about the box?"

"Lucius has it."

"And...? It's like pulling teeth to get you to talk, Skye! What about Aidan? What part does he play in all this?"

Skye closed her eyes and sighed. "I wish I knew."

Rachael came stumbling in a few minutes later. Skye was still in her pajamas, sipping a coffee with cream.

"Hey," Rachael mumbled, as she grabbed herself a cup and dropped down beside Skye on the sofa.

"Have you been at the hospital all night?"

"Yeah. I slept some, but I'm still exhausted."

"How's Starr?"

"She's going to be fine. They gave her blood transfusions, then disinfected and bandaged the wounds. She's taking antibiotics. I think she has to stay in the hospital another night, but then she can go home."

Skye took another sip of her coffee. "Did they believe her story about psycho-vampire wannabe guys?"

"Yeah, but it's good they'll never find them." Rachael managed a smile. "I told the police how you and I went looking for her and found her. They wanted to know about Tommy. I told them he must've felt guilty because he told us where to find her, but then he took off."

Skye made a very unladylike snort. "They'll never find him either, thankfully."

"They'll probably want to talk to you too, so I wanted to make sure you knew what I'd already told them."

"Okay. Thanks. Preston called. When I told him what happened, he was worried she'd lost her glamour."

"No, it's still fine. No problems there."

"How do you guys do that? How do you keep up the glamour even if you're sick or unconscious?"

Rachael smiled. "It's an ancient Elfae secret. I'd tell you but then I'd have to kill you."

"Oh, well I wouldn't want that!" Skye snickered. "You think you could take me?"

"I think I could fry your ass," Rachael laughed. "But, seriously, Skye. Thank you so much for what you did last night. I told Starr's parents the truth. I hope you don't mind. I know your being an Assassin is a secret, but there was no way they were going to believe a human and an Elfae took out four Blood-Hunters. And even if I could've done it by myself, I would've had to burn the place down to kill them."

Skye thought about it for a minute. "How come Starr wasn't able to protect herself better? Doesn't she have a magical power like yours?"

"Different Elfae have different sorts of talents. Starr's ability isn't like mine. She can make things grow. Like flowers and other plants." Rachael shrugged. "It's great if you want a garden, but not helpful if Blood-Hunters are attacking you. Happy birthday, by the way. Tonight, we have dinner with your parents. What are you going to wear?"

Skye shrugged. "I don't know. I hadn't thought about it. You?"

"Oh, I dunno, for tonight I thought maybe…pink," Rachael grinned.

Skye rolled her eyes. Why did she even ask? Pink was Rachael's default color.

Rachael left the room, and Skye lounged. She listened to her phone calls, and scrolled through text messages from family, Sarah and Angela.

Skye's parents and brother called and sang happy birthday to her over the phone. It was kind of cool. No, it was really, really nice actually. They confirmed what time they'd meet and where to go eat. Almost as soon as she hung up, Preston called.

"We've really got to get going with this box situation. Find Aidan. See if you can—"

"Whoa! It's my birthday today, remember? I have the day and the night off," Skye replied.

"Oh, yes, happy birthday. That's right. Well, I'll see what I can find out from here then. Ben is back, and Natalie should be back this evening as well. I'll see if either of them might be of some assistance in the matter."

Skye frowned. She'd almost forgotten about Preston's other Assassins. "This is my deal though, right? You're not giving it to one of them to—?"

"No, no, of course not. But the box must be found before it's opened. Someone has to deal with Lucius, and if Aidan is a hindrance, then he must be eliminated also."

"Well, sure but—"

"I'll set Ben on Lucius' trail. He'll be looking for *you* now, so he won't notice Ben lurking about. And Natalie, she's top-notch. She and Ben have worked together before and they have been very successful as a team."

But Skye was only half listening. Instead, she pawed through her closet and her drawers, looking at clothes. The blue floral jersey wrap dress or the green A-line? The pale-yellow slacks with the matching sleeveless silk top, or the red blouse with the—

"Skye? Are you listening to me?"

"Yeah, yeah, sure! Of course."

"Fine. Well, have a good evening, and again, happy birthday."

"Thanks. Talk to you later." She disconnected and made a final decision on what to wear. It would be her new, above the knee, swirl skirt in red, orange and yellow, paired with the red blouse and some red heels. She held the red blouse up to herself as she stood in front of the mirror. She had to chuckle when, against her will, the image in her mind shifted to a black blouse instead of the red one. She imagined herself going out wearing solid black instead, with her stakes strapped on, her hair in a braid. Skye shuddered and shook off the thought. She could keep both parts of her life separate. She had to.

⋅⋅✦✦✦✦✦⋅⋅

That evening, Skye, her parents and Rachael, sat at a window table in Chateau Elegante, a French restaurant, known for their five-star cuisine. The evening had gone well, the food was, of course, excellent, and it was nice to talk about regular, ordinary things like the apartment, movies, and upcoming classes in the fall. This was a far cry from discussing Blood-Hunters and Spell-Masters, magical boxes and the potential end of the world.

As the evening wound down, and their dessert was almost finished, Skye felt the tingling sensation that meant a Blood-Hunter was nearby. Rats! She couldn't even have a nice dinner with her parents, without something from her new life intruding.

She looked around and spotted Aidan, but he wasn't alone. He was with a woman. They followed the hostess and settled into a booth across the room from Skye's table. She wondered if the woman was human or a Blood-Hunter? She concentrated, trying to make the determination.

Her dad twisted around in his chair to follow her gaze. "Someone you know?" he asked, once he'd turned back around.

"No," Skye answered, at the same time Rachael answered in the affirmative. They looked at each other.

"He's just an acquaintance, actually," Rachael amended. "A friend of a friend. Sort of."

"Oh, it's the young man who you know!" Skye's mom had caught a glimpse of them, at the same time as Skye's dad. "I thought maybe you knew the girl."

"Nope," Skye shook her head. "Don't know her." But she kept her eye on her. The girl was gorgeous, with long cascading strawberry blonde curls flowing down her back. She wore a copper-colored dress, which was short and tight, showing off her curves and setting off the red tones in her hair. Gold hoops adorned her ears and she wore a gold charm bracelet. Her strappy sandals were also gold. She looked fantastic. But was she human or Blood-Hunter?

While Skye continued to try and make small talk with her parents, she also slid furtive glances across the room. At one point, Aidan stared straight at her. He smiled, then turned back to his lovely companion. Was this girl about to become his next blood meal? She remembered him saying, that blood wasn't on his menu for a couple more days. Maybe he got hungry for blood a little early.

Skye saw the young woman at the other table, get up and head to the restroom. This was her chance. She had to take it.

"Excuse me." Skye stood. "Ladies room. Be right back." Now she'd be able to discover if the girl was human or not and maybe even warn her about Aidan without giving away what he was in the process.

When she entered the bathroom, she felt no vibe to indicate a Blood-Hunter was there. Okay, that answered that question. The young woman stood at a sink, washing her hands. She looked to be about mid-twenties, maybe four or five years older than Skye.

"Hi," Skye began, when she joined her at the sinks. "Your shoes are fantastic!" She figured giving a compliment was always a good way to start a conversation with a stranger.

The woman smiled at Skye in the mirror. "Thanks! I got them at Nordstrom's." She started out the door.

"You're having dinner with Aidan?" Skye asked, and the woman turned to look at her, suspicion in her hazel eyes. "I just wanted to warn you that he can be dangerous," Skye continued.

The other woman gave Skye a tight smile. Not the open and friendly smile she'd shown when Skye had complimented her shoes. "I've known him for quite a while now. I know what he's like." She turned once again and headed for the door.

"Just be careful," Skye called out as the door banged shut. She sighed. She'd done what she could to warn the girl. Hopefully it was enough. Then again, maybe the girl knew what she was doing. She'd said she'd known Aidan for quite a while. If that was true, and she obviously wasn't dead, then maybe it was fine. Skye headed back to her table.

CHAPTER FOURTEEN

"**S**O. WHAT WAS UP WITH AIDAN AND THAT girl?" Rachael asked, once they were back at their apartment. "Do you think she has something to do with the box?"

Skye shook her head and dropped down onto the sofa. "No. She's human, and there's absolutely nothing special about her. Well, except for the fact that she's gorgeous."

Rachael sat beside her. "So, what's the connection? Is she a girlfriend? His next meal? What?"

Skye hardly heard Rachael's questions. Instead, she thought about how different Aidan had looked tonight. While he still wore black, he certainly wasn't wearing leather. On the contrary, he wore an Armani suit and a tie. He hadn't looked like Creepy Goth Guy at all. In fact...

"Skye?"

"Oh, sorry. Um, I have no idea what their connection is, but she said she'd known him for quite a while, so..." She shrugged.

"Oh well, just forget about it then. She probably isn't important." Rachael stood.

There was a knock at the door and Skye frowned. "Not Preston again," she muttered as she marched over to the door. "I told him it was my birthday and I didn't want to be—" But then she felt the now familiar prickly sensation. She yanked open the door and saw Aidan standing there in his very sharp looking Armani suit.

Her eyes narrowed. "That was a short dinner."

"Just a drink and an appetizer, actually. You going to invite me in?" he asked.

"No," Skye snapped.

"Well then, I'll just have to say what I have to say from here. Unless, of course, you shut the door in my face first."

Skye's eyes narrowed, but she didn't slam the door.

He nodded. "I'll take that as a go-ahead. So, you met Tara."

"I see she told you about our conversation in the ladies' room," Skye countered.

"Yes, she did." He paused. "What are you worried about, Skye? Are you worried I'll drain her lovely body of all its lifeblood, and leave her in a dumpster somewhere?"

"She said she's known you for quite a while, so I guess if you haven't done it already, then you probably aren't going to."

He gave her a wry smile. "Well now, you never can be sure with our kind."

She glared at him.

"But as it so happens, she and I have an understanding."

Skye's lip curled in disgust. "An understanding? So, how's that work? You buy her dinner and then she lets you drink yours?" She just wanted to end the conversation, and end it fast. "Why did you come here, Aidan?"

"I came here to reassure you that Tara is in no danger from me; although I don't owe you even that much. My life is none of your business."

Skye's eyes narrowed. "And what about Lucius? What about the box? Have you already forgotten about that?"

"On the contrary. I think of little else." He gave her a lopsided smile. "Good-night, Skye." He turned and walked away.

She shut the door with a slam, just as her phone began to sing its merry tune. Skye didn't even look to see who it was before she answered.

"I know it's your birthday, but this can't wait. I'd like to stop by with Ben and Natalie and introduce you."

It was Preston. Skye was stunned. "Now?"

"I thought you'd be interested in meeting them."

"Well, yes, but—"

"Are your parents there at the moment, or any of your friends?"

"No. Well, just Rachael, but—"

"Good. There are some important developments, regarding the box and Lucius, which you need to know about. I don't mind if Rachael is present, in fact it might be better if she is."

Skye glanced over at Rachael. "So, how soon are you going to be here?"

"About five minutes or so."

Skye sighed in frustration. "Preston, I really, really, don't want to do this. Can't we just all get together tomorrow morning over coffee or something? I really wanted this one day to myself. Just one day!"

"No. This is too important to-"

"If it's so important, then can't you just tell me over the phone?"

"No. We'll be there soon." He disconnected.

"Argh!" Skye gasped. "He is infuriating!"

Rachael frowned. "What's going on? And why was Aidan here?"

"Preston is on his way over, and he's bringing two other Assassins. They'll be here in five minutes. Aidan stopped by to make me insane, just like he always does." She turned in time to see Rachael's smile. "What are you smiling at?"

She stared at Skye, wide eyed. "Nothing. Who are these Assassins? Why are they coming?"

"Preston is their Handler. I don't know why they have to come along, except that he thinks we should meet. I guess he thinks I need help. Oh, and he said for you to be here too. I guess he meant like, sit in on the conversation."

"Me! Why?"

"I have no idea."

They didn't have long to wait. Skye went to answer the door, not knowing what to expect, and when she opened it, Preston breezed by her, wearing black slacks and a button-down shirt in a shade of deep eggplant. Two other people filed into the room as well. The first was a girl who was bit shorter than Skye. Her skin was a rich, warm, mocha and her eyes milk chocolate brown. She wore her shoulder length dark hair in multiple braids.

The second person nodded and smiled at Skye as he passed by. He was tall, and by the slant of his eyes she guessed he had some sort of Asian ancestry. His black hair was close cropped. He looked muscular but not bulky. Lean and mean.

"Skye Falco, this is Ben Takei and Natalie Brewster. Ben has been with me for three years, and Natalie for four." Preston turned to Ben and Natalie. "And this is Skye's friend and roommate, Rachael Perry."

Everyone murmured their hellos, and then Rachael, filled in the ensuing awkward silence by ushering everyone into the tiny living room to have a seat.

"So, ah, not that I'm not happy to meet you both, but what's so important it couldn't wait until tomorrow?" Skye asked.

"Let me explain," Ben began. "I've done some follow up on Lucius the Spell-Master." His voice was deep and smooth. "I've learned where he is now staying, and that he is talking to some Blood-Hunters from Nikolai's Coven, about opening the box."

"And the Blood-Hunters you staked last night were from that same Coven." Natalie added. "The same Coven as Nikolai."

Skye was confused. "So, I still don't see—"

Preston joined the conversation. "The two situations are connected."

"How?"

Preston gave her a level gaze. "Have you asked yourself how it is that Aidan and Nikolai and the Blood-Hunters from Nikolai's Coven, all know how to open the box?"

Skye stared at him, waiting for him to get to the point.

"Aidan is a loner, but he has blood ties to other Blood-Hunters who are in a Coven; again, Nikolai's Coven. They are family."

"So, all these Blood-Hunters are blood related. So?"

Rachael looked over at her. "Skye, Aidan said the box had been in his family for generations and it was his to look after, right?

Skye began to get an idea about where this conversation was headed. "But wait a minute. If Nikolai and Aidan are from the same bloodline, then they would have equal rights to the box, right? So what was the big deal about Aidan saying the box was his and all that?"

"Blood-Hunters are a weird species. Who can fully understand the way they think? My advice is to stake Aidan as soon as possible. Especially if there's any chance he can open that box," Natalie replied.

"He says he doesn't want to open it; he wants to destroy it just like we do." Though right at the moment Skye wasn't one hundred percent sure of that.

"Rule number one," Ben said. "Don't trust a Blood-Hunter."

Skye sighed. "And rule number two?"

Natalie frowned. "There is no rule number two. That's it. Just don't trust them."

Ben leaned in. "And since you've angered the leader of Aidan's family Coven, by staking four members of the group, Aidan is the perfect choice to come after you and take your life as payback, since he already knows you and can get close to you."

Skye closed her eyes. So, the Blood-Hunters who kidnapped Starr were part of that Coven. She wished Preston and the others would all just go away. Here she sat, still in the pretty skirt and blouse she'd worn to a lovely, expensive restaurant, and instead of enjoying what was left of her happy, carefree, relaxing birthday, she was discussing death and destruction with people she'd rather never have met.

She opened her eyes. "Okay, thanks for the warning. I need for all of you to leave now."

"Skye..." Rachael cautioned.

"No, I'm serious." She stood. "You're all leaving, right now. Right this very minute."

Rachael leapt to her feet, and thankfully both Ben and Natalie had enough common sense to do the same. Skye walked to the door and held it open, as Preston, Ben and then Natalie trooped out.

"Good bye. Good night. Talk to you later," Skye said as she closed the door. She turned to Rachael. "I'm still not clear about why you were supposed to sit in on that."

"I think it's because of Starr. I think Preston wanted me to know what was going on so I'd be careful. Lucius is still out there, after all."

"Like I wouldn't have told you!" Skye shook her head and stormed by Rachael. "I'm going to bed."

"But it's still early!" Rachael called after her.

"I know, but I just want some time to myself. I've got a lot to think about."

Skye stripped off her clothes and put them away, then got ready for bed. After she crawled in, she lay there, and stared at the ceiling. Was Aidan going to try and kill her? But he'd just saved her life when Lucius attacked her. That made no sense. Who was Tara and how was she involved with Aidan? Was she in danger, or was she also someone Skye now had to keep an eye on as a potential threat? Who was the leader of Nikolai's Coven of Blood-Hunters? And how much influence might he have on Aidan, if any? Did Aidan really want to destroy the box? At this point she truly believed she could not trust him, in spite of the fact that she had wanted to. Natalie and Ben were right. She should never trust a Blood-Hunter.

By the next morning, Skye had put it all behind her. Sort of. She'd awakened early but Rachael had left a note to say she'd gone to visit Starr. So, Skye decided to try and get a hold of some other friends, to see if any of them wanted to hang out and maybe go to the beach. Her plans didn't get very far, however, because Preston called.

"Before you say anything," Skye began. "I know I was rude last night but—"

"Never mind that now," he snapped. "The box is going to be opened today."

"Today! When? Where? How do you know?"

"Natalie was killed last night."

Skye felt as though someone had punched her in the gut. She couldn't form a coherent thought. Couldn't catch her breath. "Last night? But... you...she...what happened?"

"Blood-Hunters. She found the location of their Coven. There were too many of them."

"She was by herself?"

"Initially. She contacted Ben when she realized she'd found the spot, but by the time he got there, it was too late. She was dead and they were gone."

Skye sat in silence for several seconds. "Preston?"

"Yes."

"I don't think I want to work alone anymore. I've been lucky so far, but—"

"I'll have Ben contact you. I'm sorry for the short notice, but the two of you should really try and find where the remaining Blood-Hunters have gone. And then there's Lucius and the box."

"I know. And don't worry about the short notice. I'll be ready in an hour. Just have Ben call me or come over."

"All right."

"And, Preston. I'm sorry about Natalie."

"Thank you, Skye. I am too." Skye detected great sorrow in his voice. He'd obviously grown attached to her over the few years they'd known one another.

As soon as she disconnected, Skye went straight to her room to get dressed, and as she did she was wracked with guilt. She should've gone with them last night. Maybe if she'd been there, Natalie wouldn't have died. Skye was disgusted with herself. Instead of being a baby about her birthday being ruined, she should've been out with the other Assassins, looking for the Blood-Hunters' lair. It amazed her how only a couple of weeks ago she'd have done almost anything to get out of being an Assassin, in spite of the fact there was no choice in the matter. Now she was solidly entrenched. She wouldn't want to turn back now even if she could. Her friend, Joe, had been killed by a Blood-Hunter, and so had Natalie. Rachael had almost died at the hands of a Spell-Master and her friend, Starr had been minutes away from death too, thanks to those apartment-dwelling Blood-Hunters. Plus, there was a demon that could be loosed on the world at any time. Yeah. Enough was enough. She was one hundred percent in and she was determined not to let anyone else be harmed or killed. Not on her watch.

The phone rang and she snatched it from atop her nightstand. The number was unfamiliar. Probably Ben.

"Hello?"

"Hello, Skye." It was Aidan.

Skye's heart started to pound. "How did you get this number?"

"I have my ways. We need to talk. Meet me in an hour at—"

"I'm not going anywhere to meet with you. Do you hear me? If you have something to say, say it now."

"All right. Some of my blood relations have recently disappeared. I'm attributing that to the recent influx of Assassins in the area. Although there is one less of them, I understand."

"You bastard. If you had anything to do with that..."

"Me personally? Nah. But you're pressing your luck with me, Skye."

"Do you want that box destroyed or not?"

"I do. But I don't want everyone in my bloodline destroyed along with it."

"Well then tell them to turn the box over to the Bureau. Or to me. I'll—"

"They won't do that. They want it opened. They have the same fool ideas that Nikolai did."

"I can't let that happen!"

"And I can't allow you and your Bureau friends to kill off my bloodline. Back off!"

"No! Where's Lucius? Does he still have it?"

"How the hell should I know?"

Skye sighed and curbed her temper. "Why did you even get involved with me in the first place?"

"You involved yourself with me, remember?" He too had calmed down. At least he was no longer shouting.

"Yes, but since then. Why did you help me, then turn me over to Lucius? If it hadn't been for Rachael that night—"

"I know, I know, but that's the way I roll. I have to play the hand that's dealt to me, even if I don't like it."

"If I can never count on you, then I don't want to—"

"But then I saved you from Lucius at the parking garage, don't forget."

Skye rubbed her eyes. She was so tired of all this, but it was her life now and she'd have to learn to deal with it. "I don't know what to think about you, Aidan. All I know is that you'd better stay out of our way, or you're going to get staked."

"Our way? Does that mean you've been assigned to work with another Assassin?"

"If you get to the box before we do, you damn well better destroy it. That's all I'm going to say. Good-bye, Aidan."

She disconnected and finished getting dressed. By the time Ben arrived she was ready for battle, in dark indigo blue jeans, a black t-shirt and some black, low-heeled ankle boots. She strapped on her stake holster as she headed for the door to let Ben in.

He entered and gave her a quick once over with his eyes.

"Yeah, I know," Skye replied to his unspoken comment. "I look different like this than I did last night in my party clothes. I have a life besides this one, but this one is the only one that counts right now. Hang on. Let me go braid my hair. I'll be right back."

When Skye returned, it was to find Ben staring out the window. He had on faded blue jeans that fit him like a glove, and a drab, army green colored t-shirt. He also wore a shoulder holster, similar to hers.

Before she had a chance to speak, he turned. "I'm pretty sure I know where the Blood-Hunters have gone. They're most likely with Lucius."

"And where is he?"

"On Coronado Island."

Skye's eyebrows shot up. "My parents live there. And Rachael's family."

"It's a small island. Let's hope they don't get caught up in this."

CHAPTER FIFTEEN

SKYE WAS REALLY WORRIED ABOUT HER FAMILY and Rachael's, but she had to stay focused. "What's the plan?"

"Surveillance first. Then we'll decide the best approach."

"Do we have any idea how soon they're going to open the box?" Skye asked as she climbed into Ben's black, Chevy Silverado 3500. She noticed he had two shotguns in the back.

The doors slammed closed and Ben looked over at her. "For all I know, it's already open. I mean, we don't know for sure what will happen, only that the box will release a demon. By all accounts that demon is called Mortmal the Destroyer. That doesn't bode well regardless." He put the key in the ignition and they were off.

"You have guns in the back. What're they for?" Skye asked.

"Mostly for killing crazed Shape-Shifters, why?"

She shrugged. "I guess I just wasn't expecting to see them since we mostly kill Blood-Hunters. Isn't that true?"

He nodded. "Yep, but you never know what you might be up against."

More questions raced through Skye's mind, but she sat in silence and waited to follow Ben's lead. He was more experienced with this sort of thing, and to be honest, her confidence was shaken. Natalie was dead. Dead! And she had just been in Skye's living room last night; only a few short hours ago. And Ben, what must he be thinking, feeling about her loss? He'd known her and worked with her. Skye glanced over at him. He looked completely focused, like Natalie's death didn't matter, but Skye suspected the opposite was true; that his intensity was all the greater because of her loss.

As they drove, Skye again thought of Aidan. She might have been confused about his intentions regarding the box and confused by her misguided attraction to him, but whatever his game was, it would end soon, and most likely with her stake in his chest.

Skye heard a vibrating sound, and Ben reached for his phone. "It's Preston," he said, as he switched to speakerphone.

"Are you with Skye?" Preston asked.

"Yes, she's here with me. I have the phone on speaker so she can hear. We're on our way over to the island."

"Good. Bureau contacts have been able to put together a team of Elfae who are reasonably sure they can contain the demon spirit to the island, should the box get opened. They're working on it now. Some sort of a force field."

"How do we fight it?" Skye asked.

"You two just concentrate on the Blood-Hunters. Let the Bureau focus on the magical aspects." Preston paused. "And Skye, chances are you'll encounter Aidan on the island. Don't hesitate to stake him if he threatens you. We don't have time to query him on his true intentions, since they're probably shifting from moment to moment anyway. He's not to be trusted."

"I understand." Although she'd been ready to stake Aidan, if necessary, when she'd heard Preston present the order in such a way, it made her stomach clench. She hoped she wouldn't run into Aidan in the first place for surely, they'd argue and perhaps that argument would turn into a fight and then she'd have no excuse not to stake him; none at all.

"How many Blood-Hunters should we expect to encounter?" Ben asked.

"We're uncertain. The Coven itself isn't very big now; probably less than a dozen, but other Blood-Hunters may be present. You might be in over your heads, but I've got no other Assassins to send in with you. We don't have the luxury of time for others to arrive from nearby cities. You're on your own."

Ben's hands clenched the steering wheel. "How soon will that shield be set up?"

"Soon."

"Can we get in after it's up?"

"No. No one in, no one out, so you'd better hurry."

Ben increased his speed. "Just give us twenty minutes and we'll be there."

"I'll see what I can do. Good luck you two." Preston disconnected.

"See ya on the other side," Ben murmured.

As they crossed the bridge onto Coronado Island, Skye glanced up at the sky and frowned. "Look at that, it's kind of shimmery. Is it an optical illusion?"

As they came off the other side of the bridge, there was a 'boom' and then a 'snap'. Ben looked up too. "No. I think it's the shield. I think it just snapped into place."

"I don't see anything different now. The sky looks just the same."

He shrugged. "You won't notice any difference. You're not supposed to. I don't know why I looked up there. Just an automatic reaction, I guess."

The phone vibrated, and he put it to speaker again.

"Ben? Where are you? Are you on the island?" It was Preston.

"We're here. We just heard the shield lock in."

"You're on your own now. Keep us informed."

"I will. Any further instructions?"

"No. Not at this time. You have good instincts. Just do what you do best. Skye, I hope I don't have to tell you to follow Ben's lead. He—"

"Don't worry, Preston. I'll follow his lead. I'll back his play, and all that."

Ben signed off with Preston, and then disconnected. Moments later he pulled up to the curb in one of the residential areas and shut off the engine. The truck pinged a couple of times and was quiet.

"Now what?" Skye asked.

"Follow me." Ben got out, and Skye did likewise. They started up the sidewalk just as a balloon of what looked like black smoke, rose above a two-story home not three houses away from where they stood.

Skye stopped and stared. "What the—?"

"The demon is out." Ben started to run toward the house. There was no time for surveillance, but it wasn't necessary anyway. Blood-Hunters bolted out the front door with looks of glee on their faces. Others darted from the back yard and headed in the opposite direction.

Skye wondered where they were headed, but then she forgot about it in the melee. People came out of their homes to look at the darkening sky, and were immediately attacked by Blood-Hunters. Skye was shocked. She now understood the magnitude of the situation. No one in, no one out. These people couldn't even flee for their lives if they wanted to! They were trapped and the Blood-Hunters had free rein to do as they pleased. How many humans would die today? Would her family and Rachael's be among them?

A Blood-Hunter lunged at her from behind a hedge. Out of the corner of her eye she caught the movement and leapt out of the way. The Blood-Hunter's long coat momentarily blinded her as it brushed across her face, and Skye felt an instant of panic. She conquered it and whirled, stake in hand. The Blood-Hunter came at her again, but he didn't stand a chance. She avoided his clumsily thrown punch and plunged her stake into his chest. She didn't have time to enjoy watching him crumble then vaporize, though, as there was too much going on all around her. She joined Ben in the fight, and they punched, kicked and staked their way forward through the throng of marauding Blood-Hunters. Skye was amazed at how instinctive her movements were. She'd never been in a fight like this, with multiple opponents, yet each kick, each punch, felt completely natural. She was quick and her movements flowed from one thing to the next as though she'd trained for this all her life. Somehow, she sensed when a Blood-Hunter was at her back and a well-placed kick would hit its mark. She knew when to duck and when to lash out. Very soon she forgot to be amazed. There just wasn't time.

At one point she and Ben stood back-to-back against four Blood-Hunters. They fought as a team, protecting each other's blindsides until each of the four was dust and vapor. Another time Skye fell when her leg was kicked out from under her. The Blood-Hunter descended upon her before she could raise her arms in self-defense, but Ben was there. He staked the Blood-Hunter and pulled her to her feet in one smooth motion.

Skye tested her leg and found it to be undamaged. She heard sirens in the distance. "Thanks for the save."

"No problem."

The two of them looked around. The Blood-Hunters they'd fought were either vaporized or they'd run off.

"There are some people who are injured." Skye pointed to a huddle of men and women, bloodied and weeping, across the street.

"You heard the sirens. The police and medical teams are sure to be here soon. We have other things to attend to." He studied the air above the house. "The blackness has increased in size."

"I can see a face in it." Skye shuddered.

"It's Mortmal the Destroyer."

"Is there anything more we can do here? What about inside the house?"

"No. Preston said to concentrate on the Blood-Hunters. We should go after the others who ran toward town. Let's get back to the truck."

They turned and went for the Silverado, just as emergency vehicles arrived to help the injured. Skye hopped into Ben's truck and slammed the door shut.

"I'd like to check on my family. They're not far from here."

"Nothing is far from here, that's the problem. This is a small island," Ben replied.

"So can we go there first, or not?"

"No. Sorry, but our primary responsibility is to kill as many of those Blood-Hunters as possible. Preferably all of them. If we can do that, we can then go check on your family afterwards."

Skye sat in silence, her anger simmering. Her common sense told her he was right, but her heart told her she had to do something to help her family. She took out her cell phone and used the speed dial. Her dad answered on the second ring.

"Skye? Where are you? Are you alright?"

"I'm okay Dad, but you and Mom have to do something for me. There's some weird stuff going on and you have to stay inside with the doors and windows locked."

"What's going on? Have you heard something about a storm? The sky is so black. I thought maybe—"

"Dad, just please, trust me and stay inside. No matter what happens or what you see or hear. Will you promise me that?"

"Well, yes, I suppose so, but what's—?"

"Is Derek there?"

"No, he's still in Costa Mesa visiting some friends."

Skye breathed a sigh of relief. At least her brother was safe.

"What's this all about, Skye? Are you on the island?"

"I'm here but I can't explain right now. Please, just trust me. You and Mom both have to stay inside with the doors locked. Lock the windows too. And don't let anyone inside, Dad! Do you hear me? Not unless you know them personally. If you don't know the person, don't let them in! Promise me!"

"All right, sweetheart, I promise. Are you coming to the house?"

"I will be later, but I have to take care of some things first. Call Rachael's parents and tell them what I told you, okay, Dad? It's really important."

"Sure, I'll call them and let them know. Is Rachael with you?"

"No. I have to go now, Dad. Give Mom a hug for me. Bye."

She disconnected and Ben slowed the truck. Damage and destruction were all around them. Store windows had been smashed and people ran for their cars. Blood-Hunters looted stores and attacked humans at will. Skye was shocked. She had never seen such upheaval and violence in real life, but somehow instead of frightening her, it all just made her that much more determined to kill the Blood-Hunters and to see that Mortmal the demon didn't leave this island alive.

"What do we do?" she asked.

"Same as before. We fight."

"Any particular strategy?"

"Just beat the crap out of them, plunge a stake into their hearts and vaporize 'em." He parked. "Let's go."

Skye ran toward the chaos. She leapt over broken glass, slammed her stake into one of the Blood-Hunters, and then moved on toward the fray. A shriek behind her made her pause. She turned to see a Blood-Hunter lunge toward a woman cowering on the sidewalk; shopping bags still clutched in her hand. Skye drove her stake into the Blood-Hunter and her aim was true. He exploded into dust and ash, but the woman's neck was red with blood. Skye hesitated. She wanted to stop and offer help but her usefulness lay in being an Assassin, and that's what she intended to do; assassinate Blood-Hunters.

"Keep pressure on it," she shouted before she ran on, looking for the next Blood-Hunter to kill.

There was a blur of movement to her left. She ducked then lunged toward the Blood-Hunter. The sleeve of her shirt tore as the monster tried to get a hold of her. She staked him. "That shirt cost seventy-five dollars you jerk!" she said, as the Blood-Hunter exploded into dust.

Overhead, the sky had gotten so dark it was almost like night time. Skye hoped the people who escaped the downtown upheaval and mass murder, would make it all the way home to safety. She also hoped once they were in their homes, they would lock themselves in. She hoped they would be safe. Somehow, she doubted it, what with the demon spirit unfurling across the sky.

She saw Ben trading punches with a Blood-Hunter not twenty feet away. What he didn't see, but she did, was another Blood-Hunter stalking him with fangs bared. There was no time to waste, Skye ran flat out and slammed into the Blood-Hunter, knocking him sideways, sending him to his knees. She plunged her stake into his chest and watched for a moment as he began to disintegrate, then she whirled to meet the next attacker. She was thankful for that little breather after her shirt had gotten torn. She probably wouldn't get another break however, not the way things were going. Blood-Hunters were coming out of the woodwork. Maybe some had been here already, before the group came over with the box. No matter. She and Ben would kill them all.

The next time Skye had a chance to catch her breath; the heavens were black as midnight.

Ben looked around. "Looks like we killed most of them. I lost track after a while."

"You were counting?"

"Yeah," he panted. "You're doing great, by the way." He gestured toward the Savvy Bar and Grill behind her. "Let's go in there for a minute, and make sure there aren't any more Blood-Hunters hanging around. After that we can make a sweep through the other buildings. See if we can roust anymore."

Skye followed along. Her breath came in gasps. She was winded, no doubt about that, but she and Ben would recover quickly. They were Assassins, after all.

The street was quiet now, though Skye suspected some of the Blood-Hunters still lurked about. "The poor vacationers," she said. "The city is always full of them."

Ben nodded. "I hate that we're all locked in here, on this island, with no escape, but it's a sacrifice that had to be made. If Mortmal the Destroyer leaves the island, that evil will spread across the state and then the continent and, well, you know."

"I know." Skye looked around the room. The Savvy Bar and Grill had once been a fun place to come for burgers, ribs and a taste of the wild west, with bridles and saddles displayed as decorations. Now the place looked different; sad. There were broken glasses on the floor, the mirror behind the saloon style bar was shattered, and there were broken liquor bottles strewn about.

"How many more Blood-Hunters do you think there are?" Skye got a warning through her senses, only seconds before a disembodied voice answered her question.

"About a dozen or so I'd say." The voice came from the entry into the kitchen area. Someone stood silhouetted in the faint light, but Skye didn't need to see him to know who it was.

"Aidan," Skye gasped.

Ben immediately dropped into a partial crouch, his body tense and ready for battle.

"Hello, Skye." Aidan stepped into the room, but kept his distance. "Is this your new partner?"

Skye ignored his question, and asked one of her own. "Why are you here?"

"The same reason you are, I expect. Trying to catch my breath before going back out into the fray."

"Are you the one who opened the box with Lucius?"

He made a face. "No, of course not, I—"

"Don't you, 'of course not', me!" Skye had recovered from her shock at seeing him, and now was just plain angry. "Pick a side, Aidan, and stay on it."

"Well, look at the bright side. Now no one has to destroy the box. The demon is already out, and now the thing to do is to preserve the box and try and put him back into it."

"He's not going to be put back in," Ben snapped. "He's going to be destroyed by magic, never to return again."

Aidan gave Ben a weary smile. "Good luck with that. I hope your Bureau knows what it's doing. They only have as long as that shield holds, and then zip, zap, the end. Of everyone."

"Where's your Coven leader? Is he roaming around somewhere, rallying his troops?" Skye asked.

"Who knows?" Aidan shrugged and headed for the bar. "And technically I'm not actually a part of that Coven. They *are* family, but I'm a loner. I go my own way. Anyone want some scotch? I think I'll have a little shot. Care to join me?" He reached for one of the few bottles still intact, and poured some amber liquid into a glass.

"Come on." Ben had relaxed ever so slightly, and gestured to Skye to leave. "We have better things to do than stand here chatting with a Blood-Hunter who's too cowardly to try and take us on."

Aidan downed his shot of whiskey and looked at Ben, all semblance of joviality gone from his expression. "It's not cowardice. There's more going on here than even you can imagine." He pointed a finger at Ben. "And don't you go calling out an Irishman. We don't stand down from a direct challenge. Not ever."

Ben smiled at Aidan, but it wasn't a friendly smile. "Then let's have at it." He made a beckoning motion with his fingers. "Bring it on, Irishman."

Aidan came out from behind the bar, his eyes black as night, body ready to explode into violence.

Skye jumped between the two of them. "No, no, no, please don't do this!" She looked from one to the other. Maybe she'd have to stake Aidan eventually, but she found that she wasn't up for it right now, and she didn't want to watch Ben stake him either. She was angry with herself for her persistent weakness where Aidan was concerned, but there was no time to analyze her confused thoughts. She just wanted to avoid the inevitable; put it off as long as possible.

"We have other, more important things to do right now, Ben. We have to stop the other Blood-Hunters from killing and doing more damage. And Aidan, maybe he can be of some help to us. He didn't attack us outright, remember. He's not like the others."

Aidan barked out a harsh laugh. "I'm not? Now where did you get that idea?"

Skye whipped around and pointed a finger at him. "You, shut up. You're not helping matters."

"Remember the first rule," Ben ground out.

"I know," Skye answered. "Never trust a Blood-Hunter. But for right now, at least, he's not our most important enemy since he's just hanging out in a bar having a drink. Our priority is to get those other Blood-Hunters, right? The ones that are killing all the people out there."

"Right. Fine. Let's go." Ben started for the door, but kept his eyes on Aidan.

Skye followed. She also had her eyes on Aidan, and prayed he wouldn't make a move. She just wanted them all to go their separate ways in one piece.

"It goes against all my instincts to leave that blood sucker standing," Ben muttered after they were out the door and back on the street.

"I know."

He looked at her. "I don't know why I'm listening to you. You're supposed to be taking orders from me."

"It's because we have a demon to stop and that's more important than one Blood-Hunter sitting alone in a bar."

He made a face. "I suppose."

They went up one side of the street and down the other, looking for Blood-Hunters. They found dead and wounded people and Skye made some 911 calls to an already swamped emergency rescue staff.

It pained Skye to see her small city in such disarray. Stores she'd shopped in with her mother were vandalized. Restaurants, coffee shops and bars were ransacked. It was all one big mess. Lives lost and livelihoods destroyed.

"We've been though a dozen businesses. There aren't any Blood-Hunters around, they must've—"

Skye's eyes widened as the Blood-Hunter leapt from her hiding place, fangs bared, eyes black and soulless. Ben swung to his right just in time. He whirled, but not fast enough to avoid getting grazed by a fang. He gave the Blood-Hunter a smashing punch, which might've broken a human's jaw. The Blood-Hunter went flying backwards. She crashed into a wall, but recovered quickly. As she ran toward Ben with death on her mind, Skye stuck her foot out. The Blood-Hunter took a nosedive, right onto Ben's stake. She disintegrated almost immediately.

"Teamwork," Ben said, and pocketed his stake. "I love good teamwork."

"Should we stick around to see if there are any more?"

"No. Let's get over to the Hotel Del and see what's shakin'."

"I have a feeling, nothing good."

They jogged over to the Hotel Del Coronado. Skye was saddened to think of what was most certainly going on over at the beautiful, historic hotel. Once there, they found an eerie silence had settled over the place. It usually bustled with people checking in, going to and from the dining areas or in and out from the pool, the lawn, the pier, the beach, the spa or the shops.

As they walked through the lobby they saw bodies, but no Blood-Hunters. Emergency vehicles were arriving to help any survivors, so Skye didn't bother calling 911 this time. Ben motioned for her to follow him, so she did. They made their way through the lobby and into the Crown Room dining area, then to the kitchen, which looked like a tornado had hit. Pots and pans and pieces of broken crockery were everywhere. When they went downstairs where the gift shops were located, they took care to keep an eye on every corner and doorway. It was so strange for the hotel to be this quiet. Like a ghost town. Even the other restaurants within the hotel were deserted. They soon returned to the lobby and started up the stairs toward the rooms.

"Some of them must still be here," Skye muttered. "Maybe we should check the spa."

Ben smiled at her. "In case some of them stopped for a manicure?"

Skye couldn't help but give a quiet laugh. She was so tense, she felt like she might explode. It was nice to lighten the mood with a little humor.

Ben started down one hallway toward the rooms.

"This is crazy, Ben. There're a million rooms in this place. We can't check them all."

Ben turned, and was about to say something, when Skye heard a scream. Ben bolted back down the hall to the stairs. Skye clattered down the steps by his side, just as more screams joined the first.

CHAPTER SIXTEEN

ANOTHER SCREAM CUT THROUGH THE AIR. AND then Skye saw something that made her catch her breath. Even in the darkness, she could make out five kids outside on hotel property, between the structure of the main building and the sand of the beach. They were surrounded by Blood-Hunters, and among them were Emma and Cara, Rachael's younger sisters. The Blood-Hunters darted in and out, terrifying the kids, who circled and held their boogie boards out in front of them like shields.

Ben bolted forward, headed for the nearest Blood-Hunter, a female with short blonde hair, wearing tight blue jeans and a black tank top. She looked like a female wrestler, and Skye hoped Ben would get the upper hand quickly. The other Blood-Hunters were all female as well, and they were so intent on the kids, they didn't recognize the danger until it was upon them. First one and then another fell to the Assassins' stakes. Fortunately, by the time Skye and Ben turned around to face the remaining Blood-Hunters, two of the kids had gotten free and were running for their lives. Skye hoped they would make it back to their homes safely. Unfortunately, Emma and Cara were still being held by the Blood-Hunters. Another kid, a boy, was on the ground, inching away from his attackers.

"Give the children to me." Aidan strolled across the expansive lawn toward them, his long leather coat flapping in the breeze.

Again, Skye barely had a prickly warning from her senses before he appeared, yet here he was. She could hardly believe it. Would she have to kill him after all? She was absolutely not going to let him take Rachael's sisters!

"You're no longer a member of Roark's Coven," one of the two sneered. "You have no authority over us. Never had and never will."

Aidan's eyes shifted to black. "I most certainly am of Roark's Coven. I was born to it, my blood is of it, and I have just as much authority as I choose to exert." His lip curled so his fangs were revealed. "Give me the children. Now!"

"This guy can't seem to decide if he is in or out of his family's Coven," Ben muttered.

The boy on the ground scrambled toward Ben, who caught him as the kid stumbled forward. Ben redirected him toward Skye. She was thankful the boy had escaped, but the two who mattered most to Skye were still in the hands of the Blood-Hunters.

The Blood-Hunters' attention was diverted for a moment, but then they stood back-to-back, one facing Ben and Skye, the other facing Aidan. Each with one of Rachael's sisters held hostage. Aidan charged forward in a blur. The Blood-Hunter holding Cara threw her aside and met Aidan head on.

Ben leapt toward the remaining Blood-Hunter, and Emma just barely had time to duck and run. Skye darted forward to pull Cara up from the grass, and the two of them ran back to where the boy stood waiting. Emma tore across the lawn to Skye and greeted her sister in a bear hug.

Skye was torn. Should she take Emma, Cara and the boy, right now, to the safety of the truck, or should she stay and help Ben? The decision was made for her in an instant, when only Ben and Aidan were left standing. Ben started toward Aidan, stake at the ready, but Aidan backed off, hands up in the universal gesture for surrender.

"You have the children back. That was the plan, yeah? Now take your prize and go."

Ben stopped advancing and glared at him. "I thought you said I should stop staking your brethren or you'd kill me. Now's your chance, Irish. Now's your chance."

"Someday I will kill you, for one reason or another. You can count on it. As for the other part of what I said, those two were not worth the ground they walked on. Believe me, they had it coming. Now what are you waiting for? Go!"

Ben didn't move. "What's going on, Irish? Got something better to do?"

Aidan's eyes returned to their natural color, and he seemed to have gotten control of his anger. "Yeah, as a matter of fact, I do. Now go on, before I change my mind."

"Ben, come on. Please. I want to get these kids to safety," Skye called out, and after another several seconds of Aidan and Ben staring each other down, Ben finally relented. He backed away, until they were indoors once again, then he turned to the kids.

"You three, are you alright? Any injuries?"

Cara sobbed, and Emma was only slightly less weepy. "We're okay. I think. Mostly," Emma replied.

Skye looked at the boy. "What's your name?"

"Ken. Ken Butler." His eyes were round, and he was white as a sheet.

Skye could tell it wasn't his normal skin tone. The poor kid was in shock. "Come on, Ken. We're going to take you home."

Ben kept watch while Skye guided the kids back to the truck. She figured they'd done all they could do at the moment, and wondered how Preston and the Bureau were doing. Were they making any headway with containment or destruction of the demon spirit?

After dropping the boy, Ken, off at his house and making sure he and his parents were okay, Skye directed Ben to Emma and Cara's home. She was anxious to see Rachael's parents, make sure everyone was safe, and then get to her own house. Cara and Emma were quiet during the drive. They'd stopped crying and now sat in numbed silence.

"Hey, you guys," Skye began. "This is my friend, Ben. You know about me, what I am, what I do, right?" Both girls nodded. "Well, Ben is like me, and we're trying to track down all those Blood-Hunters and kill them."

Skye paused. She didn't know if she should ask this, but she felt she had to. "What Elfae abilities do you have? Were you able to defend yourselves at all?"

"No," Cara answered; her tone sullen.

"We don't have something useful, like Rachael does. We can just manipulate water," Emma explained.

Skye could hardly believe what she'd just heard. "You were standing right near the ocean, and not very far from a swimming pool. How could being able to manipulate water not be useful? You might've been able to wash those Blood-Hunters out to sea, or submerge them under water long enough to escape."

Both girls looked at her with wide, tear-filled eyes.

Ben gave her a sharp look. "They were probably too scared to think of it, Skye. Let it go."

Skye felt a flash of guilt. He was right. She hadn't wanted to make the girls feel guilty, only to show them where they could've helped themselves.

"You're right, Skye. Why didn't we think of that?" Cara looked at her twin with a stunned expression.

"But we might've drowned ourselves and Ken and the other kids too," Emma replied.

"Well, we could've at least tried," Cara wailed. "Oh, why didn't I think of that?"

"It's okay, girls. Don't worry about it now. It's over and the two of you are safe." Ben glanced back at them in the rearview mirror, then focused his eyes on the street once more.

"Here," Skye pointed. "Pull into the driveway on your left. The one with the red flower on the mailbox."

Ben did as he was instructed. When they all were out of the truck, Mr. Perry came out to meet them and guide them into the house. Mrs. Perry waited inside, and immediately enveloped Cara and Emma in her arms.

"We were so worried!" she cried. "What's going on? Is it a storm?"

"No," Skye replied. "But it's complicated. This is Ben, he's an Assassin, too." She introduced Ben to the Perrys and he quickly explained the situation.

"Does the Bureau need any more help?" Mr. Perry asked. "I might be able to add some strength to their containment shield."

"I'll contact them to get a progress report and let them know of your offer. Excuse me." Ben stepped into the kitchen.

"Where is Rachael?" Mrs. Perry asked. "Is she all right?"

Skye nodded. "She went to visit her friend, Starr, over in San Diego. She's fine."

Ben came back into the room. "They're doing well with the shield and no help is needed at this time, but they thank you for your offer, Mr. Perry." He turned to Skye. "We'd better be going."

"Okay." Skye followed him toward the door, then turned to the others. "Remember to keep your house locked up and don't let anyone in unless you know them personally. There are still a few Blood-Hunters prowling around." She lifted a hand in good-bye, then closed the door behind her.

They climbed into the truck and Ben glanced over at her as he started the engine. "They're still working on some magic to destroy the demon." He backed out of the driveway. "Preston figures if they can make things happen before a sacrifice is made to the demon, they'll have a better chance. It won't come into its full power until it has consumed the sacrifice."

"What sacrifice?" This was the first Skye had heard about a sacrifice having to be made to the demon. "What's going to be sacrificed? A person?"

"I have no idea, but probably."

"So, where are we going?"

"Back to the house where it all started. Preston and I discussed it. They've finally gotten some intel on the number of Blood-Hunters that may be involved with this. There were more here initially than they'd thought, but that, combined with my estimate of how many we've killed so far, has led us to believe there should be less than a dozen Blood-Hunters left on the island. Most likely they're congregating back at the house. I don't know whether that figure includes your pal the Irishman, or not."

"My pal?" Skye shot him a dirty look. "He is *not* my pal."

"Whatever. Anyway, when we get to the house, we're supposed to zero in on the sacrifice and not let it take place. And this time, if that Irish Blood-Hunter gets in my way, I will stake him." Ben's hands tightened on the steering wheel. "I'm through playing around."

"Well, he did help us get the girls back," Skye muttered.

Ben gave her a sharp look. "No, he didn't. He wanted them for himself, and when it didn't work out he simply turned the tables and made it look like that's what he'd planned all along. Don't trust him, Skye. Don't ever trust him."

Skye stared out the window rather than continue the conversation. She didn't know what to think when it came to Aidan. Common sense told her Ben was right, but she couldn't shake the feeling there was more to Aidan than he let on. She'd seen him do things that could be considered selfless or even noble, but she also knew he was capable of lying, of manipulation and of betrayal.

Her cell phone sang and she reached for it. The call was from Aidan, and for some inexplicable reason, she didn't want Ben to know.

"Hello." Her voice was curt.

"I need your help."

Skye was stunned. That was the last thing she'd expected him to say. "I'm kind of busy right now."

"So am I. Tara is on the island and they've got her. I need your help."

"With what?"

"Getting her back, of course!"

"I'm sure that's something you can handle without me."

"No, really, I can't. She was over here having lunch with a friend. I came to meet her but then all hell broke loose. I didn't know they'd come to an agreement with Lucius. I didn't know they—"

"Who is, 'they'?"

"The Blood-Hunters from Roark's Coven. I didn't know they were going to open the box here, today."

"So, you weren't kept in the loop?" Skye's voice was sharp with sarcasm.

"No, Skye, I wasn't. And now they want to use her as a sacrifice to that damn demon they worship. They're doing it to punish me."

Skye was horrified to think of Aidan's girlfriend, or whatever she was, being sacrificed to a demon, but she wanted to play it cool. Especially since this didn't look good for Aidan. It certainly seemed to be a pretty huge coincidence that he just happened to be here on this particular day. "And why would they do that?"

"They're angry. They don't trust me because they think it unnatural to be a loner. I don't have time to get into this now. Are you going to help me or not?"

A part of Skye wanted to say no, disconnect and forget about it, but she couldn't do it. She glanced over at Ben who had a puzzled look on his face.

"We're on our way to the house where the demon was released. They're probably all—"

"No, no, listen to me. No one is there. They're all on the beach, somewhere off Ocean Boulevard. There should be six Blood-Hunters, plus Roark, Tara and the demon. I can't do this on my own. It would be suicide and Tara will still die anyway."

Skye was silent as Ben pulled up to the house. All was quiet. She couldn't see any Blood-Hunters and the demon she'd seen before in the billowing black cloud above the house, appeared to be gone.

Skye looked over at Ben. "I don't think they're here."

"I'm going to go have a look around. Are you coming, or would you rather just sit in the truck and talk to whoever that is?"

"I'll call you back," she said into the phone, then shoved it into her pocket. She was suspicious of Aidan's motives. How could he give her such specific direction if he wasn't in on the scheme? On the other hand, he seemed to genuinely care about what happened to Tara. Everything pertaining to Aidan was confusing and the situation was becoming more and more deadly.

Skye followed Ben and they circled the perimeter as best they could, what with walls and shrubs, trees and other houses creating obstructions to their line of sight. Ben approached the front door, which stood open, and gestured for Skye to follow him in. They entered with caution, covered the downstairs and then proceeded up the stairs to the second floor. In one of the bedrooms, they found the box, all compartments open, looking like nothing more than an ornate jewelry box. The rest of the rooms were empty.

Ben went back and closed the box, then carried it down the stairs and out of the house, with Skye trailing along behind him.

"I thought we didn't need the box anymore. I thought the Bureau was going to destroy Mortmal or whatever his name is, and they wouldn't need the box."

"That's the plan, but you never know. In any case, the Bureau wants the box to be in their possession so I'm bringing it."

Once they were back at the truck, and the box safely stashed, Skye decided to tell Ben about Aidan's call. "I think I know where they are."

Ben frowned at her. "Where?"

Skye hesitated. "Well, that phone call I got. It was a tip. They're all at the beach, somewhere off Ocean Boulevard."

"Who called you?"

"And they have a hostage. A human. She's going to be sacrificed to the demon."

Ben sighed and shook his head. "It's that Irishman. Aidan. The Blood-Hunter. He called you and told you where to go."

"Well, yes but—"

"I've told you over and over again not to trust Blood-Hunters. Not to trust *him*. It's a trap. That's all it is. A trap."

"Maybe it is, but what if it isn't? This girl will be killed and—"

"If there even *is* a girl."

"Of course, there is. You told me there would be a sacrifice." Skye glared at him, then continued her original train of thought. "And if that girl dies, the demon will be stronger and the Bureau might not be able to destroy it after all. We have to try and save her. We have to go. Even if she's not there, we can't risk staying away."

Ben closed his eyes and raked a hand through his hair. She could tell he wasn't used to operating this way. Wasn't used to having a tag-along as new to the Assassins as she was, and certainly he wasn't used to taking tips from Blood-Hunters.

He opened his eyes. "Okay. We'll go look for them." He got into the truck.

Skye grinned and ran to jump in on the passenger side. "Aidan said there were six Blood-Hunters left, not counting their leader and him. That tallies up with what you and Preston figured out, right? Less than a dozen?"

"Yeah," Ben admitted. "It does, if we can take the word of a Blood-Hunter; which I seriously doubt. So, at best it's going to be the two of us against eight Blood-Hunters."

"Seven, hopefully."

Ben heaved another deep sigh. "Skye…"

"I know, I know, but promise me you'll kill the others before Aidan, just on the off chance he is actually on our side in this. Please."

After a moment, Ben nodded. "Okay, fine. As long as he stays away from me, I'll stay away from him. At least until we're the only ones left standing. But if he lied to us, and there are more Blood-Hunters there than he told us, then all bets are off. I'll stake him the first chance I get."

Skye nodded, then hit the redial to call Aidan back. He answered on the second ring.

"Well?"

"We're on our way."

"We?"

"Yes. Just stay away from Ben and he'll stay away from you."

"Fine."

"I'm sorry your whole bloodline is going to be destroyed."

She glanced at Ben, who rolled his eyes and shook his head. "You're an idiot," he muttered.

"You're not sorry," Aidan replied. "You're an Assassin. It goes against your nature to be sorry about that."

"Well, I just meant—"

"Yeah, well, my human bloodline means more to me than that one." Aidan disconnected, and left Skye wondering at his cryptic remark.

"When this assignment is over, you're going to need some serious instruction as to proper protocol when it comes to the other species we deal with." Ben shot her a look and shook his head but smiled. He rounded a corner and they were on Ocean Boulevard. "Keep your eyes on the beach."

Skye did as she was told. She knew she still had a lot to learn. Especially since her attraction to Aidan had left her confused and wary of him. She didn't trust him, not really, not anymore, but her instincts told her he hadn't lied this time and he wouldn't harm them. He was dangerous, yes, but she was going to trust her gut and believe in him just one more time.

"There!" She pointed to a spot where a group had congregated. "It looks like there's about seven or eight people and one of them is a woman."

"I can sense them too. Good call." Ben kept going for a half a block or so, then pulled over and parked. There was a bonfire, and the darkness seemed to be heavier just above it. In fact, as Skye strained to see, she thought she could make out the same wicked face she'd glimpsed earlier in the inky black cloud over the house.

"Where's your blood sucking friend?" Ben asked, once they were out of the truck.

"I don't know. He didn't say where he'd be, and he isn't my friend. We just happen to have the same goal at the moment, that's all."

Ben looked around. "Well, come on. If he shows he'd better not get in my way."

They approached the group as quietly as they could, hidden from sight for the moment behind a wall that stretched for twenty feet or more along the beachfront. When they ran out of wall, the two of them ducked behind the cover provided by some cars and then some shrubs once they were passed the cars. By now Skye could plainly see the Blood-Hunter's captive. It was Tara all right. Her arms were tied behind her back, and she was flanked by two Blood-Hunters. Every now and then she'd struggle, but she gave up after one of the Blood-Hunters, possibly the leader, strode across the sand and backhanded her. He was a tall Blood-Hunter with shaggy blond hair.

Ben tossed a stone, which landed just a few feet from one of the Blood-Hunters in the circle they'd formed. He turned in their direction.

"What're you doing?" Skye whispered.

"They'll send a scout or two this way to check things out. Be ready."

Skye heard the leader order two of the Blood-Hunters to go check things out. He then turned back to his prisoner, as did the others. They seemed to be finalizing whatever preparations they had for the sacrifice. Their voices were low, and one of the Blood-Hunters gestured toward Tara. Heads nodded and the blackness above rippled. Skye was anxious to get Tara away from there.

Two Blood-Hunters broke away from the group and headed toward the dense brush where Ben and Skye hid.

"Here we go," Ben whispered.

After a brief, and thankfully quiet, scuffle, the Blood-Hunters dissolved into nothing and Skye and Ben were once again watching the events on the beach.

"We're going to have to go out there some time. If we wait too long—"

"I know. I'm aware of that," Ben replied.

The leader looked around, probably wondering where the two Blood-Hunters were. It was then Skye saw Aidan emerge from the opposite side of the bonfire, near the water. Where had he been? She hadn't noticed him before. Had he been in the water? Aidan darted forward, and went after the two Blood-Hunters who held Tara captive. One of them was down before he had a chance to defend himself.

Ben bolted from the trees as though shot from a cannon. Skye ran forward in his wake. She attacked one of the Blood-Hunters a mere second after Ben engaged one of the others in his path, but this time the fight wasn't over so quickly. By the time Skye plunged her stake into the Blood-Hunter's heart, she turned to find that, while both Ben and Aidan had succeeded in killing their targets, Tara was still a captive. She struggled in the grasp of the leader, Roark. Her eyes were wild, her expression one of desperation. She was clearly terrified. The demon presence hovered over them, its black hands reaching for Tara from out of the confines of the jet black cloud.

"Roark, don't you do it. Don't do it!" Aidan shouted.

Roark turned his gaze from Tara to Aidan. His eyes weren't the solid black of a Blood-Hunter, they were red; solid, glowing, red. A voice came from the dense blackness above.

"He is no longer the one you remember. He is now my servant, and she will be my salvation."

While Aidan pled for Tara's life, Ben inched forward, then around behind Roark.

"And how will she be your salvation?" Skye asked, eager to keep the demon distracted.

"I will drink her blood," the demon voice replied. As if that was enough information to explain everything!

Aidan stepped closer. "Roark, I know you're in there somewhere. You can fight this. This isn't your way. Remember? Never kill the blood source. Remember? Never—Oh, God no!"

Roark lifted Tara in his arms, toward the grasping hands of the demon in the cloud, and Ben, Aidan and Skye all rushed forward in a desperate attempt to save her life.

CHAPTER SEVENTEEN

AIDAN GOT TO THEM FIRST. HE DOVE AT ROARK, knocking him off balance and Ben's stake penetrated Roark's back, but it missed his heart. Roark staggered, but didn't disintegrate into vapor as Skye had hoped. Tara was temporarily lowered beyond the demon's reach, and a screech came from the black cloud as it swirled and writhed above. Roark ignored the stake in his back and tried to lift Tara toward the black smoke hands that reached out toward her once again. Aidan took hold of Tara's arms, while Roark held her around the waist. The two Blood-Hunters struggled for possession of the terrified girl, who held onto Aidan for dear life.

Skye leapt forward, her stake at the ready, but she couldn't get a clear strike as the two Blood-Hunters spun first to the right and then to the left with their living prize. Their movements were erratic and there was no way she could tell where Roark would be in the next second. As Aidan and Roark grappled with Tara caught in the middle. Ben jumped into the fray, and grabbed one of Roark's arms. Skye took her cue from him and grabbed the other, as the grasping hands in the cloud dipped closer.

"Ben, look out!" Skye screamed. But it was too late. One of the demon hands clamped onto Ben's shoulder. He yelped in pain and fought against it, but Skye saw the moment when he simply had to let go of Roark, whether he wanted to or not. He was lifted upwards, and she was terrified the demon would take him. She let go of Roark, and threw her arms around Ben. With a scream of agony, Ben was torn from the demon's grasp, and he and Skye fell back to the ground.

She barely had time to get to her feet before she heard a shout. Skye whirled to see someone standing a short way up the beach, and Skye realized who it was. Lucius! She'd almost forgotten about him, so focused had she been on the Blood-Hunters. Depraved laughter came from within the blackness above, and the dense darkness moved off in the direction of the Spell-Master. Lucius laughed, but it was the glee of someone clearly gone around the bend into insanity.

Ben got to his feet, with a grimace of pain. He fisted his stake and once again went after Roark. Before he got there, however, Skye heard Aidan's yell of victory. He had gotten Tara away from the crazed Blood-Hunter. Ben's stake this time found its mark, and all three of them watched as Roark disintegrated then vaporized. Tara didn't see a thing. Her face was turned into Aidan's shoulder, and she clung to him, sobbing.

Skye heard an agonized scream, and looked across the sand to Lucius. His glee had turned to terror as he was pulled up into the cloud.

"I will have my sacrifice!" bellowed the voice in the inky darkness.

"No! No! I am the one who freed you! I am the one who—" and then Lucius was gone, up into the blackness.

Skye and the others stood watching as his body fell back to earth moments later, a broken, bloodless carcass, and the blackness began to take the shape of a man.

"This is not good," Aidan said, backing away, with Tara stumbling beside him.

"The Bureau has to do something right now!" Skye gasped as she too edged backwards. "We can't fight a demon. Ben, call Preston! Tell him it has to be now, we're out of time!" But the black shape continued moving toward them, looking more man-like with each step. They turned and fled.

"Back to the truck," Ben directed them, though he was the closest to the demon, while Aidan and Tara were closest to the street.

Aidan looked around. "Which one? Where is it?" he yelled back.

"There! Past that stretch of wall." Skye pointed, as she ran. Aidan picked Tara up in his arms and headed in that direction. Skye ran after them, but stopped when she realized Ben still lagged behind. She turned in time to see him fall to his knees. Blood still poured from the wound on his shoulder. He wasn't healing nearly fast enough. Something was wrong. "Ben!"

"Skye, come on!" Aidan shouted from the road. "I can't get in the truck without the keys!"

"Ben has the keys!" she yelled over her shoulder at the same time she started back to help Ben.

"No!" Ben shook his head. "Go, Skye, go!" He gestured with his good arm. "Go to the truck. Forget about me. Go!"

He tossed her the keys, which she caught, then she stood like a statue, torn between wanting to help her fellow Assassin and her own debilitating fear.

"Go!" Ben hollered at her, just as the demon caught up to him.

Skye backed away slowly, as before her horrified eyes the dark man-shape folded into Ben's body. He jerked and let out a blood-curdling wail.

She turned and ran, tears blurring her vision, the rest of the way to the truck.

"It's about time," Aidan proclaimed. "Where's—?"

"He's not coming," Skye barked back before Aidan had a chance to finish. She choked back her tears. She'd cry more later on if they lived. She unlocked the truck, and Aidan leapt into the back seat, while Tara got into the front. Skye jammed the key into the ignition, threw the truck into gear, and floored it. The truck heaved forward, then barreled down the street. Skye had never driven a one-ton truck before, but she got a crash course in handling the brute. Luckily, she caught on quickly.

Aidan shifted in his seat and looked back over his shoulder. "What happened to him?"

"The demon got him," Skye answered, her words clipped. "Where should we go? I can't just drive around until we run out of gas."

"I don't know." Aidan turned back around. "Why don't you call your Handler? He must know how close the Bureau is to containing this thing."

"I'm a little busy right now," Skye snapped.

"Do you have the number on speed dial?" Tara asked. "Or I can dial for you. I can hold the phone to your ear or talk to him for you."

Skye stole a glance at Tara. Her face was tear stained and blotchy, but she had a look of resolve in her eyes.

"I can help you. Let me do something. Please."

Skye nodded, then focused her eyes back onto the road. "The phone is in the cargo pocket on my right leg." She jostled around to try and make it easier for Tara to get her hand into the pocket. "Push five. His name is Preston. John Preston," Skye said, once Tara had the phone in her hands. "Tell him what's going on. Tell him we need that magic mojo to work sooner rather than later."

Tara pressed the button on the phone and put it to her ear. After a few seconds she spoke into the phone. "Hello, is this John Preston?" Tara's voice was hesitant at first, but grew steadier she continued talking. "My name is Tara Donovan. I'm on Coronado Island with—Yes, with Skye. No, not Ben." She glanced at Skye. "He, um, he's dead, I think. I don't know. Yes, yes. We need your help."

While Tara continued talking with Preston, Skye caught a glimpse of something in the rear-view mirror. "Aidan, I think we're being followed. Can you get a look?"

He twisted around in his seat. "Feck! It's the demon. I can almost make out—"

"What?" Skye shouted. "What do you see?"

"It's coming for us. It's flying. It looks like—"

"Like what?" Skye tried to catch a look at it herself, but she really had to keep her eyes on the road.

"It's your Assassin friend. I think the demon took over his body."

"We're on the run, Preston," Skye shouted loud enough for him to hear. "The demon is right behind us. Whatever you're going to do, you better do it fast!"

"What's that?" Tara asked into the phone. She then turned to Skye. "He says get to the U.S. Naval Base. Take Orange Avenue to Silver Strand Boulevard. Follow it south all the way to Imperial Beach." She listened to the voice on the other end of the phone, but looked over at Skye. "He says the barrier has a weak spot there. We should be able to get through."

Skye frowned. "But then the demon could get out too," she muttered. But there was no time to debate the issue. Surely Preston had thought of that. This was probably their best and only chance for survival and she wasn't going to screw it up. She swung the truck around the next corner and continued on in that direction. "I assume you've arranged it so the Navy guys let us go through there?" she shouted so Preston could hear.

Tara nodded. "He says, yes."

"Okay." Skye gunned it, and nearly flew down the road. Luckily there was no traffic. That either meant most people were dead or in hiding. She hoped it was the latter.

"He also says the magic is almost ready to go," Tara continued. "He says timing is everything. We have a small window of opportunity to escape if we can keep far enough in front of the demon."

It was as Skye had figured and she'd have to increase their lead. Every second counted here.

Aidan put the window down. "In coming!" he shouted, then levered himself up until he was half way out the window.

"What are you doing?" Skye screamed. But he was already outside, clinging to the vehicle and working his way around to the bed of the truck.

"It's the demon!" Tara cried out. "It's coming."

So much for increasing their lead.

It was all Skye could do to stay on course and not wreck the truck, while keeping one eye on Aidan and the now-demonized Ben, who was almost upon them. Skye couldn't yet get a good look at him, but he certainly didn't look right; not at all like the handsome Ben Takei she'd come to like and respect; especially with those leathery wings.

The truck lurched and swayed as Skye sped down the road. The way was clear, with no roadblocks of any kind, and she was thankful no one tried to stop them. The water on either side was very close. The sky was black, the water was black, and it was truly creepy to be driving at one hundred miles an hour on an unfamiliar road.

Tara screamed, and Skye glanced up at the rearview mirror. "What's happening?"

"Aidan! He almost fell out."

Skye looked in the side mirror as the demon approached the driver's side of the truck. She gasped as fear surged anew. The demon had Ben's face but his eyes glowed an eerie yellow. The black, leathery wings reached out from either side of his back, which now bulged with unnatural musculature, and the look on his face was of pure evil.

The demon darted back toward the bed of the truck once again. The truck hit a bump in the road, and left the ground for a moment. Tara cried out, and Skye tried in vain to see what had happened. "What's going on? Is Aidan okay?"

"Yes, but I don't know for how long. Are we almost there?" Tara asked.

"Almost." That's when Skye's phone rang.

Tara fumbled for it and nearly dropped it. "Hello? Yes. Okay." She turned to Skye. "We're going to hit the barrier right before the spot where Rainbow Drive meets Highway Seventy-Five. He says it's going to be a rough ride going through."

"How rough? What does he mean?" Skye asked.

Tara relayed the question, listened, then looked at Skye. "He says it'll be like crashing through a wall. Then there'll be a dead zone. No air, extreme pressure and heat. We'll probably feel like we're drowning in boiling water or burning up in a sauna."

Fear struck at Skye once again. She hadn't thought she could be any more afraid than she already was, but she was wrong. "Great. Tell Aidan to get inside, right now! If he stays out there, he's a dead man."

Tara threw down the phone and leaned out the window. She called to Aidan to get in, but either he didn't hear or he didn't care, because he didn't respond. He just continued the ongoing fight with the demon. Skye could see in the rearview mirror that Aidan and the demon in Ben's body were locked in combat. Aidan's fangs were bared and both he and the demon gripped each other like Olympic wrestlers. Every now and then one of them would let go and land a punch. Skye hoped Aidan could throw the demon out of the truck and down hard enough to give him pause. It was her only chase to gain a lead once again.

She reached over and tugged on Tara's shirt. "Come back in! Sit down and buckle up, we're almost there."

"No!" Tara's eyes widened and her voice was sharp. "He can't stay out there."

She tried to lean out the window again, but Skye pulled her back. "You can't be hanging out the window when we go through. You'll die!"

But Tara wrenched away and stuck her head and shoulders out the window once more. "Aidan, you have to be inside the truck when we hit the barrier! You have to come back in now!" she screamed. "Now! Do you hear me? You'll die if you stay out here!"

Skye leaned across the seat and used all her strength to yank Tara back inside the cab of the truck. "Sit down and—"

"I can't let Aidan die. He saved me! He—"

"We're almost there!" Skye was frantic at the idea she'd lose Aidan as well as Ben, but there was nothing she could do now except drive. "Buckle your seat belt!"

Aidan's boots shot through the open window and his body followed. He landed on the seat, then scrambled up to peer out the back window.

"Where's the demon?" Tara asked.

Skye gasped as it suddenly dropped from above onto the windshield, its horrid face and body blocking her vision of the road. There was a blast, right by her ear. The windshield exploded, and the demon tumbled from the hood of the truck. Skye turned to see Aidan holding one of Ben's shotguns. Beyond them, the demon lay in the middle of the road.

"Is it dead?" Tara's voice wavered. She was wide-eyed and shaking.

"Let's hope so," Aidan muttered.

Seconds later, the entire truck slammed against an invisible wall, throwing Aidan hard against Tara's seat, then rocketing him backwards against the rear wall of the cab. Skye and Tara both flew forward against their seat belts as airbags burst into the cab to offer protection. The truck continued to move forward, and all at once Skye could hardly suck in a breath. The heat in the cab was almost unbearable. Her vision was blurred, and movement was difficult. Just when she thought she might pass out, the pressure and heat were gone. The truck came to a halt.

Skye looked to her right. Tara was slumped in her seat, still gasping for air. "Are you okay?" Skye managed.

"I think so."

All four doors of the truck were yanked open, and she and Tara were helped out by paramedics. Preston was there, as were several other people, whom Skye could only assume were from the Bureau.

"Where's Aidan?"

At the sound of Tara's voice, Skye turned to see her struggling in the arms of one of the paramedics.

"Let go of me! I have to see him. Where is he? Is he all right?"

Skye felt a hand on her shoulder. It was Preston.

"Skye? Are you okay?" he asked.

She sucked in a shaky breath and nodded. "Yeah. I think so. Where's Aidan?"

There was a commotion as Tara broke away from the man holding her, and dashed to the side of the truck. She fell to her knees, sobbing.

Skye quickly looked to Preston for an explanation.

"I'll go find out." Preston left Skye in the capable hands of a paramedic. Skye watched as he peered into the cab while exchanging words with another of the emergency personnel. He nodded, then returned to Skye. "I'm afraid he's in bad shape. His collarbone is broken. Knee shattered, leg broken, skull probably cracked, neck broken, shoulder dislocated. He no doubt has internal injuries as well.

Skye's eyes widened with each proclamation of Aidan's condition. "Will he heal?"

Preston shrugged. "He's lost a lot of blood, and no doubt is bleeding internally as well. He may recover in time, but he'll need blood."

"The paramedics, can they—?"

"Not just a transfusion. He'll need to consume blood as well, but right now he can't consume anything. He's unconscious."

Skye looked over at Tara. She sat, huddled, on the side of the road. Her arms were wrapped around herself. Her head was bowed. Her shoulders shook.

"It may be best to simply stake him right now," Preston said. "By the time he recovers, he may well not be the same individual. He may have to consume so much blood to heal himself that he becomes blood crazed."

"Meaning?"

"Meaning he won't be able to control himself and he'll start killing."

Skye shook her head. "No. No, don't stake him. He rescued Tara, he fought off the demon so I could drive. He risked his life to help that girl, and I won't have him killed right in front of her."

"She won't have to know. We can do it after she's gone."

"No, you don't understand. They know each other. They have some sort of relationship. I don't know what sort, but whatever it is, she will know if he disappears from the face of the planet. She practically crawled out of the truck herself, to bring him back inside." Skye shook her head again. "Don't kill him, Preston. Please. Aren't there any times when Blood-Hunters aren't treated like mortal enemies? Can't you please give him a chance?"

Preston looked around at the truck, the people gathered, at Tara. He seemed deep in thought. "All right. No harm will come to him. You have my word. We'll relocate him to a containment facility, give him the blood he needs to recover, and see what happens. We've done it a time or two before. If he comes out sane, we'll let him go. If not..."

Skye nodded, understanding his meaning. "Thank you, Preston."

Just then Preston's cell squawked and he immediately answered it. "Preston. Yes. Are you sure?" He nodded. "Very good, but verify that. We need to be absolutely certain. What about the populace?" Another nod. "Send in whatever resources are needed to clean up, rebuild, etc. Make sure medical aid is given to all the living, but especially make sure memories are altered on all humans present."

Once he'd disconnected, Skye peppered him with questions. "Did the magic work? Is the demon dead? And what did you mean about the memory-altering thing? How do you do that? Would it be so bad to let humans know what they're up against? What if—?"

"Skye! Stop, please!" Preston scrubbed a hand across his tired face. "Let's leave most of these questions for another time. But, yes, the magic worked. The demon appears to be dead. Some members of the Bureau are going in to make certain of it. The barrier will then come down, help will flow onto the island, and all will be well."

"But—"

"No more questions. I'll see to Aidan's care and make sure the girl gets home, then I'll give you a ride back to your apartment."

Skye looked over at Tara. "She met a friend today to do some shopping or have lunch or something. I never had the chance to ask what happened to the friend. And then Ben..." Skye sighed. She felt tears fill her eyes.

Preston sat beside her. "This is the reality of being an Assassin. Ben knew the risks and so did Natalie."

She looked over at him. "You lost two of your Assassins in less than twenty-four hours. I'm sorry, Preston. I really am. I just met them both and I can't believe they're gone. I didn't really get to know them, but I liked Ben. He was a good fighter and smart too. I think I would've liked working with him on a regular basis." Skye lifted her eyes to meet Preston's. "There's sort of a camaraderie, isn't there, when Assassins work together?"

He nodded. "Yes. Some Assassins like to work in pairs. Being an Assassin can be a lonely path. Some prefer it of course, but others prefer the companionship."

Skye considered that. "I think I'd rather work with a partner than by myself. Can I do that?"

"I might be able to arrange it. I'll see what I can do." He stood. "Let me take care of a few things and I'll drive you home." He walked away, and Skye stared at the ground. A barrage of images battered at her mind: Ben fighting the Blood-Hunters; Ben rolling his eyes at her and reprimanding her for trusting Aidan; Aidan asking for her help; battling with the demon in the back of the truck; the demon wearing Ben's face; Lucius being lifted up into the black, then dropped to the earth, a body with no life in it. Skye knew she'd have trouble sleeping tonight. Probably for many nights.

She reached for her phone and realized it was most likely still in the truck. Skye heaved her tired body up and slowly walked to the vehicle. Aidan had been moved from the back seat to a stretcher. Was he conscious? Could she talk to him? Would he be able to hear her? She veered away from the truck, toward Aidan, but before she could get there, he was whisked away by medical personnel. With a sigh, Skye changed course again and headed back toward the truck. She fished around in the front seat until she found her phone wedged between the console and the passenger seat. It, at least, was none the worse for wear. Skye jammed it into her pocket and waited for Preston to take her home.

CHAPTER EIGHTEEN

"WHAT HAPPENED? WHERE HAVE YOU BEEN?" Rachael leapt to her feet as soon as Skye came through the door. It was dark out, but this time it was natural darkness. Not a sky blackened by an emerging demon.

Skye grabbed a bottle of water from the refrigerator and dropped down onto one of the dining room chairs. "Remember Natalie from the other night? She was killed by Blood-Hunters."

"Oh, no!" Rachael sat down across from Skye.

"And, it gets worse. Much worse. The demon was released from the box. The girl who was with Aidan the other night, Tara, was kidnapped to be offered as a sacrifice. Ben and I went to stop it, and Aidan was there. He helped us and we rescued her but then…"

"But then what?" Rachael leaned forward; her eyes wide.

"Ben got killed." Skye set the water bottle down and rubbed her eyes. She could still hear his voice in her head, telling her to go on without him. And she could see him in her mind's eye, tossing her the keys. And then his transformation into—

"Skye? Are you okay?"

She nodded her head and blinked back tears. "After that, Aidan, Tara and I barely escaped. The demon was killed. The Bureau took care of it with some sort of magic."

"What about our families? Are they okay?"

"Yeah. They're okay now, but your sisters were surrounded by Blood-Hunters. If it hadn't been for Aidan—"

"Were they hurt?" Rachael's leapt up an octave.

"No, they're fine. Just scared. Preston told me that all the people on the island, or maybe it's just the humans, will somehow have their memories wiped of the events. All they'll remember is a giant storm trashed the island." She shrugged. "Or something like that." Skye got to her feet. "I'm heading for a shower."

"Are you hungry?"

"Yeah. Let's go get some Mexican. You drive. I'll be back. Just give me a few minutes." Skye turned and went to her room. Though her stomach growled from hunger, she seriously didn't know if she could eat. She had a vacant feeling in the pit of her gut that had more to do with watching a friend get killed, than it did with lack of food.

Once in her bedroom, Skye started the shower and stripped off her clothes. She stared at her reflection in the mirror. "Who are you?" she whispered. "What are you turning into?" Skye felt as though she'd lost control of her life and was now on a rollercoaster ride though a horror movie which would only end with her death. The realization that both Natalie and Ben were not much older than she was when they'd died was not lost on her. Yes, she'd made the decision to see this through, and whatever came up next as well, but she was frightened. The gritty reality was that she most certainly would not live long. She remembered Preston saying as much in one of their earlier discussions. Again, she wondered what it must be like for him to lose the young people who were his responsibility within the hierarchy of the Bureau. It must be truly horrible to watch them all die. Were there any who lived beyond just a few years? If so, could she beat the odds and become one of them?

She tore her gaze from the mirror and stepped into the warm shower. As she washed the sweat and grime from her body, the citrus scent of the shower gel refreshed her. It was as if no bad things had ever happened; as if it was yesterday morning and none of this horrible afternoon had ever occurred.

But then, quite abruptly, the events of the day once again caught up with her. A sob caught in her throat, tears blurred her vision and she sank to the floor. She sat with the warm, cleansing water washing away her tears as she cried for Natalie, a girl she hardly knew; for Ben, so brave and courageous; for Aidan, injured, confined, and under a possible death sentence if he didn't maintain his sanity; and for herself. Would she even make it to her twenty-first birthday? She was scared; no, terrified. Should she even continue to live with Rachael, now that her life revolved around such incredible danger? Wasn't she putting Rachael in jeopardy as well as herself?

There was a knock at the bathroom door. "Skye? Are you all right? You've been in there with the shower running for almost an hour."

Skye immediately pulled herself together. She got up and shut off the water. It was cold now and she realized she was shivering. "Yeah, I'm fine. Sorry. I'll be there in five minutes. I promise."

How had so much time passed since she'd entered the shower? Skye hurriedly dried off and dressed, choosing a pale blue skirt that just grazed her knees, paired with a matching short-sleeved knit top. She ran a comb through her wet hair, slipped into her silver sandals and quickly swiped her eyelashes with mascara. She grabbed her purse and dabbed on a bit of lip gloss.

"I'm ready!" she called out, then met Rachael at the door.

Rachael gave her a worried look. "You sure you're okay?"

Skye forced a smile. "No, really, I'm not, but I'm trying to be. Come on. Let's go get something to eat."

———— ✦✦✦✦✦ ————

The next morning, after spending a restless night, Skye called Preston. "How's Aidan?"

"He's healing. He's been given enough transfusions to move the process along quite nicely. But he still has a long way to go."

"I want to see him."

"That's not a good idea, Skye. Why don't you just enjoy some time off while you can."

"I intend to, but I want to see Aidan first." Skye began to get the uneasy feeling that something was wrong. Had Preston only told her what she'd wanted to hear yesterday? Had he mislead her into thinking Aidan would be cared for and released? Was he actually being held there and used for some purpose other than simply allowing him to heal? Or maybe he was already dead!

"Skye, really, I think you should—"

165

"I want to make sure, with my own two eyes that he's all right. That he's being treated well, and not like a prisoner."

"He's not a prisoner, but he is in containment. Until he regains consciousness—"

"He hasn't regained consciousness yet?" Skye was stunned and her suspicions grew. "Are you sure he's being treated well? What's going on at that place, anyway? He is alive, right?"

"Calm down, Skye. Yes, he's still alive. Until he awakens, can consume blood on his own and finishes healing, we can't be certain of his mental state. Until we're certain of that, he will remain confined, but I promise you he is not being harmed."

But Skye was skeptical and angry. "So, he'll stay confined and that'll make it easy for you to kill him, right?" Skye's tone was sharp, but she knew it was no joke. The Bureau could decide Aidan should be staked, and he would be. Just like that.

"If necessary, yes, bluntly put, but yes. However, that is not my intention, I promise you."

"I want to see him."

"Skye—"

"I'm one hundred percent serious, Preston. I want to see him and I'm going to keep calling you non-stop until you tell me where he is and let me see him. Maybe if I talk to him, it will help to bring him around."

Preston sighed. "You sound like Tara."

"Tara? You've talked to her since—"

"Yes. And as I was saying, I really don't think it would be a good idea for—"

"Come on, Preston. Please! I won't drop this. I need to see him. I need to talk to him. I—"

"All right. Fine. He's located at the Marine Corps Air Station at Miramar. I'll let them know you're coming." He gave her directions and told her whom to speak with when she got there. "I hope you realize this information is highly confidential. No one outside the Bureau and certain key Marine personnel knows we have a base of operations there. Do not let anyone know where you're going, why, or with whom you'll be speaking. This is extremely classified, Skye."

"Geez, Preston, if I'm not going to be telling anyone where I'm going, why would I be blabbing about the rest of it?"

He didn't answer her question, but pressed his point. "Don't tell Rachael. No one can know about this."

Skye rolled her eyes. "Okay, okay, I'll tell her I'm running a mysterious errand for you. I'll tell her it's perfectly safe, but I don't know when I'll be back. Is that all right with you?"

"I'm not trying to be difficult here, but you most certainly are. Just give me your word."

This time his voice held an edge, and Skye knew she had pushed his patience to the limit. She knew the man well enough, at this point, to know when to back off.

"I'm sorry, you're right. It's just been a rough few weeks, and yesterday was beyond awful. I just want to see for myself that—"

"I understand. Call me when you return home. Good-bye, Skye." He disconnected.

Rachael emerged from her room, just as Skye stuffed her phone back into her pocket. "You're already dressed. Are you going somewhere?"

"Yeah." Skye hated not telling Rachael the whole truth, but she had no choice. "Preston asked me to do something for him. Top secret and all that. I'm not sure when I'll be back." She reached for her purse.

"You're doing something for Preston wearing lime green capris, gold sandals and a white tank top? Is he aware of this? Has he approved these colors?" Rachael deadpanned.

Skye grinned. "And my hair is down too! Imagine that."

They shared a smile before Skye waved good-bye and left the apartment. She climbed into her convertible and headed off to the Air Station.

Skye followed Preston's directions and made it to the gate. The guard there checked her ID then made a phone call. She waited impatiently. Once the man let her through, she continued on to the address Preston had given her. It was an ordinary looking house. The front door was blue. The fence surrounding the place was painted white. There were geraniums in two pots flanking the steps up to the entrance. Could this be right? She'd been expecting something more...sterile. Less homey. More prison-like. She looked left and right. There were other houses on either side, along the street, though they weren't as large as this one. They all looked harmless enough with their flower gardens and their little picket fences.

Skye got out of her car and tipped her sunglasses onto the top of her head as she walked along the path to the door. She adjusted her purse to lay cross-body instead of simply hanging on her shoulder. While she was at it, she checked to make sure the stake inside was readily available. She bounded up the stairs and rapped on the door.

An elderly lady with very dark skin and graying hair answered her knock.

"Ah, I'm Skye Falco. John Preston sent me."

The lady nodded. "You can come in." She stepped back and opened the screen door. "The Blood-Hunter is popular. Two visitors," she muttered.

Skye wasn't sure she'd heard correctly. "Excuse me?" But then she turned and saw Tara sitting on a red plastic chair, not eight feet from her. Her hair was lank and damp. Her eyes were red-rimmed, and Skye suspected it was from crying. She wore faded blue jeans, a white t-shirt and sneakers. She didn't look at all like the glamorous woman from the restaurant, or even like the damsel in distress of last night. No, she looked worried and exhausted.

Skye felt deflated. This was her moment. Her time with Aidan, and she didn't want to share it. She'd become aware of her attraction to him earlier on, but she hadn't taken it seriously until this moment. She'd figured it was just a little crush because of his Irish brogue and his good looks, but now it seemed she had stronger feelings than she'd realized. But really, she could hardly allow herself to go down this path. He was unpredictable, he was a Blood-Hunter, and he already had a girlfriend; Tara. But how had Tara gotten here so quickly? Preston hadn't said he'd given Tara directions to this place too. In fact, how was it that Tara had Preston's phone number? Or had he called her? She guessed it didn't matter, but what *did* matter was that Preston had allowed Tara to come here, yet had made such a big deal out of this location being ultra top secret.

"Right," Skye muttered. "And if it's so top secret what's *she* doing here?"

Tara looked up. "Hello." She cleared her throat. "Um, Skye, right?"

"Right." Skye walked over and took a seat across from Tara in another of the red chairs."

"I got here about…" She pulled her phone from her pocket and looked at it. "About twenty minutes ago." She put the phone away. "They haven't let me see Aidan yet." She paused. "You're here to see him too?"

"Yes." Skye glanced around. She really didn't know how to make small talk with the other girl; not under these circumstances. What was okay to say and what wasn't? She had no idea.

"Ms. Donovan. Please follow me."

Skye looked up and saw a tall man, dressed in a military uniform. His hair was cut short and his demeanor brusque. He stood ramrod straight and waited. Tara glanced over at Skye, then stood and followed the man, leaving Skye to stare after her with a frown.

Five minutes later, Skye heard a scream. It was Tara. She was sure of it. Skye bolted from her chair and slammed through the doorway where Tara had been taken. Her sandals slipped on the tile floor. Oh, why had she worn them? She followed two men in suits as they entered a room on her right.

Aidan sat on a bed, with Tara draped across his lap. His eyes were closed. His fangs were in her neck. Skye fished in her purse for the stake, but prayed she wouldn't have to use it.

She shoved her way between the two men, who seemed wholly unprepared to deal with the situation. "Aidan! Stop!"

His eyes opened. They were almost solid black, but were ringed in red. Whoa. That wasn't good. Skye remembered Roark's eyes glowing red. Solid red. The sign of insanity in Blood-Hunters.

"Aidan, it's me, Skye. Stop now. Right now! You're hurting Tara. You know Tara. You don't want to hurt her." She held the stake up so he could see it. He actually snarled at her, then closed his eyes again. Skye sidled over and eased behind him, then grabbed him by the hair. She tipped his head back, until his fangs cleared Tara's throat without tearing flesh. Then she punched him in the face.

Aidan rocked back then leapt from the bed, dumping Tara unceremoniously onto the mattress. He went for Skye and she narrowly missed becoming his next victim before he turned and confronted the men at the opposite side of the room.

One held a Taser. It had hit Aidan square in the chest. He twitched and fell to his knees, then ripped the attachments from his body and charged forward. The men split apart and Aidan ran out. No one was crazy enough to take him on. Except, of course, Skye.

"Take care of her. Get her some blood. Don't let her die!" she called over her shoulder as she dashed out the door after Aidan.

Aidan cringed when the sunlight hit his eyes. Skye remembered a Blood-Hunter's eyes were sensitive to sunlight. Aidan stumbled, his hands to his eyes, shading them. He staggered forward, but it was clear he couldn't see at all well in the glaring bright daylight. Perhaps he was in pain as well. She should've taken advantage of the situation, but she didn't.

Skye skidded to a stop. "Aidan, here." She reached up and took her sunglasses from atop her head. "You can have them." She held them out to him.

He turned and studied her through squinting eyes.

"Go on, take them."

He darted forward and snatched the sunglasses from her hand. After jamming them on his face, he stood a little straighter and studied her. "Skye?"

"Yes."

"Where am I?"

"On the Marine Air Station in Miramar. You were badly hurt after we went through the barrier on the island. Do you remember?"

He frowned. "I need more blood."

"No, no." Skye shook her head. "I think you've had enough for now."

He bared fangs at her. "You have no idea what I need."

He had his hand around her throat before she could think to move. His face was close to hers. "I need fresh blood to heal. I might even start with you."

"You already started with Tara." Skye managed to say, though her voice came out high and gasping.

Aidan threw her to the ground. "What are you talking about?"

Skye rubbed her aching throat. "You nearly killed her."

"What?"

"Or maybe you did. I don't know."

"I...I don't...Where is she?" He looked so confused.

"You can't go attacking people like that. You could kill someone, and if you do, the Bureau will have you staked."

Without another word, Aidan spun on his heel and ran. Skye scrambled to her feet and gave chase, but she was no match for him. Plus, he had a head start and she had worn sandals. Not the best choice for running. When would she ever learn? Skye came to a halt and watched as Aidan yanked a man out of his Jeep, jumped in and sped off into the distance. The poor guy sprawled on the ground, then leapt to his feet, but immediately yelped and lifted his foot. He hopped around and Skye suspected the ankle was either broken or sprained. Several men and women in uniforms ran out of the building where Aidan had been housed. They went to the man and gave him aid while Skye watched the dirt, kicked up by the passing of the Jeep, as it drifted on the breeze.

CHAPTER NINETEEN

SKYE MADE HER WAY BACK TO THE ROOM WHERE Aidan had been held. Several men knelt by Tara, who was now on a stretcher and about to be moved to another room. There was an IV in her arm and bandages on her neck.

"How is she?" Skye asked.

One of the men got up and came toward her. "The medical staff has things under control. She'll probably make it. I'm Travis Smith. I'm with the Bureau."

"I'm Skye Falco. John Preston sent me."

"You're his new Assassin." He cocked his head. "His only Assassin, now, from what I understand."

Skye looked Travis up and down. He was short and skinny. He wore glasses. His hair was ash blonde…and he was a jerk. "Ben was my friend. I fought at his side. He died a hero."

Travis shrugged. "He got captured and was used as a conduit for a demon that is still out there somewhere. I wouldn't call that—!"

"What did you say?" Skye took a step forward and glared at him. "Did you say the demon is still alive?"

"Yeah. I guess Preston didn't tell you." He smirked.

As the men carried Tara out of the room, she reached out a hand and grasped Skye's arm.

"Where is he? Did you find him? Is he all right?" Tara asked. Her voice sounded rough. Her throat was no doubt sore from the puncture wounds. Blood droplets stained her t-shirt.

"I spoke to him, but he got away from me. I guess he's all right. For now. I don't think he knew what he was doing when he...you know."

Tara smiled. "Good. I'm glad he got away." She let go of Skye's arm, and the men carrying her continued on their way.

Skye stared after them. How could Tara still care about Aidan after he'd almost killed her? What was wrong with that girl?

"Well, got to run. Sorry to be the bearer of bad news," Travis said, breaking into Skye's thoughts. "Preston should've told you about the demon himself." He gave her a condescending smile, then left the room. What a jerk!

Skye didn't know what else to do, so she headed outside to her car. Once there, she called Preston. That man had some explaining to do.

"Why didn't you tell me the demon was still alive?" she began, before he even had a chance to say hello. "You told me it was dead! Where is it?"

"I only just found out myself. How did you learn of it?" His voice was cool and controlled. How could he not be panicking?

"Some guy named Travis."

"Smith?"

"Yeah."

"Overbearing, self-important, interfering—"

"Yeah, well...but he was right, apparently. So what's going on, and why did you let Tara come here? She almost got killed!"

"One question at a time, Skye. Now, what did you mean about Tara almost being killed?"

"No, you answer my questions first."

"Don't be a child, Skye, we don't have time for this! Tell me about Tara!"

Skye sighed in frustration, but gave in. "She was already waiting to see Aidan when I got here. They let her go back to see him and a couple minutes later she screamed. I ran in, separated his fangs from her neck, chased him outside, talked to him for a second, and then he took off in some guy's Jeep."

"So, he's loose."

"Yes. But I warned him not to kill anyone. I told him he'd hurt Tara, and he acted really confused. I don't think he even remembered doing it. So what about the demon? What happened? I thought it was dead."

"I thought so too. Apparently, it jumped from Ben's body to someone else's. Someone from the Bureau."

"What? Who?"

"A fellow by the name of Alan Sherwood. He went in, after the magic settled, to check on the status of the body. We were certain the magic worked. It was just meant to be a precaution."

"So where is this Alan Sherwood now?"

"Well, technically he's dead. His body is simply a vehicle for the demon now." Preston sighed. "Unfortunately, we have no idea where he...*it*, is."

"So how do you know the demon is still alive and in his body? Maybe this is all some big mistake."

"There were several witnesses. Only one of them survived."

Skye was aghast. "So, everything we did was for nothing? Ben died for nothing?"

"I know it seems that way but—"

"How are you going to find it? How can we kill it? How many more people is it going to kill before it stops?"

"You're always so full of questions." Preston uttered a weary sigh. "Look, don't concern yourself with the demon right now. We've got dozens of people working on that. You find Aidan, and keep an eye on him. We never should've brought him here in the first place. This whole thing was against my better judgment."

"I'm sorry things turned out this way, but I'll find him. Do you have any suggestions on where to start looking? He could be anywhere by now."

"I don't know, Skye. That's your job. Your only job, at the moment. Just do it. And if he's red-eyed when you find him, then stake him. I mean it. I have to go."

Skye started her car and drove slowly, while keeping an eye out for the Jeep Aidan had stolen. She replayed Preston's words over and over in her head. He'd given her a direct order to kill Aidan. The only thing that would save him was if he was sane by the time she found him. Hopefully he wouldn't kill anyone in the meantime.

She returned to the entrance of the facility, only to discover that the arm of the gate was broken. The gate guard was there, along with several other men, one who was taking notes while others worked to repair the gate.

"What happened?" Skye asked the gate guard, as she eased her car to a stop.

"Some fool in a Jeep came barreling through here about an hour ago."

Skye nodded. "Um…do you know which way he went?"

The guard pointed to the left. "That way."

"Thanks." Skye turned her car left also.

It took almost a dozen tries; stopping here, there, and everywhere she could think of, before Skye found the Jeep. It was parked behind MacGregor's Pub. Funny thing…this wasn't the first time she'd stopped there. In fact, MacGregor's had been the first place she'd looked. The Jeep hadn't been there then, but it certainly was now.

She parked and got out. It was evening, and there was a cool breeze. It would've been a fabulous night to be outdoors, if she hadn't been worrying about a demon and looking for a crazed Blood-Hunter.

Skye started toward the entry to the restaurant, but something caught her eye. It looked like someone was on the ground, between two cars. She approached with caution and her worst fears were confirmed when she saw it was a woman. Her throat was a bloody mess. Sightless eyes stared up at the sky. The woman looked to be about twenty-five to thirty years old. She wore jeans, a blue blouse and black pumps. Her purse was on the ground near her body. Skye looked around as she pulled her phone from her pocket. She hit speed dial for Preston.

"I'm at MacGregor's Pub. I've found a body. Her throat looks pretty bloody. Does someone from the Bureau handle this, or should I call the police or what?"

"You did the right thing in calling me. I'll be there in ten minutes. Have you seen Aidan?"

"Not yet, but he might be in the restaurant. The stolen Jeep is here."

"Go find him. You know what you need to do."

Skye put her phone away and after another glance around, entered the restaurant. She so didn't want Aidan to be here. So, didn't want him to be responsible for the dead woman outside, but who else could've done something like that? What were the chances some Shape-Shifter was responsible? Or maybe it was another Blood-Hunter, not Aidan? No, those things seemed unlikely. If it turned out he had killed the woman, and circumstantial evidence would suggest that he did, then she wouldn't mind staking him in spite of her attraction to him.

As soon as she entered the restaurant, she knew a Blood-Hunter was there. She could sense it. Skye looked around, and sure enough, Aidan sat by the alley door with a beer in his hand and a shot of something amber colored, in front of him. He lifted his head and homed in on her immediately. She made her way to his table.

"Skye. Have a seat." He shoved a chair with his foot.

She studied him for a moment, anger building. "I saw the woman outside. Is that what it costs to get your sanity back...the blood of two women? Or are you still crazy? How many more people do you have to assault and kill?"

"What woman? What are you talking about?" He downed the shot of whatever it was in front of him.

"Don't pretend you don't know what I'm talking about."

"I don't."

"Where did you go after you left the Marine base?"

"I went to Tara's place. She wasn't there."

"Right. That's because you nearly killed her right there on the Base." Skye realized her voice had gotten louder, so she made an effort to lower it. "You were under observation. You were unconscious. Tara came to see you and you attacked her."

"I did no such thing." He leaned in. "I would never harm her. Never!"

"Well, you did. And she has two puncture wounds in her neck to show for it. Just like the woman in the parking lot. Only she's dead with her throat torn out!" She glared at him.

"Whoever is in the parking lot is none of my doing."

"Are you sure about that? I saw you attack Tara with my own eyes."

"That can't be true. I told you, I would never—!"

"Well, if you want to live, you'd better come up with a pretty convincing story for the Bureau, because Preston is on his way right now."

He downed his beer. "Show me this woman you think I killed."

Skye rose to her feet. "Let's go. After you."

"Oh, so now you won't even walk in front of me?" Aidan pushed back his chair and stood.

"I don't trust you. Never have."

"Yes, you have."

"Have not."

Aidan glowered at her, then banged out the back door with Skye following at a reasonable distance. Once they were outside, Skye pointed toward the shadowed area of the parking lot. The two of them walked over.

"It wasn't me," Aidan insisted, as they stood over the woman's body.

"I saw your eyes back at the Marine base. They were red-rimmed. You were going over the edge. Going crazy just like Roark. You attacked Tara and you attacked this woman."

His eyes changed to solid black, from their natural brilliant green. "Are they red now?"

"No."

"Well, then, I'm fine. Not crazy. Not going crazy. I didn't do it." He turned to walk away, but two cars pulled up and blocked his path. Preston got out, along with three other men who spread out to surround Aidan, while Preston went to look at the body.

Aidan turned to Skye. His eyes narrowed. "This was a set up."

"Yeah, pretty much." She now held the stake in her hand.

Aidan lunged toward one of the men. After one hard kick to the knee, the man was down screaming. Aidan met the next man head on, with a fist to the face. He went down hard and stayed there. The third man came at Aidan, and landed one blow before having his legs swept out from underneath him. Aidan was on him in a flash. One punch and he was out cold.

Skye was there before Aidan was on his feet. He moved as her stake came down, and it glanced off his coat to skid down his arm instead. He dealt her a blow that sent her reeling. She landed on her butt.

"This wound wasn't caused by a Blood-Hunter," Preston called out.

Skye looked over at him, and so did Aidan.

"It wasn't? Then what caused it?" Skye got up and brushed dirt off the back of her capris then walked over to Preston.

"Oh, so that's it, then?" Aidan looked from Preston to Skye. "No apology? No, 'I'm sorry, Aidan, my mistake.' Just accuse the closest Blood-Hunter and send three bureaucrats and an Assassin to take his life? Stake now and ask questions later, is that it? Don't bother to get the facts first?"

Skye frowned at him. "Well, you did attack Tara! What were we supposed to think?"

He glared at her. "You're supposed to think I'm innocent until proven guilty. I am owed an apology."

"Excuse me, but could we focus on this poor woman for a moment?" Preston asked. "I know a Blood-Hunter didn't do this, nor did a Shape-Shifter."

"Then what?" Skye asked, but she had a sinking feeling in her stomach.

"Let me take a closer look," Aidan stalked over and brushed by Preston to look at the body. He crouched by the woman's head and examined her neck.

Meanwhile, the three men, who had so recently been trounced by Aidan, staggered to their feet. Preston gave them a nod and they hobbled to one of the cars and left. Skye figured they were probably on their way to the nearest hospital.

Aidan looked up at Preston. "Do you know of another demon running around? I mean besides the one from the box? It *was* killed, wasn't it?"

Skye looked to Preston, who didn't seem fazed in the least, though her own stomach churned.

Preston evaded part of Aidan's query. "No. I don't know of another demon running around. Why?" he replied.

"You see this right here?" Aidan pointed to a mark on the woman's face. It was round with another circle inside, almost like a target. It looked like it had been burned into her cheek like a brand. "That's a demon mark. See the waves on one side?" He pointed to a spot near her ear. "That's a clue as to which demon. Anyone who carries this mark belongs to that particular demon."

"But...why would the demon bother to mark her if it was just going to kill her anyway?" Skye stammered. This had turned into a never-ending nightmare.

Preston looked at her. "Perhaps as a warning."

Aidan got to his feet and directed his next comment to Preston. "I noticed you didn't completely answer my question before. What happened on the island? Is Mortmal the Destroyer dead?"

Preston studied Aidan then seemed to come to a decision. "Only once before have I trusted a Blood-Hunter with inside information from the Bureau. He was a great asset. Right up until the night he betrayed us and had to be terminated by one of my Assassins."

Aidan made a face. "Never mind. Sorry I tried to help." He jammed his hands into his coat pockets and walked away.

"Stop right where you are." Preston's voice rang out in the night air.

Aidan turned. His eyes narrowed. "What?" he snapped.

"I know from the experience I just related that trust is not something one should ever grant a Blood-Hunter. However," he was quick to add as Aidan started to turn away again. "We really need to put this demon down, and you have been in this from the start. Your ability to overcome blood lust and the subsequent insanity that often comes with it has impressed me. You seem to have knowledge of this demon to rival our experts, you've protected my Assassin and another human, namely Tara Donovan, on more than one occasion, and it appears your assistance would be most useful at the moment. Can I trust you not to kill, Aidan? Can I trust you not to betray my Assassin?"

"Is Tara going to be all right?"

"Yes."

In the silence that followed, Skye waited on anxiously to hear Aidan's answer. What Preston had said was so totally unexpected. First, he'd given her a direct order to kill Aidan, and now he seemed to be doing the equivalent of offering him a job!

Aidan gave Preston a hard look. "I only kill those who have it coming, to save myself or in the defense of others."

"And you've never killed a human?" Preston looked skeptical.

"I have. Yes. When I was young. As you may already know, Blood-Hunters don't begin to crave blood until their late teenage years. Up until that point we look like and behave much like any human, but once we reach maturity our fangs come in, and we crave blood and must have it to survive. In those early years I killed some humans, but I learned from my family and the leader of our Coven reinforced the training. I disciplined myself, and I don't owe *you* any explanations so I don't know why I'm bothering. You're going to think what you want to think about me and my kind anyway. Its rubbish and I'm done talking about it with you." He turned and walked away.

"There are Assassins for a reason, Aidan." Preston called out. "Not all of you can be trusted. In fact, the majority cannot. But if you give me your word, I'll include you in this. We could truly use your help."

Aidan stopped and turned. He appeared to consider things then walked back to where Skye stood with Preston. "Fine. You have my word. Now what's going on?"

CHAPTER TWENTY

PRESTON GAVE AIDAN A LEVEL GAZE. "THE DEmon you two encountered and fought over on the island isn't dead."

"It jumped bodies." Aidan's jaw clenched. "How long have you known?"

"Just since this morning," Skye replied.

"Well, that's just fecking wonderful. It could be in anyone's body!"

"It jumped into the body of someone from the Bureau. His name is Alan Sherwood." Preston produced a photo from the pocket of his sport coat. He handed the photo to Skye, who held it so both she and Aidan could see it.

"So now what? Where do we go from here?" Skye asked.

Preston frowned in concentration. "Demons kill at random. It won't follow a pattern, so there's no way to tell where it might go next. Unless…"

"Unless what?" Aidan asked.

Preston retrieved his phone from his pocket and walked away while punching in some numbers.

"Skye!"

Skye's head whipped around at the sound of Rachael's voice. Her friend was hurrying over with Starr at her side.

Aidan leaned in. "I remember the blonde. Who's the little redheaded pixie?"

"That's Starr." Skye scowled up at him. "Shut up and go away."

Aidan grinned. "You're mighty rude to me, darlin'."

Skye turned to Rachael. "What are you doing here?" She changed position to try and block the dead woman's body from Rachael's view.

"We were on our way to the mall and I saw your car. Then I saw you in the parking lot. Is everything okay?" Rachael asked.

"Sure. Fine. Just doing a little Assassin type work."

Rachael glanced over at Aidan but didn't say anything.

Preston returned just as two black vans pulled into the parking lot. "I have some business to take care of here. If you all don't mind…" He made a shooing motion with his hands.

Skye took the hint. "Ah, yeah. Let's go."

Rachael gave her a questioning look, but headed back to her car. "See you later then!" she called out. Aidan simply disappeared into the shadows.

Skye threw a glance toward Preston as she got into her car. Rachael and Starr had already gotten into Rachael's Murano and pulled away from the curb. Preston caught her look, and made the phone symbol with his hand. He raised it to his face, pointed to himself and then to her. He'd call her later with instructions. She had no doubt of that.

Later, back at their apartment, Rachael threw her purse onto a chair and rounded on Skye. "So, what's going on? I know you couldn't talk because Starr was with us, but now you can so…"

Skye looked her friend square in the eyes. "So much has happened, Rachael. The only thing that really is worth mentioning right now is that the demon isn't dead after all."

"It isn't?" Rachael looked stunned. Skye knew just how she felt.

"No. It jumped bodies and now is in some guy named Alan Sherwood. He's from the Bureau."

"Oh, that's not good. Not at all." Rachael stared at her. "What happens now?"

"I don't know. Preston is working on it. Just, be careful when you go out, okay?"

"What does this Alan guy look like?"

Skye realized she still had the photo Preston had handed her earlier. She pulled it out. "Here, take a look."

Rachael studied the picture. "He's dead now, isn't he? I mean, the real Alan Sherwood."

"Yeah." Skye huffed out a breath and collapsed onto the sofa.

Rachael sat down too and handed the photo back to Skye. "Do you suppose I could blast him with some fire and kill him?"

Skye gave her a skeptical look. "If it was that easy, I'm sure Preston would've already thought of it."

"Rachael?" Skye was hesitant to bring this up, but she figured now was as good a time as any. "Um...now that my life is so dangerous, I was wondering if maybe...well, if maybe we shouldn't live together after all. Maybe I should just get a place by myself. I don't want to put you in danger and I already have. I don't know what I'd do if—"

"Are you serious?" Rachael looked both surprised and slightly offended.

"Oh, please don't take this the wrong way. It's not that I don't want to live with you. We've planned this for so long and I've been so excited about it, but...I had no way of knowing this whole Assassin thing was going to happen to me, and now that it has I—"

"Whoa, wait a minute. I could be in danger any time, anyway, what with random Spell-Masters being out there along with all the regular human wackos. I mean, just because Lucius was a part of your assignment—"

"But he never would've kidnapped you if you hadn't been with me that night."

"True, but some other Spell-Master might still try. And look what happened to Starr!"

"Yeah, but—"

Rachael stood and Skye could tell she was annoyed. She could tell by the tilt of her head, her stance and the narrowing of her eyes. "I'm going to bed." She left the room and Skye watched her go. She felt bad for upsetting her friend, but she was genuinely worried about Rachael's safety.

Her phone sang and Skye lay backwards on the cushions as she examined the screen to see who was calling. She'd been expecting Preston, but it wasn't him.

"What?" Her voice was sharp.

"Nice greeting. Why are you in such a mood? Mess up your nail polish? Can't figure out which dress to wear?"

"What do you want, Aidan?"

All the humor left his voice. "I want to know where Tara is."

"Why would I know?"

"Oh, I don't know, maybe because you have an inside track with the Bureau. Call Preston. Find out."

"Why?"

"If you must know, I want to apologize to her."

"You don't need to. She still loves you. She asked me about you on her way to the hospital or wherever it was they took her. She was happy to hear you'd gotten away."

"I don't doubt she still loves me, but that's good to know."

"You arrogant son of a—!"

"Now, now, temper, temper."

His tone mocked her, and Skye wished she could smack him in the face...throttle him...drive her stake through his rotten, conceited heart!

"Skye!" Not even a trace of humor was left in his voice.

"What?"

"I want to know where she is. Why hasn't she gone home yet? Is the Bureau holding her for some reason?"

"Maybe she doesn't want to go home. Maybe she left town. Or maybe the Bureau is keeping her as their guest to make sure you play nice."

"You're jealous of her, aren't you?"

"You are the most egotistical, bigheaded, haughty—!"

"Haughty? Now there's a word I didn't expect."

"Look, Mr. High and Mighty—!"

"No, you look." His tone was menacing. "You find out where Tara is, and how she is. I mean it, Skye. I won't help you with a blessed thing until I see her and talk with her. Do it." He disconnected.

Skye pounded one of the sofa cushions with her fist. He was so infuriating! She hit her speed dial and contacted Preston.

"It's Skye."

"I can see that. Your name does come up on the screen, you know."

Skye practically growled in frustration. "I can't deal with attitude right now, Preston. I've gotten enough if it from Aidan to fill a mansion. He wants to know how Tara is and where she is. He says he won't help us until he sees her and talks to her."

Preston sighed. "Being difficult already, is he?"

"He's been difficult from the start. This is nothing new."

"She's being released tomorrow. Someone from the Bureau will drive her home."

"Do you actually trust him not to kill her?"

"Yes, in this circumstance I do. He knows if any harm comes to her he'll be the first one we suspect. Besides, I believe he really has beaten down his 'inner demon', if you will. He's sane."

"But he had his freaking fangs in her neck! I saw it!"

"Skye, I've spoken with her. She is not afraid of him."

"But—!"

"She's shared her blood with him before. Albeit, not from the neck, from the arm. She says the only reason she screamed is because he startled her. One minute he was comatose and the next he'd grabbed her. She claims she never was as close to death as we at first feared. The medical report confirms it. They're keeping her overnight just to be on the safe side. It really isn't medically necessary at this point."

Skye was stunned. She was happy to know Tara was fine, but she was upset to know the girl had given her blood to Aidan willingly. That sounded awful as far as she was concerned, and she was confused about something else too.

"All this time I've been led to believe I'm supposed to stake every Blood-Hunter on sight. I'm told not to ever trust them, and you didn't even coach me at all before I staked my first Blood-Hunter at the graduation party. But recently I've heard you say you've actually *worked* with a Blood-Hunter before! And you're talking to Aidan like he's one of the gang or—"

"Skye, Skye, calm down! Everything you've believed up to this point is true. Literally, ninety-five percent of the Blood-Hunters are callous killers. That's why we hunt them so intensely. If we didn't there would be far more gruesome deaths on record than there already are. Many Blood-Hunters learn to disguise their kills so that human serial killers get blamed, or animals, if the kills are done in wilderness areas. So, you see, there is no mystery here."

"But what about this Blood-Hunter you said you worked with, and what about Aidan?"

"Whether or not Aidan is among that rare small percentile, is yet to be determined. As for the Blood-Hunter I once trusted…he was someone I grew up with. His family moved out of state when I was sixteen and I didn't see him again until I was a grown man and a Handler. We ran into each other quite by accident and shortly thereafter I discovered he was a Blood-Hunter. I gave him a chance and he blew it. One of my Assassins at the time, Kylie, staked him."

"Oh." Skye was pretty surprised Preston had shared something of his personal life with her. That had never happened before, but now she was curious about the Assassin he'd mentioned. "Well, what happened to Kylie? You haven't mentioned her before."

"She is no longer active as an Assassin."

"You mean she's…"

"No, she'd not dead, if that's what you're asking."

"I don't understand. You told me this was a lifetime commitment. You told me I didn't have a choice. You said—"

"Skye, take a breath! Calm yourself. Being an Assassin *is* a lifetime commitment. Kylie stopped being an active Assassin because of an injury that nearly got her killed and never healed properly. Although you Assassins heal at an extraordinary rate, you can't heal everything."

"What happened to her," she whispered into the phone.

"Her pelvis was shattered in a fall and her legs broken. She healed enough to walk but not enough to fight. She works with the Bureau as a Handler. She's my niece."

Now Skye was even more taken aback. Preston had told her more about himself in ten minutes than he had in the last several weeks! She hardly knew what to say.

"Oh, oh, I see," she finally stammered. "Um, okay. I'll let Aidan know what you said about Tara. What about the demon? Any progress there?"

"Yes. I think so. The trick will be keeping it from jumping to another body."

"Yeah." Skye closed her eyes for a moment.

"Get some sleep, Skye. We'll tackle this fresh in the morning."

"Okay. Night."

She disconnected and called Aidan.

"She'll be home tomorrow. "You can contact her there."

"When? When will she be home?"

"I don't know, Romeo. Just keep calling until you get her. I'm going to sleep. G'night."

She pushed a button and ended the call.

The next morning Skye sat with Rachael at a little coffee shop around the corner from their apartment. Although she wore sparkling barrettes in her hair and a pretty yellow blouse, Skye also had on stretch blue jeans and sneakers. She wouldn't be caught without traction again, or the ability to move and fight. That was for certain.

"What's with you and Aidan?" Rachael asked around a mouthful of lemon poppy seed muffin; her annoyance from the previous night apparently forgotten.

"What do you mean?" Skye nibbled on some bran muffin and sipped her coffee.

"I heard your side of the conversation last night. Couldn't help it. You were yelling."

"I also talked to Preston."

"You weren't yelling at Preston." Rachael gave her a look.

"Yeah, okay, so what were you doing listening in?"

"Like I said, you were yelling. I couldn't help but overhear. So, what's going on?"

"With what?"

"You and Aidan! Stop pretending you don't know what I'm talking about. Do you like him? Does he like you? And wouldn't that be mighty dangerous and exciting…an Assassin dating a Blood-Hunter?"

"We're not going to be dating. I don't like him. He doesn't like me."

"He saved your life once."

"And he turned me over to someone who wanted to kill me too."

"The same person he later saved you from." Rachael grinned.

Skye rolled her eyes. "What's with you? Do you *want* me to date him?"

"Not necessarily, but he is awfully good looking."

"And he's a Blood-Hunter."

"He's smart. He's resourceful. He's kind of funny sometimes…"

"I repeat. He's a Blood-Hunter."

"Did I mention he's really good looking?"

Rachael gave her a sly smile and sipped her coffee.

"He has a girlfriend, Rachael. Or at least she's someone he hangs out with, gets blood from, and cares about enough to rescue from a demon and worry about when she's not at home."

"Tara, right?"

"Right."

"Oh, well." Rachael shrugged. "It was just a thought."

"Have you given any more thought to what I suggested last night? About us not sharing an apartment after all?" Skye's phone sang. She looked at it. "It's Preston."

"Good. I didn't want to talk about that apartment thing anyway. I'll go get some napkins." Rachael got up and left the table.

Skye answered her phone. "What's up?"

"We've cornered the demon. It's at Sherwood's home."

"Where is that?" She wrote down the information on the napkin Rachael had just brought back. "Okay, I'll be there as fast as I can."

"Call Aidan. Have him come too. We may need him."

Skye disconnected and stuffed her phone back in her pocket. "Gotta run."

"The demon?"

"Yeah. They've got it cornered." Skye stood. "Sorry about this, but…"

"I understand. Go! I'll see you later at home. Be careful!"

Skye nodded, then turned and bolted out of the coffee shop.

CHAPTER TWENTY-ONE

AIDAN SHOWED UP FIVE MINUTES AFTER SKYE. It was broad daylight, so he wore dark, wrap-around sunglasses, along with black jeans and combat boots, a black t-shirt and an attitude. The house was in a middle-class neighborhood with yards neat and tidy, lawns mowed, trees trimmed. Both ends of the street were blocked off and cars belonging to the Bureau were parked across the street.

"Geez, Aidan, do you ever wear anything but black?" Skye quipped.

"If I decide otherwise, you're just the girl to take me shopping, although I doubt I'd look good in pastels. So, what's the situation?"

"Nothing has changed. The demon is inside the house. The Bureau has surrounded the place."

Preston walked over to them. "We have a magical shield up. Much like the one we had before around the island."

"Did you recover the box from the truck?" Aidan asked.

Preston nodded. "We did, yes. It was slightly damaged."

"How, slightly?" Skye asked.

"Enough not to be able to use it, I'm afraid," Preston replied.

"Damn," Aidan muttered. "Well, that's it then. We're screwed."

"What are you talking about?" Skye faced him head on. "Are you saying there's no way to kill it? The only option is putting it back in the box? Maybe we can put it in something else."

Aidan gave her a look. "Like what, a perfume bottle?"

Skye's eyes narrowed. "You are such a—!"

"Knock it off you two," Preston snapped. "This is serious."

At that moment, there was movement in an upstairs window. "Did you see that? It looks like someone is upstairs at the window." She couldn't make out who was there, but Aidan could.

"It looks like a kid, maybe eleven or twelve."

Seconds later the boy threw a leg over the windowsill.

"Is he crazy?" Skye wondered aloud. "He'll break his legs. Preston, do something!"

"I can't. The barrier is up."

"Well, can't you have them make an opening or something and go in and help the kid?"

Preston went to talk to some of the Bureau agents while Skye watched the boy who now dangled by his hands.

"He might be all right you know," Aidan said. "He looks like a pretty stout lad."

"Do you really think—?" The boy let go, and Skye gasped. He landed on the ground in a sprawl, then got to his feet and headed for a group of agents clustered near the barrier. Skye kept a suspicious eye on the kid, as did Aidan. "I guess he looks all right." As Skye watched, the boy was flanked by agents and headed for a parked car at the curb.

Aidan kept his eyes on the boy. "I don't know. That seemed too easy."

"You mean that he made it out alive? Maybe he was hiding and the demon didn't know he was there."

Preston returned.

"Who is that boy?" Aidan asked.

"He's Alan Sherwood's son. He says his mother is in the house and his father is crazy."

"He's not crazy, he's a demon," Aidan muttered.

"So, is he okay?" Skye asked. "The boy, I mean. Was he hurt?"

"He seems none the worse for wear. I've tasked some agents to work out the best way to rescue the woman," Preston replied.

Aidan shook his head. "You're daft. She's already dead."

Skye rounded on him. "How can you be so sure? The boy escaped."

Preston kept his eyes on the house. "He may have a point. The boy was awfully lucky."

"Too lucky, if you ask me," Aidan grumbled.

"If there is someone in there, an innocent, then we have to get her out." Preston looked over at Aidan. "I have a job for you."

"Oh yeah, what's that?"

"Go through the opening in the barrier, where the boy came out. Look around. Go inside if you have to. If the woman is alive and you can get her out, then do so." He handed Aidan a small device.

"What's this?"

"An earpiece. Put it in. We'll be able to communicate. Let me know what you find."

Aidan shrugged, then reached for the earpiece. He and Preston tested it. Everything seemed to work well, and Aidan set off for the barrier.

"Is this safe?" Skye asked Preston.

"Relatively. Aidan, being a Blood-Hunter, is more likely to survive an attack by a demon, should it come to that."

"Did you tell him that?"

"I didn't have to. He's not an idiot, Skye. He's fought this particular demon before. He knows what could happen in there."

"And is anyone going to go in and help him if he needs it? Or is he on his own?"

Preston stared at her. "What do you think?"

Skye's eyes widened. "That's not fair and it's not right. He isn't a member of the Bureau. He volunteered to help, and this is how you repay him? By using him as cannon fodder?"

"He is an expendable resource."

"Isn't everyone?" Skye muttered

"Calm down, Skye. Such cynicism. I didn't mean that quite the way it sounds, but I'd rather lose a Blood-Hunter than my only Assassin, and there really is no one else here who is capable of—-Wait just a moment." Preston put a hand to his earpiece. "I'm here. Yes. All right. If you— Aidan? Aidan!"

Skye leaned closer. "What's happening?"

"He said the woman is dead."

"What about the demon? Is Aidan, okay? Did you lose contact with him?"

"I lost contact, but I think it's because he took the earpiece out."

"Are you sure? Are you sure something didn't happen to him?"

The front door of the house banged open. Aidan stood on the porch with a scowl on his face. "Where's the boy?" he shouted to anyone listening.

Everyone turned toward the parked car on the curb where the boy was last seen. He wasn't there.

"Not here!" someone shouted.

Aidan's scowl deepened. "The boy is the fecking demon!" he shouted. "Where is he?"

People scrambled to search the immediate area, but it didn't take long to determine the boy was nowhere to be found.

"The boy was the demon." Preston closed his eyes. He let out a sound of pure rage and frustration.

"What?" Skye was stunned. "But he seemed so normal. Not anything like how Ben looked after——."

Aidan came storming through the opening in the barrier and over to Preston and Skye. "He's gone, isn't he? The demon tricked us and he's gone." He paced in tight circles. "You can take the barrier down now. Your men will find Sherwood's and his wife's body inside the house. There's no point in hanging around here anymore." He stopped pacing and tossed the earpiece to Preston, then with great strides eating up the ground, he stalked away.

"You might as well go too, Skye. I'll call you when we locate the demon again."

"What's its plan? I mean, now that it's free, the demon must have a plan, right? World domination? To find another demon and start a family? Something."

Preston heaved a great sigh. Skye waited. The two of them watched the Bureau agents pack up and one by one, drive off.

"Mortmal the Destroyer is a Chaos Demon, which means he is a demon that aspires only to create confusion and obliterate life as we know it. He will want acolytes. With their help the demon can create havoc and carry out a plan of destruction. There will be bedlam in the streets."

"That's what happened on Coronado Island. The Blood-Hunters ran all over the place, wrecking buildings, killing people…"

"Yes, well, you can expect more of that if this thing isn't contained."

"So where would the demon find new acolytes, now that Aidan, Ben and I killed all the Blood-Hunters who were its followers? Is there another band of Blood-Hunters around?"

"No. Roark's bunch was it. There may still be some stragglers around but," he shrugged. "I have no idea at the moment. He might leave the area and search out another Coven of willing Blood-Hunters, or he might even target some magic obsessed humans here locally whom he can manipulate. There's no telling. Just go on. I'll call you when we know something." Preston walked to his car, got in and drove away.

Skye spent the day by herself; waiting for Preston's call. She went to the mall, but every time she saw a shirt or a skirt or some shoes, the first thing on her mind was that she shouldn't buy it because she couldn't fight in it. She got something to eat, but hardly tasted her food. All she could think about was the demon and where it might find followers. She tried to talk herself into watching a romantic comedy at the theater, but how could she really get involved in some silly fictional couple's ridiculous dilemmas, when real people were being killed in her own city by a demon?

Finally, at four fifteen she decided to go home, but when she walked into her apartment, she was shocked to see Aidan sitting on the living room sofa. "Where's Rachael? How did you get in here?"

"To answer your first question, she went out somewhere with the red-haired pixie."

"Her name is Starr. I told you that before."

"To answer your second question, Rachael invited me in."

Skye frowned. "Well, I un-invite you. Get out."

He smiled. "It doesn't work that way, darlin'. If you want me out things are going to get a little rough. You don't want your nice furniture and pretty trinkets broken, do you?"

Skye glared at him. "Don't you dare trash my place."

"I won't if you'll agree to talk to me nicely."

She dropped down into the chair across the coffee table. "Just go, Aidan. Please. I don't want to see you or talk to you right now."

"Not even if I know where the demon is?"

She sat up a little straighter. "You do? Really? Where?"

There was a gleam in his eye. "Nah, I don't know. I was just seeing if you would want to talk to me if I did."

Skye picked up a paperback book and threw it at him. He grabbed it out of the air with a grin.

"What are you doing here then? Besides ruining my evening," Skye asked.

"Come on. Let's go get a drink." He stood.

She looked up at him. "I don't drink alcohol."

"So, you can have lemonade or something."

"I don't want to go anywhere with you. Just tell me why you're here."

"This is why."

"To annoy me?"

He grinned but shook his head. "Never mind. I'll go meet Megan on my own."

Now Skye was fully alert. "Megan who?"

"Oh, *now* you're interested!"

"Just tell me who she is, Aidan."

"She's an acquaintance who knows quite a lot about demons. She can help us."

Skye stared into Aidan's emerald eyes for several seconds. "Fine. Your car or mine?"

He jangled his keys. "Mine, of course."

She remembered the last time they'd gone somewhere in his car and rolled her eyes. "Great. Just great. Well, okay, as long as you don't try and stuff a third person in there with us or deliver me to another Spell-Master."

"Oh, are you still mad about that?" Aidan chuckled.

Skye just glowered at him.

They sat at a table in MacGregor's Pub and waited.

"There she is."

Skye followed Aidan's gaze. A slender girl stood just inside the doorway. Aidan raised a hand. The girl saw it and gave a nod, then wove her way through the people clustered near the bar. As she came closer, Skye could see she had wild curling brown shoulder length hair and glasses. She wore a pleated red and black plaid skirt with black loafers and a short-sleeved red knit top. There was a tattered brown messenger bag draped across her body.

"Hi, Aidan." The girl said, then turned to Skye and stuck out her hand. "Hi, I'm Megan Tanner."

Skye shook hands with the girl. "Skye Falco."

Megan slung her messenger bag over her head and hung it on the back of the chair. "So, Aidan says you guys want to hear about the research I'm doing."

A waitress stopped by and Megan ordered a Pepsi, Skye a Ginger Ale, and Aidan a beer with a shot of whiskey. Once the waitress was gone, Megan leaned in.

"So, what do you want to hear about first?" She looked gleeful.

Skye was bewildered. Who was this girl? What sort of research was she doing? Where in the world had Aidan come up with her?

"Demonology," Aidan answered. "Remember what you started to tell me about the increased incidences of teens and college students trying to summon demons?"

"Yes, yes!" Megan nodded. Her expression grew serious. "It's horrible but true. In fact, there's a group that meets near the university every weekend." She lowered her voice. "I'm in the processes of arranging to go undercover to gain more information."

Skye glanced at Aidan. Was he actually taking this girl seriously? "Ah, Megan, how did you happen to come up with this information? About the group, I mean."

Megan looked at Skye with wide eyes. "I stumbled across one of the group's members when I was doing research at the library. Literally. I tripped over his feet. He was sitting on the floor. He had his legs out and well...you know. Anyway, that's where I met Aidan also. We were browsing in the same section."

Skye could hardly contain her mirth. Aidan at the library! "What library was this? Surely, they don't have rare books on demonology at the public library."

"Actually, Megan works in the rare books section of the university library."

Megan nodded. "But that's not where I get my information on demonology. I'm a grad student. I'm kind of young to be a grad student, I'm nineteen. But, what can I say? I test well. So anyhow, the professor I work with has an incredible private collection of all sorts of rare and ancient books. Among them are books on religion, witchcraft, demonology, and lots more."

Skye frowned. "So, let me get this straight, Aidan was in the rare book section at the university library when you met?"

"No, actually I was in the history section of the public library," he replied.

Skye just blinked at him. Things had gotten way too confusing. Plus, she was still trying to wrap her head around the notion of Aidan browsing through books at the library in his spare time.

The waitress appeared at the table. "Sorry it took so long to get your drinks. It's really busy in here tonight." She set the drinks on the table. "Is there anything else I can get you? Potato skins? Onion rings? Anything?" They all shook their heads and she left.

Skye looked over at Megan. "So, back to—"

"Right, right! So, as I was saying, I'm infiltrating a group that wants to raise a demon."

"How does that work, exactly?" Skye asked.

Megan looked around then lowered her voice again. "You mean how do they do it? That's what I aim to find out."

Skye shook her head. "No, I mean how are you going to infiltrate?"

Megan's head bobbed up and down. "Oh, right. So, I met this guy at the library who is part of the group. I asked him about his piercings and his tattoos, and the next thing you know he started bragging about doing dark magic and raising demons and he invited me."

Skye rocked back in her chair. "I don't know, Megan, but I find it really difficult to believe a guy like that would be at the library looking at—"

"Right, just like you find it hard to believe I'd be at the library in the history section?" Aidan asked, his voice dripping with sarcasm.

"Well, yes, actually," Skye replied. "I'd think you'd be more suited to go undercover in a group that wants to raise a demon than Megan is." She looked him up and down. "What with your propensity to wear all black all the time."

Aidan gave her a smirk. "Funny."

"Hey! That's a great idea! Why don't you come too, Aidan? That would be so cool."

Megan's eyes sparkled with excitement. Skye closed her eyes and wished herself anywhere but here. When she opened them again, she looked at Megan. "Maybe we can just... give you some back up or something. You know, wait around outside to come to your rescue if anything goes wrong."

Megan gave her an eager smile. "Gosh, really? That would be great!"

Skye stood up. "Yeah, so, um, Aidan and I have to be going now. But it was nice to meet you. We'll be in touch." She gave Aidan a hard look. He gave her a smirk.

"Oh, sure, sure, I understand." Megan grabbed up her messenger bag. "Well, thanks for the soda." She gave Skye and Aidan another enthusiastic smile, then turned and headed for the door.

Skye turned to Aidan. "Seriously?"

Aidan gave her an award-winning smile. "Seriously."

"Does she know what you are?"

He made a face. "Of course not!"

"Does she know about the Bureau?"

"Ah," Aidan tipped his head. "She might."

Skye sat up straighter. "What might she know? *How* might she know?"

"I don't know."

"*You don't know?*" Skye gasped.

"Come on. Let's go." Aidan drained his glass and stood, then headed for the door.

CHAPTER TWENTY-TWO

SKYE'S PHONE SANG. SHE OPENED HER EYES then squinted at the bright light slicing across her pillow through an opening between the curtains. The phone continued its happy song and Skye reached for it.

"Megan just called me with an update," Aidan said, after Skye had mumbled, 'hello'.

She blinked and rubbed her eyes. "We really need to talk to Preston about this."

"I already did."

Since when did Aidan have Preston's phone number? "What did he say?"

"He said to run with it. Be her back up, like you suggested."

"Okay...so when and where?" Skye figured she'd play along, but she planned to call Preston herself. She could hardly believe he'd gone along with this hare-brained scheme. Then again, maybe the Bureau really was that desperate.

"Tonight. Eight o'clock." He gave her the address. "I'll be there early to scout around."

"Okay. Sure. But do we really have a plan here?"

"Yes," Aidan replied. "The plan is to wait around for the demon to show up. Those kids are a readymade group of followers."

"And if it doesn't?"

"It will. Besides I don't know of any other groups in the area who are doing this sort of thing, and on top of that, even if the kids can't raise the magic the demon is looking for acolytes, right? So, he'll come."

"Okay, so then what? Did Preston find a way to kill the thing, or at least contain it?"

"One way or the other. Preston and his crew will lower the boom on the demon while you and I get those kids out of there."

"I thought we were going to be back up if something went wrong."

"And we are. But it depends on whose perspective. If the demon shows up, then things went right for us, but wrong for those kids. Though, from their perspective, if the demon shows up they'll think things went right and if it doesn't show up then things went wrong. You understand?"

"Not really. But you do realize Preston was willing to use you as cannon fodder back at the Sherwood house. He sees you as expendable."

"I realize I'm not very high in his esteem, but he's included me in this and gave me his phone number as a contact point. Even so, I trust him about as much as he trusts me. I'm not stupid, Skye."

"And why is he including you in this anyway? How did you even get involved in the first place?"

"My box, my job to see it didn't get opened, my bloodline that opened it...you need any more reasons?"

"Whatever. See you at eight."

Skye disconnected and immediately called Preston.

"Did Aidan really talk to you about this Megan chick? Did he tell you his crazy plan? Did you seriously okay it? And since when does he have your phone number? Is he a member of the team now?"

"Hello, Skye. Lose the attitude, will you? I don't respond to it any better than you do."

"Right." Skye took a deep breath, let it out and tried to relax. "Hi, Preston. Good morning. Would you please answer my questions?" She asked in her sweetest voice.

"Yes, Aidan spoke with me. I know about his idea, though he presented it as your idea. Is that not right?"

"Ah, well, yeah, the part about...but I was just kidding around about being back up. He's the one who brought that Megan girl into it. She's a little weird if you ask me."

"I understand, but I happen to know Megan's father is a brilliant man. As is the professor she works with. Both are members of the Bureau in an informal sense. They are on board as consultants. I wouldn't count her out, if I were you. Megan is quite exceptional herself."

"Oh, well—" Skye was stunned. So, it was entirely possible Megan *did* actually know something about the Bureau. Perhaps even quite a lot!

"As for your other questions," Preston continued, "Aidan is not a member of the team, as you put it, but I did give him my number. Anything else you want to know?"

"You'll be there, right? Aidan said you'd be there with some other people to take care of the demon. He also said he and I should get the kids out of there. That's our job. Is that right?"

"Correct. Anything else?"

"Um, no. I guess not. Except how are you going to do it? How are you going to kill the demon? Or contain it. Or whatever."

"I don't have time to explain all of it, Skye. I'll see you tonight." He hung up.

Skye set her phone down. Now what? What was she going to do all day that would keep her mind off—Her phone started to sing again. Now what? Skye picked it up and looked at the screen, then quickly pushed the 'answer' button.

"Derek!"

"Hi, stranger. You've barely moved out of the house and already you're ignoring us?"

"I've called Mom and Dad every couple of days. I—"

"Yes, but you haven't talked to me! I'm leaving day after tomorrow."

"Leaving? Leaving for where? Oh, no! You mean…but the time went by so fast! I wanted to see you more, but then everything happened. The moving and—How about if I come over today? I can be there in a couple of hours and spend all afternoon."

"That would be great. I'll let Mom and Dad know."

"Okay. See you soon!"

Once Skye was off the phone, she threw back the covers and got up. This was perfect. Today she would visit with family and be her old self. Regular, not-an-Assassin, Skye. Then, tonight, she'd don her Assassin garb, her weapons, and help the Bureau and Aidan hunt down a demon. She hoped they'd find a way to kill it this time. She hoped she'd live through it. She hoped they all would.

SUZANN FORTUNATO

Once back on the island, Skye looked around at the devastation, and remembered everything. Including Ben's death. It was far more heart wrenching than she'd imagined it would be. How in the world had people dealt with the deaths of family and friends? A violent storm? Marauding gangs? Those were the kinds of things that had been put into people's minds, somehow, by the Bureau. But what about the neck wounds on the victims? Those punctures from the Blood-Hunter's fangs. Were they some- how made invisible? Glamoured in some way so no one could see them?

Skye wondered if it was right to alter people's memories like that. Wouldn't it be better to let people know such things as demons, Shape- Shifters, Blood-Hunters and Elfae existed? On the other hand, if those beings didn't want to be known about, didn't they have the right to stay hidden? No, wait…Not if they were killing people! But then, if humans really would band together and attempt to kill all the Elfae, Shape-Shifters and Blood-Hunters as Rachael had told her, then it might be for the best to keep things the way they were. Skye went around and around with these thoughts until she had to just shut it all out or drive herself crazy.

While she was with her family, Skye talked about her apartment, Rachael, places they'd been and the classes they'd signed up for. She'd played cards with her brother, watched a little TV and had eaten a de- licious meal prepared by her mom: beef stroganoff, green beans, a salad and Derek's favorite lemon cake. How good it was to have a home cooked meal with her whole family. Somehow, she now appreciated these little things she'd always taken for granted before. Maybe it was because she didn't know if she'd live until tomorrow. When it was time to go, she'd said good-bye to Derek, not knowing for sure when she'd see him again, and hoped he'd stay safe.

By the time Skye got back to her apartment, she was mentally wrung out in spite of the pleasant diversion of being with her family. Rachael wasn't around and thankfully neither was Aidan. She stripped off the green, daisy print sun-dress she'd been wearing, and dug in her dresser for black jeans and a black tank top. She braided her hair, removed her jewelry, then put on socks and sneakers. Next, she strapped on the thigh holster, which held her stakes. Though she didn't know what good they would do against a demon, it made her feel better just to have them with her. Last, she tugged on a long, lightweight black jacket to cover the holster.

200

She left the apartment exactly forty-five minutes before she was supposed to meet up with Aidan. She'd tried several times, since she'd been home, to contact Rachael, but got no response. Skye hoped that meant her friend was at a movie or something, not kidnapped by a Spell-Master or scooped up by Blood-Hunters for a meal. The world was a much scarier place than she'd ever imagined. Maybe after tonight it would be just a little bit safer.

Skye arrived at the place Aidan had said they'd meet, and got out of the car. All was quiet at this time of night. The streets were lined with warehouses and some smaller abandoned buildings. There were no other vehicles around yet. Not even Aidan's Boxter. She walked toward the building where everything would take place, keeping to the shadows. It was dark out, but streetlights illuminated much of the area. She could see the name of the company who owned the warehouse, painted on the side of the building. It was a huge storage facility for a construction company called, Wilford & Son Builders.

Skye heard footsteps and backed further into the shadows. Several teenage boys walked along the sidewalk across the street from her. Every now and again one or two would look around, their eyes darting every which way. Each boy wore black clothing, and many of them had black hair as well.

As Skye continued to watch, she realized there were a couple of girls mixed in with the others. They were nearly indistinguishable from the boys except that one of them wore a short skirt and the other had a flower in her hair. The one with the flower didn't have black hair. It was brown and curly The girl looked around, and Skye saw she wore glasses. It was Megan! One of the guys said something to her. Maybe it was the guy she'd tripped over at the library. The one who invited her to the demon raising.

The group filed into the warehouse. The last person to enter, looked up and down the street, then ducked in and shut the door behind him. Skye also looked around. Where in the world was Aidan? Where was Preston? Hadn't he said he would bring others from the Bureau as well? Where was everyone?

A hand landed on her shoulder. Skye whirled and slammed her fist into her assailant as fear caused adrenaline to surge through her body. Her fist was caught in one strong hand. Aidan's hand. She looked up at him, her heart racing, her eyes wide in the darkness, her breathing ragged.

"Sorry, darlin'. Figured you'd heard my approach," he whispered.

Skye jerked her hand out of his. "Liar. You enjoyed scaring me half to death."

He shrugged, then looked from her to the door the kids had gone through. "So, everybody is in then, yeah?"

"Yeah. Where's Preston?"

"He's got some people with him. They're around the corner. They'll find another way in. Ours is through that door."

Skye frowned. "I thought we were supposed to wait outside in case anything goes wrong, and then, if—"

"And how are we supposed to know something's gone wrong unless we're inside? Come on." He gave her a cuff on the arm as he jogged past. After a moment she followed.

They slowed when they got to the door. Aidan handed her one of Preston's communication devices. Why hadn't Preston given this to her himself? Who was in charge here, anyway? Aidan? She put it in her ear.

He gestured for her to be quiet, then he slowly turned the knob and put his shoulder to the door. It creaked a little, but gave and then swung open silently. Again, Aidan gestured for her to go around to the right, while he went around to the left. Skye did as he directed, but it didn't feel right. After all, the last time she'd trusted him in a similar situation he'd turned her over to Lucius the Spell-Master. How could she know for certain she wouldn't wind up as a sacrifice to Mortmal the Destroyer this time around?

"Skye? Can you hear me?" Aidan whispered through the earpiece.

"Yes," Skye whispered back. "What?"

"Stay low, keep to the shadows and be quiet. Just watch and do nothing until we hear from Preston."

Skye crept toward the voices she heard coming from the next room. The kids were talking in hushed tones, and then one of them seemed to take over speaking while the others fell silent. He must've been the leader of the bunch. She peeked around a pallet of tile to see an area in the center of the building, cleared away, with a circle drawn on the floor. The kids stood on the outside of it. Skye looked up and saw the building was two stories high, with a walkway going around the second floor. There were more items stored up there: doors, windows, screens, rakes, shovels, trash containers and other things Skye could only guess at. She could just make out Aidan hiding in the darkness across the room. Skye returned her focus to the group of teens near the center of the space. They had lighted candles. What idiots! She hoped the whole place didn't catch fire. She'd run from one fire recently, and barely escaped with her life.

Skye watched with morbid curiosity as the boy who seemed to be the leader of the group, began the ritual process of bringing forth whichever demon they'd decided upon. What if Mortmal the Destroyer didn't show up? What if some other demon did? Would Preston and his people be able to handle yet another demon presence? Would the magic they'd prepared work to kill or contain both of them?

Skye kept one eye on Megan the whole time. The silly girl seemed fascinated. She stood in her position around the curve of the circle, and Skye guessed the only reason Megan had been invited at all, was that the group needed a certain amount of people present to make the ritual work.

The kids started to chant. Two of the boys who were not part of the circle, came forward and cut the palms of their hands with pocketknives. They dripped their blood, around the circle as they walked from point to point where each person stood. Finally, the leader of the group spoke and called forth their demon of choice, while the others chanted.

"Irina, Demon of Avarice and Desire, hear us. We call upon you. Come into the circle, as we bid. Come to us, now!"

With his final words, the boy threw something into the circle. It popped and sparked, then smoke began to rise. To Skye's utter amazement, a form began to take shape. Was this Irina, going to actually appear, or was this some magician's trick? As she continued to watch, the shape began to look more and more like a woman. Could it truly be Irina the Demon of Avarice and Desire? Skye glanced toward Aidan. She wished she could see his expression. She looked again toward the circle in time to see Megan step back; her face a mask of fear and horror. As much as she was into the research of demons, she clearly never expected to see one in real life. Where was Preston? Was he here somewhere? Watching? Listening?

"Aidan?" she whispered.

"I see it. This is bad. Really bad."

CHAPTER TWENTY-THREE

BEFORE SKYE COULD SAY ANYTHING ELSE, THE door they'd come though burst open. A man walked into the room, but not just any man. This guy was huge. Skye guessed he stood six foot eight. On top of that, as if he didn't look imposing enough, his skin was black as coal, his head was bald, and his eyes glowed yellow!

"Aidan! Who—?"

"It's our demon."

"Mortmal the Destroyer? But I thought he was in the body of a twelve-year-old boy!"

"If you were a demon, how long would you stay in the body of a twelve-year-old boy?"

"Oh. Right. Good point."

The kids were so focused on the materializing demon in the circle; they didn't notice the one approaching from behind.

Preston's voice came through Skye's communication device. "Hold your positions. Both of you. Do nothing."

"But—" Skye began.

"I mean it, Skye. Do nothing."

"But those kids!"

"Do not move from your position!"

Skye's focus was torn from the demon that had just entered the room, to the new demon now corporeal within the circle. She was really something to behold. Hip length black hair, skin the color of alabaster and eyes that shifted from brilliant green to yellow.

She practically snarled at the assembled teens. "Who are you? Why have you called me?"

The boy, who seemed to be the leader, spoke. His voice wavered a bit, then strengthened. "We have called upon you, Irina, the Demon of Avarice and Desire, to give *us* what we desire most."

"What is avarice?" Skye whispered.

"Greed," Preston answered.

The boy kept talking. "We want money and power and you're going to give us these things so the city will be ours."

"Then you should have called me!" The black skinned man bellowed, and every one of the teens turned at the sound of his voice.

Irina shrieked with laughter and the kid's heads swiveled back toward her so swiftly it was almost comical.

"The Destroyer is here, too! Perfect. Foolish human children, did you think you could simply summon me and I'd bend to your will? I am more powerful than your puny circle, and The Destroyer is more powerful than even I!" She laughed again. "You do not control *us*. No mere human has power over the demon realm."

As the teens, and Skye, watched in horror, Irina stepped out of the circle which Skye assumed was meant to contain her. Now there were two demons loose in the city.

"Somebody do something!" Skye tried to keep her voice low enough that only Preston and Aidan would hear, but both Irina and Mortmal turned in her direction.

Mortmal, in his new guise, strode to Skye's hiding spot. She tried to conceal herself amongst the building materials, but it was no use. He had her in his grasp within seconds. His grip was like steel as he held her by the arm. He turned and whipped her around with him like some terrible version of crack the whip. The teens scattered, but Irina darted after them. On the upper-level Skye saw people with their arms outstretched. The presence of magic filled the air. It was dense, sparkling, and moved through the room like an arrow shot from a dozen bows. Elfaen magic!

She heard Preston's voice in her ear. "The building has been sealed with magic. We're not leaving this place until these demons are destroyed."

"Or we're dead," Aidan muttered.

Skye felt the Destroyer's hot breath on the back of her neck. "I will mark you, little warrior. You will be one of many tools I use in my new reign."

"Not if I have anything to say about it." Skye struggled against him, but it was no use. He was too big and brawny. She felt something, maybe a claw, scrape the skin on her neck. The next thing she knew she was on the ground. When she looked up, Skye saw Aidan on the demon's back, his arms around the Destroyer's throat.

"Get those kids out of here!" Aidan shouted as the demon whirled, trying to dislodge the Blood-Hunter from its back.

Skye was momentarily frozen, but then an adrenaline surge propelled her into action. She saw Megan, cowering behind a stack of bricks, and ran to her.

"Skye?" Megan's eyes were huge. She looked like she might faint dead away at any moment.

"Yes. Come on!" Skye pulled the other girl to her feet, and ran along the outskirts of the melee, toward the door.

Preston's voice was in her ear. "Skye, you can't go that way. The building is sealed."

Skye remembered his earlier words and mentally kicked herself. "Then where can we go?"

"To the stairs on your right."

"Across the room?" Skye could hardly believe what she'd heard him say. They'd have to go through the fray rather than around it. She looked left and right. Aidan fought with one demon, the other demon, Irina, took swipes at the teens, and laughed as those teens ran every which way. "Are you sure about this, Preston? If these kids can't get out of the building, they're all going to be slaughtered and I don't see how I'm going to even make it across the room."

"Yes, I'm sure. We'll give you cover. Go!"

As Skye and Megan moved toward the stairs, the other girl, who had been with the group, ran over to join them. The three of them dodged magical lightning bolts, while gathering together as many of the other kids as they could. The distraction wasn't entirely successful, however, as Irina did manage to snatch a couple of the stragglers. Skye saw that she was no longer lovely, but had clawed hands, eyes that glowed yellow, and a jaw that double hinged in a grotesque mouth with double rows of jagged teeth to make any shark envious.

Skye heard screams, and could hardly bare to imagine what might be happening behind her. After darting this way and that, Skye and her small group managed to reach the stairs. A few of the kids were missing. Skye hoped they'd found a place to hide and weren't already dead.

"Go on. Get up there. Someone will help you." Skye shouted at the kids. "And don't screw around with magic again. Not ever!" she couldn't help adding. The guys and girls didn't need to be told twice. They nodded, then bolted up the stairs. Only Megan hung back. "I didn't know. I should have. I mean, I study this stuff, but—"

"Just go. We'll talk later. I have to help Aidan."

Megan nodded and charged up the stairs.

When Skye turned around, she saw that Irina had managed to put her mark on two of the boys. Their throats were bloody from multiple puncture wounds. Near one of the wounds was a dark symbol, almost like a tattoo. It was Irina's mark and it was different from the one she'd seen on the woman in the parking lot. This mark was jagged, like a star, but with more points. Skye couldn't count how many, and at this point it hardly mattered. What mattered was getting out of this mess alive.

The boys turned toward Skye. She was horrified to see their eyes now glowed yellow, like Irina's. She hadn't just marked them, no; she'd turned them into mindless servants. Skye's heart clenched. Those boys were already dead. Their bodies now belonged to Irina.

With a shout, the boys charged toward Skye. She did a step behind side kick which hit the first demon boy in the chest, sending him stumbling backwards. She then turned to trade blows with the other boy. A bolt of fire came from the landing above, narrowly missing Skye, but burning the first demon boy to cinders. Now she just had the one to worry about.

Skye and the other demon boy continued their battle while Irina's wicked laugh echoed through the building. More fire rained from above, but only grazed her. Unfortunately, the very thing Skye had feared from the beginning now came to pass. Some building materials caught fire, and soon one side of the room was ablaze. Skye had no more time to mess around with the remaining demon boy. She had to get to Aidan. She hoped he wasn't already dead.

Skye and her assailant broke apart. With a gleefully evil smile, the boy came at her again, but another bolt of fire came from above before he reached her. The boy turned to ash almost immediately, and Skye looked up to see her rescuer. Rachael? No, it couldn't be.

Preston's voice jerked her back into action. "Skye! Heads up. I'm throwing down a weapon."

She looked up to see a sword flying through the air. She caught it by the hilt and whipped around in time to see Irina charging toward her. Skye dodged Irina's claws and sent the blade of the sword swinging toward her neck. Irina dodged aside, and the sword hit the edge of her shoulder instead. The demon shrieked as her arm fell to the ground. Seconds later, to Skye's horror, a new arm sprouted from the wound. Skye was back to square one. How in the world would she be able to kill Irina if her limbs kept growing back?

Preston's voice was in her ear once again. "Her head! Take off her head!"

Another blast of fire came from above. Irina's hair caught fire and she was distracted enough that Skye saw her chance. She swung her blade again, and this time Irina's head separated from her body, along with one of her hands which had been entangled in her hair in an attempt to put out the fire. There was an explosion of dust and sparks, and the demon was no more. Beheading certainly worked, and in a spectacular way!

Skye whirled to look for Aidan. She spotted him across the room, fire all around him, as he fought Mortmal the Destroyer. Blood dripped from multiple wounds. His shirt was torn, and he staggered. The demon had transformed into the winged monster Skye had seen chasing them on Coronado Island, only this time without Ben's face and body, thankfully. But now it was the bald man with the dark skin who bore down on Aidan. He'd put up a good fight, but it was only a matter of time. Especially now that the demon had transformed.

As Skye ran to help him, the demon used its wing to send Aidan tumbling to the floor. Skye skidded to a stop, stood over Aidan and raised her sword.

"Are you here to help me or put me out of my misery, darlin'?"

"Get up! Get up!" Skye screamed at him. The demon now hovered, beating its wings and snarling at them.

"You can't beat me. You can never defeat the Destroyer!" the demon bellowed, then swooped down, and Skye swung her sword. It just grazed the monster, and he veered away, only to return a second later. By this time,

Aidan was on his feet. He stood next to Skye as they looked up and tried to ready themselves for the demon's next attack.

"Didn't those fecking Elfae bring more to this picnic than fireworks?"

"I can't believe you're making jokes at a time like this!"

"Who's joking? I'm serious!"

"If the demon doesn't kill us, the fire probably will. We've got to finish this. Now!"

"We'll get out of this alive, darlin'. I'm sure if it."

There was no more time for banter. The demon folded its wings and dove toward them from the top of the ceiling of the two-story building. Skye was knocked to the ground, and her sword went clattering across the floor. Aidan was thrown to the side also, and Mortmal was on top of him in a flash.

"No!" Skye screamed. She scrambled to get her sword, as the flames came closer. She lurched to her feet and ran toward the demon. She plunged her sword into his back, then leapt away to avoid his furiously flapping wings. The demon writhed and screamed in pain. In a flash, Aidan leapt to his feet and darted in. He pulled her sword free, then positioned himself for a final swing of the sword to the demon's neck. Before he had a chance though, the demon fell to his knees and toppled over onto the floor.

"Is it dead?" Skye shouted over the sound of the fire.

"No. Get back!" Aidan yelled, as something dark and fluttering departed the demon's battered and burned body. It flew directly to Aidan and slammed into his chest. He dropped the sword and nearly fell to his knees.

"No!" Skye screamed again. The demon had just jumped into Aidan's body! She inched closer, then scooped up the fallen sword.

With a cry, Aidan doubled over. His eyes went from black to glowing yellow and back again. Back and forth, back and forth. His face contorted. One minute it was the face of a handsome Irishman, gone Blood-Hunter, with black eyes and fangs. The next his eyes were yellow and his jaw tried to reshape itself into something long and double hinged.

Skye watched in horror. A part of her wanted to kill the beast as it emerged, right now before it completely took hold of Aidan, but she hesitated. Should she kill him? Should she wait and give Aidan a chance? And even if she killed Aidan, would the demon only move on to inhabit *her* body?

"Preston! What do I do?"

His words came to her through the communication device and his voice sounded calm and steady. "Give him a chance."

"A chance for *what*?"

"Just hold your position. He has a plan, Skye. Let him see it through."

"A plan! This is a plan? To let the demon have him?"

Aidan was on the ground, twitching and convulsing. If he became the newest body for the Destroyer, she would have to kill him while he lay there. That was a fact. Skye steeled herself to make the killing blow, and gripped the sword hilt tighter. She reminded herself he wouldn't be Aidan anymore if the demon took over. He'd already be dead. Like Ben. Like Alan Sherwood and his son. Like the giant man with the black skin who now lay on the floor of the warehouse.

The fire continued to rage around them while Skye waited. Either for Preston's signal or some sort of proof that Aidan was gone, and in his place was Mortmal the Destroyer. She wondered if any of them would make it out of the building alive. She hoped most of the kids had gotten out at least, and that their memories were not wiped. They needed to remember this so they wouldn't play games with magic ever again.

Skye edged closer to Aidan as the flames came nearer. The heat made standing there almost unbearable. She had to get out soon. Aidan lay still. His face no longer contorted and his eyes weren't shifting from yellow to black, but were now his natural green. As Skye watched, Aidan's fangs receded. He just looked like Aidan. But was it truly Aidan? He struggled to sit up and Skye took a step back. No way was she going to help him without knowing for certain he wasn't the demon wearing a Blood-Hunter disguise. Her body tensed, ready for a fight. Her sword raised, ready to shed more blood.

He looked straight at her and gave her a crooked smile. "Are you going to just stand there, or are you going to congratulate me on my brilliant plan?"

Skye held her pose and glared down at him, still ready, just in case, and said nothing.

"Oh, I see." He staggered to his feet. "You think I'm the demon. Well, I'm not. It's me. Aidan the Blood-Hunter. Who the feck else would think to let a demon into their head?"

"Far too many human idiots, in my opinion." Skye didn't lower the sword.

"Oh, for Pete's sake! We have to get out of here, Skye. Come on!"

Skye still hesitated. "Preston? What am I looking at here?"

"I believe you're looking at Aidan. Now get out of the building and meet us at the corner of Elm and Pine just northeast of here. The shield is down. Go!"

Aidan grabbed Skye's arm and the two of them dodged flames as they headed for the way out. Debris fell from above as the upper landing gave way, and Skye narrowly missed being separated from Aidan when a beam collapsed. He pulled her to safety at the last second, then they burst through the door, out into the night air.

Aidan dragged her along until they reached the corner where Preston had told them to meet. Skye sucked in great gasping breaths of clean air as Preston came to join them.

"Skye? Are you all right?" he asked.

"Sure. Just let me enjoy breathing for a moment." She pulled in one more breath, then looked over at Aidan. "So, what was that all about back there?"

Preston answered instead. "Aidan figured the demon might jump bodies again, so he wanted to be in closest proximity. He suspected that, since he's already got a demon, of sorts, in his makeup, it wouldn't take too kindly to an intruder."

"And, I was right." Aidan smiled, though it was a tired smile. The bleeding from his wounds had stopped, but he still looked battered and bruised. Sirens wailed in the distance.

Skye shook her head in amazement. "So, you gambled that what was inside you would be stronger than the demon coming in."

Aidan nodded. "Yes."

Skye could hardly believe he would take such a risk. "You're crazy! What if your bad-ass inner monster would've lost its battle? Why would you risk such a thing?"

"I don't want this world to fall into chaos and be overrun with demons any more than you do. I have people here I care about too. Just like you."

"Tara."

"Yes, Tara."

Out of the corner of her eye, Skye saw someone standing near Preston's car. She turned, and to her astonishment, saw Rachael.

"I thought I saw you but…What are you doing here?" Skye asked as Rachael came over and joined the three of them.

She grinned. "I was the one watching your back with the fire bolts."

"You zapped the demon boy."

"And Irina. Preston is going to use me on an as-needed basis. He's already talked to my parents about it."

Skye looked at Preston. When he nodded, she turned back to Rachael. "This is amazing! "Why didn't you tell me you were going to be in on this?"

"Because you would've told me not to and you would have worried and you already had enough to worry about."

"Enough of this chit chat," Aidan grumbled. "The demons are dead. Problems solved. Time to go. It's been a long night."

Preston nodded. "You sure you're okay? No traces of the demon remain? It's truly gone?"

Aidan nodded.

"Perhaps we should run some tests and—"

"No," Aidan snapped. "I'm fine."

Preston studied him for a moment. "Then you're free to go."

Aidan lifted an eyebrow. "Oh, gee thanks. But I wasn't asking permission." He took out the communication device in his ear and handed it to Preston. "And, our association is now officially over."

"Planning to leave town?" Preston asked.

"Maybe. Maybe not." Aidan turned and walked away.

Skye watched him go. She wanted to say something. Call him back. But what was there to say, really? He had a life before he came into hers, and she had a new life to lead. Apparently without him in it. She should be glad. All they did was argue.

Preston broke the silence. "We'd best be going. The fire department will be here any minute." And indeed, the sirens were much closer now.

They headed for their cars, but Skye noticed she still had the sword. "Here, I suppose you want this back," she said to Preston, and held the weapon out to him.

Preston shook his head. "You keep it. Consider it a gift for successfully vanquishing your first demon." He got into his car and drove off.

Skye and Rachael continued on the short distance to Skye's car. Rachael swayed a bit, and Skye grabbed her friend's arm. "Are you alright?"

"Yeah, I'm just a bit drained from using my fire talent. I'll be okay."

They reached the car with no mishaps. Rachael didn't say much, just looked out the window for a bit, then closed her eyes.

Skye replayed the events of the last few days over and over in her mind. There was a lot to think about. Most of all, she thought of Aidan; his handsome face, his Irish brogue, his insistence on wearing nothing but solid black all the time. She felt a stab of pain in her heart. But there could never be anything between them anyway. He had Tara. He was a Blood-Hunter. He annoyed the crap out of her. She would miss him.

CHAPTER TWENTY-FOUR

THE SUMMER WORE ON. THERE WERE NO MORE near disasters to avert. Apart from the occasional staking, there really wasn't much for Skye to do but hang out with her friends, shop, go to the movies, visit her parents and get a suntan at the beach. All this should've made her happy. So why was she miserable? Also, bored. If someone had told her two months ago, she'd be tired of having free time to shop and sunbathe until school started, she would've laughed in their face. Unfortunately, it was true. Still, she needed to make an effort to show some enthusiasm.

"Your birthday party last night was fun," Skye said.

Rachael grinned. "I'm glad my parents went for the barbeque idea. It was good to see so many high school friends again. Even Todd was there."

Skye rolled her eyes. "Ugh. I'm *so not* interested in Todd. Just drop it!"

Rachael laughed and changed the subject. "We start college next week."

Skye nodded. "I know. And I'm excited, but a little scared."

"Why? We've toured the campus. Our classes are all set up. We know where to park and the quickest routes to and from our classes. There's nothing to worry about."

"Still, it will all be different when there are thousands of people all over the place."

Rachael shook her head. "The girl who hunts down demons and Blood-Hunters, is afraid of college classes and crowds. Who'd have thought?"

"Ha, ha, very funny. It's not that, exactly, it's—"

Skye's phone sang and she snatched it from the pocket of her jeans. "It's Preston!"

"You sound happy about it. That's a first," Rachael teased.

Skye rolled her eyes and answered her phone. "Hello!"

"Hello, Skye. Have you recovered from Rachael's birthday party last night?"

Skye laughed. "You know neither of us drinks, so it's not like there's anything to recover from. What's up?"

"Some Blood-Hunters have moved into a house in your neighborhood. Coincidentally some young women have gone missing from the area since this group took up residence. I'd like you to go check it out."

"In my neighborhood? Huh! Well, that offends me! Sure. I'd be happy to check it out."

"Also, remember when you requested, a while back, that you'd prefer not have to fight alone?"

Skye frowned. "Well, yes but—"

"I have given it some thought and—"

"Wait, Preston. I've changed my mind. Sort of. I don't think I really need anyone to help me out. At least not now. Not unless something really bad comes along, you know?"

"Yes, I do know. That's what I was going to say to you if you'd allow me to continue." He paused.

"Oh. Right. Sure. Okay. Go ahead."

Preston continued. "I have someone in mind to pair you with in the future but until it becomes necessary, I believe you are quite capable of handling things on your own."

Skye smiled. "Well, thanks Preston. Thanks a lot."

"You're welcome. Once it's dark, head on over to the house I mentioned. I have the address for you. There shouldn't be enough of them to warrant any back up, but check it out for yourself and let me know if that information proves to be wrong and I'll send reinforcements."

Skye reached for a pen and some paper then wrote down the address. "Okay, got it. I'll let you know what I find."

They said their good-byes and disconnected.

"Got some Blood-Hunters to track down?" Rachael asked.

"Yep. Shouldn't be too hard. It doesn't look like there are very many of them. At least according to Preston's intel." Skye headed for her room. "It'll be dark soon, gotta change."

Skye could hardly contain her excitement. Now she had something real to do. Something which required punching, kicking, leaping, spinning, dodging, ducking and slamming her stake into lame-ass Blood-Hunters. If there was one thing she'd learned since Aidan had disappeared from her life, it was that Preston had been right. Most of them didn't adhere to the, just-take-a-little-but-don't-kill-them rule, which Aidan abided by. Instead, they nearly all had death on their minds. Or maybe total lack of self-control. Anyhow, Aidan truly was an exception. Too bad the others from the same bloodline all went crazy and had to be staked. She hoped that didn't mean that showing restraint now, would one day cause Aidan to go crazy too. Nah, it was the drive for power that sent Roark and his Coven over the edge.

It occurred to Skye that there might be others of Aidan's bloodline family elsewhere in the world. Maybe Aidan *did* leave town. Maybe he went to track down his other blood brothers and sisters or even is parents. Who knew how big his family might be, since they all lived for so darn long. But what about Tara? Was she still here? Would she go with him? Skye had no idea where Tara lived, but she knew she wasn't curious enough to track the girl down. It was better, by far, to let it go. Aidan was gone and she was better off. Right. She'd keep telling herself that.

Skye drove to the address Preston had given her. The neighborhood was quiet. There were porch lights on and lights showing behind closed curtains. People were probably watching TV after dinner, or reading or doing whatever they usually did on a warm summer night.

She studied the house, which supposedly contained Blood-Hunters. It too was quiet. And completely dark. Maybe they weren't even there. Skye noticed that compared to the other houses in the neighborhood, this one wasn't as well kept up. The grass was long and there were weeds everywhere. Some bushes by the walkway to the front door looked as though they could use some pruning as well as some water, and even in the darkness Skye could tell the house needed some TLC too.

As she watched, a van pulled into the driveway. The garage door went up, and the vehicle pulled in. Nothing unusual about that, except Skye thought she heard a muffled scream from inside the van, just before the garage door closed. It was time for a closer look.

She snuck between the houses and peered into the windows. She couldn't see much at first, but then lights came on from within the house.

Three girls were being shoved up the stairs. They cowered and huddled together as one of the Blood-Hunters herded them.

Skye could only see three Blood-Hunters, so the information Preston had given her was probably accurate. She circled around to the front of the house, looking for a quiet way in. But when she heard more screaming, Skye figured there was no time for stealth. She simply kicked in the front door, and headed for the stairs.

When she got to the top, she followed the sound of another scream and the thumping sounds of a struggle, followed by the crash of something. Maybe a lamp? She had a stake in one hand, while her other hand was already fisted, ready for a fight.

Skye took in the situation at a glance. One girl was up against a wall with a Blood-Hunter breathing down her neck. Another girl lay on the bed, struggling against the Blood-Hunter that was on top of her, trying to get at her throat. The third girl cringed in a corner as the last Blood-Hunter drew closer. These Blood-Hunters weren't even trying to play nice.

"Hey! Why don't you pick on someone your own size?" Skye shouted. It wasn't the most brilliant thing to say, but it got their attention.

All three Blood-Hunters turned toward her. It should've been easy. There were only three of them after all, right? But that's when the situation took a sudden turn for the worse.

Skye heard movement behind her. More Blood-Hunters? She sidled over a bit, then turned just enough to see the doorway. Immediately her heart sank and fear gripped her. She beat it back down. She could do this. She had to.

At least half dozen Blood-Hunters crowed into the room. That made nine of them all together. Skye hoped there weren't any more in other parts of the house. She maneuvered so her back was to a wall and she faced the lot of them. All had black eyes and visible fangs. There would be no negotiating with these guys. Not that she'd really imagined such a thing would be possible anyway.

Without a word they began to spread out. Each of them kept their eyes focused on her. Skye lost track of the other girls in the room. She was very much afraid they didn't have long to live, and there would be nothing she could do about it. In fact, she would be lucky to survive the night herself.

There were four female Blood-Hunters in the group and all four were dressed in short bright colored skirts, skin-tight spandex tops and high heeled black patent leather boots. Their make-up was dramatic and severe, with thick black eyeliner and dark red lipstick. The male Blood-Hunters wore pressed slacks and button-down shirts with ties no less. Even in this tough situation Skye managed to wonder how this strange crew had come together. The females looked like a cross between disco queens and go-go dancers from the 1960s' the males like savvy businessmen who had just come from a happy hour at their private club. It was bizarre. But this was an occasion for action, not contemplation. In spite of her mounting fear, it was time for Skye to make a move. She felt that strange calm come over her; the one she always felt right before the fight was on.

She whirled and ducked, kicked and punched, staked a couple of them but was seriously out numbered. There was no way she could prevail, and she knew it. She managed to plunge her stake into one more of the Blood-Hunters, before she found herself held fast on either side.

The stake was pried from her grasp. It clattered to the floor and she stood glaring at the remaining four Blood-Hunters who stood in front of her. She felt blood trickle from a cut above her eye. Her ribs ached and her split lip hurt a lot, but she knew all would heal quickly. Not that it mattered much at this point. She'd probably be dead very soon. Fear coursed through her like a tsunami. It threatened to overwhelm her and her knees almost gave way, but she refused to give them the satisfaction of seeing her cower.

One of the Blood-Hunters came forward. He might've been handsome once, but not anymore. That is, unless you like straggly, white blond hair, dark circles under the eyes, and a physique so thin he looked emaciated.

"An Assassin." He tipped his head and studied her. His voice was deeper than she'd expected. "Maybe you can be of some use to us. Maybe your Handler would like to negotiate for your release." He smiled at her and she saw that his teeth were stained with blood.

A voice came from behind her. "Negotiate this."

An arrow came zinging through the air and imbedded in the blond Blood-Hunter's chest. He gave one startled glance at the doorway behind Skye, then disintegrated into dust and vapor. The other Blood-Hunters turned in surprise, and it was all the distraction Skye needed. She broke free from the two who were holding her and scooped her stake from the floor. She didn't have time to thank the person who had intervened on her behalf. She was too busy staking the two Blood-Hunters that were closest to her.

Skye turned to meet her next attacker and was stunned to see, instead, Aidan. The remaining three Blood-Hunters were still in the process of vaporizing. They were all gone. He'd killed the last three.

Skye stared at him in surprise. When she'd heard his voice, she'd been certain her ears had been playing tricks on her. But now, here he was, standing before her.

He looked her way, gave her a crooked smile, then turned to the girls cowering in the corner. "Anybody need any medical attention?"

They all shook their heads.

"Well then, you're free to go. Do you need a ride somewhere?"

Again, they shook their heads. They inched their way around the room, bodies pressed to the wall, giving Aidan a wide birth.

"What's wrong with them?" Aidan asked, once the girls slipped out of the room and clattered down the stairs.

"Your face." Skye pointed. "It's all fangy and your eyes are still black."

"Oh! Oops!" Aidan chuckled.

His face adjusted itself and he looked, once again, like a regular guy. But Skye knew there was nothing regular about him, and her heart gave a little flutter.

He bent to pick up the cross-bow he'd used earlier. "I saw you'd gotten yourself into some trouble. Thought I'd lend a hand."

"Uh, thanks," Skye stammered. "But…Why are you here?"

He looked surprised. "Would you rather I wasn't?"

"Well, no, but—"

"Don't worry, darlin'. I've had some dealings with their leader in the past. You know, the greasy one that was doing the talking? I owed him a bit of payback."

Skye smiled. She hadn't seen him in a while, but it was surprisingly easy to fall right back into the banter. "There seem to be very few people you get along with."

He nodded. "That's true. Come on. I'll buy you a drink…a lemonade," he amended, when Skye started to correct him. "I remember. No alcohol. Come on. Let's go." He turned and walked out of the room.

Skye hung back for just a moment. Could this really be happening? Was he back? Had he ever been gone? Was this a onetime thing, or—

"Are you coming?" Aidan shouted from somewhere in the house.

Skye took a breath, then headed toward the sound of his voice.

Once outside, Skye walked to her car. His was parked just behind hers. "Where are we going?" she asked.

"To a little Italian restraint near the Convention Center."

Skye hesitated only a moment before giving him a nod and climbing into her car.

She followed him to the restaurant, and once there, walked by his side through the parking lot to the entrance of the building. Neither of them spoke, though Skye was dying to ask him about a million questions.

The smells of herbs and spices made Skye's stomach growl. She hadn't realized she was hungry. Maybe it was the near-death experience. Aidan didn't wait to be seated, but cut through the dining room toward a small alcove in the back of the room. Skye followed, but was brought up short when she saw there was another person at the table. It was Tara!

She grabbed Aidan's sleeve. "You know, I've changed my mind. I think I'll just go. I have to get up early tomorrow and I think it would be better if—"

"No, no, no. I heard your stomach growl back there. You're going to eat, and I'm going to buy your meal. That's it. End of discussion. Now come on." He threw his arm around her shoulders and ushered her over to the table. People stared at them as they walked by; two people, dressed entirely in black, looking disheveled, to say the very least.

Tara's face lit up when she saw Skye. "Skye! Oh, my gosh, this is a surprise. It's nice to see you." She made room in the semi-circular booth. "Come sit by me. How are you?"

Skye gave Aidan a questioning look, but all he did was gesture for her to sit. She slid into the booth and Aidan slid in after her.

"Ah, hi, Tara. Um, I'm fine." Skye couldn't have felt more awkward at that moment. The one thing she'd never wanted to be was a fifth wheel. Now she was one.

"Are you hungry?" Tara asked.

"Indeed, she is," Aidan replied.

Tara handed Skye a menu. "Here, I recommend the chicken piccata or the fettuccini. Both are delicious."

"Thanks." Skye took the menu and hid behind it. She tried to decide what to order while listening to Tara and Aidan talk.

"You're late," Tara began, but she didn't sound angry. "Everything okay?"

"Yeah, I just had to take care of a little something, and then Skye was in the middle of getting herself killed, so I thought I'd help out."

Skye lowered the menu and glared at Aidan.

"Oh, no, what happened? Are you sure you're all right, Skye?" Tara asked.

In that moment, Skye realized her opinion of Tara had changed considerably since first encountering her a few weeks ago. Then, Tara had seemed haughty. Now Skye realized she was genuinely friendly. Maybe she had just been protective of Aidan that night.

"Yes. Of course. I'm fine." Skye rubbed the spot on her forehead where she'd been bleeding earlier. No blood. She ran her tongue over her lip. It had also healed. Her ribs still felt a little tender, but they weren't half as sore as they'd been just a few minutes ago.

The waiter came by and took their food and drink orders. Skye tried to make conversation and stick to safe subjects, but it felt stilted and awkward to her. She didn't know how much Tara knew about her, so she didn't want to say too much when she answered Tara's questions. Also, even though she liked Tara well enough, the girl was Aidan's girlfriend, and she just couldn't shake the feeling that she'd rather be anywhere but here in this restaurant, having dinner with someone she was attracted to, and that person's girlfriend. She ran all the old arguments through her head. *He's a Blood-Hunter. Nothing lasting could ever happen between us. He's not interested in me anyway. I can't trust him. And, he annoys me. He really, really annoys me.*

The food came, and Skye had the excuse of devouring her meal as a reason to not talk anymore. Once they were done eating, she planned on leaving just as soon as she could without appearing totally rude.

Finally, the dinner ended, and Skye made her excuses. "I don't mean to be impolite, but I really need to be going now. Thanks for the dinner. Could one of you move so I can get out?"

"I think Aidan has something to tell you first," Tara replied.

Skye looked over at Aidan. "What?"

He shrugged.

"Go on, Aidan," Tara urged.

Skye looked from Tara, back to Aidan again. "What's going on? What does she want you to tell me?"

Aidan shook his head. "It's not a good time."

"Then, when is?" Tara asked.

Skye's eyes darted back and forth between the two of them. What was going on here?

Tara rolled her eyes at him, then turned to Skye. "We haven't been properly introduced. I'm Tara Donovan. I'm Aidan's great-granddaughter."

CHAPTER TWENTY-FIVE

S KYE JUST STARED AT HER FOR A MOMENT. FLAB-
bergasted. "You're not his *girlfriend*?"

Tara grinned and shook her head. "Nope."

"So, you gave him blood when he was injured because…"

"Because he's my great-granddad. I've known what he is, most all my life. It doesn't matter. He's always been good to me and I love him."

Skye looked over at Aidan, still bewildered by this new information. It had the potential to change everything if only—

He nodded. "It's all true. I have no other living relations."

"Well, why keep this a secret? Why wouldn't you want me to know?" Skye asked.

He tilted his head and studied her. "I'm not in the habit of including others in my personal life. I never have before. Except for Tara. I'm a loner. Have been for a very long time now."

"He thinks being involved with others will make him vulnerable," Tara whispered.

Aidan frowned. "I heard that. And it *will* make me vulnerable. Look what happened to you, Tara. If Roark hadn't known how much I care about you, he never would've kidnapped you to assure my cooperation."

"Well, it backfired on him anyway," Tara reminded him.

"But you almost wound up dead," he countered. "It was a very near thing. I almost lost you."

Skye settled back in her seat, no longer so eager to leave the restaurant. "Maybe you think you're protecting yourself and others from bad stuff, but you're also keeping yourself from the good stuff. Like having friends."

Aidan rolled his eyes at her. "Listen to you, darlin'. Are you saying we should be friends? You're an Assassin. You'd just as soon stake me as look at me, and that's as it should be. Easy as drawing breath."

Skye frowned. "Why? You're different from other Blood-Hunters. Even Preston admits there are a small percentage of Blood-Hunters who aren't pure, ruthless killers. Just because I'd gladly stake the ninety-five percent of them, doesn't mean I'm eager to stake you."

He lifted his eyebrows. "You're not?"

"Well, I mean, if I caught you bleeding someone dry, then sure. I'd stake you in a heartbeat, but—"

"You were ready to condemn me over that body in the parking lot."

"Yes, but—"

"You'll never be able to trust me, Skye. Not really. I might go crazy, all red-eyed, and try to release another demon from a box, or—"

"Oh, shut up. I never thought—"

"Oh, yes you did."

Skye studied him. "You said Tara is your only family, but she's human. I'd know it if she wasn't, so how does that work, exactly?"

Tara glanced at Aidan. "It's more your story than mine. Go ahead and tell it."

Aidan shifted in his seat. "I was an only child. My parents died long ago; one due to an altercation with a Shape-Shifter and the other fell victim to a man with an ax. As for me, I was married once, long ago, to a human woman. My wife, Abby, died giving birth to our son; half Blood-Hunter, half human. His name was Colin. Colin married a human woman and they had two children, Michael and Maureen. Maureen died young of something probably perfectly curable these days, but Michael, my grandson, grew up and got married; also, to a human." Here Aidan stopped and smiled at Tara. "And then my beautiful great-granddaughter was born."

"And so that's why I appear as human to you, Skye, because for all intents and purposes I am," Tara added, then shrugged. "I'm one-eighth Blood-Hunter. Nothing that would come up on your radar. My mother got cancer. She died five years ago. My father died in a boating accident about a year later."

Skye was stunned. "I'm so sorry," she whispered.

"No, it's all right, really. I don't mind talking about it now. I was twenty when my mom died, and twenty-one when my dad passed away; no longer a child. Aidan has been my rock. I don't know what I'd have done without him. He gave me a place to stay and eventually, when I was ready to be completely on my own, he helped me with that too."

"I see." Skye looked over at Aidan again. She was utterly intrigued by the conversation. "Sorry for being such a dummy about this, but...um... how do Blood-Hunters and humans manage to have children together? I thought—"

He smiled. "You thought we only could have children with other Blood-Hunters."

"Yeah."

"A human/Blood-Hunter mix seldom produces a child, but it *is* possible"

"So those kids never have a tendency to get...bitey?"

"No. Not in the least. Apparently, the human genetics always dominate the Blood-Hunter DNA. I've never heard otherwise."

Skye was so involved with the conversation she was startled to see Preston appear at their table.

He smiled. "Ah, good you *are* here. Good to know my intelligence sources are accurate."

"They're not always correct. I nearly got my ass kicked by Blood-Hunters tonight." Skye grumbled.

Preston ignored her comment and looked toward the front of the room. "Rachael and Megan should be along any minute now."

Skye frowned in confusion. "Rachael and Megan?"

"Would you like to sit down?" Tara asked. "This booth is pretty big. We can squeeze in."

Skye saw Rachael enter the restaurant, followed by Megan.

"Hi Skye!" Megan gave her an enthusiastic grin once the two girls had reached the table.

Skye gave Megan a weak smile in return as everyone slid into the booth.

Skye frowned. "So, what's this all about?" She looked from Preston to Aidan.

Aidan gave Preston a nod. "This is your show. Start talking before your Assassin blows a gasket."

"All right, well, what you see here, Skye, is our new team. Minus Tara, that is. She's here because she already knows what's going on anyway, and it would be pointless to exclude her."

Skye glanced around at everyone. "New team?"

Rachael leaned in. "You already know I'm in with the Bureau on an as needed basis, right?"

"Right." Skye nodded. "But what about—?"

Preston interrupted. "Megan has given up her position at the library's rare books department. She will work for the Bureau part time, as a researcher until she's finished with her graduate degree, at which time she will be with us full time. She will be working with you and me exclusively, as will Rachael."

"Ah, okay." Skye struggled to process this new information. "But I thought the way this worked was just Handlers and Assassins."

"Not at all," Preston replied. "It takes a fairly extensive network to keep the Bureau functioning. We add new people all the time, depending on where there is a need, and who is available."

Skye's eyes swung to Aidan. "And how does Aidan fit into this?"

He gave her a crooked smile. "I'm going to be your new partner. As needed, of course."

Skye's eyebrows shot up. "Really!" She looked at Preston. "He's the person you said you had in mind?"

"That's right. You two work well together, in spite of all the bickering." Preston gave Aidan a sidelong look. "And this recent demon business, and Aidan's usefulness, has given me cause to believe working with a Blood-Hunter could be of benefit to the Bureau. Aidan has also assured me, once again, that he is not currently, and will not in the future ever kill anyone simply for blood sport."

Rachael leaned in. "If he does, I'll torch him." But she grinned at Aidan.

He gave her a dour look. "Thanks, Elfae. I appreciate that."

"Oh, no! Not really, right?" Megan asked. She looked truly distressed. "Aidan helped save my life. You wouldn't just—"

"No, no, of course not," Rachael reassured her. "I was only joking."

Preston cleared his throat to get their attention. "So, I want everyone to make sure you have each other's phone numbers, including mine. We must be able to reach each other in case of an emergency."

They spent the next few minutes adding numbers into their phones.

"That's it then." Preston got up and everyone else filed out while Aidan lagged behind to pay for dinner.

Skye waved goodbye to Preston and Megan as they drove away in separate cars, then said goodbye to Rachael, who left moments later.

Tara placed a hand on Skye's arm. "I just want to say something to you, before Aidan gets out here. I'm sorry you didn't know about Aidan and me sooner. I actually *thought* you knew. Not in the very beginning of course, but later. He likes you, you know. Very much. I haven't seen him this way about a woman before. Not ever. I think you like him too. Don't let him slip away. He's the best."

Skye searched for something intelligent to say, but her mind went blank.

Aidan walked up. "What are you two talking about?"

"Oh, nothing much," Tara replied. "Talk to you soon...Great-Granddad." She laughed, then gave him a hug and walked to her car and drove away.

Skye gave Aidan a nervous smile. "So, ah, I guess we'll be seeing more of each other. Again."

"Looks that way."

"Thanks for saving my life. Did Preston tell you where I was tonight?"

"Yeah, he did. But I really *was* looking for a little pay back with those Blood-Hunters. That was the absolute truth. Scout's honor."

"You were a Boy Scout?"

"No, of course not, but it's a good enough pledge."

"Um, well...I guess I should be going." She pointed in the vague direction of her car.

"I'll walk you over there."

They walked to her car in silence. She unlocked the door, but hesitated before getting inside. She looked up at Aidan.

"Aidan, I..." Her words trailed off. She wanted to say something to let him know how she felt, but she really didn't know what to say.

Aidan stepped a bit closer. Skye held her ground as well as his gaze. A moment later his lips were on hers. Skye's pulse raced and her heart pounded. Her mind was in a whirl. Thoughts and sensations collided; his arms sliding up her body to cradle her head, his thumbs brushing against her cheeks, the cinnamon spice scent of his hair or his skin or...what did it matter which? His kiss was bold but somehow gentle and she didn't want it to stop.

He held her close, even after the kiss had ended; her head on his chest, her arms around his waist.

"Where do we go from here?" he whispered.

She pulled away, looked up into his eyes and smiled. "I guess we fight the bad guys and save each other's lives. Whenever it comes to that."

He grinned. "Sounds like a grand plan, darlin'."

"But you'll have to get your own sword."

His eyes widened and he laughed. "I'm sure I can come up with one."

She went up on her tip-toes and planted a quick kiss on his lips, then entwined her fingers with his. "I'll see you soon."

He squeezed her hand. "Just try and get rid of me, Assassin."

She smiled as she pulled away. "I have no intention of getting rid of you."

Skye got into her car and waved to him as she drove away. This had been a night full of surprises, but the best of all had been Aidan's kiss. She realized she was happy with her strange and dangerous life. It suited her after all, though she never would've guessed so at the beginning.

As she drove, her eyes scanned the sidewalk. Humans strolled up and down, laughing, talking, and holding hands, completely unaware of the supernatural element among them. But Skye saw them; the Shape-Shifter couple sitting on a restaurant patio, the Elfae teens crossing the street in front of her at the intersection. She smiled as the light changed and she accelerated. This was her world.

"Bring it on," she whispered, and headed for home.

ELFAEN SWORD

(Marked by Destiny Book 2)

PROLOGUE

ON THE ONE HAND, AN INBORN MAGICAL ABIL-
ity was a plus. On the other hand, being born to kill murderous
monsters was not. He looked down at the mark on his arm,
which had appeared when he'd turned sixteen. Chosen, that's what he was,
by some random gene in his DNA. Now, at nineteen, he'd been at it for
three years. His team was part of a larger organization and he was one of
the best there was when it came to slaying the Dark-Angels and the Dark
Angel-hybrids, called DAX that roamed their world. He loved it and he
hated it. Normal life was out of the question.

He tugged on his long canvas black coat, now slightly faded and
frayed, and lifted his shaggy brown hair from beneath the collar. A few
unruly strands hung in his eyes and he shoved them back then leaned
toward the mirror to examine the almost healed split in his lower lip.
He'd acquired the injury the night before. He checked out the black eye
too. Tri-colored amber, yellow and terra cotta eyes looked back at him.
Were they a little blood-shot? Maybe. He closed his eyes and called his
magic from deep within. He didn't have true healing magic but this he
could do.

When he opened his eyes again and studied his face, not only did his
lip look less puffy, but the bruising around his eye was almost gone and
his eyes were no longer blood-shot. With another gentle surge of power,
he changed the swirl of colors in his eyes to an even golden-brown tone;
something that wouldn't freak out the humans. They knew of the existence of others beside themselves living on this planet but they were always

uneasy around Elementals. He lifted his sword and snugged it into the sheath beneath his coat.

It took him only a minute to get to his motorcycle and be on the road, then just a few minutes more to arrive at Book Master's Bookstore on Main St. The humans in Monument Ridge were oblivious to the fact that the building had a hidden entrance and secret offices above the books and coffee sold below.

He parked the motorcycle at the back of the building, punched in a code and took the stairs in leaps and bounds, then punched in another code on the second keypad at the top of the stairs. Once inside he went down a long hallway, straight to the boss's office. The others on the team were already gathered. He fought best alone, so he didn't normally work with them. Seeing them all crammed into the tiny office meant that something serious must have happened in the last twenty-four hours.

Thomas Westfall, the team leader, otherwise known simply as Westfall, got to his feet.

"We have a situation that will most likely be disastrous if we don't get a handle on it immediately." His eyes scanned each face in the room. "We've discovered an opening, a portal, which leads from our world to, we believe, another one."

There was a universal gasp from those in the office.

"Recon team members from S.U. here in Monument Ridge observed someone come though. This person carried a large satchel and didn't look surprised or disoriented in anyway. He was detained and is at Ravenwood Compound; the satchel confiscated and brought to me. Inside was a sword of uncertain origin. I've given the sword to the research department for study and it seems the sword was not made from any of the various metals from our world."

Westfall handed a folder with photos in it to the closest Slayer United member and murmurs of speculation arose from around the room as each Slayer looked at the pictures and passed them on.

Westfall raised a hand to silence everyone. "We have many concerns and questions. The individual we have in our custody isn't from here and admitted that the portal leads to another world, his world, but so far, he's refused to give us any other information. Did someone knowingly open this portal or is there a veil between worlds that's thinning? And if it is thinning, will it eventually weaken and shatter completely, uniting the two worlds for better or worse? Is someone taking advantage of a dangerous situation and using it for their own purposes? And if so, then to what purpose and how long has this been going on?

"We all know we have some pretty dangerous creatures residing here in our world and who knows what's over there? You all can imagine the potential consequences for both worlds."

The room was silent as Westfall once again surveyed the team gathered before him.

"I know on any given night we have many challenges in front of us, but this must take priority. I have individual projects for each of you, either alone or in pairs. We're going to keep an eye on this portal during the daytime hours in addition to your regular slaying during the evening hours. This meeting is over, but please stay to get your assignments."

Once everyone was gone Westfall sighed and dropped into his chair and raked fingers though his dark hair. When he looked up, his green eyes met the golden-brown ones across the room.

"Well?" he asked.

He shrugged black canvas clad shoulders. "Another day in paradise, brother. Just another day in paradise."

CHAPTER ONE

RACHAEL PERRY AWAKENED TO THE SOUND OF cooing mourning doves and chirping birds. She opened her eyes and for just a moment forgot where she was; but then she remembered. Rachael checked the clock. It was 7AM, much earlier than she usually got up. Even so, she got out of bed, went to the window and brushed aside the curtains to look out at the day, and it was beautiful already.

The sliding glass door of her bedroom here at her aunt and uncle's house in Tucson, Arizona overlooked a patio with a fountain right in the center. As she watched, the timer turned on and the water began to flow. The sound of it only added to the serenity. All around the bricked patio were six-foot stucco walls painted pale yellow and everywhere Rachael looked there were blooming plants giving splashes of color to every part of the enclosure.

It was far too early for her aunt, uncle and cousins to be up but Rachael didn't feel like staying shut away indoors on her first day here. She decided to get dressed and take a walk to the nearby plaza with a grocery store, restaurant, and coffee shop. It was such a lovely day and the walk would only take her about ten minutes each way. While she was at the plaza, she planned to pick up some pastries to bring back for the others; a little thank-you to her aunt and uncle for inviting her to come to Tucson for the week. She was so happy to get out of San Diego for a while. She loved her home, but it was always nice to go away on a vacation. Her two cousins were close to her own age; Liza being a year younger at eighteen and Becca twenty, a year older than Rachael, who hadn't seen any of them for at least four years.

Once she was dressed in her jeans, sneakers, and robin's egg blue t-shirt; she grabbed her backpack purse and slung it onto her back, snatched her phone from the nightstand and headed quietly out into the main part of the house. Once she'd slipped out the door, Rachael started down the dirt path that led to the shopping plaza. Along the way she texted Skye Falco, her friend and roommate back in San Diego.

Rachael and Skye worked for a secret organization called the Bureau of the Extraordinary or B. O. E. for short, while also attending college in San Diego. Rachael's job was part time and completely different from Skye's. While Skye was an Assassin and hunted down troublesome Blood-Hunters, demons and other creatures who preyed upon humans, Rachael was simply employed on an as-needed basis. She usually didn't participate in anything too dangerous, while Skye risked her own life constantly.

As she walked and texted, Rachael stumbled over a rock in the middle of the path and nearly fell. In the process she fumbled her phone, lost her grasp on it, and watched it go tumbling down an embankment. Well, that's what she got for not paying attention to where she was going.

"Great," she muttered, then with caution descended the sandy slope to retrieve her phone.

Once at the bottom, phone safely in hand, Rachael noticed another path leading in the same direction as the one she'd been on. She wondered if maybe this one united with the other further on down the way, saving her the climb back up the sandy slope she'd just come down. With another look at the path she'd originally been on, she made her decision. She'd try this new path for a while and see where it went. If it didn't rejoin the other path after a minute or two then she'd head back to where she now stood and climb up to the original path.

Rachael didn't text anyone this time; she kept her eyes on where she was going. At first the trail led her along a parallel course to the one she'd been on, but then it became less and less distinct until she could hardly make out what was path and what wasn't. She went a few more steps and stopped.

"Well, I guess I have to go back," she muttered and was about to turn around when she spied a large jackrabbit observing her from beneath a bush.

"Look at you," she whispered then slowly maneuvered so she could see the rabbit better but as she moved to her left, she suddenly felt rather queasy. There was a flash of light so blinding, Rachael squeezed her eyes shut and brought her hands up as a shield. When she dared to open her eyes once more, Rachael looked down where the rabbit had been; no rabbit, no bush.

She frowned and lifted her gaze. Everything was different; still desert but clearly not the same desert. The landscape around her cousin's house was lush with desert plants of all sorts from tall saguaros to dense ground-cover filled with colorful flowers as well as various bushes and trees. This desert was barren with white sand all around. As she studied the terrain Rachael saw what looked like a golf course and resort in the distance; or maybe it was a mirage.

"You need to come with us."

Rachael spun around, her heart knocking against her chest. Two girls stood behind her. Where had they come from? Had they been there all along? How had she not noticed them?

They approached her slowly and moved to flank her. "Don't worry, we just want you to answer some questions," said the girl with long reddish-orange hair. She was dressed in much the same way Rachael's friend Skye would be dressed if she were going out in her official capacity as an Assassin for the Bureau; with knives strapped onto her thigh and what looked like a holster for another weapon at her shoulder, peeking out from beneath a light weight jacket. Rachael hazarded a guess that maybe these girls were from a Tucson branch of the organization where she and Skye worked.

"Are you with the B.O.E.?" she asked. "Do you know John Preston? He's a Handler with the Bureau in San Diego."

The girls glanced at each other. "Nope," said the redhead. "Not familiar with Preston or any B.O.E. but if you'll just come with us, I'm sure we can figure all this out."

Rachael frowned. "I don't understand. Who are you then? What's going on?"

"That's what we're going to sort out," said the other girl, a brunette with short hair trimmed in a pixie cut. She had dark eyeliner around her bright blue eyes. She was dressed much like the first girl who had spoken, with a knife strapped on one thigh, a gun to the other. Both girls wore jeans and boots in neutral colors of the desert; beige, tan, and army green.

The redhead lunged and grabbed Rachael's arm. Rachael jerked back but the other girl's grip was too strong for her to break away. The girl was tall too, taller than Rachael and taller than the dark-haired girl. Rachael was now really frightened.

"What are you doing? Stop it! Let go of me!" Rachael shouted as she struggled to free herself once more.

"Okay," the girl with the red hair said, but she didn't let go of Rachael's arm. "Take it easy and calm down. Let's start over. I'm Alina. That's Ariel and we're taking you someplace to answer some questions. That's all. We have no plans to harm you so just cooperate and it'll all be good."

"Questions? About what?" Rachael asked.

"About lots of things," Ariel replied.

Rachael looked the brunette in the eye. "Look, my name is Rachael Perry. I live in San Diego and I'm here visiting my cousins. Why do I have to go someplace and answer questions? I'm here on a vacation!" When neither girl responded Rachael continued. "This is ridiculous. Do I look threatening to you? This has to be a case of mistaken identity or something. There's nothing else to tell you!"

Ariel nodded. "Okay, Rachael, just relax, agree to come with us, and Alina will let go of you."

Rachael frowned at the petite girl in front of her.

Ariel's bright blue eyes looked back at her. "Do we have a deal?"

Rachael took in a breath and tried to calm herself. "My aunt and uncle live right up that hill." She pointed in the direction of the house, then realized there was no housing development or hills either for that matter. Her arm dropped and fear lanced through her. "It was right there," she whispered. "Where did it go? Where could it possibly have gone?" She looked back to Ariel. "Everything is different. How can that be?"

Rachael felt her voice quiver and tears threaten. She had to get a grip. It wasn't like she wasn't used to odd situations. When you live in a world filled with Elfae, Shape-Shifters and Blood-Hunters all keeping their secrets from humans, plus demons, magic and people who want to steal that magic as well as an organization that keeps tabs on all of it, well, she ought to be better prepared for weird things like this. She forced back her panic and tried to get control of herself.

Alina relaxed her hold on Rachael a bit. "Just come with us, okay? We all want to know what's going on and how to fix it. No one's going to hurt you."

"How to fix what?" Rachael asked.

"Just come with us, okay?" Ariel urged.

After a moment Rachael nodded in agreement. What else could she do? She certainly didn't want to use her fire magic on these girls; it would kill them. She also didn't want to reveal to them she was anything other than human until she knew what was going on.

She walked with the girls, one on either side of her, to their vehicle, a battered beige thing that looked like a Jeep Cherokee, and climbed into the front passenger side. Ariel got in back and Alina took the wheel.

They drove for about fifteen minutes and the desert quickly turned to city streets. Rachael frowned in confusion when they pulled into a large parking lot shared by two restaurants Rachael had never heard of, as well as a bookstore with an unfamiliar name; Book Master's Bookstore.

"I thought you said we were going to see your boss. Is he at one of these restaurants?" Rachael asked and realized she was actually pretty hungry. By now she should've been back at her aunt and uncle's house drinking a mocha latte and savoring a gooey cinnamon roll.

"Nope," Ariel answered. "He's in his office. It's above the bookstore. Our offices are up there."

Alina turned and shot her a look. "You shouldn't be telling her all that. We don't even know if—"

"Oh, come on, Alina. She doesn't have any more of an idea what's going on than we do."

"It could all be an act."

"Whoa! Would you please stop talking about me like I'm not even here." Rachael scowled at both of them.

The other two girls fell silent as Alina parked at the back of the building next to a motorcycle. There were a few other cars parked nearby as well.

"Should we blindfold her so she can't see the secret entrance?" Ariel muttered, smirking at Alina.

Alina blew out a breath and rolled her eyes. "Let's just get in there."

There was a PIN pad on the wall and Alina punched in a code. She stood with her body blocking Rachael's view. Not that Rachael cared.

She just wanted to get things over with and get back to her aunt and uncle's house.

A panel in the wall slid open, revealing some stairs. They went up to the top where there was another door and another PIN pad. Again, Alina punched in a code and Rachael heard the door unlock. Alina shoved open the door and the three of them entered; Alina in front, Rachael in the middle and Ariel bringing up the rear. Rachael heard the door close and lock behind them. She wondered if this group, whoever they were, were just paranoid or if there was a legitimate reason for all the security.

They were in a large, well-lit room with multiple desks and computers. There were plenty of books, the reference kind, and a map on the wall. It looked like a map of the city but Rachael only caught a glimpse of things as the other two girls hurried her down a hallway to an office at the end.

The door was open but Alina knocked on the door jam. A man with piercing green eyes and clean-cut dark hair looked up from some paperwork on his desk. He wore a blue shirt but Rachael couldn't see any more of him since he remained seated.

"Someone came through," Alina said, then stepped aside and ushered Rachael into the office. Ariel hung back at the doorway.

"Come in," the man said to Rachael. "Have a seat." He gestured toward the chair in front of his desk.

Rachael sat, perched on the edge, and waited for whatever would come next.

"I'm Thomas Westfall, and you are...?"

"Rachael Perry."

"And where are you from, Rachael Perry?"

"I'm from San Diego and I'm visiting my aunt, uncle and cousins here in Tucson."

Westfall gave her a level gaze. "Tucson?" He said no more and seemed to be waiting for her to speak.

Rachael frowned. "Yes, Tucson, Arizona." She wondered what was wrong with this guy."

"I see," he said. "And how did you happen to come through the portal?"

Rachael's eyes widened. "Portal?" Of all the things she thought he might ask her next she certainly hadn't expected him to say that. What the heck was going on here?

"I don't know anything about a portal. If I'm not in Tucson then where am I?"

Thomas Westfall looked over at Ariel. "What's your assessment?"

"We observed her for several seconds before she knew of our presence and she was clearly surprised and confused after coming through the portal. I believe she's from the other side and had no idea what she'd just stepped through."

He looked over at Alina. "And what do you think?"

Alina sighed. "I was suspicious at first, that it might all be an act, but Ariel's right. I think the girl was just in the wrong place at the wrong time and came through by accident."

Westfall turned back to Rachael. "Well, Ms. Perry, I guess you're off the hook. It seems you've travelled through a portal from…Tucson, Arizona, is it?"

Rachael nodded and he continued.

"From Tucson, Arizona to the city of Monument Ridge in the western part of the Lurra Land Mass."

Rachael sucked in a deep breath and let it out slowly as she tried to wrap her mind around things. "Which is…where?"

"Not anywhere in your world, I'm afraid," he replied. "Lurra is the name of our world. From what we know, our world is similar to yours in certain ways because humans, and others, crossed through a portal a century ago. The portals were then sealed but—"

"But I can get back though, right?"

Thomas Westfall smiled. "I certainly hope so." He turned to Ariel. "Why don't you take Rachael downstairs to the café and get her a coffee or a snack? Alina, stay here, I'd like to talk to you for a minute."

And just like that Rachael's interview was over. Ariel gestured for her to follow, which she did, and the two of them went down the hall to an elevator.

Once at the café Rachael ordered a bowl of vegetable barley soup and a bagel. She was hungry, but that hunger was somewhat eclipsed by her swirling thoughts and the anxiety that went with them.

"Do you want a drink?" the guy behind the counter asked.

"Oh, yes, a large iced tea please."

"And do you have one of our member cards?" he prompted.

Ariel stepped in. "I have one." She handed it to the guy.

"ID please."

She dug in her pocket and handed him that too, then pressed her thumb onto a pad on the counter. He examined the cards, nodded and scanned both of them with a little hand-held device.

Rachael frowned in confusion as they moved to the end of the counter. "You don't have to pay?" she asked Ariel.

"I paid. I also got a discount."

"But I didn't see you give him any money and that wasn't a credit card."

"A what?" Ariel frowned, then shrugged. "I guess things are pretty different where you're from. I gave him the member card for the discount and my ID gave him the money. The thumbprint identified me as the same person who held the card. The system identifies me, checks my bank account to see if I have enough money there, then issues funds accordingly."

"Oh." Rachael nodded but she really didn't understand any of it.

"There's your order." Ariel gestured toward the counter.

Rachael picked up the tray of soup, bagel and tea along with utensils.

"Okay, back to the office," Ariel headed toward the elevator and Rachael followed her into a room where she found Alina and a table to set her tray on.

"We'll be going back out in a few," Alina said to Ariel, then turned to Rachael who had started to eat her soup. "Westfall said we could take you back to the portal and see if it's as easy to go back as it is to come though."

Rachael nodded in acknowledgment. The sooner she finished her small meal, the sooner she'd be home. She stuffed the bagel in her backpack purse and ate the soup rapidly. If she hadn't been so darn hungry, she would've immediately leapt up and shouted, *"Let's go!"*

Ariel dropped into the seat next to Alina just as the door opened. Rachael looked up to see a handsome guy with shaggy dark hair and golden-brown eyes and a closely cropped beard and moustache. He was dressed in black jeans, black combat boots and a dark, well-worn canvas coat, but it was what was in his hand that really grabbed her attention and she stopped eating.

"Where's Westfall?" he asked.

"He's not in his office?" Alina asked. "I just saw him there."

The stranger shook his head. He lifted eyebrows toward Ariel.

She shrugged. "Haven't seen him. What's going on?"

"I gotta give him this sword. He wanted to see it after it had been examined by Kirk and the others." He eyes swung to Rachael. "Who's this?"

Rachael tore her eyes from the sword. "I'm Rachael."

"She came here by accident," Ariel added. "She's from the other side of the portal."

Rachael couldn't stop her eyes from darting back to the sword however. Could it be? Could it possibly be? It was an ancient Elfaen sword, one of only four ever made, Rachael was sure of it. But how in the world did it get here, of all places?

CHAPTER TWO

THE GUY MUST'VE CAUGHT HER LOOKING AT IT because he held up the sword. "This came from your side of the portal. Do you know anything about it?"

Rachael shook her head and then forced her eyes back onto her meal.

"Are you sure?" he asked. "You seemed pretty focused on it a second ago. You could hardly take your eyes off it."

She took a sip of her tea. "It's just an impressive sword, that's all."

Alina's eyes narrowed. "If you know something, tell us."

"No, really, I don't." Rachael looked from Ariel to Alina to the guy.

"Yeah…I think you do." The guy stalked over to her and laid the sword on the table right in front of her.

All three sets of eyes were now fixed on Rachael. The tension broke when someone else came into the small room. He had close-cropped blond hair, brown eyes and a colorful Hawaiian shirt.

"Hey guys, just a reminder, tonight's—" His eyes fell on Rachael. "Oops, sorry, didn't know you had someone in here. I'll just—"

"It's okay Kirk, we remember," Ariel said. "We'll be by to pick up the stakes."

The blond guy nodded and ducked out the door.

Stakes? Rachael wondered, or did she mean steaks?

"So, what's going on tonight that you need to stop and pick up steaks to grill?" It was a stupid, random question but she'd try anything to change the subject.

"Not steaks like s-t-e-a-k-s," Ariel replied. "Stakes spelled s-t-a-k-e-s."

"Ariel!" Alina snapped. "What's wrong with you? She doesn't need to know about everything that's going on over here. She's going back to her world and—"

"I don't see how it's going to hurt for her to know what we're dealing with and how seriously it could affect her world, as well as ours, if we don't get that portal closed!" Ariel snapped right back. "If she knows what's going on then maybe she'll be more willing to talk if she does know something about the sword or anything else that can help us."

Alina seemed to resign herself to the situation. She let out a huge sigh. "Relax, Tristan. Have a seat and put your feet up. You know how Ariel is once she sets her mind to something."

Ariel turned back to Rachael. "If you do know something about that sword then you need to tell us. It could be very important. Both our worlds could be at risk if we don't get that portal closed."

Rachael's eyes widened. "You can't open and close it when you want to?"

Ariel shook her head. "No. So far, it's just been open. Anyone or anything could come through and we can't keep an eye on it twenty-four-seven; at least not indefinitely. So, Slayer United is the name of the organization we work for. Alina, Tristan and I are three of the Slayers who go out at night to hunt down various dangerous creatures that threaten the lives of all of us. Creatures that could end up in your world if we don't figure out what's going on and get the portal closed for good. So, like I said, if you know anything at all that could help us, like about that sword, then it's really important that you tell us. Now."

Rachael frowned. If she set aside the issue of the portal for a moment this world sounded a bit like her own, prompting her to ask, "What kind of creatures are you talking about?"

Alina frowned. "Okay, enough chit-chat. Do you know something about the sword or not?"

Ariel sighed. "Let me finish explaining things, Alina."

"You're wasting time," Tristan drawled. "Speed it up, Ariel."

She turned to Rachael. "Like Dark-Angels and Dark Angel-human hybrids. We call the hybrids, the DAX; short for Dark Angel Experiment."

"Ok...," Rachael said. "What are DAX? I mean, how are they...made?"

Ariel drew a breath and continued. "Dark Angel-human hybrids are creatures that used to be human but they were, through being bitten and then managing to survive, turned into a hybrid. They live off the blood of humans and sometimes animals. They're completely savage and kill without a second thought. It's amazing anyone survives an attack but there are surprisingly a lot of hybrids roaming around the city."

"What do they look like? The Dark-Angels and the Hybrids?"

"DAX have white skin, bald heads, clawed hands and sharp teeth," Ariel said. The Dark-Angels are usually about six feet tall, black skinned, wings on their backs, clawed hands and sharp teeth."

Rachael wasn't as freaked out about it as a regular human might have been. Being Elfae and working at the Bureau and living in the world she did, gave her an advantage over a regular human with no knowledge of magic, monsters and mayhem. These people had no way of knowing it, but their world sounded more like hers than they might imagine.

"So," Tristan said, "about the sword…"

"Actually," Rachael said after a moment of silence. "You might be surprised to know that my world isn't so different from yours. We have our share of demons and there are also three races who are not human but who live alongside the humans. Some of them blend in just great and go about their business. Others…not so much. The human population knows nothing about them."

"Then how do you know about them if they're living in secret?" Alina asked.

"I work for the Bureau of the Extraordinary or B.O.E. for short," Rachael replied.

Ariel nodded. "Oh yeah, you said something about that when we first saw you in the desert. I wondered what you were talking about."

Rachael nodded. "From what you just told me about your Slayer United it seems to be similar to the Bureau. The B.O.E has Assassins that are probably a lot like your Slayers, and there's also a branch that studies things, like each of the races, and keeps track of certain individuals if they're particularly dangerous. Do the humans here know about the DAX and the Dark-Angels?"

"Yes," Ariel answered. "That's why most of them don't go out at night much unless they have to. Businesses tend to close at dusk around here because of it. People don't want to risk getting turned into a monster."

"So, the DAX and Dark-Angels are only out at night?" Rachael asked.

Alina and Ariel both nodded.

"So, back to the sword." Tristan asked. "Why would someone come over to our side and bring a sword? Is there anything special about it?"

"No," Rachael lied. "It's just a sword."

"And that's why your eyes about fell out of your head a couple of minutes ago when you saw me come in with it." Tristan drawled. "You're lying."

"No really—" Rachael began, but Alina cut her off.

"No, he's right. There's something you're not telling us about that sword. You're not going home until you tell us. You know that, right?"

Rachael sighed. What could it hurt, really, to tell them about the sword? She didn't have to tell them she wasn't human. After all, her knowledge of the sword could be strictly because she worked for the Bureau.

She looked over at Alina. "Well, I don't know why someone would bring it over here but I'm pretty sure it's an Elfaen sword. Elfae are one of the groups of non-human people in my world. If it is Elfaen then it's ancient. According to the B.O.E's records there were only four of them made and it's been decades since anyone saw one."

"So, they're valuable," Tristan said.

"Yes."

"How can you know for sure if it's an Elfaen sword?" Alina asked.

"Um…well…it has to be tested with Elfaen fire," she murmured.

Before anyone had the chance to question her further, the door opened and Thomas Westfall came into the room.

"Tristan, there you are. I heard you were looking for me."

"Yeah, you said you wanted to see the sword again." Tristan handed it over to Westfall. "Rachael here says it's an ancient Elfaen sword. They're one of the races who live alongside the humans in her world."

Alina spoke up. "And, apparently she works for an organization similar to ours."

Westfall gave her an intent gaze. "Really?"

Rachael nodded. "Yes, the Bureau of the Extraordinary; the B.O.E for short. And if I'm right, that sword is one of only four ever made and there's no record of anyone seeing those swords for decades. We were starting to think they were lost or destroyed somehow and gone for good." She glanced at Alina. "Sorry I was so evasive at first but I didn't want to tell you about it probably for the same reason you didn't want me to know details about your world and the Dark-Angels and all that."

Alina nodded. "Because it didn't seem relevant or necessary since you were going back to your world and all."

"Right."

Westfall studied Rachael. "Are you certain this is one of the four?"

She shrugged. "It would have to be tested with Elfaen fire to be sure, but I'd like to take it back home with me to give to the Bureau."

"I wonder if the prisoner knew what he had," Tristan mused.

"Regardless, the sword belongs in my world, not here. He stole it, it should be returned to the Elfaen people.

After several seconds Westfall turned to Tristan. "Take her back to the portal and send her through. We've detained her long enough. We have a problem and we need to get back to solving it. Enough of the sword business." He handed the sword to Tristan. "Elfaen or not, it's a sword. You might as well go ahead and use it."

Rachael scowled at Westfall. "Hey, wait a minute! I just said the sword should be returned to—"

Tristan took hold of the sword. "You ready?"

Rachael gasped in frustration. "That's not fair. That sword doesn't belong to you!"

Tristan gazed at her with lifted eyebrows. "You done? Come on. Let's go."

With a huff Rachael abandoned her food and drink and followed Tristan out the door and down the hallway.

He shoved the sword into a sheath strapped to his back. "You okay riding a motorcycle?"

"Yeah, I guess so," she grumbled. "Do you have an extra helmet?" she added as they banged out the second of the security doors.

"Yep." He reached inside one of the large saddlebags attached to the bike. "Here ya go." He tossed it to her and she hurriedly put it on.

He got on and started the engine. Rachael was glad to see there was a second seat as well as a backrest. At least she wouldn't fall off...assuming he was a safe enough driver and they didn't get into an accident.

Tristan maneuvered through the parking lot and Rachael squeezed with her legs and grabbed onto his coat just in case he shot into traffic like a crazy person. Luckily, he didn't.

When they arrived at the spot in the desert where she'd come through the portal, Rachael was almost sorry to have to get off the bike. The ride had been exhilarating, even though she'd been a little scared at first, and it had taken a bit of the edge off her anger at Westfall not giving the sword to her.

She took off the helmet while Tristan began to talk to two people Rachael supposed were other Slayers from their organization. One was a tall burly guy with long auburn hair worn in a braid, and the other a blonde girl with shoulder-length hair and fringy bangs.

Tristan turned to her. "This is Stefan and Amy. They've been keeping watch of the portal."

Rachael nodded at each of them and said a polite hello, but she was anxious to be on her way back home, even without the sword. She saw the shimmer to Amy's left and realized it was the portal. How had she not noticed a shimmer like that before when she'd been looking at the jackrabbit? Duh, probably because she'd been looking at the jackrabbit.

Tristan gestured toward the shimmer. "Happy trails."

Rachael nodded. "Yeah. Thanks, but that sword should've been—"

"Just go," Tristan said with a sigh.

"Fine. Good luck with everything." Rachael gave a nod to the three Slayers and walked toward the shimmer. She hoped it would be as easy to go back as it had been to come through, although she wasn't looking forward to that queasy feeling or being blinded by that brilliant light again.

As she got closer, Rachael thought she could see through the opening into her own world. The desert looked as she remembered it alongside the path near her aunt and uncle's house. And there was the bush where she'd spied the rabbit.

And then the shimmer in the air flickered and the scene before her vanished. Rachael's steps slowed and she came to a stop. She could hardly believe it. The portal had closed.

CHAPTER THREE

RACHAEL WHIRLED TO LOOKED AT TRISTAN AND the others. "It's gone! The portal closed."

They all looked as stunned as she was.

Tristan took out his phone and judging from what she could hear, Rachael realized he'd called Thomas Westfall.

"Tom, the portal closed. I don't know. Right in front of us. Yes! No. She's still on this side." Tristan was silent for several seconds then nodded his head. "Gotcha." He shoved his phone back in his pocket. "Catch you two later," he said to Amy and Stefan. "Rachael, come with me." He turned toward the motorcycle and Rachael ran to catch up.

"Where are we going?"

"We're going back to the office."

"And how am I going to get home?"

"Just put on the helmet. We need to get back before the sun sets."

Rachael shoved the helmet onto her head and worked at fastening the strap under her chin. "Sunset? But its barely afternoon. I've only been here a couple of hours."

Tristan looked at her and then helped her with the strap on the helmet when her fingers fumbled for the second time. "It's not early afternoon, it's almost 6pm."

"What? How can that be?" Rachael climbed onto the motorcycle behind Tristan. "It was early morning when I got here. I hadn't even had breakfast yet!"

He turned to look at her before starting the engine. "Obviously our times aren't matched up. Then again, why would they be? It was mid-afternoon when you got here and now it's early evening. Hang on."

Rachael clung to Tristan as the motorcycle leapt forward. All she could think about was her family and how worried they must be. What did they think when they woke up and she was gone and then never came back? And what if she ended up being stuck here forever with no way home? She was so alone here. No friends, family or even familiar surroundings. They had to find a way to open that portal. They just had to.

As Tristan drove through now deserted streets Rachael caught glimpses of storefronts as they sped by and every one of them had "Closed" signs in the windows. So, it was true, the town closed down at dusk.

She gasped and closed her eyes as Tristan sped through a stoplight, then realized it hardly made a difference since there were no cars anywhere and they wouldn't get hit. Still, they were breaking the law... weren't they?

As they got closer to the bookstore, Rachael noticed people on the streets but then she got a better look as one of them ran toward the motorcycle. She really only got a glimpse but it burned the image in her mind. He didn't look like a regular human at all. His eyes were coal black with no white around them and they looked sunken into his skull. His skin was almost white, his head bald and veiny, and his lips were pulled back in a grimace over a mouthful of pointed teeth that looked more like something you'd see in a shark's mouth than in a human's. Clawed hands reached toward her and Rachael held more tightly to Tristan as the motorcycle surged forward at greater speed leaving the hideous creature in the dust. They were DAX; they had to be.

Tristan turned sharply into the bookstore parking lot, and then raced around to the back of the building. The motorcycle came to an abrupt halt right beside the door with the security code. As Tristan leapt off the motorcycle, three of the hideous creatures Rachael had seen earlier came careening around the corner of the building.

Tristan tore off his helmet and pulled two weapons from beneath his coat. One looked like a stake, the other a short blade, shorter than the Elfaen sword at his back at least.

251

"Get behind me! Punch in the code!"

Rachael scrambled behind him. "I don't know the code. What is it?"

"Six, five, two, one, one, three," he shouted and then the creatures were there. Rachael saw Tristan duck and slash and one of the creepy looking things was down but not out.

While Rachael attempted to hit the buttons of the security pad in the correct order she got slammed into the door and her breath left her lungs in a whoosh. She couldn't turn around. Instead, she felt hot breath at the back of her neck. It smelled sour, like something rotting. Out of the corner of her eye she saw Tristan stake one of the creatures. It stiffened then crumbled.

The other creature's clawed hands held onto Rachael, tearing though her t-shirt. "Tristan!" she screamed.

He charged toward her as the horrible creature turned Rachael, its claws tearing her t-shirt and digging into her flesh. She struggled in spite of the pain, as she saw its jaw unhinge. Rachael had never been more terrified in her life. The monster paused, possibly because her helmet partially blocked him from her neck or maybe the sight of it just confused him.

Logic told Rachael that her fire magic was at the ready and now was her chance to draw upon it to save herself, but sheer terror kept her from being able to concentrate enough to use it.

Rachael gasped when the monster in front of her suddenly disintegrated. Tristan's hand latched around her wrist as he jerked her away and dragged her over to the keypad at the door.

Tristan's fingers flew over the pad and the door opened. They tumbled in but Rachael's fear mounted again when she realized they still weren't safe. As Tristan tried to shut the door closed, another creature tried to push in. Tristan barely had room to lift the stake with the monster so close and the confines of the stairway so tight. Somehow, he managed it though and struck the creature in the chest. The monster turned to dust and Tristan slammed the door shut.

"Let's get though the second door."

He charged past her and punched in the code. The door opened and the two of them staggered though. The door locked behind them as Rachael slumped against the nearest desk and wrenched her helmet off.

"Were those things DAX?" she panted. Fear still hadn't entirely abated. It was too soon after nearly losing her life…or worse.

Tristan raked a hand though his hair. "Yep. In all their grotesque glory."

"And you fight those things every night?" Rachael was beginning to feel a little steadier; at least it was easier to catch her breath now.

He nodded. "Those and the Dark-Angels, when we see them."

Rachael didn't want to imagine how awful the Dark-Angels must be when their hybrids were already terrifying enough.

"Those things are worse than anything in my world. I always thought the Blood-Hunters were awful, the way they fed on humans and left them for dead, but this…these things take it to a whole other level."

Rachael saw Thomas Westfall striding toward them.

"You made it," he said.

"Just barely," Tristan drawled. "Is anybody else here?"

"No," Westfall replied. "Kirk and the others left well before dark. All Slayers have been sent out."

"Rachael, you're bleeding."

She followed Tristan's eyes and looked down. Sure enough, the tears in her t-shirt exposed red scratches that were oozing with blood.

"Let's get you to the medic room," Thomas Westfall said. "We'll need to get that disinfected right away." He gestured for her to come with him.

Fear lanced through Rachael as she quickly followed after him. "Am I going to turn into one of those things?"

"No," Tristan said as he brought up the rear. "You'd have to survive being bitten, drained and near death for that to happen."

Rachael released a sigh of relief.

Thirty minutes later, her wounds cleaned and bandaged, Rachael sat in the conference room with Tristan and Thomas Westfall. Tristan had loaned her a clean heather grey t-shirt to replace her torn one and she felt a bit more like herself.

There were sandwiches, potato chips and some fruit on the table in front of her. She grabbed a banana and gobbled it down.

"How am I going to get home?" she asked once the banana was gone.

"I don't know, Rachael," Thomas replied. "We'll do our best to figure that out and get you back to your family and friends as soon as possible. That's all I can tell you at this point.

Rachael nodded. She wasn't happy with that answer but there was nothing she could do about it.

"So, who is this person who brought the sword over here from my world?" she asked.

Tristan shrugged. "He says his name is Lairen, but the guy isn't saying much else."

Rachael considered things. "If he took the sword just because it's a nice sword that's one thing, but if he knew it was Elfaen then why would he bring it over here when the Elfaen people would do almost anything to lay their hands on an ancient artifact like that? And if he's from my world then how the heck did he know about the portal and—?"

Thomas cut her off. "These are the types of questions we're been asking ourselves too. So far, we don't have any answers.

Rachael thought about it and decided to tell them more about the Elfaen swords and their importance. Since she was stuck in this world for a bit, the least she could do is try and help solve some of "whys" and "hows" going on around here.

"Like I said earlier, there are only four of those swords in existence." She looked from Westfall to Tristan, curious what their reactions would be to her next revelation. "But there's more. Each sword has magical powers unique to the sword."

Westfall's eyes widened. "Magic?"

"Why didn't you tell us that before?" Tristan snapped.

"Yes magic, and I didn't tell you before because it didn't seem relevant."

"Not relevant!" Tristan scoffed. "How is it not relevant? It seems pretty damn relevant to me!"

"Well, I—"

Westfall cut in. "Tristan!" After Tristan grudgingly fell silent, Westfall continued. "So, tell us now. What sort of magic might this sword have and how can it potentially harm us or be to our advantage since we're now in possession of it?"

Rachael took a breath. "Four swords, four types of magic," she began. "One sword is called the Death-Dealer, one is called Fire-Starter, one is Life-Giver and the fourth is Beast-Master. Once they're awakened, they sort of have a mind of their own and bond to an Elfaen warrior."

Tristan looked skeptical. "Really." he said, his tone dry and flat.

Thomas Westfall tilted his head as the studied her. "So, you're saying each sword is a living thing and has its own magical properties...which seem to be pretty self-explanatory; death, life, control of beasts and fire."

"Why fire?" Tristan asked. His tone indicated that he still doubted what she'd told them. "That one seems kind of out of place."

Rachael shrugged. "I don't know. I'm just repeating what I—"

"Yeah, we know," Tristan interrupted. "What you read in your books."

Rachael's eyes narrowed. "Why are you always so angry; especially at me? I haven't done anything to you. I'm just trying to help!"

"You withheld information."

Westfall raised his voice over Tristan's. "Okay, okay. Calm down, Tris. Attacking her isn't going to help anything."

Rachael continued. "My point is, in the wrong hands, those swords could give someone power over life and death, not to mention the ability to control all the animals, both great and small."

"Do you have any idea which sword we have in our possession?" Westfall asked.

"No. I can't be certain."

"How do we find out?" Tristan asked. "More of your books?"

Now the questions were getting closer to some information Rachael didn't really want to reveal about herself. "Well," she began, "like I said, the sword would have to be tested with Elfaen fire and..."

"What is Elfaen fire anyway?" Tristan asked.

"Some of the Elfae from my world have the ability to...um...call up fire."

"What do you mean, exactly?" Westfall asked. "By 'call up' do you mean that this is an innate magical power?"

"Yes," Rachael replied.

Tristan looked at Westfall. "Like the Elementals, then."

Rachael was confused. "Elementals? What are Elementals?"

Tristan looked at her. "When Ariel was giving you her little lesson on what our world is like, she didn't get around to talking about Elementals. Elementals are people who are born with the ability to call up magic to varying degrees. It's innate magic too. Like what you described with the Elfae."

Thomas Westfall nodded. "The magic varies from being able to create a disguise by changing one's appearance, which all Elementals can do, to being able to encourage plants to grow more quickly or wounds to heal at an accelerated rate. There are various other similar types of magic as well."

Tristan rejoined the conversation. "And, some Elementals can control the elements like wind or rain in varying degrees depending on how powerful their magical abilities are."

Rachael thought Elementals sounded very like the Elfae.

"Do you know any of these Elementals?" she asked. "I mean, are they good people or do you fear them or...?"

Thomas and Tristan looked at each other. Thomas gave Tristan a slight nod. Tristan turned to Rachael.

"Yes, we know quite a few Elementals. In fact, I'm an Elemental and so is Tom. In fact, all the Slayers are Elementals."

Rachael was stunned. She'd been desperate to hide her true nature from them this whole time and it turned out these very people were their world's equivalent of Elfae. She grinned broadly and started to laugh.

"What?" Tristan asked, his voice hard once more. "What's so funny?"

Rachael looked at both of them. "It's just...we have more in common than you know. I'm Elfae. I have magic too."

CHAPTER FOUR

"**S**O...YOU'RE LIKE US?" TRISTAN ASKED AND AT just that moment Thomas Westfall's phone rang. He held up a finger as he answered and both Rachael and Tristan waited in silence.

Westfall's face paled. "Get back here immediately; we'll do what we can." He put his phone back into his pocket and turned to Tristan. "Another portal opened across town. Something came though. Something worse than the DAX or Dark-Angels, according to Ariel. They're on their way back. Alina was injured."

"How bad?" Tristan asked.

Thomas raked a hand through his hair. "Bad. Bad enough she might not make it."

"Rachael, would you grab a medic-kit from that closet?"

Rachael looked where Westfall had pointed, then hurried over and yanked open the door. Inside were an abundance of various supplies but the medic-kit was clearly marked. She grabbed it and brought it to Westfall. He and Tristan had shoved desks back against the wall to make more room for however many people were coming, along with the injured Alina.

Westfall opened the medic-kit, which was well stocked with things Rachael recognized, like gauze, bandages, medical tape, and ointments. There were also other things Rachael didn't have a clue about. There wasn't time to ask though, because even as a question formed in her head people began to arrive.

Rachael heard the security lock buzz open and Tristan and Westfall both reached for weapons. She figured whatever was going on out there had certainly made them extremely cautious.

Three people Rachael didn't know entered, followed shortly thereafter by two more. Next came Stefan and Amy, the only ones Rachael recognized so far. The volume in the room increased greatly when the last four Slayers showed up. Among them Rachael recognized Ariel. Two male Slayers supported a limp and bloody Alina between them. They laid her atop two desks that had been pushed together. Alina appeared to be semi-conscious, her eyes partially open, her movement slight. She was clearly in pain, judging from the occasional gasp emitting from her lips.

Westfall took charge. "Those of you with healing abilities, please use them. Ariel, here's the medic-kit, do what you can for her. The rest of you, in my office."

Rachael had backed herself into a corner so she wouldn't be in the way. As she watched, three of the Slayers, including Tristan, remained behind along with Ariel while the others filed down the hall to Westfall's office. Tristan and the others laid hands on Alina and Rachael could feel the presence of magic building. So, Tristan's magic talent was healing, Rachael noted.

All the Slayers present had their eyes closed in concentration. Ariel worked quickly and efficiently to wipe blood from Alina's body and bandage all her more minor wounds. Unfortunately, even from where Rachael stood, across the room and in the corner, it was obvious what would kill Alina wasn't those cuts and abrasions. Along her left side, from shoulder to hip was a gaping wound. It looked to Rachael like a deep claw mark; a very huge one. She wondered what could've made that.

The Slayers' healing magic had stopped the loss of blood, which was helpful, but the wound wasn't healing. In fact, as Rachael watched in horror, tendrils of black snaked up Alina's neck and down to mid-thigh. Alina screamed and writhed. All the Slayers jerked back in surprise with wide eyes.

"Keep going," Tristan shouted. "We can do this!"

But they couldn't. Seconds later Alina released her last breath.

Silence filled the room. Rachael felt magic slip away until the air was just air once more. They'd tried and failed. What had caused this? What had come through that portal? Was it still roaming around the city? Were there more of them coming through the portal even now?

Tears streamed from Ariel's eyes. "I'll get Westfall."

She turned and left the room. Tristan and the others stared at Alina and said nothing.

Westfall and the other Slayers returned. He motioned to Stefan. "Call Kirk. Tell him what happened and that his team will have to examine her body in the morning." He turned to Tristan. "Get her moved to Kirk's lab. I'll contact her family."

"Now what?" someone asked once Westfall had gone back into his office.

"We should all stay here until morning," came a reply from across the room.

A third Slayer nodded. "Yeah, agreed."

"That's a no brainer," someone else muttered.

"I didn't sign up for this," said one of the female Slayers.

"Who did?" asked Amy. "Nobody asked for this." She shoved up her sleeve to reveal a mark on her forearm. "But it's in our DNA. We got the mark. We're born for this so we do what we do, end of story."

Tristan and one other Slayer lifted Alina's lifeless body and carried it from the room. Once Ariel returned she sat not far from Rachael, brushing tears from her cheeks while some others cleaned up Alina's blood, still smeared on the desk and floor. Those not cleaning up blood began to shed their weapons and stow them in lockers along the far wall. Each locker was large enough for a grown man to stand in and looked to be about four feet deep. It looked to Rachael like every one of these Slayers had access to multiple weapons.

Rachael brought her attention back to Ariel as the other girl brushed by her.

"Hey, I'm sorry about your friend."

Ariel turned back and sniffed. "Thanks. We've been partners in this Slayer crap for the last three years. She was from here, but I transferred in from East Lurra. Alina had been working alone but she accepted the change and helped me adjust. She showed me how things work out here in the wild west." Ariel gave Rachael a sad smile, sniffed again and wiped her nose with her sleeve. "Anyway, I better go get a tissue." She turned and walked away.

Rachael looked around for Tristan and found him talking quietly with Stefan and Amy. She suddenly felt really alone and out of place. What was her family doing right now? Did they think she'd been kidnapped? Would she ever get back to them? And what was the horrific danger out there that had come through the second portal and killed Alina? With the way things were going, Rachael wondered if she would even survive to get home.

Thomas Westfall returned to the group. "Everyone, please give me your attention. Take a seat or however you're comfortable. I have something to say."

Chairs squeaked as they were turned around and adjusted. Some people sat on chairs, while others perched on desks. Some remained standing but everyone looked toward the man who was their leader.

Westfall cleared his throat. "I've notified Alina's family. They are understandably grief stricken. That having been said, they also know the risks of this calling. Other members of Alina's family have been Slayers as well. Some have died in the line of duty as she has tonight. This situation serves as a reminder to all of us that although we have superior strength and agility, the ability to heal quickly and some have the added bonus of Elemental magic to aid that process, we can't forget that we are not immortal. Tonight's occurrence was truly unexpected and no one...I mean no one, is to blame." He looked at Ariel and then at the rest of the Slayers. "This is the beginning of a new kind of threat. We need to determine if the opening of these portals is a deliberate act and if so, who is doing it and why."

"Sir?"

Rachael turned toward the voice to see Amy rise to her feet.

"Sir, isn't it possible this opening of the portals is some sort of natural...I don't know...accident?"

Westfall nodded. "It's possible. Whatever the cause, these portals must be closed permanently. We have enough to deal with on a regular basis without the addition of strangers traveling back and forth and monsters from our darkest nightmares killing thousands."

"Is that prisoner still here?" Stefan asked. "The one who was caught bringing the sword across?"

"Yes," Thomas replied. "He's being held off site at the Ravenwood Compound."

"Well, what're we waiting for?" someone shouted. "Let's go pummel the bastard until he tells us what he's up to and who else is involved!"

Several people yelled out their agreement but Westfall shook his head. "Take it easy. Tristan and I will go there when it's light and question him again."

"But that thing! It's out there somewhere and it killed Alina!" Amy looked angry. Her eyes shot daggers at Westfall. "We should get back out there, find it and kill it!"

"And this is why you're not in charge, Amy, and Thomas is," Tristan countered. "He's got the level head, you're just—"

"Screw you, Tristan! Of course, you'd take his side, he's your brother," Amy snapped back.

Tristan smirked at her. "Half-brother, sweetness; same mother, different fathers. Which explains why his last name is Westfall and mine is Tate. And no, we don't always agree on things but he's right on this one."

Rachael was surprised to learn Tristan and Thomas were half-brothers. On the other hand, they did have similar features, coloring and build now that she studied them more carefully.

"We should stay in and regroup," Thomas said, effectively ending the verbal duel between Amy and Tristan. "A lot has happened in the last forty-eight hours. We're dealing with situations and creatures we've had no prior experience with and the learning curve is steep. We need to keep our cool, gather as much information as possible and think things through before we act. For now, try and relax, get some food from the conference room if you wish, and get some sleep." Westfall turned and went down the hall to his office.

Once again Rachael was left to her own devices. She slumped in a chair and rested her head against the wall behind her. This place, which at first glance had seemed rather like her own world, was actually far more dangerous and getting more so as the hours slipped by.

"Hey, you okay?"

Rachael opened her eyes. She hadn't realized she'd closed them. Ariel had taken the seat next to hers.

"Yeah, I'm okay I guess," Rachael replied.

"So, what's this I hear about you not being human? And magic...you have magical abilities?"

Rachael eyed her, not sure whether Ariel was accepting or being critical. "Who told you?"

Ariel shrugged. "Tristan, just now."

Rachael glanced around and lowered her voice. "I'm Elfae and Eflae seem to be roughly the equivalent to the Elementals on this world, at least as far as they've been described to me."

Ariel looked at her with eyes that were still sad at the loss of her friend, but her smile was genuine. "I'm an Elemental too. Did Tristan tell you? All the Slayers are."

"So, what's the mark on Amy's arm? She talked like it was a badge or something. Is it a tattoo? Do you all get one when you become a Slayer?"

Ariel cocked her head. "Yes, we all have one, but it's not something earned. At a certain age it just appears. For some it's on the arm, for others the back, chest or leg. Once that mark appears you're a Slayer and your duty is to work to make this world a safer place."

Rachael processed that information. It sounded very much like the Assassins at the Bureau in her world, but they didn't have a physical mark to differentiate them from everyone else. She rubbed her temples. This place was giving her a headache.

"I just want to go home," she muttered.

Tristan appeared at Rachael's side. "Westfall told me to take you to Kirk's office. There's a sleeper sofa in here. You can get some shut-eye."

"I'm not tired," Rachael said but she followed Tristan down the corridor, through the lab and into a small room with a desk, chair, computer and sofa.

"I'm sure he won't mind if you sleep in here." Tristan took the cushions off the sofa and unfolded the collapsed frame and mattress inside. "He'll be in early in the morning though so I hope you like waking up at the crack of dawn."

Rachael nodded. "Yeah, okay."

After Tristan left, Rachael could still hear voices from down the hall but they were faint. She glanced around the room. Technical scientific books filled the bookshelves along one wall. Rachael sat on the sofa and swung her legs up. She stared at the ceiling, worried that she'd never be able to fall asleep so early in the evening and with so much now on her mind, but she was wrong. After a few more minutes of snooping around Kirk's office she kicked off her shoes and lay down on the bed, pulling a lightweight blanket around her as she settled in. She closed her eyes, just to rest them for a bit, and the next thing she knew it was daylight and someone was shaking her awake.

CHAPTER FIVE

"RACHAEL. RACHAEL WAKE UP."

She opened her eyes. It was Ariel and behind her stood the guy she'd seen briefly yesterday, the guy in the Hawaiian shirt.

"Kirk's here. He needs to use his office." She held out a cup. "I brought you a mocha latte from downstairs. There are doughnuts in the conference room."

Rachael rose from the sofa. "Is there someplace I can wash my face and is there an extra toothbrush and hairbrush around here somewhere?" She rubbed her eyes and imagined she must look pretty awful.

"Yeah, sure."

Rachael took the mocha from Ariel and threw Kirk a smile just before taking a sip of the chocolaty coffee. It was really good. "Sorry to be in your way."

"It's okay," he said.

"Come on," Ariel gestured for Rachael to follow her and the two of them left Kirk's office. "We've started making plans for tonight," Ariel said. "Stefan and some of the others are going to go out during the day to assess damage from last night and see if there's any sign of the creature that came through the portal last night. Some Slayers are also going to the site of the new portal to see if it's still open. Kirk's gonna work on finding a way to close it if it is."

They arrived at the lockers. Ariel got into hers and handed Rachael a hairbrush. "There are extra toothbrushes in there." She pointed to a large bathroom with several shower stalls. "Feel free to use any toiletries in there. We share them. See you in the conference room."

Twenty minutes later Rachael felt much more awake and alert as she emerged from the bathroom. She had washed her face, brushed her teeth and fished some makeup out of her purse and applied it. After running the brush through her blonde hair, she headed toward the conference room with hopes that today the portal to her world would've opened again and she would get to go home.

She entered the room and found several boxes of doughnuts on the wide conference table along with some fruit and more coffee. A few Slayers were there and most didn't even glance her way when she'd come in. Rachael reached for a chocolate cake doughnut, grabbed some more coffee and had only finished half of it when Tristan appeared at her side.

"Come on, let's go."

"Go where?" she said around a mouthful of doughnut.

"To the portal."

"My portal?"

"No, that one's still closed. We're going to the other one."

"What? Why?"

He ignored her question. "First we're going to meet Thomas at Ravenwood Compound to re-question the guy who brought the sword over from your world; then we're going to the portal."

Rachael followed Tristan down the stairs and out into the bright sunlight. "But why are you taking me with you? I don't see why I should go with you to either of those places and how do you know my portal is still closed?"

"Amy and Stefan. They've already been there this morning; went first thing, as soon as the sun came up. There's nothing there. As for the other..." He handed her the same helmet she'd worn when riding the motorcycle yesterday. "Since the guy we have at the compound is from your world. Maybe you can find out something we haven't been able to yet."

"That's ridiculous. I don't see how." Rachael got the helmet on securely and then climbed onto the back of the motorcycle. The ride took a little over thirty minutes as it was on the outskirts of the city and when they got there Tristan had to punch in a code to get the security gate to open. Once they were inside the compound Rachael saw a huge outdoor training area enclosed by walls that must've been at least ten feet tall. Tristan drove around to one side of the building and stopped the motorcycle.

They got off and Rachael removed the helmet. "Look, I don't know why you think he'd talk to me. Why would he tell a total stranger what's going on? If he's not going to tell you then he's not going to tell me!"

"We'll see." Tristan headed to the nearby entrance and Rachael jogged after him.

They entered the building, which was huge and vacant; a giant empty warehouse.

Rachael looked around. "There's nothing here."

"Oh, yes there is."

Tristan moved a panel on the wall, revealing a keypad. He punched in a code then pressed his hand to the glass panel that popped up. A light ran from top to bottom, scanning his palm print. A door opened that Rachael hadn't even noticed before.

"Come on," Tristan said, and descended the stairs just off the landing on the other side of the door.

Rachael looked around then followed him down. The door slid closed behind her but she wasn't plunged into darkness since there were lights along the walls.

When they got to the bottom Tristan took a sharp right and Rachael followed along. At the end of the corridor on the left side was a door, which Tristan went through. Rachael could see Thomas Westfall was already there and manacled and chained to a table was the man they'd detained for bringing the Elfaen sword into their world.

Rachael gasped when the man looked up and into her eyes. It couldn't be. But it was.

"You!" Rachael said.

"Hello Cupcake," said the young man with waist long white blond hair and eyes that were piercing blue, like a Husky Rachael had seen at the annual dog rescue fundraiser back home.

"You know each other?" Thomas Westfall asked.

"I told you it was worth bringing her here," Tristan said. "But damn, I didn't think they would know each other!"

Rachael looked from the guy in front of her to Westfall and then Tristan. "I don't believe this. We go to the same university and we have a couple of classes together. This is unbelievable!"

"Right you are, Cupcake. It must be destiny." The blond guy smiled at her.

"Don't call me Cupcake. We don't even know each other."

"Sure we do. I'm the guy who sits next to you in class."

Rachael glared at him. "I don't even know your name."

"It's Lairen. Lairen Perry."

"See," Tristan said. "He's talking and we already know more than we did ten minutes ago."

"Perry?" Rachael frowned. "That's my last name."

Lairen nodded. "I know. And I know you better than you think."

"No, you don't."

"Yes, I do. Your father is Gabriel Perry, your mother is named Amelia."

"How could you possibly know that?" Rachael gasped.

"Because I'm your half-brother," Lairen replied with a smirk.

"Whoa!" Tristan bent over laughing. "Didn't see that coming."

Rachael spared one angry glance in Tristan's direction. "That's impossible," she snapped. "I have two younger twin sisters. I don't have a brother."

Lairen grinned. "Well, actually you do."

Rachael shook her head. "No. That's not possible."

Westfall cleared his throat. "Okay, you can have your not-so-happy reunion later. Right now, we have questions."

"What were you doing with that Elfaen sword?" Rachael blurted out.

"Oh, is that what it is?" Lairen winked at her. "I hadn't noticed."

Tristan had stopped laughing and now glared at the prisoner. "Cut the crap and tell us what we want to know. The sooner you do that the sooner we might let you go back to your own world."

"The operative word there is 'might', I guess, huh?" Lairen said.

Tristan bent forward and leaned in, palms on the table in front of Lairen. He looked him in the eye. Rachael thought he looked pretty threatening but Lairen just shifted back in his chair, his expression still calm and unworried.

"Where did you get that sword and why did you bring it through the portal?" Tristan asked. "How did you even know about the portal? Are you the one who opened it?"

"So many questions all at once!" Lairen glanced over at Rachael. His eyes met hers then shifted back to Tristan. "Whatever. I might as well tell you."

"Go ahead," Westfall said. "We're all ears."

"There are four Elfaen swords. That's meaningless to you, I know."

"We already know that," Thomas said. "Rachael told us about them."

Lairen's lifted eyebrows lifted and he gave her a sidelong glance. "So much for the Bureau's secrets."

"It's not a secret," she snapped. "It's Elfaen history. And what do you know about the Bureau?"

Lairen shrugged. "I know you work for them."

Rachael gasped. How the hell did this total stranger know so much about her? Had he been stalking her?

Westfall redirected the conversation. "Let's talk about this portal. How long has it been open and who opened it?"

Lairen shifted his gaze to Thomas. "There's been someone opening portals between our worlds for decades and you all just didn't know about it." He looked over at Rachael. "And neither did your precious Bureau."

"So, who opened it and why were you bringing that sword over here?" Tristan asked.

"Do you have any of the other swords?" Rachael asked.

Lairen smiled. "This is where things get really crazy. But I think I've told you enough."

"I want the swords," Rachael said. "They belong to the Elfae and I'm going to take them back when I go through the portal."

Lairen chuckled. "And you know how to open a portal?"

Rachael's face fell. "No, but—"

Thomas Westfall sat across from Lairen and studied him. "Another portal was opened last night, after the one first you and then Rachael came though had closed."

Lairen shrugged.

"This other portal didn't lead to your world. From what Rachael has described to us of your world, I doubt what came through it could possibly be from there," Westfall continued.

Lairen tilted his head. "What do you mean? What came through?"

Thomas pulled a folded piece of paper from his coat pocket and unfolded it. "This is a picture of what came through the portal. We got descriptions from the Slayers who saw it and had someone sketch it."

Rachael snatched the paper from Westfall's hand, studied it and shook her head. "No, that definitely didn't come from my world. Not unless something has been unleashed over there that I've never seen or heard of before."

Thomas showed the picture to Lairen who shook his head. "I've never seen anything like that either." He looked at Westfall. "So where did that thing come from?"

"We were hoping you could tell us," Westfall replied.

Lairen shrugged. "I have no idea."

"So, it's a portal to yet another world," Tristan grumbled. "Great. This just gets better and better."

Westfall turned to Lairen. "So, if I understand correctly, these portals are being opened by someone, they're not a natural phenomenon."

"That's right," Lairen said. "My mom and I came over here when I was a kid. My step-dad lives over here." He released a heavy sigh. "He's the one who's been collecting the Elfaen swords." He looked at Rachael. "And yes, he has three of them. The one you caught me with was the last one."

"How did you even know where they were?" Rachael asked. "Nobody has seen them in, like, forty or fifty years!"

"I don't know. He locates them and I go get them. He had one already before my mom even married him," Lairen said.

"This doesn't make any sense," Tristan muttered, then turned and shouted at Lairen. "What is he doing with them? Collecting them? Or does he have something more in mind? And what's going on with these damn portals?"

Lairen leaned forward in his chair. "Look, I don't know, alright? He sent me to get one of the swords about a year ago and I did. No big deal. This time it didn't work out so good as evidenced by the fact that I'm sitting here." He jangled the chains on his wrists.

"And you've been going to college on one side and living on the other?" Rachael gasped.

Again, Lairen shrugged. "Yeah, sort of. I mostly live over there now. Not here. I like it over there."

Thomas Westfall scowled at Lairen. "And who exactly are your parents?"

Lairen eyed him. "My mother is Beatrix Jarrett. My father is Gabriel Perry."

"He is not!" Rachael shouted.

"You know what I meant," snapped Thomas. "I want the name of your stepfather!"

Lairen's eyes met Thomas's. "My step-father's name is Sebastian Westfall." Then he laughed and began to sing. "Reunited and it feels so good!"

You could've heard a pin drop.

"The prisoner's step-father is your dad?" Tristan said to Thomas.

And then to Rachael's surprise Thomas Westfall drew back his fist and smashed it into Lairen's face. His head snapped back and he stopped singing and didn't resume.

"What is your step-father's name?" Thomas asked again.

Lairen took a breath and spoke softly. "I told you the truth. It's Sebastian Westfall. It is quite a coincidence don't you think? Here I am, in chains, talking with my half-sister and my step-brother, neither of whom even knew I existed until this very moment."

Tristan turned to Thomas. "Seriously, dude. Your dad is married to his mom and you didn't even know that?"

"You know I don't have anything to do with my father," Thomas snapped. "And even when I did, he was always so damn secretive. That's why our mother left him. You know that. I have no idea where he goes, what he does or who he does it with!" Thomas raked his fingers through his hair. After a moment he turned to Tristan. "Take Rachael and go. There's no point in heading to the other portal at this time. We have enough Slayers there to keep an eye on things."

"But what about this guy? We haven't gotten nearly enough information about—"

"Go, Tristan!" The look on Westfall's face was deadly serious. "Go. Now."

With a final glare at both Westfall and Lairen, Tristan wheeled around and headed for the door. "Come on, Rachael," he called over his shoulder.

"But I want the swords back! I can't go home without them. They're a national treasure, at least to the Elfae!"

"Well, it doesn't look like you're going home anytime soon anyway. Not unless we can get someone to open a portal," Tristan replied.

Rachael threw a glance toward Lairen. "I want those swords."

"Good luck, Cupcake," he said.

"Argh!" she balled her hands into fists. "I'm not a Cupcake! Why do you keep calling me that?"

He smiled up at her. "Because when you were little, it was your favorite food. You would clap your hands and laugh, then grab the cupcake, squish it and then get frosting and cake all over your face when you tried to eat it."

Rachael stood there blinking at him. A vague memory had surfaced… of her mom making cupcakes…and of a white-haired boy who came to stay with them for a little while.

Rachael said nothing, just turned and followed Tristan out of the room.

CHAPTER SIX

"I CAN'T BELIEVE THIS! WHAT'RE THE CHANCES? Thomas has a step-brother neither of us knew about and...so that guy's your half-brother, huh?" Tristan said as they put on their helmets in preparation for riding the motorcycle. He seemed to have calmed down a bit from his frustrated anger when they were inside the building.

She shook her head. "No."

"Well, he's either that or a stalker. He seemed to know stuff about your family that no stranger should know; assuming he was right about your parent's names."

"I don't care what he knows. He's not related to me."

Tristan laughed. "Hey, I have a half-brother. It's not so bad."

"Are you serious? You actually think I should give that guy the benefit of the doubt? Especially after he's been helping *your* half-brother's father steal ancient Elfaen artifacts and open portals to where the hell ever?"

"Nah," Tristan threw his leg over the bike and looked at her. "I'm just teasing you. And we don't know if Lairen is the one opening the portals. He sounds like more of an errand boy."

Tristan started the motorcycle and Rachael climbed on behind him.

"So where are we going?" she asked when they stopped for a traffic light. She was still feeling grouchy but tried to shake it off.

"Back to the office to talk to Kirk. I want to see that sword."

Rachael spent the rest of the ride wishing she were home and wondering how long it would take for her to get back. Days? Weeks? Months? She certainly hoped not. All she'd wanted to do was take a walk on a beautiful day and buy coffee and pastries. Instead, she'd landed in another place altogether.

And then there was the guy from her college classes, Lairen Perry. If that was even his real last name. He could be making it all up. But then who was that white haired kid she remembered from so long ago, sitting at their dining room table with her? Hadn't he had ice blue eyes? He did, if her memory was accurate. If he was indeed Lairen then he was about four years older than she was. That would make him 23. Most college students were done with school by that age but people of all ages attended classes at universities so he could be telling the truth.

Tristan stopped the motorcycle behind the bookstore and Rachael removed her helmet. She followed him inside and then waited while he tracked down Kirk. Despite freshening up this morning she felt like she needed a shower. And a change of clothes would be nice too.

Tristan came banging back into the lunchroom where Rachael sat staring at the walls.

"Here's the sword." He tossed it onto the table. "How do you activate it?"

Rachael's eyes widened. "What? Why would you want to activate it?"

"Why indeed?" Thomas Westfall appeared in the doorway and frowned at Tristan.

Tristan's eyebrows shot up. "I thought you were still with the prisoner. How did you get back here so fast?"

"Never mind that," Westfall replied. "Why do you want to activate the sword?"

"I want to know what we're dealing with. Which of the swords is this? How does it work? What does it do? Having it could benefit us," Tristan replied. "We may be up against someone with three of these things, not to mention DAX, Dark-Angels and now this...thing from the other side of the new portal."

"You're assuming the prisoner's step-father, the man collecting the swords, is also the one opening the portals. You believe what he told us."

"Yeah, I do. And he's not your average antiquities collector. I'd bet my life on it. Is he really your step-brother?"

"I'll ask Mom if she knows anything. With my dad anything is possible," Thomas replied. "But, as for the sword, we don't need to activate it, we just need to secure it so it doesn't fall into the wrong hands." He looked at Rachael. "What's your take on all this? Is the prisoner really related to you?"

"No. Well…I don't know. Maybe, but I don't see how it's possible."

"Probably in the usual way," Tristan drawled then laughed.

Rachael shot him a scathing look.

Thomas cleared his throat. "Now that we've learned that the portals are not a natural occurrence, but the work of a specific individual, we have no way of knowing when you might be able to go home, Rachael. I'm sorry but it looks like you're stuck here for the time being. But, I promise you we'll do what we can to retrieve the other three swords from my father, if in fact that's who has them, so that whenever you do return home you can take them with you."

Rachael nodded. "Thanks. I appreciate that." But she felt so discouraged. What must her family think? They must be desperate to find her. And Skye and Mr. Preston at the Bureau. They must be wracking their brains to try and find her too.

"In the meantime," said Tristan, "what sort of magic do you have?"

"What?" Rachael's head snapped up. "Why?"

He shrugged. "Maybe your magic could help us fight those creatures that came through the portal, or find the swords or…something."

"Not a bad idea," Westfall said.

Rachael frowned. "I don't see how I or my magic can be of any real help. I don't know how to fight and my magic isn't the type that would help you locate anything."

"Let us be the judge of that," Westfall said. "If nothing else you might be of help to Kirk in the lab. What sort of magic do you have?"

Rachael sighed. "Well," she began. "My talent…my magic…is fire. I can wield fire."

Westfall's eyebrows shot up. "Fire. So…you can test the sword."

"Yes," Rachael nodded. "I can. But that isn't going to help you in—"

Tristan let out a whoop. "Don't you see, your magic *can* help us! We can activate the sword! Come on, let's go test this baby and see what we've got. I'm dying to know which sword it is."

Before anyone could reply Ariel came rushing into the room. She was out of breath and looked like she'd been fighting or running for her life, Rachael wasn't sure which.

"All hell has broken loose!" Ariel gasped. "It's not even dark out and frightening things are coming through that portal. Humans are scrambling for cover. We need every Slayer, right now!"

And just like that all conversation about the Rachael's magic and the sword was over. Tristan and Thomas ran from the room.

Rachael wandered out to the main part of the offices. She found books and read a little bit to pass the time. She also went downstairs to the bookstore and peeked out the security door. The store was apparently closed for the day, with all lights off and customers and employees both gone. Rachael propped the door open with a heavy book she'd brought with her for that purpose. She didn't want to get locked out of the upstairs offices.

She wandered around for a bit but then her stomach started to growl. She took a fruit smoothie drink in a bottle and a couple of other items from the deserted café. She felt bad about that. It was stealing after all, but she was hungry and figured Thomas would settle up later on her behalf. He seemed like a nice enough guy.

Rachael ate then continued to browse the store in the semi-darkness. There were plenty of books and magazines to keep her occupied but she was restless. When would someone come back? Had more Slayer lives been lost and what about the human population? If Lairen's step-father was the one opening the portals, why would he want these monsters to run rampant in the city? What could he possibly have to gain?

Hours passed and by this time Rachael was so bored that the sound of vehicles pulling into the parking lot caused her to run to the front of the store and gaze out in excitement. Had the Slayers finally returned?

She saw Tristan's motorcycle race around to the back of the building, followed by several other rugged looking vehicles. She raced back to the secure door she'd left propped open, grabbed the book and darted up the stairwell in time to be there when they all started coming in.

A dozen people collapsed on the chairs and some on the floor. Everyone looked dirty, sweaty and exhausted, even Thomas whom Rachael had not yet seen looking anything but polished and professional since she'd arrived in this place.

"I can't believe it," Amy gasped. Her blonde hair hung in her face and she pushed it back with one violent stroke of her hand.

"How many are dead?" someone else asked. "Where's Karl?"

SUZANN FORTUNATO

"What about Sammy?" asked a man with dark skin and a shiny bald head.

"They're with the others we dropped at the hospital," someone replied.

Rachael tried to follow the conversation among the Slayers but she didn't know anyone except Amy, Stefan, Ariel, Tristan and Thomas. From what she could piece together, several Slayers had either died or were close to it.

"I don't understand how this could happen," Stefan said. "We're getting our asses kicked and we're the best fighters out there for this kind of thing."

"It's because we're totally frickin' unprepared for fighting something like this!" Amy snapped.

"They should call in the military," said the man with the dark skin and bald head. "We're tapped out."

"We're not tapped out, Daze," Thomas Westfall replied. "We can find a way to put a stop to this ourselves, besides there's hardly a military left anymore. It's pretty much every man for himself out there. There're barely even enough police to take care of the regular crime."

"Well how do we do it then?" Daze shot back. "How do we kill these things? We may have lost a half a dozen Slayers today. If this keeps up, we'll all be dead before the week is out."

"How many of those things are there?" someone asked.

"At least four," Tristan replied. "Along with those bird-like things with the foot long beaks and claws dive bombing us."

"And so far, we haven't been able to kill even one of them," Amy grumbled.

"The military should be called in," Ariel said. "Maybe their weapons... long range missiles—"

"I already told you," Thomas said. "There's no point in asking, their resources are spread too thin as it is. Our job is to figure out how to kill these monsters and close that damn portal. We also have to find the person responsible and put a stop to whatever he or they have planned. But, we're on our own. The military isn't going to be of any help." His cell phone rang and he fished it from his pocket while heading back to his office.

"Now what?" Tristan asked.

"Maybe it's the hospital," Ariel suggested.

They all waited quietly this time. There were a few hushed conversations here and there while some of the Slayers started cleaning and bandaging their more minor wounds and abrasions.

After a few minutes Thomas Westfall returned, his expression grim. "Sammy, Karl and the others...they didn't make it."

There was complete silence and Rachael's eyes darted around the room. Each face was wide eyed, some with tears beginning to fall. This was no game, no movie. The Slayers who had died today were friends of the people in this room, friends they would never see or laugh with again.

In spite of her own sorrow at being separated from her world, her family and her friends, Rachael now knew that she had to wholeheartedly throw in with these people. Their survival meant her survival as well.

CHAPTER SEVEN

RACHAEL SAT ALONE IN KIRK'S LAB. EVERYONE else was either sleeping, training or doing research, making calls or generally plotting revenge against the person or persons to blame for the open portal and the deaths of their fellow Slayers. They were all going out again as soon as it was dark. Thomas Westfall had instructed certain Slayers to concentrate on tracking down the Dark-Angels and the DAX while Kirk and his team worked on getting the portal closed. Humans were barricaded in their homes while the ten-foot monstrosities from what they'd all taken to calling the Hell World, roamed about. The bird-like creatures, similar to pterodactyls, perched on houses and looked for stray people or pets to devour.

Rachael's eyes fell upon the sword. It lay, forgotten for the moment, on a metal table not three feet away. She was alone in the room. She glanced toward the door. Would she have time? She really was just as curious as Tristan about the sword. Was it truly Elfaen? She could test it, right here, right now, and if she were lucky nobody would even know. With one more glance at the door, Rachael closed her eyes and focused, calling up the fire always inside her.

The door opened and Rachael's eyes flew open as well. She forced her internal fire to quickly extinguish. She turned to see Kirk in the doorway.

"Oh hey, I just came in to get some stuff," he said as he gathered up some papers and books from his desk. "You okay in here?"

"Yeah." Rachael nodded. "Sure. I'm good."

"Ok." And with a nod good-bye he was gone.

With a sigh Rachael, very quickly this time, centered herself and tapped into her ability to call fire once more. She walked over to the sword and stretched her arm out, palm facing the blade. Fire flowed in a direct line from her hand to the surface of the blade and Rachael waited with excitement to see if anything would happen. Seconds later it did.

Slowly markings began to appear along the length of the metal. Rachael recognized them as ancient Elfaen and her excitement grew. Once the sword's name appeared she shut down her fire magic and stared at the glowing blade. She'd been studying ancient Elfaen history for a while now, ever since gaining access to the resources at the Bureau. She could make out the first few letters of the sword's name and that was enough.

"Fire-Starter," she whispered. "You really are one of the missing Elfaen swords."

She reached out her hand again, this time to take hold of the sword to examine it more closely. Her palm wrapped around the hilt and she lifted it, being careful not to touch the sharp edges of the blade. The sword was heavier than she expected. Rachael glanced at the door. Maybe she should set the sword down now. She didn't want Tristan to suddenly come striding in and start hassling her about it, but then her hand started to tingle and the sensation traveled up her arm. Rachael could feel something in the sword calling to her, or more specifically to her magic.

The sword now felt alive in her hand. Rachael felt something course though her body and down her legs. It wasn't painful though, just odd. She heard a voice speak the word, *Chosen,* but there was no one else in the room. The voice was inside her head. She looked down at the sword. Again, she heard the voice. *Yes.* Was the sword talking to her?

"Oh crap!" Rachael muttered. "What have I done?" She tried to drop the sword but it seemed to be fused to her palm. She shook her hand to try and dislodge the sword. "Let go!" she said aloud.

"What?"

Rachael whirled to see Ariel standing in the doorway.

"Nothing!" The sword fell from her hand onto the metal table. Rachael glanced down at it with a sigh of relief, then back to Ariel. "Just looking at the sword. You startled me."

Ariel nodded. "Oh. Well, I just came in to tell you…it's time. We're all heading out."

Rachael nodded. "Good luck."

Tristan loomed behind her. "Let's go, Ariel."

Ariel gave Rachael a halfhearted smile. "Hopefully I'll see you later… If I'm not dead." Then she brushed past Tristan and was gone.

Tristan turned away but Rachael called his name and he turned around. Rachael gave him a sad smile. "Good luck."

He nodded in acknowledgment then turned and left, closing the door behind him. Moments later Rachael heard the sounds of all the Slayers leaving the building and then she was alone once more. She glanced over at the sword but something caught her eye. She noticed a shimmer in the air to her right. Immediately her attention was riveted to the small gleaming spot, which steadily became more translucent as she stood watching warily. If this ended up being a portal to her world, she'd be a fool not to grab the sword, step through and leave this place and its people to their problems. Immediately she chastised herself for that thought. Just a few hours ago she'd decided to commit herself to this fight.

Rachael wondered if she should stick around to see what this glinting, rapidly expanding portal had to offer or flee. But where could she go, really? She was relatively safe here in the confines of the building but if she went outside…

The portal continued to open. At first Rachael couldn't see through to the other side. She remained hopeful but cautious. Eventually the space within the gleaming oval cleared and she saw a face looking back at her.

The man's steely grey eyes narrowed. His expression was grim. There was a scar from his temple to the corner of his mouth to the point of his chin. His hair was to his shoulders; black, straight, with streaks of grey. Behind him stood a woman. She had white flowing hair and was small and delicate of build but her eyes held the same flicker of anger as the man's.

His eyes darted to the metal table near Rachael. "My sword," he said, his voice gravely and deep.

The woman stepped forward. "Where is my son?"

The portal continued to widen and Rachael was afraid the two of them would step through as soon at the opening was large enough. She did the only thing she could think of. She grabbed the sword, whirled and ran for the door.

Down the hallway and through the empty office she ran. She clambered down the stairs and shot through the door leading to the bookstore. It closed softly behind her. She was now locked out of the upstairs offices but the man and woman could still come down the stairs in pursuit.

After a quick glance over her shoulder, she ran to her left through the middle of the darkened store, all the while looking for a place to hide. She ran to the front of the shop and crouched behind the checkout counter.

She stayed there, cowering, for several minutes. She chastised herself for her fear. She had fire magic. She could take care of herself. Unless, of course, Sebastian Westfall, if indeed that's who she'd seen, had powerful magic of his own…something to counter or disable her magic all together.

She thought she heard the door to the stairwell open but she was so far away from it that she couldn't be sure. Then again, the store was deathly quiet so it was possible she had heard someone enter the bookstore from above.

"Where are you, girl?"

Rachael's heart leapt in her chest. She tried to figure out from which direction she'd heard the voice. On her left? Straight ahead?

"I will find you, little girl. You can't hide forever."

She recognized the voice and it most certainly was the man from the other side of the portal.

Rachael reached within and called her fire magic. She was frightened but she wasn't going to let her fear run away with her like she had when the DAX attacked her. She gripped the sword in one hand and maneuvered to better ascertain where the man stood.

"Come out and give me the sword, girl. I won't harm you if you turn it over to me. I'm the rightful owner, you know. It was stolen from me just days ago."

Rachael peeked between a display of bookmarks and one of magnifier reading glasses. He stood near the bargain books displayed not twenty feet from her. She ducked back into hiding but must've made some slight sound that he could hear because there was a rustle of movement, and the next thing she knew he was on her side of the counter she'd been hiding behind.

"Give me that sword!" He reached for her but she sprang away nearly falling as his hand just missed closing on her arm.

"It's not your sword!" Rachael shouted as she scrambled away.

She felt magic build to her right. She turned. The white-haired woman held Rachael's gaze, then released the magic…air magic. A strong wind slammed into Rachael, causing her to lose her footing. She stumbled and grabbed onto the counter but she kept sliding across the floor, her legs barely able to keep up as she was propelled backward. Eventually she fell and dropped the sword.

The man strode forward to get the sword which now lay six feet from Rachael. She crawled forward in an effort to get there first and stretched out her arm, willing the sword into her hand, she was stunned when it actually skittered across the floor and right into her palm.

Unlike the last time she held the sword, Rachael felt power surge through her. The sword was alive in her hand and her every cell felt electrified.

Rachael felt the woman's air magic building once again but then the sword blade glowed orange, yellow and gold. Rachael felt the moment when she and the sword merged into one and noticed that neither the man nor the woman advanced on her. Sparks flew from Fire-Starter and amazingly, from her own body.

The woman's magic dwindled. She looked at the man.

"Let's go," he said. "This changes things." He drew symbols in the air and Rachael saw the shimmer where a portal began to open.

"Why are you opening portals to other worlds?" she shouted at him. "What do you want with these swords? What do you have to gain?"

He stepped through the portal then turned back. His eyes held a maniacal gleam. "Why should there be three separate worlds when there could be just one?"

The portal closed. The man and woman were gone.

Almost immediately the sword felt heavy in Rachael's hand. She staggered and caught herself as the overwhelming presence of Fire-Starter left her and retreated back into its metal home. But she could still feel its essence; its magic had joined with hers on a very deep level. It was a bond that couldn't be, wouldn't be shattered. She and this sword were now bound together for life; she knew it with a strange certainty.

Seconds later Rachael heard vehicles coming into the parking lot. She went to the window at the front of the store so she could look out and see who was there. When she saw the Slayers she ran to the back of the store, to the door that led to the stairs and to the office, then remembered the door would be locked. Was the code on this door the same as the one to the outside? What was that number again? She tried to remember but it was no use. She hadn't a clue and she was locked in the bookstore. Would Tristan or anyone else think to look down here for her? Would anyone even notice she wasn't upstairs?

As Rachael stood contemplating these things, the door in question burst open. "Rachael!" Tristan called out. "Are you down here?"

"Yes!" She hurried through the store to meet him at the doorway but when he saw her, he drew is own sword and crouched ready to do battle.

Rachael whirled around to see where the threat came from but there was no one there. She turned back. "Tristan, what's wrong?"

A look of confusion passed over his face. "Rachael? Is that you?"

Now Rachael was confused. "Yes, of course it's me. Who else would it be? I don't have a twin here that I know of." She started to walk toward him but he kept his guard up and looked at her suspiciously.

"Prove it."

Rachael stopped and frowned at him. "Why should I have to prove it? You know what I look like. You probably even know the sound of my voice by now. What's wrong with you?"

"You have the sword."

"Yeah, so?"

"And you don't look like you."

Rachael didn't know whether to be angry or scared. What the crap was he talking about? "What do you mean I don't look like me?"

"Your hair."

She lifted a hand to her hair and felt it. It's not like it was standing on end or anything and it felt the same as always. What was his problem? "What about my hair? Why you're all freaked out?"

"Look at it. Look at the color!"

Rachael scowled at him and pulled a chunk of hair forward so she could look at it. The room was in semi-darkness but even so Rachael could tell her hair wasn't blonde anymore.

"What the...?" She darted passed Tristan and into the woman's bathroom just a few feet away. Before the door shut, she felt around for the light switch and flipped it on then turned toward the mirror. Immediately she saw what Tristan had referred to.

Rachael gasped. Her hair was red; and not just red but bright red, shot through with highlights of equally bright yellow and orange. Her hair looked like the flames of a raging fire.

CHAPTER EIGHT

RACHAEL SUCKED IN A DEEP BREATH. "OKAY, okay," she muttered. "I can fix this. I can glamour it back to blonde. It might not be a permanent fix but…it'll be okay. This is going to be okay."

She called her glamour magic, the magic that hid her extra pointy ears and her tri-colored green eyes from the humans in her world. Surely, she could cover this crazy hair too. But nothing happened. The glamour didn't work. For the first time in her life, since she was a very small child, she couldn't disguise her appearance; at least not her hair.

Rachael staggered out of the women's restroom in shock. She looked up at Tristan and the look on her face must've told him what he needed to know because he put away his sword.

"I can't make it go away! It's permanent!" she gasped.

"What happened? And why are you carrying around that sword?"

Rachael looked down at the blade in her hand. "I fire tested it."

Tristan sighed. "What? When?"

"Just before you all left to go out tonight. How did it go, by the way? Did you get the portal closed?"

"Before we get to that, tell me about the sword."

Rachael shook her head. "It's always about the sword with you."

"Just tell me! How did your hair end up like that? And what are you doing down here?"

"Well, after you all left a portal opened upstairs in Kirk's lab."

"What!" Tristan's eyes widened. "Right inside the offices?"

"Yes." Rachael explained about the man and woman she'd seen and her fear of them coming through the portal to get the sword.

"And she asked about her son?" Tristan asked.

Rachael nodded.

He frowned. "What did she look like?"

"Long white hair, petite."

"Hmm, and him? What did he look like?"

"He had grey eyes, black hair to his shoulders with streaks of grey in it and he had a big scar." She indicated how it looked by tracing a line down her own face with her finger.

Tristan's eyes widened. "It's true then. You just perfectly described Thomas's father. I don't know if the woman is Lairen's mother but I don't know why he'd lie about that part. What the hell are they after? What is it they're trying to do?"

"They want to rule the world," Rachael said. "Or in this case, worlds. I asked him. He told me."

She told Tristan about her confrontation with Mr. and Mrs. Megalomaniac there in the bookstore and what had happened with the sword.

"Whoa!" Tristan exclaimed.

She nodded. "I know!" She then had a thought. "I wonder if he realizes that it's me who activated the sword. If he knows that—"

Tristan followed her train of thought perfectly. "He'll try and kidnap you to activate the other swords."

Rachael's eyes widened and she grabbed Tristan's arm. "But he can't know that for sure and he can never find out!"

"He won't. I'll talk to the others and make sure they know not to breathe a word of it."

Rachael relaxed a little. "Okay. Okay, good."

"So, this sword is Fire-Starter."

Rachael nodded.

"And it's bonded to you."

Rachael nodded again. "Yeah. I didn't know that would happen when I picked it up after I tested it." She made a face. "And I guess I got a makeover I didn't want too because now I can't even magic my hair back to its regular color. Or any other color either for that matter. I tried while I was in the bathroom."

Tristan sighed. "Well, let's go back upstairs and I'll fill you in on our end of things and you can let the others know what happened while we were gone."

"No wait, tell me now. What happened out there? Is the portal closed?"

"Yes. That's one thing we got right tonight. The portal is closed. Of course, that doesn't mean another one from that damn fire-filled place can't be opened again somewhere else."

"You saw through it to the other side?"

"Yeah, pretty horrible."

"How did Kirk get the portal closed?"

Tristan shrugged. "Some sort of science stuff. I don't know. I'm a Slayer not a scientist. That's why he gets paid the big bucks and I just get blood on my clothes and run through a lot of laundry detergent."

"And what about the Dark-Angels and the DAX? Any sign of them?"

He shrugged. "They seem pretty scarce lately."

"Maybe that's because these new monsters have scared them all away," Amy said from behind them. "If we're lucky the new badass monsters will wipe out the old ones and save us the trouble. And what the hell happened to your hair?"

"Long story," Rachael said with a sigh.

"Come on," Tristan gestured for them to go back upstairs. Once they were back in the offices Tristan went looking for Thomas while Rachael explained what had happened in everyone's absence, to Amy, Stefan and Ariel and some of the other Slayers.

Tristan returned shortly. "Where's Westfall?"

"Dunno," Stefan answered.

"He probably went home," Ariel suggested.

"What?" Amy shook her head. "No way. He's usually the first one in and the last to leave. And he was just here a minute ago."

"What's up with him lately? Half the time I can't find him when I need to talk to him and now is one of those times," Tristan grumbled.

Amy looked barely able to contain her anger and frustration. "I feel so useless. Here we are, Slayers who are supposed to be protecting this city and we can't even protect ourselves and our own damn office space!"

"I think maybe I should go talk to our prisoner again," Tristan said. "He holds the key to all of this, I'm certain of it. If we could just find out where his conniving parents live—"

Thomas came striding toward them from the direction of his office.

"Where the hell have you been?" Tristan snapped, interrupting himself. "I'm going back to Ravenwood to question the prisoner."

Rachael looked up at Tristan. "I want to go with you."

Thomas finally looked at her and was clearly startled. "Rachael? What happened to—?"

"Amy can fill you in," Tristan didn't wait for Thomas' approval; he just headed for the door. Rachael followed him.

"Be careful," Thomas shouted after them. "It's well after sunset now."

They passed the lockers and Tristan veered right to grab something out of one of them. Once they were outside, he strapped Rachael into a scabbard that would allow her to carry the sword at her hip, then got on the motorcycle.

"This is the weirdest thing," she muttered. "I'm not a warrior. Why did the sword pick me?"

"Maybe we'll figure that part out later. Right now, I want to get over to Ravenwood." Tristan started the motorcycle.

"Why is your prison or whatever it's called so far away from your office?" Rachael asked.

"We're just above the book store temporarily," he replied. "But soon we'll all be at Ravenwood and we'll have a lot more room over there too. We might've been there already if that portal thing hadn't happened." He inclined his head to the right. "Incoming."

He snapped his visor down and Rachael did the same as she turned to see a couple of DAX heading their way. Tristan shot out of the parking lot and through the intersection. Compared to the last time they'd gone this way, there weren't nearly as many hybrid creatures lurking along the road. Maybe the larger monsters that came through the portal really had scared them all off...or killed them.

Once they reached their destination, Rachael pulled off her helmet and followed Tristan back through the security points to the facility below ground. They rounded the corner to the cell where Lairen was supposed to be, only he wasn't there.

Tristan scowled. "What the hell?"

He darted through the entire level, looking in one room after the other while Rachael waited. A thought suddenly came to her.

"Crap! I should've thought of it sooner!"

Tristan hurried back in her direction after searching all the cells and the room where they'd conversed with him before.

"What?" he snapped. "What did you think of?"

"If Lairen's parents know how to open portals, then he does too. He let himself out."

Tristan shook his head. "But even if he knows how to open portals, why wait this long? He's been in here for...what...four days now? Why would he stick around if he was always able to set himself free?"

"Or, maybe his parents just finally found him," Rachael suggested. "They could've done some sort of locator spell or something and—"

"Damn it!" Tristan pulled his cell phone from his pocket and hit a number on speed dial. "He's gone!" he barked into the phone. There was silence for a second or two. "I don't know! How the hell should I know?" He shoved the phone back in his pocket. "No point sticking around here. Come on, let's go."

"Who were you talking to?" Rachael asked as she trotted after Tristan.

"Thomas."

They emerged from the building and headed over to the motorcycle but Tristan stopped dead in his tracks and Rachael nearly ran into him.

"Son of a bitch," Tristan muttered. "This just keeps getting better."

"What?" Rachael asked as she sidestepped and stopped at his side. "Oh."

There were three DAX hovering around the motorcycle. They turned, one by one, and stared at Tristan and Rachael.

"What do we do?" Rachael asked.

"You go back inside. I'll take care of this."

"Um, Tristan?"

"Yeah, what?"

"I'm not going back to the building."

"This isn't the time to argue, Rachael. Get in there."

"No, you don't understand. The way is blocked. We have more visitors."

Tristan cursed but Rachael was undaunted. She had her fire magic, she had Fire-Starter and she had Tristan at her side. This was going to be a piece of cake.

CHAPTER NINE

RACHAEL WAS AWARE THAT HER THOUGHTS weren't entirely her own. Sure, she was more confident than she'd been before the confrontation in the bookstore with Lairen's family, thanks to the sword's assistance, but fighting a half a dozen DAX didn't seem to her like a "piece of cake". She reached behind her for Fire-Starter, which slid comfortably into her hand, and unsheathed the sword.

Piece of cake. Bring it on.

That was most definitely Fire-Starter talking, yet Rachael heard the words mingle with her own thoughts and come out of her mouth as well.

"Piece of cake. Bring it on." She felt infinitely more confident having said it aloud.

Tristan threw a glance her way. "Okay then. Here we go."

He unsheathed a long blade from the holster along his thigh and pulled a stake from within his coat. The nearly full moon gave them all the light they'd need to save their lives.

"Just remember, no mercy."

"Don't worry," Rachael said. "I got it."

"We're going over to the motorcycle, slowly. Follow my lead."

Rachael, sword at the ready, followed Tristan while keeping an eye out behind them. She'd hoped the three by the building would stay out of it. No such luck, they were stalking her.

She focused her power and called up her magic, then lifted her arm. "I'm going to take care of these three following us," she said to Tristan. "Get ready for some fire."

Rachael released her magic, fire shooting from her palm. There was an extra punch to it since she also held Fire-Starter in her other fist. Flames hit the closest DAX, then reached for the two behind. All three shrieked.

"Watch your back!" Tristan shouted to her.

She shut off her fire magic and whirled to see Tristan battling two of the DAX at once, while a third DAX eyed her hungrily. Rachael turned her head to keep an eye on the DAX on fire. Two of them were dust in the wind but unfortunately one of them still staggered toward her; now just an arm's reach away. The fire seemed to have singed him but not torched him.

Rachael felt the sword press her mind. It wanted to take over. She was more than happy to turn over the reins since on her own she was clueless.

Power surged up her arm along with heat, strength, and the cunning of Fire-Starter's magic. She ducked, ran past the DAX and struck, using both hands on the sword for extra support. The smoldering DAX's head left its shoulders. The hybrid turned to dust but Rachael didn't waste time watching it happen. Instead, she turned to see that Tristan had already bested two of the remaining DAX. Only one remained. The horrible creature was right next to the motorcycle when Tristan slashed it across the chest, causing it to stagger backwards. He staked it and the DAX disintegrated.

Tristan looked around. "Wow, I'm impressed. You really held your own and then some." He glanced down at the motorcycle. "Ugh, now there's DAX blood and dust all over my bike."

Rachael made a face and held up her sword. "Is there something I can wipe the blade on? It's got DAX blood on it."

Tristan chuckled. "Ah, the girly girl appears after the battle is won."

Rachael grinned. "You should talk! You're all worried about your precious motorcycle getting DAX dust on it too."

"Touché." He pulled a couple of rags from the saddlebags on the motorcycle. "Here." He tossed one to her. "And let's get out of here before any more show up."

They put on their helmets and climbed aboard the motorcycle. As Tristan maneuvered the bike back onto the main road, Rachael caught a glimpse of something dark moving in concert with them; perhaps stalking them.

"I think there might be another one," she said and pointed in the direction of the shadow.

Tristan looked where she pointed then gunned it and the motorcycle leapt forward. Rachael was very glad her seat had a sissy bar as a back support or she might've gone right off the back of the bike.

"Whoa!" she yelled. "Don't do that."

He shouted something back to her but she couldn't hear it over the rushing wind and the sound of the engine.

"I couldn't hear you before," she said when they finally reached the bookstore parking lot. "What did you say back there after you took off like a rocket?"

Tristan hurriedly punched in the code for the door while Rachael looked around. Luckily there were no DAX skulking behind the building.

"That wasn't a DAX," Tristan said once they were safely indoors.

"Then what was it?" Rachael asked as they trotted up the stairs leading to the next security keypad.

"It was a Dark Angel."

Rachael suddenly realized she hadn't yet seen one of those. In fact, she'd almost forgotten about them what with all the other monsters roaming about, not to mention the portals, Sebastian Westfall and his wife, and of course the shock of finding out she might have a half-brother as well as simply trying to adjust to the fact she was in another world so different from her own.

"I didn't get a good look at it," she said while unstrapping the scabbard and sword from her hips.

Tristan had shrugged off his coat and now leaned on one of the desks. No one else was around.

"Be glad you haven't seen one up close and personal yet. If you think the DAX are horrific, just wait 'til you come face to face with a Dark Angel."

"How are they different from the DAX?" Rachael yawned. Yawned! "Gosh, I'm sorry. I just got so tired all of a sudden. It's because I used my magic. It always drains me."

"Maybe you should go get some sleep. It's been a long day. I'll tell you about the Dark-Angels tomorrow."

"What about you? Do you always stay here? Don't you have a home to go to?" Rachael asked.

"Yeah, I do but," he shrugged. "I'm just gonna stay here tonight. I don't think you should be alone here now that we know Sebastian Westfall can open a portal right here in the office." He shook his head. "I still can't get over the fact that Thomas's dad is involved in all this."

His cell phone zinged and Tristan looked down at the text. "It's from Thomas. He talked to our mom and she confirmed that the woman Sebastian married years ago is named Beatrix and she already had a son; a blond boy. Well, I guess we already knew it was all true but still…"

Rachael raked her now flame-red hair back. "Sorry, I don't mean to be rude but I really do have to get some sleep. I can hardly keep my eyes open."

"No problem. Go back to Kirk's office where you were last night. I'll catch some sleep in Thomas's office. There's a pretty decent couch in there."

Rachael got to her feet, grabbed the sword and scabbard from the table and staggered back to Kirk's office.

"Just yell if you need anything." Tristan shouted after her. "And stash that sword somewhere so it's out of sight!"

"I will!" she said with a wave of her hand but without bothering to turn around.

When she got back to Kirk's office, she peeled off her clothes, except for Tristan's t-shirt, slid the sword under the mattress near the head of the bed, and dropped down onto the fold out bed. Her last thoughts before drifting off to sleep were that she really needed to go shopping for clothes but how would she pay since her money would be no good here…and then she fell asleep.

Rachael awakened to the sound of someone walking around and shuffling papers. She opened her eyes and saw Kirk near his desk.

"Hey," she said in a sleepy voice. "Sorry I'm in your office again."

He looked over at her. "No problem. I just came in for some things.

Someone knocked on the door jam and both Rachael and Kirk turned.

"Morning," Ariel said. "I come bearing gifts."

She strode over to where Rachael had been sleeping and dumped a pile of clothes on the bed.

"Looks like you're going to be here for a while so I brought you some things."

"Wow, thanks!" Rachael sat up and brushed her hair back. She caught a glimpse of it lying over her shoulder and was startled to see red instead of blonde. She made a face. "Ugh. I don't know if I'm going to be able to get used to this."

Kirk slipped out of the room and Ariel sat on the edge of the bed. "Actually, I think it's kind of awesome. You look good with red hair."

Rachael made a face. "Thanks, but I'm not so sure. It's hardly natural looking and bold and brash is not generally my look. If you know what I mean."

Ariel nodded. "I understand, but it really isn't so bad. So anyway, look through the clothes and see what you can wear. I think the tops should all fit and we can go out today and buy you another pair of jeans and whatever else you need."

Rachael smiled. "This is so nice of you. You totally read my mind. I so need to go do something normal for a little while and I really could use some extra clothes."

Ariel stood up and headed for the door. "Come to the conference room when you're dressed. There's stuff to eat."

After she was gone Rachael sorted through the selection of t-shirts (both long and short sleeved), button down shirts, sweatshirts, and there was even a well-worn beige denim jacket. All she'd need to buy were jeans and some undergarments for now.

She got up, tugged on her jeans, grabbed a chocolate brown long sleeved t-shirt as well as the beige jacket and headed for the bathroom to shower and dress. While she was there, she washed her hair too.

Once clean and clothed Rachael stood in front of the mirror and combed her hair. Wet, it was darker, not quite so brilliant a red but she could still see the orange and yellow streaks throughout.

She stared at herself in the mirror. Who was this girl who looked back at her? Where was her soft blonde hair, her delicate jewelry, and the pretty pastel colors she usually wore? Instead, this girl in the mirror looked incredibly different. The only familiar thing was the necklace Rachael wore. Her mom hand given it to her as a gift, a white gold heart with a blue topaz in the center. Rachael fingered the necklace and tears blurred her vision. She wanted to desperately to go home. She missed her parents, her sisters and her friends at the Bureau; especially Skye, her best friend.

Amy barged into the communal bathroom. "Hey, there you are. You okay?"

"Yeah," Rachael sniffed and grabbed a tissue to wipe the tears from her cheeks and to blow her nose. "I'm okay. What's up?"

Amy's blonde bangs hung in her eyes and she brushed them back. "Argh, gotta get these things cut. Anyway, Ariel is saving food for you since the others are in there scarfing everything down. Just thought you should know. I heard you handled yourself pretty well fighting some DAX last night. Tristan is impressed which makes me impressed coz not much is newsworthy with him."

"Oh, well thanks," Rachael couldn't help but smile. Knowing she'd scored some points with both Tristan and Amy made her feel a little better...a little more accepted within this group of natural born fighters. She was definitely the odd girl out, yet here she was, like it or not. But hopefully she wouldn't be here for too long.

She shrugged into the beige jacket and noticed it was just like the one Amy wore.

Obviously, Amy noticed it too. "I see you have one of Ariel extras."

"Yeah, she loaned me some shirts. I need to go get another pair of jeans though. I just don't know how I'm going to pay for them."

"I'll talk to Westfall about putting you on the payroll for clothing expenses. And maybe for food expense too."

Rachael's smile broadened. "Thanks. That would really help."

The two of them walked together to the conference room where Ariel flagged them down. Rachael made her way to the seat next to Ariel while Amy veered off to speak with Stefan and Daze about something.

"Here, I saved you some food," Ariel said.

Rachael reached for the coffee, bowl of mixed fruit and plate of hot food.

"Sorry the potatoes and stuff aren't very warm anymore but there's a microwave over there," Ariel pointed and Rachael saw it on the counter to her right.

"Thank you. And for the clothes too. I really appreciate it."

"No worries. Eat up. Westfall should be here in a few minutes."

Rachael went to the microwave and heated the food. "Where's Tristan?" she asked once she'd returned to the table.

Ariel glanced around and shrugged. "Dunno."

Just then Thomas Westfall and Tristan entered the room and without being told everyone took a seat. Some were still eating remnants of their breakfast. Others sipped coffee. The room fell silent. Tristan took an empty chair near Stefan and Amy. Kirk sat along the far wall; separate from the rest of them. Thomas stood at the head of the table and addressed them all.

"I want to bring everyone up to speed on everything. Kirk and his team have found a way to close any portals that open in the future." He gestured for Kirk to speak.

Kirk stepped forward and addressed the group. "It's complicated but basically what we do is run an electrical current to the opening of the portal and shock it. That causes the magic to be disrupted and the portal to collapse." He stepped back and Westfall continued.

"So, that's one hurdle. As for the flying bird-like creatures we've seen come through the portal. Those of you with archery skills, meet with Kirk after this meeting. We're going to set you up with explosives that will be attached to your arrows. Next up are the DAX and Dark-Angels. For the time being we're going to stop looking for them specifically. If you come across them, kill them but don't go looking for them. Our focus is going to remain on the newest threats."

Thomas gestured toward the three Slayers sitting closest to him. "Daze, Stefan and Tristan are going to work together to bring down those ten-foot-tall behemoths, one at a time." He turned to Kirk. "If you can come up with any adjustments to weapons or create something new that will work on these monsters it would be much appreciated. The sooner the better."

Kirk nodded and Thomas Westfall surveyed the room. "Some of you may not be aware that we've identified the person opening the portals. There may be more than one person, but at this time we know only that..." he paused and took in a breath, eyes downcast. His eyes snapped up. "My father, Sebastian Westfall is the one at fault."

There was a bit of murmuring around the room. After opening a folder he'd carried in with him, Westfall continued.

These are photos of Sebastian Westfall and his wife, Beatrix. Who, by the way, is *not* my mother in case anyone is not clear on that. My parents were only together for two years."

The photos were passed around.

"If anyone sees either of these two people you have my permission to do whatever it takes to prevent them from opening any more portals. I would prefer for them to be captured and held for questioning, but if that isn't possible…" He didn't finish his sentence but Rachael figured everyone in the room got his meaning.

"Alright," he said. "Meeting is over." He turned and left the room.

CHAPTER TEN

A FEW MINUTES PASSED AS THE ROOM CLEARED out. Rachael had no idea what she should do. Was she expected to go out and fight with the rest of them?

"Rachael!" Ariel called out as she hurried into the room. "Amy spoke to Westfall and he okayed you a line of credit to buy some clothes and stuff. I thought I'd come tell you the good news and take you out shopping. Do you want to go now?"

Rachael smiled. "Sure! But are you sure I shouldn't be…I don't know, doing something more productive?"

Ariel shrugged. "Well, you'd actually be doing me a favor."

"I would?"

Ariel's eyes dropped. "Yeah, if I keep busy, I'm less likely to think about Alina and all the others who, you know…died."

Rachael's eyes widened. She'd been so busy thinking about her own troubles that she'd almost forgotten that Ariel was grieving the loss of her friends.

"Hey Rachael," Tristan strode into the room. "I want to talk to you about something."

"Can it wait?" Ariel piped up. "We were just about to go out."

Tristan looked slightly taken aback. "Oh, okay. It can wait. Where are you going?"

"Ariel is taking me to get some extra clothes. I really don't have anything much with me except what I was wearing when I came here and I—"

"Yes, absolutely. Go. I'll see you guys back here later. Be careful out there though," he warned. "Remember, these newest Hell-Spawn are out in the daytime, not just at night."

"How could I forget," Ariel muttered as they walked away from him.

They went outside and got into the battered beige Jeep-like vehicle that Ariel drove.

"Where're we going?" Rachael asked as she buckled up.

"We'll try the mall first but a lot of stores haven't reopened since those, Hell-Spawn, as Tristan says, came through the portal."

They drove about three miles to the mall and Rachael saw very few cars along the way. She figured most people were playing it safe and staying indoors. When they got to the mall Rachael caught her first glimpse of one of the 'Hell-Spawn'. One of the bird-like creatures that had come through the portal was perched on the roof of the mall.

"Uh, oh," she pointed and Ariel followed her gaze.

"Well, crap." Ariel pulled the car over and stopped before the creature spotted them.

"It looks like one of those flying dinosaurs we learned about in school," Rachael whispered. "A pterodactyl, I think they're called. What're we going to do? Do you think it'll chase us if we keep driving?"

"Yeah, that's why I stopped the car."

As Rachael mulled that over and wondered what the best thing was for them to do next, some people came out of the main entrance to the mall. There were only a few cars in the parking lot and all of them were parked as close as they could get to the entrance.

"There must be some stores open in there," Rachael said. "Those people have shopping bags."

Before she could draw another breath to speak, the pterodactyl's head swiveled to the left. He'd spied the people rushing to their car. Its body lifted, wings spread.

Rachael gasped. "Oh no."

The pterodactyl let out a screech and dove toward its prey. The people saw the giant bird-like creature coming and ran but it was no use. One of the monster's claws grabbed one of the women, bags and all, while the other woman dropped her purchases and made a mad dash for the car door. The pterodactyl plucked her from the side of her car with its beak.

"No!" Rachael screamed as the beast swallowed its prey and flew off with the other person, most likely already dead, still fisted in its clawed foot.

Ariel took this opportunity, while the creature flew back to the roof, to wheel the car around. She took off, leaving a cloud of dust behind.

"Is it following?" she asked.

Rachael twisted in her seat to look out the back of the vehicle. "No."

Ariel sucked in a deep breath and released it. "We'll try Hampton's."

Rachael faced forward once again. She could hardly breathe. Her heart pounded and her mind searched for some way to deal with all she'd just seen.

She turned to Ariel. "You're so calm. How can you be so calm? We just saw two women get killed and eaten by that thing!"

Ariel kept her eyes on the road. "I'm more shaken up than you think, I'm just around this stuff more than you are so I've learned to deal with it better."

"No." Rachael shook her head. "No, you don't deal with *that* every day. That belongs in a horror movie, not in real life!" Rachael felt the panic in her voice but she didn't care. "I can't do this, Ariel. I can't. Someone has to find a way to send me home. Now. Today. I want to go home. I have to go home!"

Ariel pulled the car into another parking lot, this one without a pterodactyl hovering. She shut off the engine and turned to Rachael.

"Rachael, take some deep breaths and try to calm yourself down." She laid a hand on Rachael's arm. "Everyone is doing the best they can to solve all these problems we're facing, including getting you home. I promise. We'll get you home somehow. We will."

Rachael took a few calming breaths and tried to quell the panic that had risen so quickly.

"That's right, there you go," Ariel murmured. "It looks like Hampton's is open so we're going to walk in there, buy you some jeans and whatever else you need and then we're going to calmly walk back to the Starfleet and go back to the office. Okay?"

Rachael nodded and took one last deep calming breath. She let it out. "Okay. Right. What's a Starfleet?"

"It's the kind of car I'm driving," Ariel replied. "Come on. Let's go."

Ariel and Rachael got out of the Starfleet. Ariel came around and walked by Rachael's side, her eyes scanning their surroundings. Once they were inside Rachael released another breath, she hadn't realized she had been holding. Her body relaxed.

"How do I pay? I don't have a bank account here and my fingerprint won't be on file here." To her embarrassment her voice got that panicky sort of hitch to it again.

"Here," Ariel maneuvered Rachael over to a chair. Rachael sat and Ariel knelt in front of her and took her hands. "Look. Everything is going to be okay. Westfall gave me a pre-paid card to give to you." She fished it out of an inside pocket in her jacket. "See? This is how you'll pay for your clothes." Ariel smiled at her. "Now come on, let's shop." She stood up and so did Rachael.

Rachael nodded. "Okay. Sorry. Thanks for being so patient with me. It's just…I've never seen…" Her voice trembled.

"I know. It's okay. Let's go look at the jeans." Ariel headed down the nearest aisle and Rachael followed.

Forty-five minutes later Rachael had selected two pairs of jeans, some new undergarments, a package of black socks, some pink cotton floral print pajamas to sleep in and a sturdy black duffel to keep her things in.

"Is there enough money on that card to cover all this?" she asked.

Ariel nodded. "And then some. Do you need make-up or anything? We've got plenty of shampoo and conditioner back at the office but we take turns buying it so if—"

Rachael's eyes widened. "Oh, I didn't know that! Yes, let's definitely get some. I want to contribute."

They spent a few more minutes in the store and were then ready to check out. For a while Rachael had been able to block out the image of those two women being killed by the pterodactyl but as she and Ariel checked out those images came flooding back. Rachael told herself to get a grip. She wanted to be more like Ariel. Be horrified at what had happened but then put it behind her.

As they left the store, Ariel paused to scan the sky. She also surveyed the parking lot for anything threatening. Rachael did the same.

"Looks good. Come on," Ariel said.

Rachael followed her lead and the two of them made it back to the Starfleet safely.

"Where did you stash the sword?" Ariel asked on the drive back to the Slayer United office.

"Under the mattress of the foldout bed."

"I think maybe you should carry it with you all the time."

Rachael frowned. "It's kinda big to be carrying around everywhere."

Ariel shrugged. "Yeah, but with all that's going on it might be a good idea."

Rachael thought about that. "Yeah, I see what you mean."

They pulled, once again, into the parking lot and drove around to the back. Ariel parked and Rachael gathered her things. They went through both security doors quickly and entered the office.

Several Slayers were there and most seemed to be discussing strategy.

"There you are," Thomas Westfall said as he approached them.

"See ya later, Rachael," Ariel whispered, and veered off to speak to Stefan and Amy.

"You can put those bags in my office, then gather the rest of your things and bring them there too," Thomas said once he and Rachael were face to face.

"Ah, sure," Rachael replied. "What's going on?"

"I've decided it's not a good idea for that Elfaen sword to be here all the time now that we know Sebastian can open a portal here. If he gets his hands on that sword…Well, anyway, Tristan and I have discussed it and you're going to be staying at his place, with him, starting tonight. The sword will be safe there and so should you be."

Rachael nodded. "Oh, okay." Still shaken up by what she'd seen earlier, she had a hard time switching gears.

Rachael went to Westfall's office to drop off her bags, then went back to Kirk's office to gather what she had back there. Most of what she had actually belonged to Ariel but Rachael also grabbed her backpack purse, then decided to make another trip to get the sword. When she arrived back at the entrance to Thomas's office, Tristan was there.

"I guess he gave you the news that we're going to be roommates," Tristan said.

Rachael dropped the rest of her belongings onto Thomas's sofa. "Yeah. Is that what you wanted to talk to me about before?"

He nodded.

Rachael didn't know if she liked the idea of rooming with a guy. "Um, no offense, but weren't there any girls who I could—?"

There was some sort of commotion is the other room and Tristan dashed out the door with Rachael hot on his heels.

Another portal had been opened right there in the office.

"Get back," Tristan shouted and threw his arm out to block Rachael from running past him headlong into a whirlwind.

Papers flew all around and Rachael felt the wind pull at her, causing her to inch forward in spite of Tristan's arm. Her hair whipped around her face and she struggled to grab it all and keep it out of her eyes.

"It's them, isn't it?" she shouted above the roar. "Sebastian Westfall and Beatrix?"

And then to Rachael's utter shock something huge came through the portal; huge and terrifying. The thing stood ten feet tall at least, had enormous muscles, black shaggy hair, a pronounced brow bone, large jagged teeth and eyes that were an eerie yellow. It lumbered through the portal carrying a weapon with a claw on one end and a blade on the other. Rachael suddenly realized that this weapon was what had caused the claw marks on Alina's body.

As the beast passed through the portal the wind turned hot. The temperature in the room rose considerably and Rachael didn't think anyone close to the portal could possibly stand it. And then the wind was gone but the heat stayed; along with the monster that started swinging its fists and its weapon.

The Slayers were caught completely off guard and many didn't even have time to grab a weapon; especially while that wind had been whipping though the office. Even those who did manage to get something to fight with couldn't get close enough to the monster to do any damage.

"Get back in the office!" Tristan shouted at her then ran into the fray to help the other Slayers.

Rachael was torn. On the one hand, fear told her to seek cover until this was over, but on the other hand she was a little offended that Tristan had so little confidence in her. Hadn't she fought three DAX and won? Of course, she'd had the sword with her then but still…

She maneuvered around fallen chairs and overturned desks. The sound in the room was deafening, what with shouts, grunts of exertion, clanging of metal on metal, screams of pain and the roar of the beast from the hellish world.

Tristan was right in the thick of it and came very close to being slashed by the clawed end of the monster's weapon. Rachael saw Stefan fly through the air after being hit by a giant fist. He was a rather large guy himself, which made it all the more shocking that he would be disposed of so easily by the monster; like brushing a crumb from the table. When he hit the far wall and slumped to the ground Rachael was afraid he'd been killed. But then he staggered to his feet and rejoined the fight.

Ariel and Amy worked in concert to slash at the hell creature's legs from behind. Others engaged the monster on the other three sides but no one was making any real headway. Rachael cringed as two and then three of the Slayers were felled; one run through by the beast's blade and two torn apart by the clawed end of the weapon. They didn't get up.

Rachael knew she had to do something to help. She called up her magic, raised her arm and directed fire right at the monster's broad back; an easy enough target. There were no Slayers in the way to get burned, and the ones who were nearby backpedaled to stay well out of the way.

The beast whirled and for a moment Rachael thought it might charge at her and that the fire wasn't actually causing it any harm after all. But then Tristan and Stefan both plunged swords into the hell monster's back. It let out a roar, turned and fell back through the still open portal, which closed with a snap.

The Slayers, at least the ones who were left standing, stood still for a second or two in silence, catching their breath and assessing their own wounds and the condition of their comrades as well as the room, which was pretty much destroyed. There was a small amount of fire damage, caused by Rachael's fire magic, but at least the whole place hadn't caught on fire. That had happened once before when Rachael had used fire magic. Luckily the torched monster had fallen back through the portal.

Three of the Slayers didn't get up and weren't even moving.

Thomas went to each of the bodies and crouched down beside them. He shook his head after checking for vitals.

"Do what you can to heal any of your injuries," he said. "And get something to cover the bodies. I'll notify families." He got up. "Don't bother straightening this place up," Thomas instructed as he looked around and assessed the damage. "We're going to relocate to Ravenwood immediately. This location is compromised."

"You should've thought of that yesterday after the first portal was opened in here!" someone shouted. "If we'd done what we should've and moved right away then Daze and the others wouldn't be dead!"

Rachael's eyes widened. Daze was dead? She felt a wave of sadness. She'd known him, if only just a little bit.

Thomas looked at the guy who had spoken out. "There is a time and a place to vent your frustration and anger about what's happened, but right here right now isn't it. There's too much to be done and the more quickly the better. Let's do what we have to do to take care of the wounded and the dead and get our things transferred over to the Ravenwood Compound. Save the anger for our real enemy; the monsters and the man pulling their strings."

"He's your father!" someone else shouted. "How can we trust you when your own father is trying to kill us?"

"And doing a damn good job of it too!" a third person added.

Rachael watched Thomas turn his steely gaze to the new hecklers. "I said, this isn't the time or the place. Attend to your fellow Slayers and get this place packed up." He turned and stormed passed Rachael and Tristan, straight into his office and slammed the door.

CHAPTER ELEVEN

WITHOUT A WORD, TRISTAN WENT TO HELP the others. Rachael also left her spot along the far wall to see how she could help. She was happy to see that both Amy and Ariel were alive and unharmed. Stefan had a cut above his eye, which was bleeding, but he seemed okay too.

After a minute or two Tristan returned. "Go get the sword and keep it with you at all times from now on."

Rachael nodded and hurried back to Kirk's office. The sword was right where she'd left it, thankfully. She buckled it on, then quickly headed back to join the Slayers. Kirk met her half way.

"Hey, would you help me box up some stuff?" he asked. "Unless you're supposed to be doing something else."

"No, I can help," Rachael said and walked back to the office with him. Kirk showed her where some boxes were and what to pack.

"That was some pretty fancy magic back there," he said while they worked. "Is everybody able to do stuff like that where you come from?"

"No. Just the Elfae."

"They can all throw fire?"

"No, no. Some control air, some water…very few wield fire."

"Sort of like the Elementals then. Did Thomas or Tristan tell you about them…us?"

Rachael nodded.

Rachael made a few trips to carry boxes to one of the vehicles outside, then went back to the room where the portal had opened to see what else she could do to help.

Thomas emerged from his office. He looked tired. Tristan was with him.

"Come on," Tristan said to Rachael. "Grab a box. There's more to go down to the trucks."

"Sure." With a worried glance in Thomas's direction, she followed Tristan.

"Is he going to be okay?"

Tristan handed her a box. "He'll be okay. We'll get through this and everything will be okay."

"Are you sure about that?"

"If I keep saying it often enough it helps," Tristan replied.

Rachael didn't think that was a very confident answer but she understood.

They maneuvered around other Slayers who were also carrying things out of the compromised and demolished office, and down to the waiting vehicles. One by one boxes of paperwork, books, equipment, weapons, furniture and even the communal bathroom toiletries all got packed and transported to the Ravenwood Compound. Those who were injured had been tended to, either healed by their own quick healing bodies or by the healing magic of others.

By the time late afternoon rolled around Rachael was exhausted but at least they'd managed to remove everything from the office above the bookstore and were now at Ravenwood.

"Rachael," Thomas said when the two of them happened to be alone in his new office for a moment. "I want to thank you for what you did back there. You know, attacking with your fire like you did. It gave the others an opening."

"I'm just glad it worked," Rachael said and gave him a weary smile.

Tristan rounded the corner and entered Thomas's office. "Everyone's gone. Half of them wanted to go out tonight and kill anything that moves. The other half didn't feel like doing anything at all, just going home and letting the city rot, at least for a night."

Thomas shrugged. "And what about you?"

Tristan gave him a puzzled look. "Aren't you angry that no one even consulted you about what to do? We usually have a plan, some sort of structure for how we're going to proceed each night."

"Let them do what they want for tonight. Let them sleep on it and their tempers cool down. Tomorrow I'll call a meeting and we can hash things out."

"What about the Slayers who died today?" Tristan asked. "Daze and the others."

Thomas sighed. "I've contacted all the families and the coroner has their bodies." He looked around. "There's a lot of unpacking to do but not now. It's time to call it a night."

Tristan looked over at Rachael. "You ready to get outta here?"

Rachael nodded. "Yeah."

She scooped up the new duffel she'd purchased earlier while out shopping with Ariel. It was now stuffed with the new items she'd purchased as well as the clothing Ariel had given to her. She also grabbed her purse. Her phone battery no longer had a charge, but her phone wouldn't work over here anyway.

"All set," she said.

The three of them walked out together.

"Let's just hope Sebastian doesn't find this place," Tristan said just before he and Rachael split off from Thomas.

"He better not," Thomas replied. "We have nowhere else to go if this place gets compromised. We have to run him to ground and stop all this. Too many lives have been lost."

The three of them stood there in silence for a minute, then Thomas opened up his car door. "We best get going before darkness falls." He got in, shut the door and started the engine.

Rachael noticed the make and model of the black sedan. It was an Ulterra Bullet. Once again, she was reminded that she was far from home. None of the car models, stores, or restaurants were familiar. She felt a pang of longing for home but brushed it aside as best she could. There was no point in dwelling on something she couldn't do anything about right now.

"Let's go," Tristan handed her what she'd come to think of as 'her' helmet.

"What about my duffle?" she asked while putting it on.

"Wedge it between us and hang onto it."

He got onto the bike and she did as he suggested.

"Ready?" he asked.

"Ready!" she shouted above the noise of the engine.

Twenty minutes later they pulled into a neighborhood and down one of the narrow streets that ended in a cul-de-sac. Tristan drove into one of the driveways on Rachael's left at the very end of the road and parked in a garage made for two cars. The motorcycle was the only thing in it. Apparently, Tristan didn't own a car.

He shut off the engine and used a pulley to manually close the garage door. "I lost the remote," he said, then strode over and unlocked the door leading into the townhouse.

Rachael looked around as they entered directly into a laundry room, which led to a kitchen. There was a small dining area just beyond the kitchen.

"Come on. You can put your stuff in here."

Tristan led her out of the laundry room, to the right, beyond the front door to a hallway. He turned left.

"Here's the bathroom you can use," he indicated an open door to his right after they'd gone a few paces. "And the guest bedroom is right here." He inclined his head to the room in front of them with a view of a screened porch. "In case you're wondering, this was my parents' house. I grew up here. Make yourself at home. I'll be in the kitchen."

He left and Rachael stepped into the bedroom. There was daisy print wallpaper and she couldn't help but smile. Yeah, this was definitely not the way a guy would decorate; more like a mom's touch.

She plunked her duffle on the bed, unzipped it and unpacked her things. She folded everything and arranged the clothes in the large dresser across from the bed. She did put a few of the shirts in the closet along with the beige jacket Ariel had given her. Next Rachael carried her recently purchased toiletries into the guest bathroom. The daisy theme continued there with a flower print shower curtain.

Finally, all her things put away, Rachael walked back out to the main part of the townhouse. Across from the front door was a living room where French doors led to the same screened in porch that was just off the guest bedroom. Rachael wandered over to the doors and looked out. There was no real yard, just a small brick patio. There were no flowers or any other plants, which made the little area look rather sad and colorless. Rachael thought of her aunt and uncle's house with their beautiful big patio and sparkling fountain. She closed her eyes and willed the image away since it made her feel an almost unbearable longing for home.

"Hey, you want something to eat?"

Rachael turned toward his voice. Tristan stood there with a menu in his hand.

"I was thinking of ordering from this place. They'll probably still deliver since the sun hasn't set yet. It's getting close though. After that… no deliveries."

Rachael took the menu and looked it over. The food seemed to be a lot like what she'd find at a Chinese restaurant back home. "I'll have this one." She pointed to it. "Number forty-six."

He nodded. "Okay, be right back."

After Tristan left the room, Rachael continued to survey her surroundings. There was a large screen in the wall, which she figured was a television, and a comfortable looking sofa right across from it. There was also a fireplace with a prominent mantle over it. Above the mantle was a photo of a young couple, their arms around each other.

"Okay, the food is ordered," said Tristan as he strode back into the room.

Rachael turned to him but he'd obviously noticed her starting at the photo.

"They're my parents. They were both Slayers."

"Were?" Rachael asked and was almost afraid to hear the answer.

"Yeah, they're both dead." He dropped onto the sofa and switched on the screen in the wall. Every channel had a symbol indicating the station was off the air. "Damn vid stations. Just when we need them most, they've closed up shop." He switched it off again.

"I'm sorry about your parents."

"Yeah…well," he shrugged. "It comes with the job, as you've seen first-hand these last couple of days." He pulled up one sleeve of the army green t-shirt he wore and showed her the mark on his arm. "This appeared when I was sixteen. Every Elemental knows what it means. It means the person is Chosen." He pushed the sleeve back down before Rachael got much of a look at the mark. "Chosen to be a Slayer," he added.

"And you have no choice."

"None."

Rachael thought about her friend, Skye, and how she too was chosen… to be an Assassin for the Bureau. Skye hadn't wanted anything to do with her calling, but once Skye had accepted the responsibility, she'd become an excellent fighter and killer of demons, Shape-Shifters turned vicious and murderous Blood-Hunters.

"You're good at what you do. All of them seem to be."

He sighed. "Even so, Slayers don't last long."

"Nobody ever…retires?"

"Sometimes. My parents did. They married, had me. But in the end, they were killed anyway."

Rachael wanted to ask how it happened but she wasn't sure if she should ask something like that. While she was trying to decide if she should ask or not, the doorbell rang.

Tristan jumped up and went to look out the window by the front door. There was a narrow atrium and at the other end was a heavy metal security gate.

"It's the food," he said. He opened a narrow drawer in the long skinny table under the window and lifted out a handgun, then put it in the waist-band of his jeans, at his back.

Rachael watched as Tristan went out for the food, unlocked the gate and paid the delivery guy with a card and a fingerprint, just like Ariel had done that first day when Rachael got food in the bookstore cafe.

He waited until the delivery guy had driven away before coming back into the house. Once Tristan was inside Rachael could smell the food and her stomach growled.

Tristan grinned. "Hungry?"

"Very."

He got out plates and forks while Rachael dished up the food.

"All I've got is water," he said as he pulled glasses from the cupboard.

"That's okay."

They sat in the little dining area at a dark brown wooden table with four matching chairs.

"So, I noticed you didn't go back into Thomas's office when I told you to. You know, when that Hell-Spawn came through the portal," he said around a mouthful of food.

Rachael set down her fork. "Yeah, about that. I'm surprised you told me to go hide after I helped you kill the DAX the other day. I was kind of insulted, actually."

"I'm not used to the idea of you being a fighter. And, you didn't have the sword with you so…" he shrugged.

"But I still had my fire," she pointed out.

"Yes, but still…"

"Still, what?" Rachael was feeling a little angry and defensive. She picked up her fork again and stabbed one of the vegetables on her plate with a viciousness that wasn't really necessary. "Remember I work for an organization that's similar to yours and I sometimes am called upon to help out in dangerous situations. Situations where some fire would come in handy."

"The operative word there is "sometimes". You're "sometimes" called to help. And you even said yourself that you're not a fighter. I wasn't wrong to try and protect you."

Rachael shot him a scathing look. "Well, I appreciate your wanting to keep me safe but I'd also like some credit for not being totally helpless."

"Oh, I'll give you that," Tristan smiled at her. "You're definitely not totally helpless."

CHAPTER TWELVE

AFTER THEIR MEAL RACHAEL HELPED CLEAN up, then sat with Tristan on the screened in porch.

"Don't worry, we're pretty safe here. It's the closest you can get to being outside at night without taking your life into your hands," he said.

"It's nice out here but you could use some flowers in pots or something to brighten up the patio."

Tristan didn't say anything and she glanced at him.

"My mom had that whole patio surrounded by pots with plants in them. I don't have time for stuff like that."

"What happened to your parents?" The words were out before she could stop them.

"Dark-Angels." He looked at her. "You need to know about them and I might as well tell you about my parents too. Like I said, they'd stopped being Slayers, at least officially since once a Slayer always a Slayer. Anyway, they'd married, bought this townhouse, had me, and then one night Dark-Angels killed them. I was here with a friend. They never came home. I found out early the next morning they'd been killed."

"Oh my gosh, that's horrible," Rachael said softly. "How old were you?"

"Fifteen. The following year the mark appeared on my arm and I went to train with Slayer United. That was three years ago."

Rachael thought of her friend, Skye and how steep a learning curve there was for this sort of thing. "You've learned a lot in three years."

"I had to if I wanted to stay alive."

"So, what do they look like, the Dark-Angels? How are they different from the DAX?"

Tristan sat up a little straighter. "For one thing they're generally bigger than the DAX and more muscular. The thing with the DAX is how they look is somewhat dependent on how they looked as a human; tall human, tall DAX, short human, short DAX. But the Dark-Angels are all big. And they have huge black wings, which makes them more mobile and harder to kill. Their bodies are black too, so they blend in with the night better than the DAX with their pale flesh."

Rachael made a face. "They sound awful. I could hardly imagine anything more frightening than the DAX until I saw that horrible thing that came through the portal. That weapon with the blade at one end and the claw at the other…that's how Alina was killed, wasn't it?"

"Yeah. There must be some sort of poison or venom of some kind on it. Remember how those black lines traveled up and down her body and we couldn't heal her?"

Rachael nodded. "Did Daze die like that?"

"Broken neck."

"Broken neck! But he was a big guy, like Stefan!"

"Which just goes to show you how strong those Hell-Spawn are."

"Is that what we're officially calling them? Hell-Spawn?"

"That's what I'm calling them."

Rachael sighed. "I saw one of those pterodactyl-type things eat a person when I was out shopping with Ariel."

"She told me. She said I should take good care of you while you're staying with me or I'll have to answer to her. What's a pterodac—?" He made a face. "Whatever!"

Rachael grinned. "A pterodactyl. It was a type of flying dinosaur from way back in my world's history. They don't exist anymore. I've just seen pictures of how they must've looked."

"Oh, well I've been calling them Flying Hell-Spawn," he laughed. "It's easier to say."

Rachael laughed too and then yawned. "Oh no! I'm always yawning and cutting the evening short. Sorry, how rude of me."

"That's okay. You go get some sleep. Your schedule has gotten all turned around. I'm used to staying up almost all night but I'm going to try and get some sleep pretty quick here too. I'll be here when you wake up or if I have to go somewhere I'll leave you a note...or just wake you up and drag your ass outta bed," he grinned.

Rachael got up and started back inside, then turned back.

"When I first met you, you seemed like a real jerk; always angry and yelling. But you're actually pretty okay." She smiled at him and slipped indoors.

When Rachael woke up it was late morning. She took a quick shower, and pulled on her new jeans and one of Ariel's tops. It was army green, much like the one Tristan had worn the day before. She tied her bright red hair back in a ponytail, put on socks and shoes and went to find Tristan.

"Oh good, you're up," he said when she wandered into the kitchen. He stood there in snug fitting dark wash jeans and was in the process of pulling on a long-sleeved black t-shirt. "Come on, we have to get going. Thomas called a meeting."

"Do I have time to eat?"

"Here," he tossed her an apple. "There're oat bars in that box on the counter and fresh coffee in the pot. Grab a mug and let's go."

"But I can't drink coffee and eat on the bike!"

He rolled his eyes. "Put the apple and oat bar in your pocket and eat them when we get there. And here's a travel mug. You can sip as we go." He handed her a blue and red striped travel mug with a lid.

"And what about the sword. Should I bring it?"

"Oh yeah, don't leave home without it. Not now, not ever."

Rachael ran back for the beige jacket Ariel had given her and quickly zipped the oat bar and apple into the two inside pockets. She grabbed the scabbard and sword, buckled it on, then poured coffee into the mug once she'd gotten back to the kitchen.

Tristan waited for her in the garage, the door already open and his helmet on.

"Here."

Rachael set her coffee down and put on the helmet he'd handed her, retrieved her coffee and climbed aboard the motorcycle. Tristan had already locked the house door and was once again waiting for her.

They sped off through the relatively quiet city streets. A few people had ventured out in cars but Rachael knew the dangers they faced. She scanned the sky for Flying Hell-Spawn and was especially afraid one would fly up behind them and snatch them off the road before they knew what had happened.

They made it to Ravenwood without any trouble. Tristan got them through the security and once they were down the stairs to the lower level, they just followed the sound of voices until they found the room where the meeting was to take place.

Rachael slid into the first empty chair she saw, while Tristan walked over to a seat on the other side of the room near Thomas. Rachael nodded at Amy and Stefan then gave Ariel a small wave and a smile. There were only nine people in the room, including her. Were the others late or—?

"Let's start," Thomas said. He rose to his feet and looked at each of them individually. Today he wore black jeans and a blue button-down shirt and a blue and black tie. His short hair was neatly combed. He looked like the perfect 'business casual'. If only, Rachael thought, this were an ordinary weekly meeting of some bank tellers or something. Unfortunately, it wasn't.

"First I want to fill you in on some things," Thomas continued. "The families of Daze, Stella and Rand were all notified yesterday and their bodies were collected by the coroner's office."

Rand and Stella, Rachael hadn't known the names of the other two Slayers who had been killed but now she had names to put with the faces.

"And now we're down to only seven of us," said a dark-haired woman across from Rachael. Her hair was pulled back in a sleek bun and she looked like she was angry enough to spit fire.

"I'm aware of that, Sophia," Thomas said.

"We're losing Slayers right and left, man," said a lanky guy with shaggy blond hair and a scar across his nose. "And we're no closer to stopping Westfall, the other one," he added which drew a chuckle from Amy, "or killing these damn monsters."

"And where's Kirk and his team?" asked Stefan. "Why aren't they here?"

"You're right, Mickey," Thomas said to the blond guy. "But Kirk and his team have been working on the tools you'll need to kill the flying creatures."

"Flying Hell-Spawn," Tristan said.

"Yes," Thomas gave him a nod then glanced at Stefan. "And that's why Kirk and his team aren't here. They're working."

A large guy who was quite muscular but also looked like he could lose a few pounds, stood up and confronted Thomas.

"And where the hell are you most of the time? Not fighting with us. Hell no! This girl," he gestured to Rachael, "is more willing to put her life on the line then you are."

"Hey now—" Tristan began but he was quickly cut off.

"Shut up, Tristan," Sophia said. "Hulk is right, and you've even noticed it. Half the time when we're looking for Westfall he's not around. Where does he go?" She turned from Tristan and faced Thomas. "Where do you go?"

And from there the meeting went from being rather civil to devolving into a shouting match between those who thought Thomas was no longer fit to lead them and others defending him.

"Everyone shut the hell up!" Stefan shouted over the din and Rachael was thankful that they all listened. The room quieted down. Stefan looked at Thomas.

"Look, no offense but the fact that your father is the one causing all the problems, the fact that you do seem to disappear on us often and the fact that you're nowhere to be found when there's actual fighting taking place, makes some of us wonder if maybe you're not the best man to be leading us right now."

"That's putting it tactfully," Mickey said. "Actually, some of us wonder if maybe you're in on it, you know, what your father is doing."

"Now just a minute," Tristan said as he shot to his feet. "Thomas hasn't had anything to do with—"

"Tristan, he's your brother, of course you're going to defend him," Sophia snapped. "But we have valid concerns."

"Excuse me," Ariel lifted her hand. "May I say something here?" Everyone looked at her. "It seems to me that we're dealing with a situation that none of us is really prepared to deal with. At least Westfall… Thomas…has leadership experience. That's why he was given this city to protect. Why don't we just let him continue to lead? I'm sure he's doing the best he knows how with the limited intel and resources that we have."

"And who would you suggest would lead us anyway if Thomas didn't?" Amy asked. She looked around the room at each of them.

"Not me," Mickey muttered which got a snicker out of nearly everyone.

317

Thomas finally spoke. "Look everyone, I know this has been the most discouraging few days of our lives. We've lost friends we cared about, the humans we're supposed to be protecting are in greater danger than ever before and we're up against something we've never faced before and it seems to be kicking our butts. But I promise you that I and Kirk and his team are doing everything possible to get us some kind of an edge. And I am not on board with anything my father is doing. I haven't spoken to him in over ten years. The man is evil incarnate and I intend to take him down in any way possible; even if that means giving the order to kill him if necessary. Which, as of now, is an order I'm giving."

The room was silent and Rachael looked around at everyone's faces. Would they believe him or would they remain disgruntled?

"Well, about damn time," Hulk muttered. "Let's go kill the bastard."

"First we gotta find him," Mickey reminded everyone.

"Can we get any help from Slayers in other Cities?" Amy asked.

"I've tried," Thomas replied. "No one has any suggestions other than to say they'll set up a perimeter around their own cities."

"Good luck with that if those things decide to leave Monument Ridge," Sophia said. "They just don't want to get involved. Cowards."

"So, what's it gonna be then?" Tristan asked. "Are we all satisfied that Thomas continues to act as Overseer?"

Rachael noticed he glared at everyone, one face at a time. Ariel and Amy nodded approval immediately. Hulk and Mickey seemed satisfied and gave their nod of approval.

Stefan shrugged. "Fine by me."

Sophia was the last to give her agreement. "Yeah, okay."

Seconds later Kirk appeared in the doorway. "The arrows are ready. Come down to the lab whenever you're able and I'll show the archers how they work."

"Which brings me to something else," Thomas said. "Daze was to lead one of the archery teams but now he's gone and so are many of the archers. Since there are only seven of you left, each of you will be carrying a bow and arrows along with your swords, stakes and any other weapons you usually carry. We're going to have to adjust, people, so if you're not particularly good with a bow and arrow then you need to get out there and practice immediately. From now on you'll be divided into two teams.

Hugo…sorry…Hulk, you, Mickey, Stefan and Sophia will be a team and Tristan, Amy, Ariel and Rachael will be a team."

"Me?" Rachael gasped.

Thomas nodded. "Yes Rachael. You've proved yourself competent and we need you."

"But I don't know the first thing about archery!"

"So, practice!" Thomas replied.

CHAPTER THIRTEEN

RACHAEL REMOVED THE SWORD AND ITS SCAB-bard from her hips and slumped down onto the ground with her back to the wall of the building. From here, under the protection of the roof, she could watch the others train until it was her turn. She munched on her oat bar and apple. Her coffee had gotten cold during the meeting and she didn't much feel like drinking it anyway. She'd brought a bottle of water up from the shelter of the underground office and lab and sipped it while scanning the sky. She hoped the Slayers were keeping an eye out as well. You never knew when one of the Flying Hell-Spawn might swoop in and grab a snack.

The day was sunny but the training grounds were partially covered by a canopy. Tristan and Mickey sparred with swords, Amy, Sophia and Ariel worked on their archery skills and Stefan and Hulk fought each other in hand-to-hand combat.

While Rachael watched, her mind wandered. She wondered about Lairen, her supposed half-brother. Was the ability to open portals something learned; something outside of the natural magic an Elemental was born with? Could Lairen create portals too? Had Sebastian taught him? If so, could she persuade Lairen to open a portal to her world so she could go home? That is, if she ever saw him again. Or was the ability to open portals something Sebastian was born with? And would other Elementals who were blood related to him be able to open portals also? Rachael sputtered when a sip of water went down the wrong way. Thomas. Thomas Westfall was Sebastian's son. Could *he* open portals?

As if conjured by her thoughts, Thomas rounded the corner of the building, watched the others train for a few seconds and then came over to where Rachael still sat on the ground. He dropped down beside her in the shade of the building.

"Have you had a chance to practice yet?"

"Not yet, but we've got all day, right?"

He nodded. "I suppose so. How are you holding up?"

"Ah, good, I guess. You?" She suddenly felt very awkward around him and boy did she want to ask him some questions now that she'd thought of them.

"You know, if we can locate Sebastian's home base, we might be able to find the other Elfaen swords too. You could potentially go home with all four."

Rachael's eyes widened. "You're really going to let me take them? That would be awesome." She paused and looked down, then back up at Thomas. "But if your father is killed there may not be any way for me to get home. I mean, who would open a portal?" She waited, hoping he'd say something revealing.

Thomas frowned. "Ah. I hadn't really thought of that."

"Maybe Lairen?" Rachael suggested, as she revisited the same thoughts she'd had a minute or two ago. "Maybe Sebastian taught him how to do it. Maybe I could talk him into opening a portal to my world. He seems to like it there. Maybe he'd want to go back and stay."

Thomas seemed to be considering her words although his eyes were on the Slayers who were still training. They'd rotated however and now Tristan and Mickey were doing archery, Amy, Sophia and Ariel were working on hand-to-hand combat and Hulk and Stefan were practicing with swords.

"Maybe," he finally said but then remained silent.

Rachael was so disappointed. She'd really hoped he'd reveal something without her having to ask a direct question.

"What about his wife, Beatrix? Do you think she knows how to open portals?"

Thomas gazed out across the training area for several seconds before turning toward Rachael.

"Excuse me." He got up and went to speak to Tristan and that was the end of Rachael's conversation with Thomas.

She frowned at him as he walked away. Was he hiding something? Did he actually know more about this portal business than he was letting on? What if Sophia and the others were right about not trusting Thomas?

A shadow covered the training area. Rachael looked up and what she saw nearly froze the words in her throat; but not quite.

"Look up!" she shouted and everyone did. Those who were underneath the canopy came out from under it for a moment to scan the sky and then ducked back underneath. The other Slayers who had been out training in the sunshine immediately joined them.

Rachael held her position in the shadow of the building and hoped the Flying Hell-Spawn didn't see her. When it banked and turned to fly away from them, she snatched up her sword and ran across the open field to the others.

"It's too high up," Ariel said. "Unless it comes closer there's no point in using the arrows."

Thomas boldly came out from under the canopy and searched the sky. "Well, it's coming back and it looks lower."

"Low enough?" Stefan asked.

"That's debatable," Thomas replied as he returned to the canopy covered area and grabbed one of the practice bows and altered arrows. "Kirk said he adjusted the arrowheads for those things having tougher skin and mechanized the bow for accelerated speed and greater distance. Let's see if they work."

He went back out into the open field and kept his eyes focused on the sky.

"The hell with it," Amy muttered. She snatched up a bow and a couple of arrows and joined him, Sophia hot on her heels.

Stefan grinned. "I'm in." He too lifted a bow and some arrows from beside the archery targets.

"It's seen us," Thomas shouted.

Tristan ran out, followed by Ariel, Mickey and Hulk.

"Are you all crazy?" Rachael muttered to herself. She didn't dare come out from under cover and make herself vulnerable, not after what she'd seen the other day. She saw the shadow of the creature as it came swooping toward the Slayers. She heard the boom of huge, heavy flapping wings that kicked up the dust and she was terrified of losing more of her companions.

Everyone had their bows lifted, arrows ready to fly, but Thomas was the first to release his arrow, followed rapidly by everyone else. The beast let out a piercing scream.

"Yeah!" Stefan and Hulk shouted almost simultaneously.

Tristan turned to her. "Rachael, get out of there!"

The others were making a mad dash back to the building but Tristan waited for her, his hand held out, his body tense and ready to flee.

Ariel had stopped a few feet behind Tristan. "Come on Rachael! Run! Run!"

It took Rachael a second to realize what was most likely happening. The beast was falling and would land on the canopy...right on top of her! She bolted straight out from under the canopy and didn't even bother looking up. She kept her eyes on Tristan and ran like her life depended on it; which it did.

She grabbed his outstretched hand and he pulled her along. Ariel turned and ran too, the three of them joining the others at what Rachael hoped was a safe distance. She heard a loud thump and when she turned, she saw the pterodactyl-like creature sprawled on the ground; it didn't move.

"Thankfully that thing didn't land on the building," Mickey said.

Hulk nodded. "Yeah, that would've really sucked."

"That's an understatement," Thomas muttered.

Stefan, Amy, Tristan and the rest of them cautiously approached the downed beast. After several tense moments Rachael was relieved to learn that the monster was truly dead.

"Weren't there just two of these things?" Ariel asked.

"Yeah," Sophia answered.

"One to go then," Amy said.

"This is the first real progress we've made," Thomas pointed out. "The canopy was destroyed but so was the beast. Good going, all."

"And Kirk will be happy to know his new and improved bows and arrows work great," Stefan added.

"Are you okay?" Tristan asked Rachael as the two of them walked back to the main building.

"Yeah, fine, thanks to you. If you hadn't yelled at me, I would've been squashed."

They followed the others and went down the stairs to the underground facility.

"What happens to that thing's body?" Rachael asked. "Is there someone who can move it?"

There was an explosion outside. Tristan and Rachael looked at each other and ran back up the stairs.

"What's going on?" shouted Ariel.

Everyone had stopped on the stairway.

"Hold on," Tristan yelled back.

He pushed through the door and Rachael arrived a second later and went to stand next to him. Rachael was amazed to see the Flying Hell-Spawn in flames.

"Well, that solves that problem," Tristan said. "They spontaneously combust when dead."

"Handy," Amy said. She and Ariel had joined Tristan and Rachael.

Thomas too came to observe the cremated creature. "Come on. Let's get downstairs," he finally said. "The others went to see Kirk."

"How many people are on Kirk's team?" Rachael asked as she followed Tristan back indoors and into the conference room where they plopped down on two of the chairs. "I keep hearing about Kirk and his team but I don't think I've ever seen anyone except Kirk."

Tristan gave her a lopsided grin. "That's because there is no team. At least not in the way you're probably thinking. Kirk's 'team' is a girl."

"A girl? Just one girl?"

"Yep. The team thing started as a joke but it stuck. She's good. Super smart. Probably smarter than Kirk."

Rachael grinned as she thought of Megan Tanner, the geeky super smart girl who was part of the Bureau at home in San Diego. "We've got someone like that at the Bureau too. She's brilliant but sort of...different."

"Different how?"

Rachael shrugged. "Oh, nothing bad. She just dresses sort of different from the rest of us and dances to the beat of her own drum, if you know what I mean."

"I think I do."

Ariel wandered into the room. "Rachael! I've been looking for you. Are you okay?"

"Yeah sure. I little shaken up, but...you know."

Ariel looked at Tristan. "Westfall wants to talk to you."

"Where is he?"

"With Kirk and Miko in the lab."

"Miko?" Rachael said.

"Yeah," Tristan said as he got to his feet. "Kirk's team. The girl I was just telling you about. I'll be back."

He left the room and Ariel dropped down into the chair he'd vacated. "I knew when I joined up that we all might die at some point but you always think 'not me, not my friends'. You know?"

"Did you know all the Slayers who died? I mean, did you know them well?"

"I didn't know the two who died the same day as Karl and Sammy. Even Karl and Sammy I didn't know real well, but still...and I didn't really know Rand but Daze and Stella, yeah. I knew them pretty well. And of course, Alina."

Rachael felt so bad for Ariel. She could only imagine how awful she'd feel if Megan, Skye or Aidan, Skye's boyfriend, were killed; especially Skye, her best friend and roommate. Actually, she really didn't want to think about it so she changed the subject.

"Um, Ariel, why do you think Sebastian Westfall hasn't just opened a bunch of portals to my world and to the hell world and just let whatever's going to happen, happen? He says his goal is to have no boundaries between the worlds so what's stopping him?"

"Maybe he doesn't have the power to open a bunch of portals all at once. Or maybe he can't keep them open for very long."

"But that portal I came though was open at least twenty-four hours. Surely that's enough time to do the kind of damage he wants to do."

Ariel shrugged. "Maybe not. Or maybe he's not sure he'll be able to control all the chaos. He seems like the sort who wouldn't be satisfied with destroying the worlds but he'd also want to take charge once the destruction is done."

Something nagged at the back of Rachael's mind and then it solidified. "The swords. He's been collecting the Elfaen swords for a reason. Now I have one that's been activated. At the bookstore, when he realized I could use the sword, he said that changed things. It changed things because he knows even if he gets the sword, he won't be able to use it because it's already bonded with me! He won't have the power of Fire-Starter!" She looked at Ariel wide-eyed. "He can't move forward because he hasn't been able to activate the swords. He can't control the beasts without Beast-Master. He can't control life and death without Death-Dealer and Life-Giver. He's stuck!"

CHAPTER FOURTEEN

"TONIGHT, BOTH TEAMS WILL BE OUT LOOKING for DAX, the Dark-Angels and that last Flying Hell-Spawn," Thomas said later when all of them were gathered together.

"I thought we weren't bothering with those right now," Stefan said. "They seem like the least of our worries."

"I changed my mind," Thomas replied.

Kirk walked into the room followed by a Japanese girl who looked to be about seventeen or eighteen. She was tall, maybe five-seven Rachael thought, with long black hair that lay over one shoulder in a side ponytail. She wore round glasses and had on khaki trousers, dark brown hiking boots and a white button-down shirt.

Thomas smiled. "A rare visit from Kirk's 'team', the elusive Miko. To what do we owe the pleasure?" He didn't sound sarcastic, more like a big brother teasing a little sister.

She rolled her eyes then nodded a greeting to them all. "Here's something that should help you guys out." She reached into the well-worn, army green messenger bag slung across her body. "We've created devices for each of you to carry which will close a portal should you find one open. They're like the one Kirk used a couple of days ago but these are smaller." She pulled out a metal object, oval in shape, which fit in the palm of her hand. "You press the button here." She indicated a black button on one end of the device. "And then you touch the other end of the device to the edge of the portal, right where it shimmers. It'll short out the magic that's keeping the portal open and it'll close quite quickly." She handed each of them one of the little devices.

While they looked at the little metal objects in their hands, Miko continued and what she said caused everyone to give their full attention once again.

"My family has decided to evacuate along with most of the other people in Monument Ridge."

"What?" Tristan said. "Evacuate? When did this start happening?"

"You probably haven't seen anything about it because all the vid stations are shut down," Miko replied.

"I noticed," Tristan replied. "Every time I try and switch on I get nothing but static."

"People have been leaving since yesterday," Kirk added. "That's why so many stores have remained closed, including the bookstore."

Tristan looked puzzled. "I figured it was because of these new monsters rampaging around."

Kirk looked nervous about something. "Yeah, um, and well…" He looked down, then back up at Thomas. "I'm leaving too. I'm evacuating with the others."

"What!?" said nearly everyone else in the room.

Kirk raised his hands. "I know, I know, I'm sorry but I'd rather move somewhere where these new hell monster things aren't. Preferably someplace where there aren't so many Dark-Angels and DAX either."

"Like where?" Ariel asked.

"My family is heading north," Miko said.

"Yeah," Kirk added. "Everyone knows there are fewer Dark-Angels up north and fewer Dark-Angels means fewer DAX."

"When are you leaving?" Thomas asked.

"In the morning," Miko replied. "First thing."

Kirk nodded. "Me too."

"And that's why we were in a big rush to get these things finished so we could give them to you before we left," Miko added.

"That's it," Mickey said and rose to his feet. "I'm done with this. I'm outta here."

Thomas frowned at him "What are you talking about?" Thomas asked.

Mickey looked him square in the eyes. "Other people are smart enough to leave this place. Why the hell are we still here? This is suicide. I'm evacuating with them."

"You can't be serious?" Tristan said.

Mickey looked at him. "Oh, I'm very serious, man."

"But we need you, Mickey," Ariel pleaded. "There's only seven of us left and we can't defend the city without your help!"

"Look around you, Ariel," Mickey snapped. "This city is done for. Wise up and get the hell out." He turned and headed for the door.

"Mickey!" Thomas yelled at his back. "Slayers are protectors. How dare you desert your calling and your fellow Slayers when they need you the most?"

Thomas looked to Rachael to be as angry as she'd ever seen him. His face was flushed, his body tense and there was fire in his eyes.

Mickey looked back at Thomas. "I dare because I'm sick of this; all of it. Being a Slayer in this town is a losing proposition." And then he rounded the corner and was gone.

Tristan leapt to his feet. "Son of a bitch. I'll go after him."

"No, don't. Let him go," Thomas said. "With that attitude you don't want him guarding your back anyway." He glanced around at the others. "Anyone else?"

No one said a word.

Thomas turned to Miko and Kirk. "Don't worry. I'm not angry with you. You two aren't Slayers. It's not your responsibility to stay and fight against these new, admittedly terrible odds. We'll miss your assistance but…" he held up the device Miko had handed him earlier. "Thank you for these. Go now if you wish and travel safely."

Kirk and Miko both nodded their good-byes and left the room.

Miko had seemed like a girl Rachael would've liked to get to know and now she was gone. It seemed that lately most of the people Rachael met were gone before she had a chance to even learn their names—or shortly thereafter.

Thomas slumped in his chair and ran a hand through his hair. "Alright, it's time I joined the fray. I'll take Mickey's place on the team."

Tristan scowled at him. "But you can't. You never train. You're out of shape. No offence, but you've become a paper-pusher."

"Well thanks, Tristan," Thomas snarled. "I think that's overstating things just a bit."

While Tristan and Thomas continued to argue, and the others joined in, Rachael closed her eyes and tried to tune them all out. She felt small and insignificant and she was tired of it. She'd known her place at the Bureau and she'd slid into the same position here; always in the background, staying in the shadows of the other more aggressive team members, but she was tired of being a background person. She had fire magic and could burn down buildings and even kill if she had to. She was the only one who could activate the other Elfaen swords so that alone made her a valuable asset, and she and Fire-Starter had bonded so she had that going for her too. She had more to offer here and it was time she put her fears aside and stepped up to the plate.

Rachael rose to her feet. "Everyone shut up!" she yelled and smacked both hands on the surface of the table. Every set of eyes was on her. "This is ridiculous." She pointed at Thomas. "He's in charge and he wants to fight alongside you and so he should, so quit arguing about it. Our first priority should be finding Sebastian Westfall and his wife. They have to be stopped and the reality is that Sebastian most likely will have to be killed. If his wife knows how to open portals and she stands against us then she goes down too. So, let's focus our efforts on finding Sebastian and stop wasting time."

She looked at Thomas. "Does your mother know where he is? I ask this because lots of times woman know exactly what's going on in their ex's lives even if they won't admit it. She knew about Beatrix and she knew about Lairen, she might know more."

He gave her a bemused smile and nodded. "Good call. I'll check."

She turned to Tristan. "I need to test out what Fire-Starter and I can do. The sword will direct me but I want to make certain I can do what I need to in any situation. Will you spar with me?"

He nodded. "Yes, of course."

"Alright, so like I said, instead of sitting here complaining and arguing let's find Sebastian and go end this."

"We still have some rather large and vicious monsters to deal with," Amy reminded her.

"And we will, but our priority is to make sure no more of them come through a portal into this world." Rachael looked all around the table. "Are you all with me on this? What's it going to be?"

There was silence for a moment while everyone looked around at each other; except for Tristan who grinned at her. "I'm in."

"Me too," Ariel said.

Stefan chuckled. "Right on, girl. You can count on me."

Rachael glanced around the table at the rest of them. Hulk and Sophia nodded.

"Yep," Amy said. "Sounds like a plan."

Thomas tipped is head as he studied her. "Alright, Rachael. Spoken like a true Slayer. You may not have the mark but you have the heart."

"More than that wuss, Mickey," Sophia muttered.

That broke the tension and they all laughed.

Thomas got to his feet. "Tris, why don't you and Rachael do some sparring while I see if I can begin to get back in some semblance of fighting shape." He glanced at Rachael. "And then I'll talk to my mother and see what she knows. Good enough?"

Rachael nodded.

"I'll spar with you," Amy said to Thomas. "It shouldn't take you long. You *are* a Slayer after all. You're just a little rusty."

Rachael followed Tristan out of the room as everyone dispersed.

"Good going back there," Tristan said. "I didn't know you had it in you."

"Well, I'm sick of this; sick of watching people die all around me and wondering if I'll be next, sick of being scared, sick of—"

"Sick of letting other people call the shots too, apparently." Tristan laughed.

She gave him a sideways glance. "I guess so."

They climbed the stairs and emerged back into the mid-afternoon daylight.

"Amazing how that Flying-Hell-Spawn just burned itself to nothing," Rachael said as the studied the area where the beast had gone down. "It's almost like it never happened."

"The crushed canopy indicates otherwise," Tristan quipped. "Well, get out that Elfaen sword and let's see what you can do." He retrieved his sword from its scabbard.

Rachael put her hand around Fire-Starter's hilt and pulled the sword free, blade gleaming. She felt the jolt of power run from her hand to her shoulder and down through the rest of her body. The expression on Tristan's face caused Rachael to stare at him.

"Is something wrong?"

"Rachael, you should see yourself."

She looked down at her body and saw the sparks she'd seen before when she's held Fire-Starter in the bookstore. "Yeah, it does that." She grinned.

"But I didn't see them after we fought the DAX."

She shrugged. "Maybe it dissipates or shuts off after a while. I don't know." She felt the unmistakable pull of the sword. It wanted to fight and so did she. She leapt forward without warning and Tristan barely had time to get his blade up in defense.

Rachael let the sword take over, as she'd done before when fighting the DAX. She didn't really know what she was going to do next or how it all worked but her body knew what to do and was faster than she ever could've imagined. The sword, normally heavy in her hand, felt light and easily maneuverable. She ducked and spun, lunged and retreated, whirled like a dancer to well-learned choreography.

Finally, Tristan stepped back and called it quits but Rachael wasn't even tired. She felt like she was just getting started. Fighting with this sword was absolutely exhilarating. Still, she followed Tristan's example and stepped back as well, ending the sparring match. It was then she realized the others stood in a circle around them, their eyes wide, and a couple of them had their mouths hanging open.

Rachael blew a strand of hair out of her eyes then pushed it back when it failed to rearrange itself. "What's going on?" she asked.

"Well, you, sister. You're what's going on," Amy said.

Ariel gaped at Rachael. "I thought you hadn't ever fought before. That was amazing."

Rachael was a little embarrassed. "It's the sword. Since we're bonded it sort of…leads me."

"It does a damn good job of it," Hulk laughed. "Wish I had a sword bonded to me!"

"Well, this makes my practice session look sort of silly in comparison," Thomas said.

"You did just fine," Amy replied. "You have nothing to worry about."

Thomas shrugged. "Even so, looks like it's time for me to go have a little chat with my mother about Sebastian and see what I can dig up. You all carry on with your practice." He strode away and Rachael grinned at Tristan.

"Wanna go another round?"

"Ah, no. I think I'll move on to something else. Besides, from what I can see you don't need any practice. Unless you want to work on something other than sword fighting."

"Like what?"

He shrugged. "I don't know. Between your fire magic and your ability with that sword I think you're just as battle ready as the rest of us. Maybe you don't need to work on anything else after all. Come on, let's take a break."

Tristan headed over to a large tree in the far corner of the compound and Rachael followed, after putting Fire-Starter back at her hip. There was a wooden bench underneath the tree and the two of them lounged in the shade while the other Slayers continued practicing.

"So, what sorts of magic does everyone have?" Rachael asked. "I guess you're a healer. I saw you trying to help Alina."

Tristan shrugged. "Yeah, well my healing magic isn't strong. It's good enough for minor wounds though, and since being a Slayer already gives me a natural ability to heal quickly, my magic just adds to that. As for the others…" He looked out across the compound at them. "Ariel's magic is air based."

"Like Beatrix Westfall's magic. What about Amy?"

"She and Hulk can manipulate water. Thomas has magic that's related to yours in a way, it has to do with electrical impulses. He can bring lightening, light a fire, start cars—"

"Oh! Start cars! I can do that," Rachael said. "I once started a fire by accident and Skye and I had to run for our lives to get out of it. Then, we couldn't start the car because it was actually Aidan's car and we didn't have the keys and…well, anyway, I can start a car too."

Tristan gave her a thoughtful look. "Skye is…"

"My best friend and roommate. Aidan is her boyfriend. They're Assassins for the Bureau."

He nodded. "Oh, right. Well, anyway then there's Sophia. She's a healer too, like me, but it also manifests in a way that she can grow things like plants. So, if you want a garden or an instant jungle, she's the one to call."

"What about Stefan?"

Tristan chuckled. "He has a very non-Elemental type of magic. It enables him to locate things."

Rachael's eyes widened. "Locate things? Well, that's different."

"Yeah, he used to get teased about it all the time when he was a kid, but then he grew taller and more muscular than any of us and started kicking ass."

"So, you've known him since you were a kid?"

"Yep."

"And what about all the others?"

"Ariel transferred here so I didn't know her but I knew Alina, Stefan and Amy. The others came from around here mostly, but I didn't know them until we all became Slayers."

Rachael had scanned the sky for the remaining Flying Hell-Spawn, just in case it showed up. She noticed Tristan did as well. She was doing one of those quick scans when she saw Thomas hurrying over to them.

"Jack-pot," he said once he was in front of them. "I talked to our mother. She scolded me for not telling her Sebastian was the one behind the portals and the Hell-Spawn. She said of course she knows where he is."

"Really?" Rachael nearly jumped up she was so excited. "Let's go get him!"

"Not so fast," Thomas cautioned.

"Why?" Tristan drawled. "Where is he?"

Thomas sighed. "He lives about an hour outside of Monument Ridge city limits."

"So?" Tristan asked. "What's the big deal?"

"The big deal is that it's a secure compound, sort of like this one, except that he built it right smack in the middle of Dark Angel Valley."

"What?" Tristan frowned. "How is that even possible?"

"He obviously had it built during the daylight hours when they wouldn't be around."

"But the Dark-Angels could just fly into the compound at night and—"

"He had a roof built over the entire compound," Thomas said.

"So, there's no way in?" Rachael asked.

"None," Thomas replied.

334

Chapter Fifteen

S O INSTEAD OF GOING TO SEBASTIAN WESTFALL'S
compound that night as Rachael had hoped, they went back to
Thomas's original plan of hunting DAX, Dark-Angels and the
Flying Hell-Spawn; if they could find it. Rachael was disappointed. She'd
really hoped to end this terrifying nonsense that very night.

They went out at dusk in two groups of four. Rachael had been told to
join Amy, Stefan and Hulk and she was alright with that. She would've felt
more comfortable with Tristan or Ariel since she knew them better than
the others but at least she wasn't going to be alone out there.

As dusk turned to dark the four of them walked the deserted streets of
Monument Ridge. The other team had taken a different part of town but
both teams were in areas where DAX and or Dark-Angels were known to
be prevalent. What they were unprepared for was an encounter with one
of the three remaining Hell-Spawn.

"Oh, crap," Amy muttered. "Do you see what I see?"

"How could we miss it?" Stefan replied.

They'd walked around a corner and not fifty feet away, half obscured
in shadow, was a Hell-Spawn. It sat on its haunches and seemed to be
eating something.

"Is that a DAX it's eating?" whispered Hulk after the four of them
melted into the shadow of a deserted building.

"Judging by that pasty white skin I guess so," Amy whispered back.

"Looks like we just missed seeing it happen," Stefan replied.

"Uh, oh," Rachael said, her voice low, "It looks like it's seen us. Now what?"

"No sense running. That thing would probably catch us anyway," Hulk said. "Let's do this."

"But I thought we weren't supposed to—" Rachael didn't get a chance to finish because Hulk took off running toward the Hell-Spawn.

"Well, crap," Stefan muttered and ran after him.

"Damn Hugo. That's why we call him Hulk. No brains, all brawn. What an idiot." Amy darted after Stefan.

Rachael brought up the rear, pulling Fire-Starter from its sheath as she ran. She instantly felt the sword's power mesh with her own and saw the resulting sparks surround her body. They dissipated quickly this time, though she wasn't really paying all that much attention to it once she got closer to the monster.

Attacking a Hell-Spawn at any time was probably a bad idea but running right up to one that was in the middle of a meal was truly insane. The beast roared at them and scooped up its double-bladed weapon, which had been lying on the ground at its feet.

Hulk lunged for the beast but was blocked by a giant arm swung in his direction. He went flying, which stunned Rachael, although it shouldn't have. She'd seen a beast like this in action at the old offices after all. But still, seeing a big guy like Hulk airborne…

Stefan and Amy engaged the Hell-Spawn together, as it growled and swung the blade end of its spear-like weapon at them. Rachael ran around behind the monstrous beast and tried to find a vantage point. She knew she could use her fire magic as a distraction like she'd done before in the office with the other Hell Beast, but with Stefan and Amy causing the distraction this time there was no need.

Unfortunately, before she could find an opening the clawed end of the spear came whipping back as the beast maneuvered to keep Amy and Stefan at bay. Rachael threw herself sideways and the claw just missed her.

She kept one eye on the claw while getting to her feet once again. There was really little finesse to this fight, just brute force. Rachael readied herself and kept pace with the Hell-Spawn's movements so she could stay behind the creature while avoiding stepping in DAX remains. She figured later she might throw up, it was so disgusting, but now all her focus had to be on helping her friends stay alive. And there it was. When, exactly, had they become her friends? Again, something to think about later.

The beast flung out a meaty arm at Stefan, who leapt back to avoid Hulk's fate. Meanwhile, Rachael saw that Hulk was on his feet and had entered the fray once again. Unfortunately, at the same time Rachael saw her opening and lunged forward to stab her sword into the Hell-Spawn's back, the beast swiped the clawed end of its spear right across Hulk's stomach. Rachael still managed to drive her sword into the monster's back and the beast let out a deep bellow of pain and rage. Rachael released her fire magic, through Fire-Starter, increasing the sword's proclivity to burn whatever it touched. She just barely had time to yank the sword free before the Hell-Spawn erupted in flames. They all had to backpedal quickly to avoid being scorched.

Rachael felt exhilarated by the power of the sword yet drained from using her fire magic. Somehow the two managed to balance each other leaving her feeling pretty even as far as her energy level went. She skirted around the burning Hell-Spawn and over to where Stefan and Amy were crouched beside Hulk. When Rachael got there she saw the same dark marks traveling up and down his body. It was just like what she'd seen happen to Alina.

"It's some kind of venom," Stefan said. "It has to be."

"Can we save him?" Rachael asked.

Amy looked up at her. "You saw what happened to Alina and we had several healers working on her. Still, we couldn't save her. Besides, he's already gone."

Rachael realized then that what Amy said was true. Hulk wasn't breathing. She reached down to take his pulse just to be sure but Amy was right. Hulk was dead. Whether from the venom or from the deep gashes that had torn open his stomach leaving it a gruesome mess, Rachael wasn't sure.

Stefan rose to his feet and pulled his phone from an inside jacket pocket. He scanned their surroundings while he talked.

"If you guys aren't in the middle of something we could use transport for Hulk," he said into the phone.

Rachael heard Thomas's voice speaking on the other end of the conversation, though she couldn't make out his exact words, and then Stefan briefly explained what had happened. After he put his phone away, he looked at Rachael and at Amy who was now standing at his side.

"They're on their way."

"Geez," Amy muttered. "The poor bastard. He was a good guy but…" she sighed. "Well, he didn't deserve that."

While the three of them waited for Thomas and the others to show up, they kept an eye out for other threats.

"Guess the Hell-Spawn have thinned the group," Amy remarked. "There don't seem to be very many DAX around."

"And no Dark-Angels either," Stefan added.

About thirty minutes later Thomas, Tristan, Ariel and Sophia showed up with one of the utility vehicles. Rachael thought it looked sort of like a Suburban. The guys lifted Hulk's body into the back and then Thomas and Tristan took the front seats, Rachael, Amy and Ariel sat in the back seat while Sophia and Stefan rode crouched in the very back with Hulk. Rachael thought about poor Thomas having to give yet another family a call with bad news.

"Well," Tristan said with a sigh, "at least you killed one of the Hell-Spawn so Hulk didn't give his life for nothing."

"Rachael is the one who actually killed it," Stefan said. "The rest of us just kept the brute busy so she could have an opening to use that amazing sword."

Tristan turned in his seat to look at Rachael and Thomas, who was driving, met her eyes in the rearview mirror.

"Good going, Rachael. You're an asset to Slayer United," Thomas said.

"Very much so," echoed Tristan.

Rachael looked away from them. She was embarrassed. "I couldn't possibly have done anything useful if Amy, Stefan and Hulk hadn't been there. It was a team effort. I shouldn't get all the credit."

Amy clamped a hand on Rachael's shoulder and gave her a gentle shake. "That's okay, Rachael. I'm happy to be the distraction as long as you continue to torch those monsters. Two down, two to go."

"Let's hope the one Rachael torched in the office actually died," Ariel said. "It went through the portal with two sword wounds in its back, but it might still be alive."

Stefan shook his head, "Nah, I seriously doubt it."

"Well as long as it isn't alive in our world, I don't care what happened to it," Sophia said.

They pulled up to Mountain Ridge General Hospital and Rachael was relieved to see there were still people working in the emergency area. Thankfully not everyone had evacuated, at least not yet.

Thomas got out and talked to someone inside the building and within just a couple of minutes four men came with a stretcher to unload Hulk's body. Rachael and the others stayed in the vehicle.

"His real name was Hugo," Ariel said to Rachael. "Did you know that?"

Rachael nodded. "Yeah, I remember Thomas calling him that. And Amy too, mentioned it in passing."

Ariel looked Rachael in the eyes. "I'm glad you're here. I hope you can get back home when all this is over but right now...I'm really glad you're here."

Rachael smiled at her. "Thanks."

They drove back to the compound in silence. When they got there Thomas disappeared into his office and Rachael knew he was calling Hugo's family, just as he'd had to do so many times in the last few days.

"Couldn't he wait until morning to tell Hulk's family?" she asked. "You know, rather than wake them out of a peaceful sleep."

"It's better to get it over with," Sophia said. "Even though it's the wee hours of the morning, they'd want to know."

Tristan nudged Rachael. "You wanna go home?"

She nodded.

"We're outta here people," Tristan said.

"Be careful out there," Ariel warned.

Amy smiled, although it was a weary smile. "Yeah, we don't want anything to happen to wonder girl here."

Rachael sighed. "I'm hardly that."

"Well, right now you're coming pretty close," Stefan said. "Safe journey home you guys."

"What about all of you?" Rachael asked. "Are you staying here?"

"I'm too tired to go anywhere else," Sophia said.

Stefan shrugged. "I'll be heading out."

Amy looked over at Thomas who had just joined them. "I think I'll stay here for a while," she said.

"I notified Hugo's family." Thomas dropped down into the nearest chair. "I'm getting so tired of doing this." He closed his eyes, put his elbows on the table and put his face in his hands, fingers threaded through his hair. "I'm tired of telling families that their child is dead."

Amy put a comforting hand on Thomas's arm then looked at Rachael and everyone else who stood around the table. "You guys go on. We'll be okay."

Sophia immediately took the hint and stood up. "I'll be in the bunkhouse if anyone needs me."

Rachael looked up at Tristan. "There's a bunkhouse?"

He nodded but looked over at Thomas. "Maybe I should stay," he whispered.

Rachael put her hand on his arm and tried to give him a meaningful look. "Let's go. Amy has this."

Tristan looked over at Amy. She gave him a nod.

"Good night, Thomas."

Thomas lifted his head. "Night, Tris."

With a sigh Tristan turned and left the room. Rachael followed him as did Stefan and Ariel.

"Be safe you guys," Ariel said once they were outside by their vehicles. She gave Rachael a hug and Rachael hugged her back as Stefan started his car and headed out of the compound. He stuck his hand out the window and waved. Rachael waved back.

Ariel got into her car too. "Seriously, take care driving home."

"You too," Tristan said as he and Rachael put on their helmets.

Tristan and Rachael left the compound and sped through the empty city, back to his townhouse. Once they were safely inside, Tristan closed the garage door and made sure everything was locked up tight. He dropped down onto the sofa and tried the vid stations. No luck. He tossed the remote onto the sofa and looked at Rachael.

"I've been here how many days?" she asked.

He shrugged. "Three, four? I don't know."

"It seems like I've been here forever. I want to go home so badly but then…I don't know if that's even going to be possible." She flopped down onto the sofa beside him. "And I'm starving."

"It's dark out so we can't order anything delivered but there's peanut butter and bread." He shrugged. "Maybe some cans of soup."

Rachael shook her head and sighed. "It's a wonder you don't starve. You need some real food in this house." She got up and went to the kitchen. Tristan followed her.

"I'm hardly ever here!" He handed her some jam from the refrigerator, opened the cupboard and grabbed a couple of cans of soup. "Tomato or tomato?"

Rachael chuckled. "Uh, tomato sounds good."

"You know," he said. "I think we originally got off on the wrong foot. I didn't trust you. I yelled at you a lot and—"

"Yes, you did," Rachael said. She spied the bread and took out four slices.

"You want a sandwich too, right?" she asked as she reached for the jar of peanut butter on the counter.

He nodded and handed her a knife to spread the jam and peanut butter on the bread. "And yet now I find myself really admiring you and—"

"Really?"

He took her by the shoulders and turned her to face him. He looked her right in the eyes and his expression was serious. "I'll do whatever it takes to get you back home, Rachael. I promise. I'll kidnap Sebastian Westfall and force him to open a portal if I have to."

Rachael felt something break loose in her heart. For the first time since being here she felt that knot in her stomach begin to relax. She sighed and smiled up at him.

"Thanks, Tristan. You don't know how much that means to me."

He pulled her to him, his arms around her and it felt like the most natural thing in the world to embrace him, her head against his chest. They stood like that for several seconds until Tristan finally stepped back.

He smiled at her. "We better eat and get some sleep."

"Yeah," Rachael said as her lips curved into a smile. She went back to making sandwiches while Tristan heated up the soup.

CHAPTER SIXTEEN

RACHAEL AWAKENED TO THE SOUND OF SOME-
one repeatedly pressing on the front door bell. She got out of bed
and staggered, still in her pajamas, out of her bedroom to see
what was going on. Tristan had gotten there first. He wore black jeans and
no shirt. His feet were bare. He was looking out the window and down the
corridor of the atrium to see who was there.

He turned when Rachael approached. "It's my next-door neighbor's kid."

Rachael peeked out the window to get a look. A young boy stood there.
He looked to be about twelve. His hair was dark; he wore a grey t-shirt,
faded jeans and sneakers. She looked up at Tristan. "So let him in. I'll go
make coffee."

Tristan went out to let the boy in through the security gate. Rachael
set the coffee maker to brewing and came back to see what the boy wanted.

Tristan and the boy stood just inside the front door. "Jeff, Rachael.
Rachael, Jeff," he said as an introduction. The boy nodded at her.

"So, you guys just woke up?" the kid asked.

"Yeah, we did. We stay up late," Tristan said. "What brings you to my
door at one in the afternoon, ringing my doorbell like a crazy person?"

Jeff's eyes widened. "Oh, yeah, I came to tell you there's a giant…thing
sitting on the roof of the house down the street! I figured you'd want to
know because you kill stuff like that and—"

Tristan bolted out the front door and through the atrium with Rachael
right on his heels.

"Well, crap," he said as they stood underneath the awning.

There, four houses down, perched the last of the Flying Hell-Spawn.

"We don't have bows and arrows," Rachael commented.

Tristan sighed. "Nope. We'll have to let it go. If we run out there with nothing but swords, stakes or long-knives it'll eat us for lunch. We definitely need archers to take that thing down."

He ducked back into the atrium and Rachael followed suit. When they got back into the house Tristan pointed a finger at Jeff.

"You stay here until that thing is gone; you hear me?"

"Sure. No problem," Jeff said. "You got any donuts?"

"Donuts? You want donuts for lunch?" Tristan asked.

"Yeah, my mom makes me eat all healthy when I'm at home so, ya know, I'm not at home right?"

Rachael laughed and went to check on the coffee. "We don't have any donuts but we can make toast and peanut butter." It wasn't exactly what she wanted to eat after just having peanut butter and jam sandwiches the night before.

"Okay," Jeff called back. He didn't sound too thrilled about toast and peanut butter either.

At some point she really wanted to go to a grocery store and buy some fruit, veggies, decent cereal, pasta and sauce, some different varieties of soup and maybe some stuff to put in the freezer so it would be there for Tristan after she was gone.

She poured the coffee, put bread in the toaster and thought about how Tristan's life, all of the Slayer's lives, would go on as usual after she was gone. Would any of them think fondly of her from time to time? Would Tristan? She found the thought of leaving not quite so appealing as it had previously been, not that she wanted to stay here. She wanted to go home with every fiber of her being but…Rachael realized that she liked some of the people here and would miss them if she couldn't ever see them again. The toast popped up.

"Here's the coffee." She took a steaming mug out to Tristan and turned to Jeff. "The toast is ready. There's peanut butter on the counter. Help yourself."

The kid wandered into the kitchen and Rachael could hear him opening drawers, probably looking for a knife.

"The knives are in the drawer to the left of the stove," she called out.

"Got it," came the reply.

Tristan was on the phone. "Yeah, we'll be in as soon as it's gone. Don't want to risk traveling the roads. That thing'll scoop us up in a heartbeat. Right. Okay, see ya later." He ended the call and put his phone in the back pocket of his jeans.

"You better get dressed. As soon as that winged monstrosity is gone, we're outta here."

"Okay," Rachael said. "But we have to stop for some decent food along the way."

"It's a deal," Tristan said with a smile.

Rachael went to shower and dress. She was still startled to see her new orange and yellow streaked red hair. Oh, how she missed her beautiful blonde locks. She wondered if all the swords changed the people they bonded with or if this was just Fire-Starter's way of saying 'hello' and 'you're mine'.

After showering and washing her hair, Rachael twisted it into a braid that hung down her back. She then selected some clean jeans and one of Ariel's loaned shirts; this one a black V-neck t-shirt. She put on socks and sneakers, shrugged into the beige jacket and went to find Tristan who lounged on the sofa. He was fully dressed now, in black jeans and boots and a deep red t-shirt. He had one arm flung over his eyes. He was asleep.

"Tristan?" She waited a couple of seconds. "Tristan!"

He removed his arm from his eyes and sat up. "Ready?"

"Is the pterodactyl thingy gone?"

"Yeah, and Jeff went home, or wherever," he waved a hand.

Rachael went to get Fire-Starter and met Tristan in the garage.

He lifted up the door and scanned the sky. "Seems safe enough."

She put on her helmet after buckling the sword to her hip. "Where are we going to eat?"

"Depends what's open," Tristan replied and climbed aboard the bike. He started the engine and Rachael climbed on behind him.

"Well, I don't care, as long as it's someplace that has real food," she shouted over the roar of the engine as they accelerated onto the street, and then snapped her visor down. She craved a huge salad with tons of veggies and red wine vinaigrette. Or Mexican food. That would be nice too. Her thoughts drifted next to pasta primavera, but she also searched the sky for the Flying Hell-Spawn.

Tristan passed by several restaurants that were clearly not open, but finally pulled into the parking lot of a place that was. He parked close to the door and then got off the bike.

Tristan removed his helmet. "I hope this is okay with you. It's pretty good. I've eaten here before."

"What kind of food do they have?" she asked as she tugged off her own helmet.

"Kind of like what we had for take-out but the seasonings are a little different."

They went inside and Rachael slid into a booth. After looking at the menu she decided this place was rather like a Thai restaurant. She saw a dish that reminded her of Pad Thai so she ordered it.

"With extra veggies," she told the waiter.

After Tristan had ordered and the waiter was gone, she looked over at Tristan. "So, what's the plan tonight? Did Thomas say?"

"Actually, the plan is for this afternoon. He wants us all to go out to Sebastian's house and confront him during daylight hours when the DAX and Dark-Angels aren't going to be a problem."

"By confront do you mean attack or sneak in or what?"

"He wants to try and talk to his father. He mostly just wants us there as back up."

Rachael stared at him. "So, he's going to knock on the front door and hope to have a civil conversation with the guy who is responsible for most of the death and destruction over the last few days?" She couldn't wrap her mind around it. She shook her head. "That's crazy. That is not going to end well."

Tristan shrugged. "That's Thomas for ya. At least he thought of bringing back up instead of driving out there by himself."

The waiter arrived with their food and Rachael dug in. The food was really tasty, warm and delicious. It was nice to have a hot meal other than soup.

When they were done eating, Rachael and Tristan rode the rest of the way to the compound, passed the security checkpoints and met with the others in the conference room.

Rachael thought Thomas looked more relaxed than he had since she'd gotten there. She noticed Amy stuck close by him and Rachael smiled to herself. Thomas and Amy. Was this something that had been going on and she just hadn't noticed or was this something that had begun during these treacherous last few days?

Judging by everyone's quiet conversation they all had been informed of Thomas's plan and all of them thought it was a ridiculous idea. Still, here they were, ready to go.

"At least we have something to do instead of just waiting around for darkness to fall," Sophia said. "Maybe we'll spot the Flying Hell-Spawn and take it down. That would keep the afternoon from being a total waste."

They took two vehicles; Thomas, Amy and Stefan in one, Tristan, Rachael, Ariel and Sophia in another. The drive was actually kind of pretty, with rolling hills and plant life everywhere once they got outside the city limits.

"There it is," Ariel said and pointed to a wall in the distance. "That must be it. And I can see the sun shining on the roof."

Rachael saw it too. How out of place the ugly gray walls looked in the midst of all the desert beauty.

Tristan followed Thomas's vehicle when he turned down a dirt road. There was a sign posted that read, *'Private Property Enter At Your Own Risk'*. They drove right by it and kept going about a mile more until they were right in front of a huge walled-in complex with a domed roof.

They all got out of the vehicles and looked around for a moment, then dispersed to their separate lookout points around the compound.

Rachael saw Thomas walk up to the security gate and push a buzzer. Once she got to her assigned place along the far wall, she could no longer see the front of the compound or any of the others. It made her a little uncomfortable. Still, she had her magic and she had Fire-Starter. She'd be okay.

She looked up at the sky. No sign of the Flying Hell-Spawn. All was quiet around her. She wondered what in the world she was supposed to do if there was a problem inside. Fire magic wouldn't do any good on a block wall, nor would her sword. Even if she could somehow manage to get on top of the ten-foot wall, how was she going to smash through the roof?

Rachael sighed. There was something wrong about all of this. Thomas wanting to talk to his dad, spreading all the rest of them out so that no one could see each other, each of them staring at a solid wall with no way to get in should Thomas need them.

And then a hand covered her mouth and an arm wrapped around her torso, pulling her against the body of someone taller and stronger than she.

Rachael struggled but it didn't last long. There was something in the person's hand, something that smelled sickly sweet. The person lifted her and swung Rachael around and the last thing she saw was the shimmer of a portal, then everything went black.

CHAPTER SEVENTEEN

RACHAEL REGAINED CONSCIOUSNESS SLOWLY. Her head hurt and when she opened her eyes the room swam. At least there were no bright lights. That would've made things all the worse.

She tried sitting up but a wave of nausea caused her to groan and she lay back down. She closed her eyes until the sensation passed then tried again. This time she was able to sit up. She leaned against the wall behind her and looked around. The room was small and there were no windows. She sat on a bare mattress on a blue-carpeted floor. There was nothing else in the room.

After a little while longer Rachael's head had cleared and her vision was steady once more. She got up and the nausea didn't return. Hooray. Now where the heck was she? She remembered the shimmer of a portal so she knew she could be anywhere. What's more, Rachael suddenly realized she no longer had the Elfaen sword. It was gone. She no longer even wore the scabbard.

She hurried across the room and tried the door, not really expecting it to be unlocked. It wasn't. She banged on the door.

"Hey! Is anybody out there? Where am I?" But she had a horrible feeling that she already knew. She was inside Sebastian Westfall's compound, brought in through a portal, right into his house. Where was Thomas? Maybe he would hear her if she kept yelling. He was the only one who might stand a chance of knowing she was here.

"Hey! Somebody! Help me! Thomas! Thomas! Can you hear me? I'm trapped in the house!" She screamed again and again but nobody came.

Finally, Rachael gave up and looked all around her, trying to see if there was anything around that would help her; something she hadn't noticed when she'd looked around before. But no, there was nothing that would help her, although she did find an attached bathroom with a sink, toilet and narrow shower stall. She considered it but then decided there was no point in using fire magic here. She was locked in so she'd only succeed in burning herself up in an inferno.

She lifted her fisted hand to begin knocking on the door again when it suddenly burst open. Rachael leapt back so she wouldn't get hit. Her suspicions were confirmed once she saw who had come through the door. She recognized him from the time she'd seen him through the portal and then in the bookstore. It was Sebastian Westfall.

"Thank you for returning my sword." He stood there with an evil, twisted grin on his face. He was lean of build and wore gray slacks, and shiny black shoes and a black button-down shirt.

Rachael glared at him. "I didn't return it. You took it."

"Well, if that's the way you wish to view it..." he shrugged. "And now you will come with me. But first," he made a gesture with his hand and two huge men came into the room.

Rachael backed up and lifted her arm to use her fire magic. At least the door was open now so if she started a fire, she stood a decent chance of getting out of the room and hopefully to safety. But it wasn't meant to be. The two men lunged at her before she could do anything useful. They each grabbed one of her arms, and although she struggled, they managed to place some sort of device on each of her wrists. They let go and stepped back. Rachael immediately lifted her arm again and called her fire magic but this time no one stopped her. And then she realized why. Her magic was a no show. She tried again and got the same result. The devices on her wrists were somehow blocking her magic. She pulled at the metal bands but couldn't get them off.

"Don't bother," Sebastian said. "They won't come off unless I take them off and the only time that's going to happen is when you fire test the other swords for me."

"You aren't going to get away with this."

Sebastian laughed. "Why do people always say that? Of course, I'm going to get away with it. I'm also going to reopen both those portals and leave them open permanently, and I'm going to have the swords I need to control the beasts, and have control over life and death. You can keep the fire sword, dear. Let that be my gift to you for assisting me in making my dreams come true."

He gestured again to the two hulking men and they grabbed Rachael's arms and frog marched her from the room and down a long hallway. They turned right and continued down another corridor to an elevator. The men forced her in and they all rode up to what Rachael thought must be ground level. When the doors opened, they entered a huge living room with a fireplace at the far end. Books lined the walls from floor to ceiling on either side of the fireplace and to Rachael's right was a desk. In front of the desk sat two people, a young man and an older woman, her hair was long and brown, streaked with grey, tied to the side in a low ponytail. They rose to their feet as Rachael and the others approached and when they turned around Rachael realized the young man was Thomas.

"Thomas! He tricked you and kidnapped me." Rachael struggled to get free and go to him but the two men at her back held her firmly.

Thomas almost cringed when he saw her and the look on his face told Rachael something she could hardly believe but then his words confirmed it.

"I'm sorry Rachael. It had to be this way."

Rachael felt the sting of betrayal deep in her heart. She was angry—oh so very angry.

"You did this. You set this whole ridiculous thing up just so you could turn me over to him."

"He had my mother, Rachael, and he wasn't going to release her unless I turned you over."

The woman beside him laid a hand on his arm but spoke to Rachael. "It's true. Sebastian kidnapped me just as he did you. Thomas didn't want to betray you but—"

"You're despicable," Rachael spat out. "I've done nothing but help you this whole time and this is how you repay me? Tristan will figure it out. He and the others will—"

Sebastian cut her off. "Tristan will do nothing. Jeanette is his mother too and he wouldn't want her to suffer. He would've done the same things Thomas did, I simply got to Thomas first."

Rachael shook her head. "That's not true. I don't believe you."

Sebastian chuckled. "It doesn't matter what you believe, all that matters are the facts, and the fact is that you are mine, you will do what I tell you to do and then I will open a portal and send you through it, back to your vulnerable and soon to be conquered world, along with Fire-Starter. Or maybe I'll decide to keep the sword if you prove to be uncooperative."

He turned to Thomas and his mother, Jeanette. "You two are free to go." He made another gesture and a man emerged from another hallway, which lead into the room. "Serge will show you the door."

Serge herded Thomas and his mother from the room but Thomas turned back and looked at Rachael.

"I really am sorry, Rachael. But he promised me he'd send you home after you activate the—" His words were cut off by the closing of the hall door.

Rachael glared at the closed door. She'd lost all respect for Thomas. At first, she'd thought him to be very cool and professional. He was, after all, in charge of about a dozen Slayers as well as the protection of an entire city and that was quite a responsibility. Then she'd felt sorry for him and the pressure he was under. She'd been glad to see that he and Amy had made a connection. She wondered what Amy would think about Thomas if she knew what he'd done. But now, Rachael had no more respect or sympathy for Thomas. She simply hated him.

"Well now," Sebastian said. "Why don't we go up to the roof top lounge and watch the Dark-Angels. Did you know I had a special viewing room where we can sit in perfect safety and observe them in all their glory?"

He turned and headed out of the room. Rachael's two escorts followed him, shoving her along with them. They returned to the elevator and went up a level. This time Rachael stepped out of the elevator into another large room but this one had a glass ceiling and offered three-hundred-and-sixty-degree view of the surrounding desert. She could look straight up and see the stars. It would've been amazing and beautiful if she weren't being held prisoner.

There were comfortable seats all around, chairs, loveseats, and full-sized sofas. Small end tables were also scattered about next to the chairs. Glass topped coffee tables sat in front of each of the sofas.

"Would you like a drink, my dear?" Sebastian asked as he walked over to a semi-circular bar at one end of the room. "I have wine, beer, hard liquor…oh, wait, Elfae don't drink alcoholic drinks, do they? You might lose your ability to hold your glamour!" He laughed. "Isn't that right, my dear?"

Sebastian walked over to the woman who sat at the bar. Rachael recognized that super long platinum blonde hair. It was Beatrix Westfall, Lairen's mother who was, Rachael guessed, an Elfae herself.

"Hello Rachael," Beatrix said. "We meet again. Would you like some juice? Water?"

"Release the girl," Sebastian said. "She can no longer do us any harm." The two men who held Rachael's arms released her.

She shrugged them off. "No, I don't want anything to drink."

Beatrix got off her bar stool and approached Rachael. "We won't harm you as long as you do as my husband wishes. You'll be very comfortable here, safe from the DAX, the Dark-Angels and the Hell-Beasts. And then you'll get to go home. You see? All will be well."

Rachael's eyes narrowed. "Is Lairen really your son? Is he my half-brother?"

She smiled. "Why, yes. He is; on both counts."

"Why are you doing this? You're from my world and he's going to destroy it. Doesn't that bother you?"

She shrugged. "He's promised me a better one; one where I will be queen."

Rachael could hardly believe her father had once loved this woman. Or maybe he hadn't. Although she had a difficult time imagining her father would have had a one-night stand with this horrible woman, he just wasn't the type. They must've had some sort of relationship for her dad to let Lairen spend time at Rachael's house when they were young.

"Come now," Sebastian said. "Dark is approaching. Let's settle in to watch the Dark-Angels come alive."

Rachael didn't know what to expect but she wandered closer to the glass. The moon wasn't full but it did give off enough light for her to see movement beyond the window. She hoped Tristan, Ariel and the others were long gone. She didn't want them harmed by the Dark-Angels. Well, maybe it would be okay for Thomas to be attacked, nearly killed and turned into a DAX. Yeah, she was still angry and figured she would be for a very long time.

As Rachael watched, dozens of creatures took flight. They rose up to the sky and Rachael could see them in silhouette. One or two that were close by must've been attracted to the little bit of light in the observatory because they came nearer. One perched on the ledge just outside of the glass and looked in. It was magnificent; a beautiful angelic being with snowy white wings. Its form was very like Rachael's own, but larger and seemingly genderless. Its body looked strong but not particularly masculine, its facial features appeared somewhat feminine because the face was so pretty that it didn't seem to belong on a male body. The creature's hair was a soft gold color and hung to its shoulders. Its eyes were blue, like a summer day. Why were these beings called Dark-Angels? They weren't dark in any sense of the word; they were beautiful…stunning…gorgeous. There just weren't enough words to describe them. She felt a peacefulness come over her like nothing she'd ever felt before. If she could only stand closer to this perfect being…if only she could feel the comfort of its embrace, the gentle touch of its glorious velvety wings against her skin…

Rachael took a step closer to the glass.

CHAPTER EIGHTEEN

I N AN INSTANT EVERYTHING ABOUT THE ANGEL
changed. White wings turned black, golden hair vanished leaving a gleaming hairless pate, its body was no longer lean and lithe but muscular in a
most unnatural and distorted way. It lunged at her with a mouth full of pointed
teeth, abnormally long fingers with curved claws scratched at the glass.

Rachael jumped back and fear tore through her. She'd been lulled, as if
in a trance, drawn to this creature, an innocent to the slaughter. Now she
understood why they were called Dark-Angels and they were all the more
deadly because a person would be lured by them with an illusion of all that
is good and wonderful, beautiful and comforting, straight to their death.

She heard Sebastian laugh. "Ah, that was priceless." He turned to
Beatrix. "We should invite guests here more often."

His comment annoyed Rachael but she was too busy trying to catch
her breath and calm her racing heart to come up with a scathing comment.
The Dark Angel had flown away and Rachael hoped no more of them
would come close to the window. She had thought she would be watching
them, but in truth she now felt like she was the specimen under glass.

As the Dark-Angels flew by, they gazed in the window with glowing
yellow eyes, at her and at Sebastian, Beatrix and the two bodyguards who,
Rachael noted, looked a little nervous.

"They can't get in, you know," Sebastian said. "I have special glass. It's
incredibly strong. Paid a lot for it too." He grinned at a passing Dark Angel.

Rachael plopped down into a nearby chair with a sigh and remained
there, without saying a word, until Sebastian had tired of the observatory

and ordered everyone back downstairs. This time no one grabbed Rachael's arms. They simply flanked her to escort her back to her room with Sebastian leading the way.

"I will have food and water brought to you shortly and then again in the morning. Sleep well, dear, tomorrow we will see to those swords." He smiled at her. "Aren't you excited to see them? Imagine, all four of the legendary Elfaen swords together in one place and you are the lucky girl who will get the privilege of being the one to activate them all for me, the future king of three realms!"

He left, followed by his two henchmen and Rachael was alone, once more behind a locked door. Immediately she tried to get the cuffs off her wrists but she finally gave up. She couldn't slide them off or get the latch to open. She was so frustrated; his whole situation as impossible. How was she ever going to get out of here? She didn't know what methods Sebastian had planned for forcing her to activate the swords but she sure wasn't going to do it voluntarily.

When the door opened about thirty minutes later someone brought in a tray of food and a bottle of water. The person who brought the food and drink was one of the burly men from earlier. He eyed her as he came in but she didn't bother getting up off the mattress on the floor where she was seated. The man set the tray on the floor and left.

With a sigh Rachael got up to investigate. There was a sandwich with a bag of chips and an apple. She hoped the meal wasn't drugged but either way she decided to eat.

She thought about Tristan, Ariel and the others. Would any of them care that she was gone? Would Thomas pretend he didn't know anything about her disappearance? Would anyone come for her? And how was she going to get out of activating the swords? Finally, from sheer exhaustion and total boredom, Rachael finally fell asleep.

The next day Rachael woke up when someone once again came into the room bringing another tray of food. This time the tray held hot cereal with berries on top. At least she was being well fed. She ate, and then tried to freshen up a little in the bathroom by throwing some water on her face. If nothing else it got the sleep out of her eyes. There were no towels so she dried her face with her jacket and wiped her hands on her jeans. She wondered when Sebastian would demand her presence. She didn't have long to wait. The door opened and there stood her two escorts from the previous night.

After a ride in the elevator Rachael found herself in the presence of both Sebastian and Beatrix once more. This time they were in a bare room with no adornments of any kind, just a cement floor, ceiling and walls. Sebastian held a case, which he opened. Inside laid all four Elfaen swords. Fire-Starter was here. If only she could open her hand and call the sword to her right now. But Sebastian quickly shut the case after taking out the three swords he wanted activated.

The other swords looked just like Fire-Starter. They would, as there was nothing to distinguish them from each other without the use of Elfaen fire to reveal their names.

Sebastian took one of the swords out of the case and placed it on the ground about six feet from where Rachael stood, then came over to stand in front of her.

He smiled. "Let's start with this one, shall we?"

Rachael shook her head. "I'm not going to activate those swords for you."

"Of course, you are," Sebastian replied.

She frowned at him. "No, I'm not. I don't want my world destroyed by Hell-Spawn monsters and I don't want it taken over by someone like you."

A moment later Rachael felt sharp pain on her face and in her neck as he backhanded her and sent her sprawling. She looked up at him in shock and touched her cheek as tears sprang to her eyes.

"You are going to get up and you are going to activate this sword, and then the next and the next," Sebastian ground out.

Rachael could see his eyes flash with anger and the sneer on his face confirmed it.

"There, there now," Beatrix said, and put a calming hand on Sebastian's arm.

Rachael expected him to shrug it off but he allowed it, although anger still burned in his eyes.

"Why don't we start small?" Beatrix suggested. "How about activating just one sword for us today, hmm?" She smiled at Rachael. "You are being promised safe return home after all. And Sebastian has also promised to let you keep the Fire-Starter sword. Now aren't those two things worth activating one sword?"

Rachael slowly got to her feet. "Is this how it's going to be? Are you going to hit me every time I refuse until I've activated all the swords?"

"That's a possibility," Sebastian said. "But you'd be bringing it upon yourself. I have no real desire to harm you as evidenced by the fact that you have your own room with an attached bathroom, you have food brought to you, and as my lovely bride has reminded you, I've promised to open a portal for you and send you home. The sooner you activate all three swords the sooner you will see your family and friends once again."

Rachael realized she was between a rock and a hard place. Sebastian and his wife were clearly crazy, it was unlikely anyone would come to rescue her, and she had no desire to be beaten. Plus, she did want to go home, with or without Fire-Starter, but preferably with. On the other hand, maybe since they'd have to take the cuffs off her wrists to enable her access to her fire magic, she'd be able to torch the two of them and get out of here. She wondered if her two escorts were right outside the door. She might have to torch them too.

"Okay," she finally said. "I'll fire test one of the swords."

Beatrix beamed at her and then turned to her husband. "You see, everything is going to be alright." She stepped over to Rachael and removed one of the cuffs.

Rachael frowned. Why was it so easy for Beatrix to take them off? Must have something to do with magic.

Once the cuff was off, she quickly called up her fire magic and lifted her arm, palm out, toward the sword. She stood like that for a couple of seconds then quickly swung her arm toward Sebastian and his wife as she released her magic. Fire burst from her palm straight for them but her fire hit an invisible shield of some sort. Rachael lowered her arm. Sebastian and Beatrix were unharmed.

"You didn't actually think I was stupid enough to make the mistake of being without protection." He gave her a smug look. "You can't harm us, dear. Now do what you promised. Activate the sword."

Rachael lifted her arm. There was no point in refusing. He'd only hit her again and again until she complied with his wishes. She released her fire onto the blade and watched the sword's name appear. She wondered if

Sebastian or Beatrix could read what appeared on the blade or if she was the only one who could make out the sword's name. Life-Giver.

Beatrix came and put the cuff back on Rachael's wrist. When she was done, she went to more closely examine the sword then looked over at Sebastian. He gave her an enquiring look.

"Life-Giver," she said.

Sebastian approached the sword, now cooling on the floor, and crouched to pick it up. Rachael hoped he'd burn his hand, but he didn't. His fingers wrapped around the hilt and he lifted the sword a look of rapt expectation on his face. Rachael waited for the bonding process to begin but nothing happened. At least nothing she could see.

"Why don't I feel anything?" He stared at the sword as though willing it to connect to him. "How do I know when I'm bound to it?" Sebastian turned suspicious eyes her way. "Well?"

She shrugged. "I don't know anything about how this works."

"But you've bonded to the Fire-Starter sword."

"Yes, but I wasn't expecting to. It just happened."

His eyes narrowed. "I saw the sparks. I saw your hair change color. Surely something happens to affect anyone who bonds with one of these swords."

"I don't know," Rachael said. She tried to keep any sign of happiness at bay. What a stroke of luck. He wasn't bonding with the sword. Maybe he wouldn't be able to bond with any of them.

"Let me," Beatrix said.

Sebastian handed her the sword but nothing happened at her touch either.

"Damn it!" Beatrix shrieked. "It's not working!"

Sebastian rounded on Rachael. "You must activate the other two."

Rachael frowned at Beatrix. "But you said only one sword today."

Beatrix glared at Rachael. "That was before. I've changed my mind. We're going to bond with these swords today and you will make it happen!"

Rachael felt Beatrix's air magic start up. "What're you going to do, blow wind at me until I comply?" she said. "You can blow me all over this room but it's not going to make me use fire magic on—"

Sebastian held up his hand. "Silence!"

Beatrix shut down her air magic and glanced at her husband who strode to the door and opened it.

"Bring the girl," he said to someone outside the door.

Rachael frowned. Now what? Who else did Sebastian have here at his house? Her question was answered moments later when the door re-opened and one of Sebastian's henchmen came in dragging a stumbling, blindfolded girl.

"Ariel!"

Sebastian marched over and ripped the blindfold from the girl's eyes. She blinked a couple of times and then her eyes narrowed as she focused on Sebastian.

"You won't get away with this," she ground out, eyes narrowed in anger.

Sebastian laughed. "There it is again. 'You won't get away with this'," he mimicked, then laughed again. "Oh, but I am getting away with it you, silly little girl, and very soon you will be bowing before your king and queen of the three realms." He smiled at Beatrix. "Yes, that does have a very nice ring to it. King Sebastian and Queen Beatrix of the Three Realms." She grinned back at him.

Sebastian turned to Rachael; his smile now gone. "You will activate the remaining two swords. Right here, right now. And if you don't...well, you may be willing to take a beating but I doubt you'd let your friend take one for your sake. Shall we see?" He hauled off and smacked Ariel across the face. She didn't fall because the man who stood behind her held onto her arms.

Ariel glared up at Sebastian. "Is that all you got?"

He smiled. "Absolutely not." And then he hit her again, this time in the stomach.

Ariel doubled over and groaned. It took her a while to straighten and when she did there were tears in her eyes. She looked like she was having trouble breathing.

"Okay, okay, stop it!" Rachael cried. "I'll activate the swords!"

Ariel looked at her and shook her head. "No, Rachael, don't do it."

"Oh, so you want to get hit again, is that it?" Sebastian asked. He lifted his hand to hit her but Rachael stopped him.

"No! Don't! Never mind what she says. I'll fire test the swords. Right now. Let's do this."

Sebastian dropped his raised arm and smiled at her. "Very well. I'm so glad you've seen reason. I knew snatching this girl would prove to be useful." He walked over to the case and took out both the remaining untested swords. "Let's begin."

CHAPTER NINETEEN

A FTER HAVING THE CUFF TAKEN OFF HER WRIST once more, Rachael summoned her magic and raised her arm. She directed her fire at one of the swords and waited for the lettering to appear on the blade. Beast-Master.

Once again Beatrix attached the cuff to Rachael's wrist and then she and Sebastian stepped forward to examine the sword.

Beatrix looked at Sebastian, her face alight with excitement. "Pick it up!"

He did, and although Rachael had hoped maybe this sword wouldn't bond with him either, it did.

Sebastian's entire body went rigid as the sword pulsed in his hand. His facial features twisted and contorted and the pupils of his eyes elongated into narrow ovals like cat's eyes. His irises went from light hazel green to brilliant cat-eye green and although his face returned to normal his eyes remained the eyes of a cat. It looked truly eerie and Rachael could hardly stand to look at them. He now looked alien, like a creature from outer space.

"It worked!" He shouted, arms raised, one hand still clutching the sword. "I am the Beast-Master. I can open the portals and control the beasts!" He looked at Beatrix. "And now, the last sword, Death-Dealer. And it shall be yours, my dear. It must be yours and then together we shall rule the three realms side by side!"

Rachael and Ariel glanced at each other. Rachael wished somehow she could get to Fire-Starter but even if she did, Ariel was still captive. Sebastian and Beatrix had the upper hand.

"Well, what are you waiting for?" Sebastian snapped at her. "Activate the remaining sword!"

Rachael held up her arm to show him her wrist and lifted her eyebrows.

"Oh, right," Sebastian muttered. He gestured to Beatrix who came and removed the cuff.

With a sigh of resignation, Rachael focused her magic once again. Boy, was she beginning to get tired from all this use of her innate talent. She flexed her wrist, palm toward the remaining sword and released her fire. About thirty seconds later the sword's name shone clearly on the sword but they all knew what it was going to read well before this. Death-Dealer.

Rachael shut off her magic and this time Sebastian put the cuff back onto her wrist while Beatrix went to pick up the sword, a look of anticipation on her face. When nothing happened that look on her face turned to rage.

"It won't respond to me!" she shrieked. "Make it work. Make the sword bond with me!" She shook the blade in Rachael's direction.

Rachael was quite exhausted at this point but she put up a good front and glared back at Beatrix. "I have no control of the swords! They have a mind of their own and bond with whomever they choose."

Sebastian went to the door and flung it open. Two more big guys in suits entered the room and grabbed Rachael by the arm. They shoved both Rachael and Ariel toward the door.

Sebastian called out, "Wait!" then glared at both Rachael and Ariel. "Put them together in the room and lock them in. No food. No water until I say so. Now get out!"

Rachael didn't bother struggling, she was too tired, but Ariel did; not that it got her anywhere. A few minutes later they were locked into the room where Rachael had been held since the previous day.

Ariel smiled at Rachael as she gingerly touched her split lip and swollen eye. "That guy packs a punch," she muttered. "What I'd give to have healing magic instead of air magic right now."

Rachael dropped down into the mattress. "I'm so sorry you got involved in this."

Ariel sat beside her. "I was already involved. I'm a Slayer. I had no choice but to be involved. So how did you wind up in here? All we knew was that Thomas came back out and when we went to get back in the vehicles you were nowhere to be found."

"It was a set up. While we were all out of each other's sight Sebastian opened a portal, used some kind of drug to knock me out and then snatched me. I woke up in this room and some of his security guards, or whatever they are, took me to him. Thomas was there and so was his mother."

Ariel's eyes widened. "What? Thomas saw you? He didn't say anything. He acted like he had no idea where you were!"

"Oh, he knew," Rachael sneered. "Apparently Sebastian held his mother hostage so he'd turn me over. Thomas set up the whole trek out here and split us up just so his father would have the opportunity to take me and then he lied to all of you about it."

Ariel shook her head. "I don't believe it. This is…How could he do that? He's a Slayer and an overseer of Slayers, his job isn't just to protect the city but to safeguard his team."

"Yeah, well obviously he didn't care about anything except getting his mother out of there and the hell with betraying me. After all, I'm just someone from another world and not really a part of his team. Sebastian let them go after he had me. You didn't see her come out?"

"No. Maybe she left after we did so Thomas wouldn't have to explain anything to us about it."

"Probably one of Sebastian's guys took her home. How did you end up here?" Rachael asked.

"Snatched by a couple of Sebastian's guys. I was out patrolling with Sophia. We thought we heard something down a neighborhood alley and split up. Sophia cut through between two houses and I entered the alley from one end. They were waiting for me. One grabbed me from behind while I confronted his pal. They drugged me too. I passed out and here I am. I guess they brought me here as insurance that you'd do what they wanted you to do."

Rachael sighed. "I guess so. Sorry."

"You have nothing to be sorry about, girlfriend. Thomas betrayed you. He betrayed all of us."

"Was anyone even looking for me?"

Ariel grinned, then winced and touched her tender lip. "Oh, yeah, Tristan about went nuts. He wanted us to immediately search the area, which we did but then Thomas said we all needed to get back because it would be dusk soon and we didn't want to get caught outdoors what with all the Dark-Angels and all that."

Rachael shuddered. "I saw one up close. Sebastian has a viewing room on his roof. Those are the scariest things I've ever seen. Worse than the Hell-Spawn and they're pretty terrifying too."

"Oh, speaking of Hell-Spawn, we killed the other flying one last night. That was before I got taken and brought here." Ariel made a face and then winced again. "Ouch," she gasped and must've seen concern on Rachael's face. "Don't worry. I'll be okay by morning. Slayers heal pretty fast even without healing magic. So now what? How do we get out of here?"

Rachael looked around. "We don't."

"Well, there must be some way."

"I've checked the room and the bathroom but there're no windows and nothing to jimmy the door with so…" Rachael shrugged. "I'm tired from using so much of my magic and Sebastian has my sword with the others anyway. Plus, I don't have the energy to try and escape right now."

"I wonder what the others are thinking now that I've disappeared too." Ariel lay back on the mattress and closed her eyes.

"I don't know, but I bet they'll never guess Thomas is behind any of it."

"Oh boy, the crap's gonna hit the fan when Tristan finds out."

"I just hope we can get out of here to let him know." Rachael leaned back against the wall. "You know, Sebastian told me he'd open a portal and let me go home after I helped him. I seriously doubt he's going to keep that promise."

"What's his agenda anyway?"

"He wants to open portals to my world and the hellish one, let all the monsters into this world and mine. Then for he and Beatrix to rule all three as king and queen."

Ariel opened her eyes and looked at Rachael. "And now he's got the Beast-Master sword to control the beasts."

"Yep."

"Good thing none of those swords bonded with Beatrix. Imagine her with the Death-Dealer sword."

"I don't even want to think about it," Rachael mumbled. "Sorry but, I'm so tired. I think I'm going to snooze for a little while. We have nothing else to do anyway." Rachael closed her eyes and drifted off to sleep.

Rachael awakened to Ariel gently shoving her shoulder. "Rachael, wake up," she whispered.

"What? What's going on?"

"Shh, someone is trying to get in."

Rachael got to her feet just as the door slowly swung open. The room was dimly lit and Rachael was surprised to see Lairen's head peer around the edge of the door.

He smiled. "Hello Cupcake. Time to go."

Rachael frowned. "Lairen?"

"Hey," Ariel said. "Isn't he the prisoner who escaped?"

"Yes, I am, but we don't have time to chat right now. We've got to get out of here." Lairen entered the room. He was dressed entirely in black and his white blond hair was pulled back in a low ponytail. "I've got something you'll be needing."

Rachael looked down to see the case in his hand. "The swords! You have the swords!"

"Shh, yes, but only the three. He didn't even bother to lock them up since they're useless to him so I snagged them. Come on, let's go."

"And why should we trust him?" Ariel whispered to Rachael.

Rachael shrugged. "I trusted Thomas because I thought he was a good guy but he turned out not to be. I thought Lairen was a bad guy but...who knows? And I really do want to get out of here so it's worth a try."

"Ladies," Lairen said. "We really gotta go."

Rachael and Ariel followed Lairen into the hall and over to the elevator. Lairen held a finger up to his lips then flipped over a small panel in the wall to reveal a button. He pressed the button and closed the panel as a larger panel opened up in the wall. Lairen gestured for them to follow him and they did.

Once in the passageway and after the large panel was closed, the girls followed Lairen down a series of hallways, straight to a door. On either side there were boxes stacked about half way up the wall and some old furniture that looked like it had seen better days.

"Once we get outside," Lairen whispered, "we'll have to make it to my car, which is just down the road. I couldn't take the chance of starting it up so close to the house in case my step-dad or his goons wake up and try to stop us."

"But what about the Dark-Angels?" Rachael asked.

"Yeah, that's the other thing. There're a lot of them around and we have to get to the car without getting killed or worse."

Rachael waved her hand in front of Lairen's face. "What about these cuffs? I have no access to my magic with them on."

"Oh, right." He reached over and used a small key he'd dug out of his pocket to remove them.

Ariel nodded. "Okay, let's do this, but first give me one of those swords."

Rachael gave her a hard look. "One of them might bond with you, you know that."

"And maybe they won't," Ariel replied. "I don't really care and either way I need a weapon."

Lairen opened the case and looked at Rachael. "How do you know which one is yours?"

Rachael reached toward the swords and Fire-Starter flew into her hand. "That's how."

Lairen's eyes were like saucers. "Wow."

Ariel grabbed one of the swords and Rachael gave her a guarded look.

Ariel hefted the blade. "The weight and balance are good. I can use this."

"You don't feel anything?" Rachael asked.

Ariel shook her head. "Let's get out of here."

Lairen closed the case, leaving the one remaining sword inside.

"What about you?" Rachael asked.

"I have a longbow," he said and reached behind a dresser with a couple of boxes on top of it. He pulled out a quiver with arrows and a bow. "I stashed them here earlier." He slipped the quiver onto his back. "Okay. Here we go."

Ariel held her sword in one hand and picked up the case with the remaining sword in the other. "You can't carry it," she said to Lairen. "You need both hands free."

Lairen nodded and then opened the door.

Chapter Twenty

HE THREE OF THEM QUIETLY SLIPPED THROUGH
the doorway into the darkness of the night.

Lairen gently closed the door behind them. "This way," he
whispered.

They hurried down the dirt road that led to the house, being careful to
scan the sky as they went. There were some shrubs large enough to blend
into their shadows but the moon was bright and Rachael knew Dark-
Angels could appear at any time.

"How far to the car?" Ariel asked.

"Just around the bend," Lairen replied.

"Incoming!" Rachael whispered. "Dark-Angels."

Lairen readied his bow while he ushered Rachael and Ariel behind
him. "Keep going. I got this."

Rachael and Ariel kept moving but more Dark-Angels appeared in the
sky and headed in their direction as though called. And perhaps they did
have some sort of telepathy because it seemed as though once the first Dark
Angel had seen them; the rest were eerily quick to appear.

Ariel kept one hand wrapped around the handle of the case holding the
remaining sword. "Don't let them trick you," she said to Rachael. "They
may look harmless but they're—"

"I know, I know. I've seen one up close," Rachael replied. Even as she
ran to the car, which she could now see in the distance, perhaps fifty yards
away, she kept her eyes on the approaching Dark-Angels.

Lairen let one of his arrows fly and it pierced the chest of the closest Dark Angel. The creature screamed then fell to the ground. What had started out as beautiful and golden as it approached, now returned to its true nature; that of horror and dark malevolence.

"Run!" Ariel cried. She slashed with her sword as several more of the Dark-Angels swarmed them; each one looked hauntingly beautiful, but it was all an illusion.

Rachael felt Fire-Starter respond to the threat; its power rushed up her arm and flooded her body. She saw sparks fly as the blade bit into the flesh of one of the Dark-Angels. Rachael pushed her fire magic through the sword and into the creature that even now tried to beg for mercy with its winsome eyes and wholesome expression. Once the fire took hold though, Rachael saw the beast change to its natural form. Guttural sounds emanated from its throat, its glowing eyes condemned her and its clawed hands reached for her.

More were on their way but they no longer kept up the pretense of looking like peaceful emissaries of the heavens. They approached in all their terrible viciousness; mouths open to show hungering jaws of pointed teeth and long clawed fingers grasping.

Lairen let a few more arrows fly in rapid succession. Unfortunately, some only injured and didn't kill the creatures.

They reached the car and Rachael continued to fend off one Dark Angel after another, while Lairen attempted to hang onto his bow while pressing the button that would unlock the car doors.

"Get in!" Lairen shouted once the doors were unlocked.

Ariel threw the case with the sword into the back seat, climbed in and quickly slammed the door. Rachael took a final slash at one of the Dark-Angels then ducked into the front passenger seat.

Lairen was already behind the wheel. He locked the doors and started the car, pushed down on the gas pedal and the car shot forward. Rachael was afraid that the Dark-Angels might try and get into the car or even work together to lift it off the ground and fly off with it, but they seemed to lose interest once their prey was no longer readily accessible. As the car sped away Rachael looked out the back window and watched the remaining Dark-Angels fly away, leaving their dead brethren to whatever fate befell Dark-Angels that died.

She turned back around. "Whew. That was…"

"Yeah," Ariel echoed from the back seat. "Everyone okay?"

"I'm good," Lairen said. "You?"

"Fine," Ariel replied. "What about you, Rachael?"

"I'm okay." She turned to Lairen. "Where are we going?"

He glanced at her. "You tell me. I just planned the break out, didn't get any further than that."

"We could go to the compound," Ariel suggested.

"I think we should go to Tristan's place," Rachael replied. "I want to tell him about Thomas and I don't want to take the chance of running into that traitor."

Lairen nodded. "Just tell me how to get there once we get closer into town."

Ariel grabbed the backs of the two front seats and leaned forward. "So how did you get out of the compound before? Can you open portals?"

Rachael heard the suspicion in Ariel's tone and she also was curious. "Yeah, how did you manage that? Did Sebastian get you out?"

"Actually, it was neither. Thomas got me out."

"Thomas!" Both girls said at the same time.

"He can open portals?" Rachael exclaimed. "You mean he could've sent me home any time?" If she thought she'd been angry with Thomas before, now she was really steamed.

Lairen shook his head. "No, he can open them, but not to other worlds like Sebastian can. Thomas can only open them to take him to other locations in this world. Have you ever noticed him showing up out of nowhere or seeming to vanish from the premises when no one saw him leave and you were just talking to him a minute ago?"

Rachael nodded.

"Well, that's how he does it."

"So, he let you go?" Ariel asked.

Rachael frowned. "But he acted like he didn't even know you!"

"Yeah," Lairen chuckled. "Acted is right. We're not exactly the best of friends but we most definitely know each other."

Rachael felt like she wanted to punch something. "Tristan is going to be so angry when he hears this."

"If he even believes it," Ariel said. "He may not. He grew up with Thomas and he's not going to take the word of this guy," she tipped her head toward Lairen, "over the brother he's known his whole life."

"But after I tell him about how Thomas arranged my kidnapping, I mean, Thomas even admitted it and so did his mom, who is also Tristan's mom, I might add. He'll have to believe it." Rachael felt a little less certain than she sounded but even if he didn't believe her right away, she hoped he'd come around.

As they followed the main road into the city, Rachael gave Lairen directions to Tristan's townhouse. She hoped Tristan was home but it was still dark out so it was possible he was out hunting DAX.

Lairen parked on the street and Rachael went to the door while the others stayed in the car. She rang the doorbell and waited. Tristan's face appeared at the window alongside the front door. She saw his eyes widen and then he disappeared, probably to get his gun before opening the door.

The front door opened and Tristan came out. He wore faded blue jeans, black boots and a deep burgundy long sleeved t-shirt.

"Rachael?"

"Yes, Tristan, it's me. Ariel is with me and so is Lairen. May we come in?"

He frowned and halted his walk toward the security gate. "Lairen? The escaped prisoner?"

"Yes, it's a long story and I want to tell it to you so could you please let us in?"

Tristan walked the rest of the way and looked past her to the car in the road and its occupants. She saw a cut on his brow and bruises on his face as well. She thought he must've had a tough night.

He looked back down at Rachael. "Did he kidnap you?"

"No, he helped us escape. Please, Tristan let us in and I promise Ariel and I will tell you everything that's happened since we disappeared."

Tristan studied her for a moment. "Alright, but if he's coercing you in any way—"

Rachael shook her head. "He's not coercing me or Ariel. We just escaped from Sebastian Westfall's compound, had to fight off Dark-Angels to get to the car and then drove all the way here. Now would you please let us in?"

Tristan unlocked the gate. "This better not be a trick."

Rachael sighed. "It's not." She turned and gestured for Ariel and Lairen to come inside.

Once everyone was indoors, Tristan studied Lairen warily then glanced at Ariel. "What's in the case?"

She set it down and opened it. "The fourth Elfaen sword. And this…" She said as she began to place the one she'd been using in the case as well, "is one of them also. But don't flip out, it didn't bond to me."

"Wait," Tristan said. "Let me see it."

"There's a window of opportunity after a sword has been fire tested for it to bond with someone," Rachael explained. "Maybe you shouldn't—"

But her warning came too late. As soon as Tristan touched the sword Rachael's eyes widened and she was instantly silenced by what she saw. The cut on his face healed and the bruises faded to nothing.

Rachael looked up into his startled eyes. "Tristan? I think the Life-Giver sword just chose you."

He turned to her. "How is that possible?"

She shrugged. "I don't know. I didn't expect Fire-Starter to bond with me either but it did. How do you feel?"

He looked at her, his face alight, his smile contagious. "I feel better than I have in years…maybe ever. Like I just had an infusion of energy and well-being."

"Unfortunately, Sebastian has the Beast-Master sword," Ariel said, a look of disgust on her face. "It bonded with him."

"And what about the last sword?" Tristan asked.

"Well, that just leaves Death-Dealer," Rachael replied.

Ariel closed the case. "Okay, this was unexpected and really nice for Tristan and all but let's get back to the reason we're here."

"Jealous it didn't bond with you, Ariel?" Tristan teased.

Ariel sighed and shook her head, a smile on her face. "No, not really, but we do have some serious stuff to talk to you about and we shouldn't put it off any longer."

"Right," Tristan set the sword aside but Rachael thought he seemed reluctant to do so. He looked over at Lairen and his eyes narrowed. "Start from the beginning."

Rachael and Ariel explained what had happened to them right up to when Lairen pulled his car up to Tristan's home. They had to stop and start a few times though, first, when Rachael got to the parts about Thomas and her interaction with him at Sebastian's compound, and then again when Lairen explained how Thomas had opened a portal and broken him out of the Slayer United compound.

Tristan shook his head. "No, I just don't believe it. This is my brother we're talking about. I've known him my whole life. He wouldn't do something like this. He's not capable of it."

"Well, I'm sorry but he is and he did," Rachael said.

"And my mother was there?" Tristan asked, a look of incredulity on his face.

Rachael nodded.

Tristan was quiet and the others gave him time to think. Finally, he glanced at Lairen. "So, you're telling me you weren't in on any of it."

Lairen shook his head. "No. I did retrieve a couple of those swords for Sebastian, I admit that, but I had no idea what he was going to use them for. I thought he just wanted to collect artifacts from other worlds."

"But you had to know he was stealing them," Tristan countered.

Lairen shrugged. "Look, the guy was good to me and to my mom and I guess I just didn't pay that close attention to things. I trusted him."

"And when, exactly, did you stop trusting him?" Tristan asked.

"When I found out he was holding my sister and her friend against their will, that he smacked them both around. I also overheard my mom talking with him about their plans and I realized he was psycho."

"I hate to say it but your mother is psycho too," Tristan corrected him.

Lairen looked angry for a moment but then the tension left his body and he shrugged.

"So, what're we going to do?" Rachael asked. "Sebastian is going to open more portals now that he has the Beast-Master sword and can control the Hell-Spawn."

Lairen looked at her. "Hell-Spawn?"

"That's what we call them," she said.

"Well, first off I'm going to go talk to Thomas privately," Tristan said. "I want to see what he says when it's just the two of us, you know, if he admits to his part in all this or not." He glanced at Lairen. "And I'm still not entirely sure I trust you."

Lairen looked at him, his face impassive, and just shrugged.

"Well, I want to go get some real sleep now that I don't have to keep one eye open waiting for Sebastian or his goons to come get me for some reason," Ariel said.

"You can sleep in my room," Rachael offered.

"And Lairen can take the sofa," Tristan suggested.

Ariel frowned. "Well, where are you going to sleep, Rachael?"

"Well, I—"

"She can stay in my room," Tristan said as he grabbed the Life-Giver sword and stood up. "Besides I want to talk to you a little more in private, Rachael."

"Oh, okay." Rachael got up and was about to leave the room when Lairen put a hand on her arm and stopped her.

"I've been meaning to ask you, Cupcake, what happened to your hair? It was blonde and now it's crazy red, yellow and orange!"

"The Fire-Starter sword happened to me, that's what," she smiled at him and realized she wasn't as irritated with him for calling her 'Cupcake' as she once had been. Rachael turned and followed Tristan from the room, bringing her sword with her.

CHAPTER TWENTY-ONE

A S SOON AS THEY WERE BEHIND THE CLOSED
door, he rounded on her.

"Is he for real?" he whispered.

"Yeah, I think so. I mean, I don't trust him completely but I trusted your brother and look where that got me."

"Do you have any idea what I've been through trying to find you?" Tristan asked. "We searched all around Sebastian Westfall's place and I've been keeping an eye out all over this city for any sign of you. I didn't know if a Dark Angel killed you or turned you or what. Every time I saw a DAX, I was afraid it might be you!" He raked fingers through his hair and started to pace. "And then Ariel disappeared too!"

"Ariel told me you guys killed the other Flying Hell-Spawn."

"Rachael, are you listening to me? I was terrified you were dead or worse. I've been going crazy." He grabbed her shoulders and looked into her eyes. "And now you come waltzing in here, with our former prisoner at your side, telling me my own brother is to blame for your disappearance."

"I'm sorry Tristan. I don't know what else to say but it's the truth."

Tristan let go of her. "I'll find out more tomorrow."

"We have to move quickly though. Now that Sebastian has Beast-Master, he could start opening portals at any time."

"Well, isn't there a learning curve or something with these swords?" Tristan asked.

"Not much. You saw how quickly and effectively I fought the DAX. It's going to be the same way with Sebastian. And with you for that matter." She smiled. "You have the Life-Giver sword, Tristan."

"Let's hope I won't have to use it. I'd rather we all stay unharmed."

"Me too. But it's a big deal that the sword chose you! You're not even from my world. You're not Elfae."

He made a face. "Neither is Sebastian and he's bonded with a sword too. I just hope one of our people can bond with the remaining sword. We may need it."

Rachael nodded. "That's a good point."

Tristan had been pacing the room again but he stopped. "Sorry, you must want to get cleaned up, into some different clothes and... are you hungry?"

"No. Not really. I'm good. But I do feel kind of grubby."

"You can use my shower if you want to get cleaned up." He pointed to around the corner to the attached bathroom. "Help yourself."

"Thanks. I don't have any of my clothes in here though. I'd better go—"

"No, here, you can borrow one of my shirts to sleep in." Tristan rummaged in a dresser drawer and pulled out a black V-neck t-shirt. "How's this?"

"Uh, okay I guess."

"And these." He pulled out some lightweight pants made out of cotton knit; like a t-shirt. "They'll be too big for you but maybe you can make them work."

Rachael took the offered pants. "Ok. Um…I'll be back." She ducked into the bathroom and turned on the shower.

Twenty minutes or so later Rachael looked at herself in the mirror as she towel-dried her hair. She'd never looked worse, in her opinion. First off, she still had a faint mark on her face from where Sebastian had smacked her. Second, she had on two items of baggy clothes that left her shapeless, and third, she had on no makeup and her hair was a damp straggly mess from the shower. And even worse, she wanted her own hair color back. She didn't even look like herself and there seemed to be nothing she could do about it.

With a sigh she hung the used towel on the bar and opened the door. Tristan stood by the window but turned as she entered the room.

"Here," he gestured to the bed. "Lay down. You can sleep under the covers and I'll sleep on top of them."

Rachael suddenly felt pretty awkward as she realized that somewhere along the line she'd become attracted to this guy, and now here she was about to share his bed. It was only to sleep, nothing more, but still…

She walked over to the bed and climbed in, feeling more like a child being tucked in than a college student sharing a bed with a hot guy. Because he was, after all, a very good-looking guy even though she'd been too interested in getting home and then surviving this place, to think about it too much.

She pulled up the covers as Tristan lay down on top of them and snapped off the light. The room was now dark, with only a little moonlight peaking in from the shuttered window. She could see his face, partly shadowed, once he turned in her direction.

"What are you going to do about Thomas?" she asked.

"After I talk to him, and if I'm convinced that what you've told me about him is true—"

Rachael felt a flare of irritation. "Of course, it's true. I know he's your brother but why would I lie?"

"I don't know, but I've known him my entire life and I have to give him the benefit of the doubt."

Rachael roped in her annoyance. "Okay, I understand that."

"Anyway," Tristan continued. "If he's capable of creating portals then I want him to open one right into Sebastian's house or where ever he's going to be so we can stop him. If you and I, Stefan, Amy, Ariel and Sophia all converge on him at once and completely unexpectedly, then we might stand a chance of taking him out of the picture for good."

"What if we get there too late and he's already opened the portals?"

"Then we close them with the devices Kirk and Miko gave us. By the way, does Lairen know how to use that longbow?"

Rachael nodded. "Yes, definitely."

"Good. Then we might be able to use him, that is unless he's going to double cross us somehow."

Rachael frowned. "If Thomas opens the portals for us to go through, then he'll be there too. That could be a liability. I'd like to be able to trust him but I just don't. That is unless he's seen the error of his ways and wants to make it up to you and all the rest of us, not to mention the whole freakin' world. And even then, I don't know if I'd trust him. He might help his father escape or actually fight against us."

"I said I'd talk to him. That's all I can say about it right now."

She sighed. "And I have to get that last sword back too; the Beast-Master one."

"Speaking of the swords, and specifically the one we have, the Death-Dealer sword…maybe Stefan or—"

"I don't know how long the window of opportunity is for bonding. I might have to reactivate it."

"Okay, well we'll cross that bridge when we come to it. I'll get Stefan, Amy and Sophia over here tomorrow and we'll see what's what."

Rachael closed her eyes and thought about how the next couple of days might play out. If Sebastian Westfall was killed then who would open a portal so she could get back to her own world? But if he were kept alive, would he even open one for her anyway? Was it too much of a risk to let him live? But if no one else could open a portal to her world then she'd never get home.

Somewhere in between all these thoughts Rachael realized Tristan's breathing had slowed and deepened. She figured he was asleep. If only she had met him back in her world. If only, if only, if only…but they weren't destined to be together so there was no point in even allowing herself to think about the possibilities. It was funny though how feelings could turn around on a person.

She hadn't liked him all that much when they'd first met and he seemed to only grudgingly accept her presence but then things had changed. Somewhere along the line she'd come to think of Tristan, Ariel and even Amy and Stefan as friends; Thomas too, but not anymore. She remembered the hug she'd shared with Tristan in the kitchen not so long ago. He'd initiated it. And he admitted to being crazy worried about her disappearance so maybe he was attracted to her as well.

Rachael rolled onto her side, facing away from Tristan. But there was no point in allowing her thoughts to wander in that direction. They all had to work together to survive and that's probably all this was; an attraction born of life and death situations. It wasn't genuine. Not like the stuff real relationships were built on, right? Her eyes closed and her mind wandered into sleep. The next thing she knew, bright light flooded the room and Rachael hid her eyes.

"Wake up!"

Rachael turned over and put the pillow over her head.

"Come on, Rachael," Ariel said. "Time to get up. How was your night with Tristan?" she teased.

Rachael sat up and threw the pillow at Ariel who caught it easily from over at the window where she'd opened the blinds to let the light stream in.

"What time is it?" Rachael asked.

"After two. Tristan went to talk to Thomas. He said for us to wait here until he got back."

Rachael crawled out of bed and staggered into the bathroom. She splashed water on her face then came back out feeling a bit more awake.

"My sleep schedule is all turned around," she grumbled. "Where's Lairen?"

"He's out in the kitchen making us sandwiches."

Rachael eyes widened. "Really. Where did he get the food? Tristan keeps his cupboards pretty bare from what I've seen."

"I guess he shopped while we were gone. Hope you don't mind but I borrowed back one of the shirts I loaned you," Ariel said with a grin.

"Fine with me." Rachael left Tristan's room and went back to her own. There she fished some clean clothes from the dresser and got dressed while Ariel went out to the kitchen to see how the food was coming along.

Rachael put on a little bit of makeup and brushed her hair, then pulled it back into a neat braid. It was easier to deal with the crazy bright red color when she didn't have to look at it cascading over her shoulders all the time.

She left the bathroom and headed out to the kitchen to find the table set for three. There were even placemats and napkins. Rachael gazed wide-eyed at Lairen.

"Here you go," he said and set a plate with a sandwich, chips and macaroni salad in front of her.

She slid into the chair next to Ariel. There was a jug of what looked like lemonade on the table as well.

Lairen returned to the table with bowls of soup for each of them.

"Wow!" Rachael could hardly believe it. "This looks great!"

"You're welcome, Cupcake. Are you ready to acknowledge me as your brother yet?"

Rachael smiled at him as he took a seat across from her. "Well, my opinion of you has certainly improved, that's for sure, but I don't know about the rest."

"I'm going in the right direction then at least," he said and took a bite of sandwich.

They were just finishing up washing the dishes and putting everything away when Tristan returned.

"Well?" Ariel said.

"How did it go?" Rachael echoed.

Tristan looked drained. "He admitted it. He said he never wanted either of you to get hurt and he's glad you escaped, but getting our mother away from Sebastian was his priority. In fact, she's leaving town today; going to the coast somewhere."

"So will he do anything to help us or are we on our own?" Rachael asked.

"He says he'll help us and do whatever we need him to do. He's stepping down as overseer of our Slayer United branch and he turned it over to me." Tristan sighed. "Technically he can't do that. There are people up the ranks at Slayer United that make those kinds of decisions. You can't just hand the position off to—"

"But they've abandoned us," Ariel pointed out. "They've stayed well away from everything that's going on here."

"They've thrown you all to the wolves and I don't understand why," Rachael said. "Your whole world and mine could be destroyed by Sebastian and they don't even care!"

Lairen cleared his throat to get their attention. "I don't mean to rub salt on your wounds but…"

"But what?" Tristan snapped.

"Well," Lairen continued. "Who was the person who contacted your higher ups to let them know what was going on here?"

Rachael's eyes widened. "Thomas."

"Did he really call them?" Lairen asked. "And if he did, how do you know he gave them the whole picture? Maybe your Slayer United people don't have any idea what's going on here."

"Son of a bitch!" Tristan shouted and leapt to his feet. His phone was out of his pocket and in his hand in a flash. "I'll be back," he said and left the room.

"Wow," Ariel said. "I hadn't thought of that."

"Me either," Rachael replied.

CHAPTER TWENTY-TWO

HEY FINISHED CLEANING UP FROM THEIR LUNCH and then waited in the living room for Tristan to return. He'd gone out onto the back patio and Rachael could hear bits and pieces of his phone conversation. Finally, he came slamming back into the house.

He looked at Lairen. "You were right. They didn't know the full extent of what's been going on here. They're sending a team to do routine patrols in the area for DAX, Dark-Angels and the two remaining Hell-Spawn. That frees us up to go after Sebastian. They're also sending a second team to back us up in case a portal gets opened and Hell-Spawn start flooding in. So, in all, they're sending about twenty Slayers."

"That's a relief," Ariel said. "We'll need that many if those Hell-Spawn start flooding in. Now we can just concentrate on Sebastian Westfall, his wife and those hulking goons he has working for him."

"How many of them are there?" Rachael asked Lairen.

"Just the three plus someone who does the cooking and another person who cleans the house. Those last two you don't have to worry about though. They'll stay out of your way. They just cook and clean and mind their own business."

"What sort of magic do the goons have?" Ariel asked.

"One has air, one water and one earth," Lairen replied.

Rachael made a face. "So, things could get messy between our magic and theirs unless we can take them out quickly and quietly before they see us coming."

Ariel nodded. "Right. Stealth is going to be really important in all this. We want to take out the guards first, quickly and quietly."

"Yeah," Tristan nodded in agreement. "No magic or Sebastian will know something's up. And while I was on the phone I also talked to Stefan and filled him in. He'll talk to Amy and Sophia and then the three of them will be here as soon as possible. I want to see if any of them can bond with the remaining sword before we go after Sebastian."

"And what about Thomas? How's he going to fit into this? Or is he?" Ariel asked.

Tristan explained what he'd talked to Rachael about the night before.

"So, you're going to trust him to open a portal for us?" Ariel asked. "You realize he could tip his father off and we'd be walking right into a trap."

Tristan scowled at her. "I know. I'm aware of that but having him open a portal for us, straight into Sebastian's stronghold is also our best chance at catching them all off guard."

Ariel made a face. "Let's just hope he doesn't open a portal into a locked room where we'll all be prisoners."

Rachael turned to Tristan. "You really do trust him not to betray us again?"

"He said he'd help us. I believe him."

"I'm all for giving people second chances," Lairen said. "But there's a lot of risk involved here. You better be absolutely certain about this."

Tristan turned his scowling countenance toward Lairen. "Yeah, you just keep your mouth shut unless you have inside info for us. Thomas was quick to betray the Slayers to protect our mother and I have no reason to believe you won't change sides once we get there to protect yours."

"I admit," Lairen said. "That I don't want to see any real harm come to my mother but then again, she's not really a very nice person. Never has been. My childhood was not a picnic. She's always been selfish and manipulative and being with Sebastian has only made her worse. All I ask is that you make an effort to stop her without killing her. Is it so wrong for me to want that?"

"No, Lairen," Rachael said. "It's not." She looked at Ariel and Tristan. "I think we can make that promise, don't you? To not kill her unless there's no other way?"

After a moment Ariel nodded. "Yeah, I think that's reasonable."

Rachael looked at Tristan who continued to study Lairen through narrowed, suspicious eyes. "Yeah, okay," he finally said.

The doorbell rang and Tristan went to look through the window. "It's Stefan and the others." He went out and unlocked the security screen to let them in.

"Hey," Stefan said with a smile when he saw Rachael and Ariel. "Glad to have you two back."

Amy smiled. "Good to see you, Warrior Princesses."

Sophia nodded toward Ariel and Rachael. "So, the band is back together again, ready to kick some ass." She turned to Tristan. "What's the plan?"

The doorbell rang again and everyone looked over at Tristan with questioning eyes.

"That should be Thomas," he said.

"Really?" Sophia said, her voice had a sarcastic tone to it. "Why the hell is he here? He's about the last person we should be—"

"He's here because I asked him to come," Tristan said, cutting her off. "He's key to our plan."

"Because he can open portals," Rachael said, just to clarify.

Tristan nodded. "Right. So, play nice, everyone."

He went to let Thomas in. Rachael could feel the tension in the room and it only increased when Tristan returned followed by Thomas.

Rachael had been used to seeing Thomas looking very professional in button down shirts and his short hair perfectly combed. Today his hair was messy, as though he'd run his fingers through it repeatedly, and he had on well-worn jeans and a denim jacket over a faded red t-shirt.

Thomas briefly glanced around the room, barely meeting the eyes of those who stared at him. Rachael almost felt sorry for him. He was certainly not getting a warm welcome.

"Hello everyone," he said to the room in general, and then looked over at Rachael. "I'm sorry. I really am. I'm glad you got away from my father. And you too," he said to Ariel. "I never meant to—"

"Save it," Sophia snapped. "You betrayed them so you betrayed all of us. Now you have a chance to make it right so don't blow it."

Rachael studied Amy's reaction to Thomas. It seemed to Rachael that Amy and Thomas's romance had just begun but she doubted it would continue. At least judging by Amy's expression. Her eyes shot arrows through

Thomas. Good thing she didn't have any real arrows with her or Thomas might be bleeding on the floor this very moment.

"Okay, so, I've explained everything to all of you," Tristan said. "Now it's just a matter of executing our plan." He looked over at Thomas. "This is your chance to make it up to all of us. Can we count on you?"

Thomas's expression was solemn. He nodded. "Yes. Absolutely. I will make sure you get into my father's house safely. No tricks," he added. His eyes landed on Lairen. "It seems our roles have reversed. You're on the inside and I'm the one under suspicion now."

"I didn't know what I was doing when I helped Sebastian get his hands on the swords and I didn't betray anyone," Lairen said.

"But now you're going to betray your mother."

"Not really. They've promised to try and spare her."

"I didn't," Sophia said.

"Nor I," Stefan added.

Amy looked over at Tristan. "Is that part of the deal then? To spare Beatrix?"

He nodded. "If possible, yes. Non-lethal force unless absolutely necessary."

Amy shrugged. "Okay. I can do that."

"Yeah, alright," Sophia said, but she didn't look happy about it.

Stefan grunted. "Sure, okay."

"Now, on to the next thing." Tristan went over to the case, which held the fourth Elfaen sword. "What do you think?" he asked Rachael.

"Let me go ahead and reactivate it just to make sure."

"Where?"

Rachael gave it some thought. "How about on the patio out back?"

Tristan nodded and headed for the patio. "Come on, everyone. We'll give Stefan first crack at it."

Rachael figured Tristan had already filled the others in on what they'd be doing next because none of them looked confused or asked any questions; they simply followed him out to the covered porch. They waited there while Tristan and Rachael continued on out onto the little patio.

Tristan laid the sword on the brick. "Try not to scorch my patio or set my house on fire, okay?" His little joke was a relief after all the tension she'd been feeling for the last half hour or so since Thomas had arrived.

Rachael waited until Tristan had returned to the porch and joined the others, then she took a breath and centered herself. She raised one of her arms straight out, palm facing the sword, and released her fire magic. The sword glowed, absorbed the flame and soon Rachael could see its name forming on the blade. She dropped her arm as her magic died away and walked over to the sword.

"Yep, definitely Death-Dealer. No surprise there." She looked at Stefan. "Want to give it a try?"

Stefan separated himself from the others and came outside to stand next to Rachael.

"Go ahead and pick it up," Rachael said. "The heat from the flames is absorbed quickly and then it cools quickly too so it won't burn your hand."

Stefan bent down and picked up the sword. Nothing happened, that much was obvious to Rachael.

"Well?" Tristan asked, though he had to have realized nothing had happened.

Stefan looked at him and shook his head. "Nothing. It feels just like any other sword." If he was disappointed, he didn't show it. He set the sword back onto the ground.

"Okay, who's next?" Rachael asked.

"Tristan, why don't you try?" Sophia asked.

"He already has bonded to one of the swords," Ariel said. "I don't think he wants to try for another."

Those who didn't already know this turned to look at Tristan.

"It's true," Tristan said. "The Life-Giver sword bonded with me when I picked it up to look at it. I didn't realize...well...anyway. Somebody else."

"Me," Amy said. She came out to the patio as Stefan stepped away from the sword. She glanced at Rachael who gave her a reassuring smile.

Amy bent down and picked up the sword. A second passed and then Amy's eyes widened.

Rachael became frightened when Amy's eyes went dark; and not just dark but black, solid black alien looking eyes. Rachael stepped back and so did Stefan, as Amy's expression became the snarl of a wild creature. She now held the sword in a two-fisted grip, her eyes moving from Stefan to Rachael and then to the others on the screened in porch.

"Oh crap," Rachael muttered. "Maybe we shouldn't have done this."

"Rachael, Stefan," Tristan said, his voice soft and low. "Move very slowly toward the porch. Very slowly."

They inched their way across the patio with Amy's eyes tracking them, her body tense and ready to attack like any predator after prey.

And then quite suddenly Amy's eyes cleared, her stance relaxed and she took a deep breath. "Well, that was interesting."

Rachael blew out a deep breath, her hand to her heart. "You had us really scared."

"So, I guess the sword bonded with you?" Stefan asked.

Amy gave him a funny look. "Ya think?" She chuckled and then examined the sword. "I'm looking forward to seeing what this baby can do."

CHAPTER TWENTY-THREE

"OKAY. HERE'S THE WAY THIS IS GONNA GO." Tristan said once they were all back inside the townhouse. "Sophia and Stefan, I want you guys to go back to our compound and wait for the other Slayer teams to arrive. You'll be in charge of making sure the right amount of people are on the streets and then get back over to Sebastian's compound with the rest. Fill them in on the number of Dark-Angels they're likely to expect out there and prep them for what might come though the Hell World portal if one gets opened."

Both Stefan and Sophia nodded their agreement.

"Okay," Stefan said. "Do you need us for anything else right now or do you want us to head over to the compound now?"

"You can go ahead," Tristan said. "We'll see you later."

"Assuming we're all still alive after this," Amy muttered.

Sophia raised a hand in farewell. "Kick some ass for us."

Seconds later they were gone.

"Okay, let's do this," Tristan said. "Thomas?"

"Hold on," Rachael frowned. "Shouldn't we wait until the other Slayers are here so we have back up?"

"No," Tristan replied. "They won't be on the inside anyway. We're doing this with just the six of us." He looked over at Thomas who nodded and stepped away from the rest of the group.

Thomas lifted both arms until he was reaching up, about head height, hands next to each other palms out. He slowly brought his hands down and to the side until they met at the bottom, forming an oval. Rachael saw a shimmering trail follow his hands all the way down. Thomas stepped aside.

"It'll take a minute to open fully, then you can step through," he said.

Rachael, Ariel, Lairen, Amy and Tristan watched as the oval lengthened and widened. As it did, Rachael began to see through to another place. She hoped Thomas had kept his word and wasn't leading them into a trap.

"Okay," Tristan began. "We take out the three guards first. Thomas will open portals and all we have to do is push the guards through. Thomas will close the portal and the guards will be someplace else, far from the house and no more trouble for us."

Amy smiled. "Brilliant!"

"And then we do the same with my mother," Lairen said.

Tristan nodded. "Yes, if possible. If we can get her alone it shouldn't be too difficult but if she's with Sebastian and things get crazy—"

"Yeah, I know," Lairen said.

"Hopefully," Tristan continued. "We confront Sebastian last after everyone else who could cause trouble for us is taken care of."

"The portal is open," Rachael said, redirecting everyone's attention. Through the portal she could see a hallway and an elevator. "It looks like the corridor outside the room where I was being held."

"Yes," Thomas said. "It's usually pretty quiet down here so I figured it was a good place to start out. You can take the elevator to the other levels."

Lairen approached the portal and was about to step through when they saw one of the burly guards exit the elevator."

"Can he see us?" Ariel asked.

"Not yet but he will," Thomas replied. "You better get through. And don't give him a chance to double back to the elevator."

"We don't have a portal to put him through," Rachael said.

Thomas shrugged. "Put him through here."

"In my house?" Tristan gasped. "I don't think so."

"We don't have a choice, Tristan." Rachael stepped through the portal. Lairen, Ariel and Amy had already gone through.

Lairen ran straight at the guard with Tristan close at his heels. There was a brief scuffle and the carpet beneath their feet began to shake.

"Earth magic," Tristan muttered, then knocked the guard out cold. The floor was still once more. Tristan and Lairen dragged the unconscious guard up to the portal and tossed him through.

"Do you think anyone upstairs felt that? The ground shaking, I mean?" Lairen asked.

"Nah. It didn't last that long and if they did, they'd probably think it was a tiny earthquake. Tristan frowned. "I'm not real happy about this. I don't like the idea of that guy in my house."

Thomas rolled his eyes. "He'll probably leave as soon as he comes to. He'll leave, your security door will slam shut behind him and he won't be able to get back in. Your house will be fine."

Rachael watched Thomas close the portal. He ran one hand across the shimmering edge of the oval, erasing it as his hand moved along and the portal was gone.

"Where next?" Amy asked.

"Into the elevator," Lairen said. "We'll go to the main part of the house. Keep an eye out for the cook and the maid, though. I don't want them to be collateral damage."

"Won't this thing ding when the door opens?" Ariel asked once they were all in the elevator.

"No. It's silent," Lairen replied.

A few seconds later the doors slid open and Rachael saw the living room where she'd previously confronted Thomas and his mother. Someone looked up as they exited the elevator. It was the maid. Her eyes went round and she looked like she was about to scream but Lairen hurried toward her with his finger against his lips.

"Shh, Mara, it's okay. They're with me."

The tiny woman, who looked to be about forty years old, was slightly plump. She put her hand to her heart.

"Lairen, you scared me," she whispered. "What is this all about?"

"You need to leave the house," he said. "It's not quite dark yet so you can make it to town before nightfall. Or at least go to your room and lock yourself in."

Mara gave Lairen a solemn look. "There's going to be trouble."

"Yes. So, leave now and if you see Alphonse—"

"I'll tell him to get out of here too," Mara finished for him.

"Right," Lairen nodded. "Now go."

The little maid scurried off.

As she exited the room through one door, a door at the other end of the room opened. One of the guards, Serge, if Rachael remembered his name correctly, came in. His eyes fell on their group and he immediately turned to leave the room, presumably to alert Sebastian.

Amy darted forward and grabbed one of his arms as Ariel got a hold of the other.

"Oh no you don't," Amy said.

Thomas quickly opened another portal as Tristan went to help the girls. His way of helping was to punch the guard in the face, but not before the guard's water magic caused the pipes under the little wet bar in the corner to rupture. Water burst from beneath the sink and water sprayed all over the room.

"There goes our element of surprise," Tristan grumbled as the girls shoved Serge though the portal. Thomas closed it quickly and as he did someone else came barreling through the door. It was the other guard.

"Here we go," Tristan muttered. He charged forward but this guard wasn't as easy to overpower, possibly because he'd heard a commotion and had come in expecting trouble. He'd also had his magic at the ready.

A fierce wind kicked up almost immediately, blowing Tristan back and nearly knocking Rachael right through the new portal Thomas had just created. He caught her by the arm and shoved her away from the opening.

Rachael watched as Tristan and the guard slugged each other. Tristan was lighter on his feet and avoided many of the punishing blows sent his way while delivering several to the guard's face and stomach. Finally, with a sweep of his leg, Tristan knocked the guard's legs out from under him.

The guard's magic waned when his head hit the floor. Immediately Tristan was on him and punched him in the face a couple of times until the guard's head lolled from side to side, blood from his nose smearing his face. Tristan stood up and wiped the blood from his hand then dragged the downed guard across the floor and through the waiting portal.

"Where did you send him?" he asked Thomas.

"The Palms restaurant. I go there to eat occasionally. It's the first thing that came to mind."

"And the other guard? Where did you send him?" Ariel asked.

Thomas shrugged. "Gold Medal Gym on Third St."

"This place looks like a tornado hit it," Amy muttered.

Water still sprayed from the broken pipe and more and more furniture was getting drenched along with the curtains. In fact, they were all getting wet. At least the wind had stopped blowing but there were papers strewn around the room and crooked pictures on the wall.

"Split up then meet back here," Tristan said. "I want to check this whole level before we go anywhere else. Shout if you need help."

Rachael paired off with Ariel while Lairen and Amy moved off in a different direction. Tristan went with Thomas.

"This place is huge," Ariel whispered as they began to investigate various rooms. "I had no idea."

"Yeah, it was hard to tell with that big wall around the whole place," Rachael replied.

"There's nobody here," Ariel finally concluded. "I wonder if the others found any—"

"Over here!" someone shouted.

Rachael and Ariel ran toward the voice; Rachael with sword drawn and Ariel with arrow to bow, ready to fly. When they got to the place where they thought they'd heard the shout there was no one there.

Rachael froze. "Listen."

She and Ariel stood absolutely still and waited but there was nothing. No sounds of a scuffle, no cries for help.

"Let's go back to where we split up," Rachael whispered.

Ariel nodded and they went back the way they'd come, weapons still at the ready, their eyes scanning each room for danger. They reached the room where they'd all separated into pairs, at nearly the same time that Amy did. Rachael saw her enter the room from the opposite direction. Amy had the sword, Death-Dealer in her hands and her eyes were that eerie black Rachael had seen back at Tristan's house. She grabbed Ariel's arm and both girls froze.

"Amy?" Rachael whispered. "Where is Lairen?"

Amy's eyes went back to their normal color and she lowered the sword a bit.

"I don't know. We were searching one of the rooms. He was on my left and a little behind me. He said something and I turned toward him but he was gone. So, I came back here."

"Who called out?" Ariel asked. "We heard someone shout."

"I think it was Tristan," Amy replied.

Rachael frowned. "Well then where is he? And where're Lairen and Thomas?"

"I do not have a good feeling about this," Ariel muttered.

CHAPTER TWENTY-FOUR

THE THREE OF THEM WENT THROUGH THE ENTIRE area again, room by room, but couldn't find any of the guys.

"What the hell is going on?" Amy growled.

"Maybe they found a secret passage somewhere," Rachael suggested. "They wouldn't leave this level without telling us but if—"

"So, someone popped out of a hidden door somewhere and snatched Lairen without Amy seeing or hearing a thing? And then did the same thing to Tristan and Thomas? That sounds pretty crazy." Ariel shook her head. "That seems unlikely."

Rachael shrugged. "I don't know, but they didn't just disappear into thin air."

"What if Thomas opened a portal and pushed them both through to get rid of them?" Amy suggested.

"It could happen," Rachael said. "But I really don't think Thomas would do—"

A door closed behind them and all three girls turned toward the sound. Tristan and Thomas came into the room.

Rachael scowled at them. "Where have you been? We've been going crazy trying to figure out what happened to you!"

"We found a secret passageway," Thomas said.

"See! I told you!" Rachael gasped and grinned at Amy and Ariel.

"Is Lairen with you?" Amy asked.

Tristan frowned. "No. I thought he was with you."

"Nope," Amy said. "The two of us were clearing a room and he vanished."

"Vanished?" Tristan's voice turned hard. "I don't trust that guy." He shook his head. "If he's compromised what we're doing here—"

"So where does this secret passageway lead?" Ariel asked.

"We don't know," Thomas replied. "We followed it for a while but—"

The spraying water stopped and everyone turned to look at the sink.

"Now what?" Rachael muttered.

Lairen stepped into the room from the hallway. "I shut off the water main."

Amy scowled at him. "So, you went to turn off the water without telling anyone? What the hell is wrong with you? We're in the middle of a mission and you leave without telling anyone?"

He rolled his eyes. "Sorry."

"Did you see anyone? Talk to anyone?" Tristan asked.

Lairen shook his head. "No, why—?"

"Where does the secret passageway lead?" Tristan asked.

Lairen's eyes widened. "There's a secret passageway?"

"Forget it," Rachael said. "Let's go to the observatory and finish this."

"Lead on, Cupcake."

"Shut up, Lairen," Rachael snapped as she passed him on the way to the elevator.

"Ouch!" Lairen grinned as she walked by. "Those words hurt."

Rachael whirled on him. "You're not funny, Lairen. People have died because of your stepfather and your mother and we're here to make it stop. That might mean killing your mother, by the way, so start taking this seriously."

"Thank you, Rachael," Tristan said as they walked over to the elevator side by side. The others trailed along behind them, slogging across the damp floor. "I couldn't have said it better myself."

"Do you suppose the elevator is going to work?" Ariel asked. "I hope the water didn't reach all the way into the electrical system."

"We'll find out." Lairen pushed one of the buttons, the doors closed and the elevator began to move.

Amy gave Lairen a sideways glance. "I hope Sebastian and your mother aren't going to be standing there waiting for us when we get off the elevator."

He gave her a hard stare. "If they are it won't be because of me."

The doors slid open. The observatory seemed to be empty. Rachael saw that the sky was darkening. It was now twilight and full dark was coming fast.

Thomas was the first to step off the elevator. A second later something flew from across the room, went straight through his chest and knocked him to the ground, half in and half out of the elevator. An arrow.

"Thomas!" Tristan and Amy both shouted.

Amy darted forward but Ariel held her back and pulled her away from the open door.

"There might be more arrows for the rest of us," Ariel whispered to Amy.

Lairen and Rachael already stood with their backs against the side of the elevator so as not to be seen. There was no real cover in the elevator so it was the best any of them could do.

"But someone has to help Thomas!" Amy pleaded.

Tristan reached out and dragged Thomas the rest of the way into the elevator. Lairen hit the button and the doors closed.

They all fell to the floor to see to Thomas. His eyes were open but it seemed to Rachael that he was most certainly dead. He wasn't moving at all. She couldn't even see him breathing.

Tears ran down Amy's cheeks but she brushed them away and turned to Lairen. "This is all your fault!" she screamed. "You did this!" She hit him repeatedly in the face, the shoulders and the chest.

All he did was back away and then try to restrain her so she couldn't keep hitting him. "I didn't do anything. I swear to you. I didn't."

"Amy!" Tristan called to her and she whirled around. "Amy, come here. He's still alive but just barely."

Amy knelt beside Thomas with Tristan on the other side across from her.

"I'm sorry," Thomas whispered. "I'm sorry for everything."

"Don't die on me, Thomas," Amy said. "Don't you dare die on me."

Thomas smiled at her but it turned into more of a grimace. His eyes flicked over to Tristan. "You have no one to draw the portals now. I'm sorry, Tris. I'm so sorry."

Tristan had his hands on Thomas as he tried to send healing into his body. "Don't even think about it, brother. All that matters now is that you get well."

"I'm not going to get well."

"Yes, you are," Tristan insisted. He looked at the Life-Giver sword. "Maybe, somehow, with the help of this thing—"

"Thomas! Thomas!" Amy gasped and shook him gently. But it was no use. Thomas took his last breath and Tristan fell back against the elevator wall, a hand over his face. His shoulders shook.

Rachael closed her eyes and looked away, confused and sad. She wanted to blame Lairen but did he really betray them? And who had shot the arrow? She'd been angry with Thomas but she'd liked him and he was Tristan's brother. What would Thomas's death do to Tristan? Would he even want to continue with the mission? Or would he continue but become a maniacal risk taker, living only for revenge and get himself and the rest of them killed in the process?

Ariel sat next to Amy and put her arm on her back, gently rubbing, as Amy cried, her face in her hands.

Rachael went to Tristan. She put her arms around him but didn't say anything. She didn't even know what to say. A few seconds later he rubbed his face and brushed away tears then got to his feet.

"I really didn't have anything to do with this," Lairen said, but Tristan lifted a hand to silence him.

"Save it, Lairen. If you didn't, then help us do what we came here to do so Thomas won't have died for nothing. And if you did have something to do with my brother's death then I swear to you that I will make sure you die along with your mother and step-father before this night is over."

"He wouldn't kill his own son," Lairen said. "Think about it. Why would Sebastian kill Thomas?"

"He has a point," Ariel said as she and Amy got to their feet.

"Well, someone did," Tristan growled. "Because that wasn't an accident!"

"So, then what happened out there?" Rachael asked. "I mean, if someone didn't deliberately kill Thomas then was it a booby-trap, set to shoot whenever someone stepped off the elevator, regardless of who it was?"

"Or, you said there was a secret passage," Ariel mused. "Maybe the passageway goes up here too and maybe someone peeked out, shot the arrow and then ducked back in with none of us catching a glimpse of him."

"Or her," Amy added with a sniff. Her eyes were red and puffy but she seemed to be pulling herself together.

"Do you think we should still go into the observatory?" Rachael asked.

"No," Tristan said. "I don't want to risk it."

Ariel looked at him. "Then what? What do you want to do, Tristan?"

"The passageway that Thomas and I found earlier," Tristan said. "Let's go back to it and see where it leads."

"Oh, right," Lairen drawled. "Then we'll be trapped in a narrow hallway with no place to hide if someone attacks us. That sounds smart."

Tristan launched himself at Lairen, knocking Ariel and Amy out of the way in the process. He punched Lairen who hit back and then the two of them struggled to get in whatever damage they could inflict in the tight space of the elevator.

"Stop it! Stop it!" Amy screamed at them. "You're stepping on Thomas!"

Immediately Tristan stopped and looked down. Rachael could see he was horrified at the thought he'd further harmed his brother. Amy was crying again.

Rachael placed her hand on Tristan's arm. He looked at her.

"What are we going to do about Thomas?" she asked as gently as possible. "We can't just leave him here but it's night time now and we can't carry him out because of the Dark-Angels. And we don't have a portal," she added, although it pained her to point that out.

"We can take him to the kitchen for now," Lairen suggested. "In the morning you can have someone come for his body."

Tristan scowled at him and said nothing for several seconds. Finally, he nodded. "Yeah, alright. Let's ride this elevator to whatever floor the kitchen is on."

Lairen punched the button and the elevator began to move.

When the doors slid open Lairen stepped out and looked around and Rachael was glad he'd decided to be the first one out this time.

"It seems safe enough," he said then stooped to pick up Thomas's legs while Tristan lifted his upper body. Together they brought him out then laid him on the floor by the refrigerator.

Rachael heard a click behind her and whirled around. The pantry door was ajar. Had it been that way before? She gestured to the others to step to the side and once nobody was directly across from the door Rachael yanked the handle. She made sure she was well out of the way in case an arrow came flying through the air, but nothing like that happened.

Tristan was the first to approach and Rachael joined him. They looked into the large pantry filled with canned goods, boxes and bottles of various items.

"Looks like an ordinary pantry," Rachael said.

Ariel, Amy and Lairen now stood behind them, peering in.

"I guess it was nothing," Rachael said. She started to turn away but Tristan grabbed her arm.

"No, wait. If I'm not mistaken..." He stepped into the pantry and placed his hands on the back wall. "I think maybe..." He ran his hands along the wall and fiddled with the corners a bit. He then pressed in along the left side of the wall and Rachael heard something click. "There," he said and nudged the door open.

Behind the door was a dark, fairly wide corridor with steps leading both up and down.

CHAPTER TWENTY-FIVE

LAIREN SIGHED. "LIKE I SAID—" BUT THEY ALL
glared at him and he stopped speaking.

"Maybe we should split up with one some of us going up and some
going down," Rachael suggested.

"No." Tristan replied. "We all stay together. Come on."

He started down the steps and they all followed. There was room for
two people to walk abreast so Rachael came alongside Tristan.

"You and Ariel go next," Amy said to Lairen. "I don't trust you at
my back."

"Fine," he huffed and stepped into the corridor along with Ariel so that
Amy could bring up the rear.

The passage wasn't as dark as it had first appeared. There were dim lights
spaced several feet apart all along the way and the path leveled out so they
weren't going down, down, down to some dungeon far beneath the earth;
at least Rachael hoped not. Still, she wondered how much farther it would
be before they discovered where the passage would take them. She didn't
have long to wait. After walking about fifty yards or so they came to a door.

Tristan looked back at the rest of them. "Okay, here we go. Be prepared
for anything. Stay low in case there are more flying arrows."

He slowly opened the door and Rachael could hear movement on the
other side.

Lairen peered out the door. "We're outside the house," he whispered.
"But still inside the compound. We don't have to worry about Dark-Angels
though, it's all roofed."

As Tristan opened the door wider Rachael caught her first glimpse of what they were up against. Her eyes widened and her breath caught in her chest.

"Oh, no," she whispered.

The compound yard contained dozens of Hell-Spawn beasts of various sizes and types. There were more pterodactyls and some monsters like the ones Sebastian had already loosed on the city but there were some other types as well; some small as a Cocker Spaniel but far more terrifying than any dog. Others slithered on the ground. Many were misshapen creatures of various sizes; beasts that didn't look at all like anything Rachael had seen before in this world or her own.

They shuffled about but all kept their eyes on Sebastian, like soldiers waiting for orders and since Sebastian had the Beast-Master sword, Rachael knew that was exactly what they were doing.

"He's putting together an army," she whispered.

"What're we going to do?" Ariel asked Tristan.

"Whatever it is, it isn't going to be pretty," Amy muttered.

"I say we get out of here, notify your other Slayers and have them all meet us just outside in the desert, and as soon as Sebastian releases these things into the world, we all attack," Lairen suggested.

Ariel shook her head. "That's not a great idea. It would be better to attack them while they're contained."

"Plus, we'll have to fight the Dark-Angels too," Amy added. She looked at Tristan. "What do you think?"

"I think we should close that portal before any more come through. But first, I'm going to call Stefan. I have an idea."

Rachael had been so caught up in staring at all the Hell-Spawn that she hadn't really paid much attention to Sebastian. While Tristan made his call to Stefan, she studied him. Even at this distance she could see his lips moving. He was talking to the creatures, controlling them, and as more came through the opening of the portal they fell under his control too.

Tristan ended his call and looked at Rachael and the others. "Stefan and Sophia are going to bring all of the Slayers here. They're going to scale the walls and join us. We'll have back up."

"That's great!" Ariel whispered.

"But the Dark-Angels!" Rachael gasped. "They'll pick them off while they're climbing the walls!"

"It'll be okay," Tristan assured her. "We're talking about seasoned Slayers and Stefan knows what he's doing. He'll handle it."

"But it will take them a half an hour to get out here so we have some time to kill," Amy reminded them all.

Tristan shook his head. "Less than that. They're on their way already. Stefan decided not to have any city patrols tonight. He thought we might need the help and the city is mostly evacuated anyway."

"Good!" Ariel said, and Rachael echoed her.

"There's my mom," Lairen said. "I didn't see her at first but she's on the other side of the portal."

"You realize we can't shove her through some benign portal anymore," Amy said. "She's either going through that one or she's getting killed here in this world."

Lairen looked stunned, as if that reality had only just hit him and Rachael figured it probably only just had.

"So, we agree that closing the portal is our first priority," Tristan began. "We need to slip around the edges, stay in the shadows as much as possible. This area isn't well lit so that shouldn't be too hard."

"And hopefully no monsters will give us away or eat us before we get half way to the portal," Amy added.

"What if we can't close it?" Rachael asked. "The portal I mean. What if—?"

Tristan fished in one of his pockets and brought out a device. "We have these, remember? The little gadgets Kirk and Miko gave us. They'll close the portals, no problem."

"Oh yeah," Rachael said. "I'd forgotten you guys had those."

Tristan reached into his pocket again. "I have an extra." He held it out to her and she took it. "Now," Tristan continued. "Let's see what else we've got going for us here. What magic do we have between us?"

"I'm fire," Rachael said.

Ariel lifted a hand. "Air."

"Water," Amy said. "But I don't think that's going to do us any good since there aren't any lakes or storm clouds around. Plus, with our luck I'd probably just end up drowning everyone."

Tristan's eyebrows shot up. "That's actually a pretty good idea! Maybe we can drown some of these things. Can you try and call water from the ground? I know we're in the desert but if you reach down deep enough—"

"Maybe," Amy shrugged. "I can try."

"I shut off the water main to the house, but the water is still there and available. You could use that." Lairen added.

Tristan nodded. "And I'll let Stefan know to have the other Slayers come in ready with their magic too. I'm sure with so many Slayers there will be some who have water magic and they can assist you in pulling water from the ground."

"My magic is earth, by the way," Lairen said. "I can be of some help with that."

"Okay, see this is good," Tristan said. "We've got water, fire, air and earth. Perfect. All bases covered." His smile wavered. "I'm only sorry my form of magic isn't too useful in this situation but it is what it is."

"And don't forget," Rachael said. "We have three of the Elfaen swords." She smiled at Amy and Tristan. "And Ariel and Lairen have their bows."

Tristan nodded. "Let's get as close to the portal as possible; stealth mode. Tap into your magic before we get out there and then let it loose as soon as we're discovered. If nothing else, we can create confusion."

Tristan's phone vibrated. He looked at the text. "Stefan says they're just heading up the drive. They'll wait until they hear a commotion in here before scaling the walls." He put his phone away. "Okay. Are we ready?" When there were nods all around, he gave them a wry smile. "Magic and weapons at the ready. Stealth mode. Close the portal, disable Sebastian and Beatrix, and kill as many of Hell-Spawn as possible. Let's go."

They started out the door but Rachael hung back.

"Wait, one thing," she said, and everyone looked at her. "Um, well...if we kill Sebastian, I won't be able to get home. He's the only one who can open a portal so...if he hasn't already opened one to my world then how—?"

Tristan's eager expression fell away. "Oh crap, I forgot about that. Rachael, I'm sorry. Of course, we have to get you home, but I don't know—"

"Look!" Ariel whispered. She'd moved a little bit away from the group and could see further into the holding area for the Hell-Spawn. "Come here!" she whispered and gestured for Tristan and Rachael to come over.

"You see?" she pointed to the far side of the compound. "There's another portal open! Maybe it's to your world."

Tristan grabbed for his phone again. "I'm going to tell Stefan not to use his or Sophia's devices to close that portal. I'll tell him to guard the portal instead." He turned and went back to the others and then further down into the passageway to talk.

"See," Ariel said to Rachael. "Everything is going to work out okay."

Rachael smiled but she was still doubtful. "I hope so but there's a lot we have to accomplish between here and there."

Tristan came back. "All set. They're getting ready to scale the walls right now instead of waiting. Everybody has their magic primed, right? Are we ready?"

There were nods all around and the five of them crept out quietly. They moved slowly and kept low to the ground and into the shadows when possible. Tristan and Rachael went around to the right and the others went to the left.

Rachael was worried that the most difficult part would be not drawing the attention of the Hell-Spawn, but luckily, they were all being controlled by Sebastian with meant their eyes were on him all the time, not looking around for prey.

They'd made it about halfway there when the first of the Slayers crested the wall and then a minute later the entire area was in chaos. Magic roared in from all sides. Wind kicked up, blowing in all directions at once. The earth began to shake and Rachael feared she might fall and get trampled. There was a deep rumbling from underground and water began to spurt upwards like geysers.

As more of the Slayers dropped down inside the compound the sounds of battle began. Rachael lost track of her companions but she drew her sword and felt the surge of magic within her, both her own and the sword's. They almost immediately joined together and Rachael started throwing fire at anything that kept her from reaching the Hell-World portal. She knew Tristan, Ariel and Amy would also make their way there since it was their first priority and they also held the devices that would close the portal.

About halfway there Rachael fell. A combination of the heaving earth, the muddy ground and the strange looking Hell-Spawn's tail caused her to lose her footing. The thing was snake-like, long and low to the ground. Rachael had stumbled over its reptilian body and now lay sprawled in the mud. She'd dropped Fire-Starter but as the Hell-Spawn reared up before her, jaw unhinged, ready to strike, Rachael spied her Elfaen sword and held out her hand. Immediately the sword slammed into her palm and with both hands on the hilt she swung the blade. The Hell-Spawn's fangs were just inches from her face when the sword bit into its flesh, transferring fire along with the cut of the blade. The Hell-Spawn jerked sideways then fell over; its entire body twisted as it lit up from the inside, then quickly burned and turned to ash.

Rachael didn't have time to watch. She leapt to her feet and continued on toward the Hell-World portal. There was enough chaos all around her and she was within twenty feet of the portal when Beatrix confronted her.

"You are not ruining our plans, little girl," Beatrix screamed at her over the din of swords clashing, monsters roaring, wind blowing and water gushing. She lifted her hand, sending a whirling windstorm toward Rachael. She instinctively countered with fire, realizing too late that it was a bad idea. The fire blew back in her direction and she only avoided being burned because she leapt out of the way in time.

Rachael once again found herself on the ground but she released a blast of fire from her downed position and Beatrix wasn't ready. Her clothing caught fire and she screamed. Rachael jumped to her feet to avoid being trampled by friend or foe and continued on toward the portal. She tried to tune out Beatrix's screams of pain and was almost to the portal when she met yet another obstacle.

Lairen stood in front of her, his bow up, ready to let an arrow fly into her chest. "Take my mother and me with you to your world," he shouted.

"Lairen, get out of the way. Let me close the portal. We can talk about this later!"

"No! Promise me now that you'll let us both come with you."

"Or what?" Rachael asked. "You'll kill me? I'm your sister, right? Why do you want to kill me?"

"Because you have the life I should've had all these years!"

Rachael could hardly believe what she had just heard. "We're in the middle of a frickin' battle for our lives and you want to talk about this _now_? Are you frickin' kidding me? Get out of the way, Lairen!"

And then Tristan slammed into Lairen from behind, and knocked him to the ground. Lairen's bow fell from his hand as he fell headlong into the mud. The arrow had been released from the bow as he fell but it flew wide and missed Rachael completely.

"Go, Rachael!" Tristan shouted. "Close the portal!"

Rachael turned and ran. She had the device that would short out the current and close the portal right in her hand and then something jumped into her path and before she knew what had happened the device was gone. Rachael could hardly believe it. A small doglike Hell-Spawn with blood red eyes and black fur had stolen the device right out of her hand. The creature turned to look at her, the device in its mouth. If it were a dog, it would've been cute, but not that creature, not now. The beast turned and ran. There was no point in chasing it. There were too many monsters, too much mud and influx of water making the area more of a soupy bath every minute, and too many people with weapons. Rachael couldn't afford the lost time.

She ran back to Tristan who had knocked Lairen unconscious and had propped him up against the wall in the corner. He looked up at her in surprise.

"Give me your device!" she yelled.

"What happened?" he asked as he fished it from his pocket.

Rachael didn't take the time to explain, simply grabbed the device, switching it on as she ran. This time no one hindered her and she pressed the device to the edge of the portal and prayed Kirk and Miko were right, that it would close down the portal. And then she saw it flicker. A Hell-Spawn was about half way through, when the portal shut down. The Hell-Spawn was cut in two. The front half twitched once and then disintegrated.

Rachael looked at the bedlam all around her but especially at the portal that would hopefully take her to her own world. Tristan came up alongside her.

"We better get over there. Stefan and Sophia are doing their best to keep the Hell-Spawn out but—" Rachael's quick intake of breath silenced him.

"Sophia is down!" Rachael ran toward the portal with Tristan at her side. She threw fire in every direction, clearing a path for them. All this use of her magic was beginning to take its toll on her in spite of the surge of power Fire-Starter given her.

They were almost to the other portal when a gust of wind knocked Rachael into Tristan causing them both to stumble. Rachael turned to see Beatrix standing there. She stood ankle deep in water and was covered in mud, which must've put out the fire, but even so Rachael knew she had to have some serious burns on her flesh.

"You bitch!" Beatrix screamed. "You're ruining all my plans!"

She lifted her arm to throw another gust of wind at them and this time Rachael knew better than to throw any fire in her direction.

"Run!" Tristan shouted, but then quite suddenly Beatrix's head was no longer on her body. It went flying one way while her body crumpled to the ground. Behind her stood Amy, her eyes solid black and a triumphant smile on her face.

CHAPTER TWENTY-SIX

"**G**ET TO THE PORTAL!" TRISTAN SHOUTED.
Amy whirled and ran, shadowing Tristan and Rachael as they headed to the portal, sloshing though water now almost knee deep. By the time they got there it was clear that Sophia wouldn't last much longer. She'd been badly clawed. Other Slayers had taken over guarding the portal and not letting any beasts slip by into the unsuspecting world on the other side.

Stefan held Sophia so she wouldn't slip to the ground and under water. She was clearly in a lot of pain; her body clawed open and bleeding heavily. Tristan joined him at Sophia's side and Rachael suspected he was reliving Thomas's recent death, judging by the look on his face. She turned away as Amy joined Tristan, Stefan and Sophia, to give the others time with their friend in the last few minutes of her life.

Rachael scanned the compound for Ariel. She hadn't seen her since they'd left the secret passageway. As she looked the realized it was now much easier to see individual people and monsters, as there were fewer of them in the compound. Many of the Hell-Spawn were gone, had been killed and had either flamed out, drowned or disintegrated. But where was Ariel? And where was Sebastian Westfall?

She sensed Tristan at her side even before she saw him.

"Sophia is gone," he said. "Stefan will take her body and Thomas's when he leaves. I told him where to find him...it...his body."

Rachael put her hand on his arm and gave it a squeeze of sympathy. "I haven't seen Ariel. Have you seen her?"

Tristan frowned. "No, I haven't." He scanned the area like Rachael had only moments ago.

"I haven't seen Sebastian either. You don't suppose—?"

Tristan tensed. "We have to find her."

The last of the Hell-Spawn, a pterodactyl, crashed to the ground dead, and flamed as the remaining Slayers moved well out of the way. Knee-deep water helped put out the flames. The earth no longer shook, the water had ceased to gush like a fountain from the ground and the wind had died down to nothing.

Tristan turned to Stefan. "You and a few of the others take Sophia and Thomas and go. We still have to find Ariel and take care of Sebastian."

"I should stay and help you," Stefan said.

"I'd rather someone who knew them bring their bodies back to the compound and notify their families," Tristan replied. "And if the other Slayers would stick around, at least until tomorrow, that would be a big help."

Stefan nodded. "I understand. I'll take care of it."

"Be careful," Tristan added. "Remember there are a lot of Dark-Angels out there once you get outside these walls."

"Yeah," Stefan said. "I know. How could I ever forget? Damn treacherous things."

Tristan glanced at Rachael and pointed at the portal. "Can you tell if this is your world?"

Rachael stepped closer to the opening and peered through. "I don't know. I suppose it is because that was Sebastian's plan. Of course, the chances of this opening being anywhere near where I came though is..." She gave a cynical laugh. "Highly unlikely."

"Do you want to go through?" Tristan asked. He glanced at Amy who now stood beside him. "We can give you our swords and at least you'd be able to go home with three of them."

Rachael hesitated. "But then you won't have any weapons to fight Sebastian."

"We can scrounge around and find something," Amy shrugged. "A sword someone dropped...something."

"No." Rachael shook her head. "You shouldn't give them up. This isn't over yet. You have to find Ariel and I want to help you. I can't go home not knowing if she's alive or dead and I can't leave wondering if Sebastian is still around to open more portals later. I'm staying until this is finished."

A look of immense relief passed across Tristan's face. He nodded. "Okay. Good." He turned to Stefan. "Make sure someone guards this portal. We'll be back."

Stefan nodded. "Done. I'll take Sophia now and come back for Thomas." He gave Tristan a nod and lifted Sophia into his arms, then joined some of the other Slayers as they all headed for a way out of the compound.

"Where's Lairen?" Amy asked.

Tristan looked back at the place where he'd left Lairen unconscious. He was gone. "I have no idea but wherever he is he could still be trouble for us so keep an eye out."

Tristan started to walk toward a regular entrance into in house. It was about twenty yards away from where the secret passageway came out into the compound. Rachael and Amy fell into step on either side of him.

"So, the three of us against Sebastian." Rachael said. "But what if he's already opened another portal and escaped to another realm? And what if he's taken Ariel with him?"

The thought of Ariel, the first person to really befriend her in this world, being kidnapped and taken away by that madman, or killed by him, made Rachael feel sick.

"Let's hope that hasn't happened," Tristan said.

"So where are we headed?" Amy asked.

"We're going to go through this place room by room until we find him," Tristan replied. "We'll check the secret passages too if we have to."

As Rachael and the others neared the doorway into the house, they saw a couple of Slayers carrying Thomas's body out from the secret passage.

"You okay?" Rachael said to Tristan.

"Yeah. I have to be."

The three of them entered the house and began the search but after going through every room on the level where Rachael had been locked up previously, they still hadn't seen Sebastian or Ariel anywhere.

"To the main level we go then," Tristan said, and they got into the elevator.

When they reached the main part of the house, they quickly searched the room where water had sprayed everywhere and then continued on to other rooms. Eventually there was nowhere else to look but the observatory.

"I hate the idea of going up there," Amy said. "After what happened to Thomas..." she shook her head and Rachael saw her blink back tears.

"I know," Tristan replied, "but we have to. It's the only place left to look for Sebastian and Ariel and if he isn't there then he might be hiding in one of the secret passages and we'll have to search those next."

They got back into the elevator and Rachael pushed the button. All three of them were silent during the ride up to the top level. The door slid open and nobody moved.

Tristan took a deep breath. "I'll go."

Rachael watched as he quickly stepped out and to the side, away from the opening of the elevator where Thomas had stood when he'd been pierced through by the arrow. But then he stood, frozen, staring off across the room somewhere.

"Tristan?" Rachael said. "Is everything okay?"

He didn't reply. She and Amy exchanged puzzled looks, and then cautiously came out of the elevator. It was then Rachael understood why Tristan had behaved the way he had; Sebastian was waiting for them, and he wasn't alone.

One of the windowed doors of the observatory was open and Sebastian stood out on the balcony, one arm around the neck of a woman.

"Mom?" Tristan said, his voice uncertain. "What are you doing here? I thought—"

"You thought she'd evacuated with the other poor frightened people of this city," Sebastian said. "Well, as you can see, she didn't. Jeanette is here with me."

"Tristan, I'm sorry," Jeanette whimpered. "Thomas told me to leave and I was getting ready to go but Sebastian—"

Sebastian's arm tightened around her neck. "Hush my dear. Your son doesn't need to hear the whole story. All he needs to know is that you're here with me now."

"Let her go," Tristan said.

"Now why would I do that?" Sebastian replied. "My Beatrix is dead and I need someone to be my queen."

Tristan scowled at him. "Your queen? What are you going to rule over? Your beasts have been killed and your portal has been closed."

"I will simply open another one."

Sebastian smiled at Tristan and Rachael could see the maniacal gleam in his eyes. The man was truly deranged.

"Where is Ariel?" Amy asked.

Sebastian's eyebrows lifted. "Oh, your adorable little Slayer friend? She's around here somewhere."

"Where is she?" Amy shouted and advanced on Sebastian. He tightened his hold on Tristan's mother causing her to struggle for air and Tristan grabbed Amy's arm to stop her from approaching them.

"Let her go, Sebastian," Tristan said.

"Or what? You'll use magic to stop me? You'll come at me with your swords? You'll shoot me?" He laughed. "I don't think so because I am the one in control here. I am the king of this world and the next. I rule the beasts and the creatures of the air." He became more agitated, his eyes glazed and his face a mask of fury. Spit flew from his mouth as he shouted to the heavens.

"I am all powerful in this realm and in every realm! I am all-powerful! Me! Only me!" he threw his arms wide and flung Jeanette from him as he did. She spun away and slammed into the balcony railing. It burst apart with a sharp crack and Jeanette went tumbling over the edge with a scream of terror and then there was silence.

"Mom!" Tristan rushed to the balcony and gazed over the edge. For one moment both Tristan and Sebastian stood there, just a couple of feet from each other, looking over the railing, each of them stunned and silent, and Rachael saw her chance. She thrust out her arm, palm forward and blasted Sebastian with fire. Tristan leapt back as Sebastian shrieked and twirled in an attempt to put out the flames, and then plummeted over the same railing Jeanette had just fallen through.

Rachael and Amy ran out to the balcony and looked down along with Tristan. Jeanette was dead but so was Sebastian. Horrified, Rachael watched as Dark-Angels crowded around the two broken bodies but then left them alone. Apparently, they didn't have any use for the already dead.

Tristan turned to face Rachael and Amy, his face pale, his eyes wide. Rachael could hardly believe he'd lost both his brother and his mother on the same day. It was beyond awful, beyond heartbreaking.

411

Rachael gently led Tristan back inside as Amy reached into her pocket and pulled out her phone.

"I'm going to let Stefan know what's happened," she said. "He'll have to send someone back for...for Tristan's mother."

She stepped away to make the call and Rachael looked up at Tristan. "Tristan? You're going to be okay. Do you hear me? You're going to get through this and you're going to be okay."

"What was he doing on the balcony anyway?" Tristan asked. "There are all kinds of Dark-Angels out there. Dark-Angels could've killed them both. What was he thinking?"

"He was probably thinking that since he had the Beast-Master sword that he could control them," Rachael replied.

Amy returned and she had an extra sword in her hand. "Is this the other Elfaen sword?" She held it out to Rachael who took it.

"Yep. Looks like it," she said after a quick examination.

Amy glanced over at Tristan then reached out and placed her hand on his arm. "I'm sorry about your mom. First Thomas and then your mom. I just don't know what to say."

He nodded and gave her hand a squeeze before letting it go. "Thank you." He ran a hand across his face and sighed. "We still have to find Ariel." He went to shut the door to the balcony and Amy walked around the room, looking for places Sebastian might have hidden Ariel.

Rachael's head snapped around. "Wait, I heard something. A thumping or...there it is again. Over here!"

All three of them rushed to the wall across from the elevator.

"It's coming from inside!" Amy ran her hands across the wall in an attempt to find a latch.

"Here, let me," Tristan said.

Rachael stood aside and waited. Was Ariel really behind the wall? Was she okay? What if they'd left this floor, this house, and never found her?

Tristan found the latch and a panel in the wall slid open. Inside was Ariel, bound and gagged, and next to her some sort of device with arrows in it. It was the booby trap that had killed Thomas!

CHAPTER TWENTY-SEVEN

"TRISTAN. LOOK." RACHAEL POINTED OUT THE device with the arrows.

"Yeah," he said as he pulled Ariel to her feet. "It was a booby trap that killed Thomas after all."

He and Amy untied and ungagged Ariel then Rachael rushed to embrace her friend in a hug.

"Are you okay?" she asked.

"Yes, yes, but I feel so stupid. I let him get the best of me." Ariel reached for her bow and quiver of arrows, which lay on the floor beside her. She looked at Tristan. "I'm sorry. I failed you. I let myself get caught."

"Don't worry about it," Tristan said. "What's important is that you're alive and okay and we found you."

"I have bad news though," Amy said. "Sophia is dead."

Ariel's eyes widened. "Oh, no! What happened?"

"It was during the fight outside," Amy replied. "She fought well but…"

Ariel looked up at Tristan. "Was anyone else hurt? Stefan?"

"Stefan is fine. He and the other Slayers took Sophia and Thomas's bodies away from here. He's notifying the…families."

Rachael noticed Tristan had stumbled over that last part. The only person to notify of Thomas's death had been their mother but now she was dead also.

"We'd better get out of here," Tristan said. "Come on. Let's go."

"What happened to Sebastian?" Ariel asked as they walked to the elevator. "I could hear some stuff but it was muffled and I couldn't figure out what was going on."

"Rachael flamed him," Amy said. "It was awesome."

"I can't think of anyone more deserving," Ariel replied.

Amy's phone chimed and she answered it. After a brief conversation she disconnected the call. "Stefan is waiting for us at the portal that leads to Rachael's home. Stefan left a couple of Slayers guarding it."

"You're going home now?" Ariel asked.

Rachael nodded.

"But your clothes! Your purse and phone! Everything you have is back at Tristan's house," Ariel reminded her.

"I know, but the longer I wait the greater the chance the portal will close and then I won't be able to go home at all." As Rachael said that she wondered what had become of Lairen. He'd wanted to go back to her world so much he'd been willing to threaten her about it, so where the heck was he now?

"But those portals stay open for days!" Ariel exclaimed. "The one Alina and I were guarding when you first got here was open forever it seemed. Do you really have to go now? This minute?"

Rachael nodded. "Yeah. I don't want to miss my opportunity just in case this portal doesn't stay open as long as the other ones."

They got in the elevator and rode in silence.

"Hold on a second," Tristan said once they'd gotten off the elevator. "Before we go to the portal, I have something I have to do."

He veered off and went out a different door.

"Where's he going?" Ariel asked.

"Tristan and Thomas's mom died tonight," Rachael said.

"Was she the lady who was here?" Ariel asked. "The one Sebastian was holding hostage too?"

Rachael nodded. "Yeah. It was an accident really, Sebastian shoved her and she hit the balcony railing. It broke and she went over."

"From the observatory?"

"Yes. I think that's where Tristan is going. To try and see her before some of the Slayers take her out to the cars."

Amy sighed. "Yeah, they already took Sophia and Thomas."

They waited a few minutes and finally Tristan returned. He was wiping his eyes with the back of his hand.

"Okay," Tristan said. "Let's go meet Stefan at the portal."

"Here, before we go," Amy handed Rachael the Death-Dealer sword. "I can't say I'm not going to miss this sword. It's been a rush to use something like that. I'll never forget it."

Rachael already had Fire-Starter at her hip. Now she held Death-Dealer in her right hand and Beast-Master in her left.

"You might as well take these too," Amy said as she unbuckled the sword belt at her waist and shrugged out of her baldric. "You better not be walking around your world with naked blades. I don't know how things are where you live but here, they frown on that sort of thing."

Rachael took what Amy offered and sheathed the blades. The swords seemed to fit well enough even though they were a bit smaller than whatever was supposed to be carried there.

As they got closer Rachael frowned. "I see Stefan but where are the guards he posted? Is that them on the ground?"

They hurried over to find the two Slayers who had been left to guard the portal were indeed on the ground and both of them were wounded. One of the Slayers had an arrow in his leg and the other held an arrow in his hand, which seemed to have come from his arm since he had a bloody sleeve and a hole in his shirt.

"What happened?" Tristan asked.

One of the Slayers looked up at Tristan. "Some son of a bitch shot us and took off though the portal. He could've killed us but he didn't. Still, it's embarrassing."

"And painful," the other Slayer grumbled.

"What did he look like?" Stefan asked.

"Tall, long white-blond hair to his waist tied into a braid. Blue eyes."

"Yeah," said the other Slayer. "They were bright blue. Kind of eerie looking."

"Lairen!" Rachael gasped.

"Well, now I guess we know what happened to him," Amy muttered. "He went through the portal. He's back in your world."

"Great," Tristan muttered.

Stefan looked over at Rachael. "I hear you're leaving us tonight."

She nodded. "Yeah," she said, voice soft as sadness filled her. She was excited to go home but these people had become her friends and she would never see them again. She gave both Stefan and Amy a hug then turned to Ariel who had tears in her eyes. Rachael hugged her.

"I'm going to miss you," Ariel said as she hugged Rachael back.

"I'll miss you too. Thanks for loaning me clothes and for being my friend."

Rachael stepped away from Ariel and looked over at Tristan. She had a lump in her throat and tightness in her chest. This was going to be more difficult than she'd imagined.

"Tristan…thanks for everything," Rachael began but Tristan interrupted her.

"I'm coming with you," he said, his voice soft but unwavering.

Rachael's eyes widened. "What? Really?"

He nodded. "Yes." He looked over at Stefan. "Take care of Thomas and my mom's bodies for me. Make sure they have proper burials."

"I will," Stefan said and clamped a big hand on Tristan's shoulder. "Good luck."

Rachael thought he didn't seem surprised by Tristan's decision, but Amy and Ariel were clearly in shock; their mouths open, their eyes wide.

"Tristan, are you sure about this?" Amy asked.

He nodded. "Yes, absolutely." He looked over at Ariel and included her in what he said next to Amy and Stefan. "Don't let the higher ups at Slayer United push you around," he said to them. "You all can be leaders; if not overseers of a division, then certainly leaders of a team. Don't forget who you are and what you've accomplished."

Ariel rushed forward and hugged him and then Amy did the same. Stefan shook his hand, then embraced him.

"Good luck," Amy said.

Ariel just smiled though her tears and nodded her head in agreement.

Tristan looked at Rachael. "I'm ready when you are."

Rachael glanced at Ariel, Stefan, Amy and the two wounded Slayers. She lifted a hand in farewell then grabbed ahold of Tristan's hand and together they walked through the portal.

There was the familiar sensation of nausea, the flash of bright light. When Rachael turned back, she could see all of them on the other side, now a bit blurry.

Amy stepped forward, the portal closing device in her hand. "I suppose we have to do this," she said, although she didn't look like she really wanted to.

Tristan nodded. "Yes. It's the only way to keep both worlds safe."

"Good-bye!" Ariel called out. She was really crying now and Rachael began to cry as well.

"Good-bye," she called back as tears clouded her vision. "I'll miss you all."

And then Amy placed the device along the shimmering edge of the portal and with a snap and a spark the glimmer was gone and the portal closed.

Rachael covered her face with her hands and continued to cry. Tristan put his arms around her and held her for a bit. Finally, she pulled back and wiped away the tears.

"You okay?" Tristan asked.

"Yes, fine. I'll be fine."

He looked around. "Where do you think we are?"

Rachael surveyed the area as well. "I have no idea," she said after a minute.

There were a few buildings not too far away. They looked like shops. There was also a road with a few cars parked at the curb and a small parking lot adjacent to the shops.

She turned to Tristan. "Come on. I need to make a phone call. Hopefully someone will let me borrow a phone." She sniffed and wiped her nose on her sleeve. "And I could use a tissue," she added.

Tristan walked with her most of the way but then hung back. "I better wait here with the swords. If people see us with weapons like these, they might call your law enforcement or whatever they're called here."

Rachael paused. "You're right. Okay." She took off the swords she had strapped to her hips and slung over her shoulder then handed them to Tristan. "I'll be right back."

She walked around the corner of the nearest building and saw a pizza parlor. She went inside, went to the bathroom to get a tissue to blow her nose. Afterwards she went to the counter and asked if she could use their phone.

"It's not long distance, is it?" the teenager behind the counter asked.

Rachael thought about that. "Um, I don't know."

The boy gave her a stern look. "Well, if it's a long-distance call, I can't let you use the phone."

"What city is this?" Rachael asked.

He gave her a weird look. "It's Portland."

Rachael's eyebrows shot up. "Portland, Oregon?"

"Yeah," he nodded. "That one." He was still giving her a strange look.

"Oh, then I guess it is a long-distance call. But I'm stranded here and I've got to call someone to come get me. Couldn't I please use a phone?"

"You can borrow my cell phone," he said with a sigh. "But... you have to keep it short and you have to stay right here. I don't want you stealing my phone"

Rachael smiled. "Thank you! Yes, absolutely. No problem."

He fished the phone from his pocket and handed it to her.

Rachael took the phone from the boy and punched in a number. The phone rang a few times and then a familiar voice came on the line. It was John Preston, Handler for the Bureau of the Extraordinary. Rachael was so relieved she almost started to cry again.

"Mr. Preston, it's Rachael. Rachael Perry."

"Rachael!"

"Yes, it's me! I'm in Portland, Oregon and I need someone to come get me."

"Yes, yes of course! I'll get someone there right away. What happened to you, Rachael? Your parents, your family in Arizona, Skye, Megan, we've all been going crazy trying to find you!"

"It's a long story but right now I'm at..." she looked at the boy.

He supplied the answer. "Carmine's Pizzeria." He handed her a takeout menu with the address on it and she repeated the address to Mr. Preston.

"I'll have someone there as soon as possible. Before nightfall that's certain," he said.

"Oh, and, um, I don't have my phone or any ID with me," Rachael said. "I don't suppose you could use your credit card over the phone to buy us something to eat, would you?"

Mr. Preston laughed, something he didn't do very often. "Yes. I can do that but you said "us". Who's with you?"

"That's part of the long story I'll have to tell you when I see you all." She glanced at the boy who was gesturing for her to give him back his phone. "I'm giving the phone to the pizza guy. Hold on while I give him the order. And thank you!"

She handed the phone to the boy, placed her order and waited until he'd gotten off the phone with Mr. Preston.

"Thanks," she said. "I'll be back in a minute with my friend."

She ducked out the door and ran around the building. Tristan stood waiting right where she'd left him.

"I called home. They're sending someone to pick us up and I ordered us something to eat. It's probably going to be a long wait. Mr. Preston said someone would be here to get us before dark though."

They walked together back to the pizzeria and Tristan looked up at the sky while they walked.

"Are there Dark-Angels here? Do we have to worry about that when night comes?"

"Nope. No more Dark-Angels to worry about," Rachael replied.

They took seats inside the pizzeria. Tristan had kept all the swords tucked underneath his long coat, but then slid them onto the seat of the booth once they were settled.

Rachael felt the giddiness of having talked to Mr. Preston start to ebb away and her thoughts turned back to Tristan, all he'd lost today and the fact that he'd come here with her.

"Tristan, I'm so sorry about Thomas and your mom."

He nodded. "Thanks."

"And I'm really glad you decided to come here with me, but you've given up all your friends and everything you knew to come to a strange place and you can never go back. I hope you don't already regret what you did."

"No. No I don't. I have no family left there."

"What about your father?"

He shook his head. "He's a stranger. I don't even know him."

"But—"

"No, Rachael, really, it's alright. I was tired of working for Slayer United anyway. Tired of the hierarchy and the bullshit, tired of the Dark-Angels and the DAX." He sighed. "I was ready for a change."

"But your friends! Stefan, Amy—"

"You know, we weren't even really friends before all the stuff with Sebastian and the portals happened. I always fought alone and I didn't socialize much with the others. We all knew each other, sure, and respected each other too for the most part, but actually friends?" he shrugged.

The boy brought two plates of food over and set them on the table. "Here are some glasses too. The fountain drinks are right over there," he said, and then left.

Rachael got up. "What do you want to drink?"

Tristan shrugged. "As long as it's cold, I don't really care."

Rachael went over to the soda machine and got them two root beers. She returned to the table and set the drink in front of him. "I hope you like it."

He took a sip and nodded, then looked down at their food. "So, what's this?"

"It's a calzone. They can be made with all sorts of different ingredients inside. Take a bite."

Tristan did and a smile appeared on his face. "This is good," he said around the mouthful.

After they finished eating Rachael and Tristan took a walk then sat beneath a huge shade tree and talked. The hours ticked by. Finally, Rachael dozed a bit, her head in Tristan's lap. When she awakened the sun had travelled farther across the sky and Rachael figured it had to be late after-noon. She looked up at Tristan. He'd fallen asleep too, his head against the trunk of the tree.

She sat up and Tristan immediately awakened.

He looked around. "Everything okay?"

"Yeah. I hope nobody from the Bureau came while we were asleep." She got up and stretched. Rachael was anxious to call her family and see her friends again, especially Skye. She wondered what Skye would think of her newly red, orange and yellow hair. What would her parents think? Especially since she so far hadn't been able to change it back using glamour.

"Hey, an official looking car just pulled up to that place where we ate."

Rachael turned and saw first Mr. Preston and then Skye got out of the car. He was dressed to perfection, as usual, in steel grey slacks and a dove grey button-down shirt, black shoes and dark glasses. He was a little grey at the temples but it only served to make him look more elegant and distinguished.

Skye was dressed in blue jeans, black sneakers and a raspberry hued sleeveless blouse. Her dark auburn hair was pulled up in a high ponytail.

Rachael grinned. "It's them! Come on!" Then she took off at a run.

CHAPTER TWENTY-EIGHT

"**S**KYE!" SHE SHOUTED AND THE OTHER GIRL turned her head. Mr. Preston was about to put his hand on the door to the restaurant but he dropped his arm and whirled around.

Rachael ran right up to her friend Skye, threw her arms around her in a bear hug and started crying again, she was so happy. After releasing Skye, Rachael launched herself into Mr. Preston's arms. It was something she'd never done before and would probably never do again but she was so very happy to see them both, so hugs all around seemed appropriate.

"Your hair!" Skye gave her a puzzled look. "What—?"

"I'll tell you on the way home," Rachael laughed through her tears then looked at Mr. Preston. "When you said you were sending someone to pick us up, I didn't think you meant the two of you!"

"Well," Mr. Preston said. "I figured who better to come retrieve our lost girl?"

About that time Tristan finally joined the group.

"Mr. Preston, Skye, this is Tristan Tate. He came with me from the other world where I've been."

Skye's eyebrows shot up. "Other world?"

"Yes. I'll explain it all, I promise." She then glanced at Tristan and continued the introductions. "This is John Preston, my Handler and Skye Falco, my best friend. She's an Assassin with the Bureau."

Tristan greeted Skye and Mr. Preston. After shaking hands with Tristan, Preston gestured toward the sleek black car at the curb.

"Let's head back to the airport. I'm sure you're anxious to get home and you can call your parents from the plane. I already let them know I'd heard from you so they'll be expecting your call."

The four of them got into the car and as they did Rachael retrieved all four of the Elfaen swords from Tristan. She handed them to Mr. Preston.

Skye laughed. "You're collecting swords now?"

"No," Rachael grinned. "They're the lost Elfaen swords."

Mr. Preston examined the hilts of the swords. "So, these have been in another world this whole time?"

Rachael nodded.

"I'm looking forward to taking a closer look at these when we get on the plane," Preston said.

During the drive to the airport Rachael explained how she'd come to find herself in a different world. She told Skye and Mr. Preston about Slayer United, the discovery of the swords, and how she and Tristan had each bonded with a particular blade. She also talked about Sebastian and his plans and how she'd fought with the sword on more than one occasion.

Skye beamed at her. "Rachael, you're officially an Assassin now like me!"

"Hardly," Rachael said. "It's the sword doing all the work. If you put any other sword in my hands, I wouldn't have the faintest idea what to do."

"And you, Tristan, you're an Assassin for your Slayer United. I'd like to hear more about that," Preston prompted.

"Well sir, I guess I'm the equivalent of one of your Assassins from what Rachael has told me, but we're called Slayers."

"It sounds like you've seen your share of fighting."

Tristan nodded.

Preston glanced at Tristan in the rearview mirror. "Which weapons are you most familiar with?"

"Sword, of course, bow and arrow, various firearms and knives," Tristan shrugged. "Plus, I'm used to using a stake too."

"Sounds to me like you'd make a pretty good addition to the Bureau," Skye said.

Preston nodded. "Yes, I was thinking the same thing."

Skye looked at Rachael. "Okay, I've waited long enough. How in the world did your hair go from blonde to red, orange and yellow? Was that intentional or—"

Rachael shook her head. "No, definitely not intentional and I can't even change it back with glamour. It happened when I bonded with the Fire-Starter sword."

"What'll happen if you don't use the sword anymore and someone else bonds with it?" Skye asked.

"I don't know," Rachael replied. "This might be permanent or…" she shrugged. "Who knows?"

"We can discuss this more at a later date," Preston said. "But you may want to hang on to that sword, Rachael. You'd be an asset to us. And you, Tristan, perhaps you would like to continue using the sword you bonded with as well and join the Bureau."

"It's too soon to make a decision about that but I appreciate the offer, sir, and I'll think about it," Tristan replied. "For now, I think I'd just like to take a break from killing things and get used to being here."

"Certainly," Preston said.

After they arrived at the airport and boarded the Bureau's private plane, Preston handed Rachael his phone and she called her parents. Naturally she had to go through the entire story of what had happened to her all over again, but it was so thrilling for Rachael to speak to her parents and her younger sisters. Her parents promised to fill in her Arizona relatives and when the call neared the end Rachael brought up the topic that had been most on her mind.

"Dad, while I was there in the other world, I met a guy who was going back and forth between that world and this one. He was actually in one of my college classes too. That's how I first recognized him. He said his name was Lairen and that he's my half-brother. Is that true? Could it even be possible?"

There was dead silence on the other end of the line.

"Dad? Are you there? Did you hear me?"

"Yes." Her dad sighed. "Yes. You do actually have a brother named Lairen. A half-brother. I haven't seen him since he was just a little boy. Tell me…what does he look like?"

Rachael was stunned. To have it all confirmed blew her mind and also caused her to have so many questions.

"Um, well, he's tall. He has long white blond hair and intense blue eyes."

Her dad sighed. "Yes, that sounds like him."

"He said his mother's name was Beatrix. I met her. She was awful." That was an understatement, but Rachael didn't want to admit to her dad just how close she'd come to being killed by the woman.

"Beatrix was always a difficult woman. Luckily my relationship with her ended almost before it began. My only regret is that a child was brought into this world during that time and I wasn't able to be the one to raise him."

"What happened, Dad? I can't even picture you with someone like that."

"It was a long time ago, Rachael. An awful mistake that I made before I knew your mother. I tried to be a part of Lairen's life but Beatrix fought me every step of the way and then she disappeared, taking my son with her."

"Well, he slipped though the portal before it closed so he's somewhere around, here in our world. Maybe you'll see him again one day but I'm not sure it will be a happy reunion. He seemed jealous of me...my life growing up...all that."

"I'm not going to worry about it now. I just want my daughter home. We're looking forward to seeing you, Rachael."

"I'll come see you tomorrow and I'll be bringing a friend; the guy who came with me from the other world."

"Tristan?"

"Yes. I hope that's okay."

"Of course. We'd love to meet him."

Rachael said good-bye and handed the phone back to Preston.

"Everything okay?" he asked her.

"Yeah but..." She looked over at Tristan. "It's true. Lairen is my half-brother."

Tristan's response was to make a face.

"It's so weird to think you have a brother," Skye said.

"Yeah, I know," Rachael frowned but then shifted gears. "Tristan is going to need a place to stay. Where—?"

"There're apartments available in the complex next to ours," Skye suggested.

While Rachael and Skye talked, Rachael noticed Mr. Preston gesture to Tristan and the two of them went to sit in another part of the plane.

"Rachael, are you listening to me?" Skye asked.

"Uh? Oh, yes, right. Maybe we can go take a look at them tomorrow after I see my parents. I wonder what they're talking about."

"Preston's probably trying to talk him into being an Assassin." Skye grinned at her. "He's very good looking."

Rachael smiled and looked down. "I know. I think so too. And I think he likes me but…"

"But what? How could you possibly say no to that guy? Don't tell me he's a jerk."

"No! No not at all. I thought so at first but it was because he was just so focused on the task at hand, you know, the mission, the threat. But now I think he's great."

"Then what's the problem?"

"Well, we've been through a lot and maybe part of the attraction is the 'two people fighting for their lives' thing. Maybe once everything calms down, he'll go his way and I'll go mine and—"

"Uh, I don't think so. I've seen the way he looks at you. He's got a thing for you and he's got it bad."

Rachael knew she was blushing; she could just feel it. "So, how's Aidan?"

"Aidan is good." Skye smiled. "Yeah, he's the best."

"I wonder what he'll think of Tristan."

Skye shrugged. "I wonder what Tristan will think of Aidan once he finds out Aidan is a Blood-Hunter. Doesn't Tristan kill things like Blood-Hunters where he's from?"

Rachael grimaced. "Ugh, the DAX. They're really nothing like Blood-Hunters. They're hideous and they're mindless killers. They're horrible."

"I can see you don't like them much," Skye chuckled.

Rachael shuddered. "No. The DAX make Blood-Hunters look like the most civilized people around. I'm sure Tristan will like Aidan just fine once I explain things."

The rest of the journey home was quiet. By the time they got back to San Diego Rachael was both tired and excited and more than ready to get off the plane and back to her own apartment and bed.

When they got off the plane Tristan grabbed Rachael by the arm. "Can I talk to you for a minute in private?"

She glanced at Preston and Skye's retreating backs as they walked from the plane to the nearby entrance to the airport.

"Hey, um, we'll be just a minute, okay?" Rachael called out.

Both Preston and Skye turned around. Preston nodded.

Rachael looked up at Tristan. "Is something wrong?"

"I don't think so, but your Mr. Preston offered to pay for a motel for me to stay in overnight. The thing is…I'd rather stay with you if you don't mind and if there's room."

"Oh! Well, sure. That would be great. Um, Skye and I share an apartment and you could sleep on the sofa, I guess. If that's okay with you."

"Yes. I'd rather do that and I'd like to get a change of clothes too." He glanced up at the dark sky overhead, then back down at Rachael. "Sorry. Old habits die hard. I just keep expecting Dark-Angels to swoop down."

Rachael smiled. "That's okay. And sure, we can go shopping and get you some clothes. I have to get my driver's license replaced and get a new phone too. Also, I promised my parents I'd come see them tomorrow too and you're coming with me."

"I am?"

"Yes. You are."

CHAPTER TWENTY-NINE

A FTER RACHAEL AND TRISTAN ATE BREAKFAST the next morning, they went to a motor vehicle office and Rachael applied for a replacement license. After that, they went to the mall. Rachael got a new phone and they shopped for clothes for Tristan so he'd have something else to wear besides what he'd had on when he'd walked through the portal. He now wore blue jeans, a sapphire pullover knit shirt, new black boots and a lightweight jacket that hung to mid-thigh. Not long enough to hide swords, but a nice jacket nevertheless. His rather shaggy dark hair was clean and behaving well; not too wild in spite of the breeze trying to rough it up.

Rachael had on blue jeans as well. She'd chosen a pretty blouse with a swirl of green and blue to wear and she'd added a lightweight blue cardigan, which coordinated with the blue in her blouse. Her long hair was braided. She figured that would be best when going to visit her parents. She hoped they wouldn't react too badly to the color, especially since she couldn't change it. Perhaps she could go to a salon, like the human girls, and get it lightened again. On the other hand, if magic couldn't change the color, she didn't think some chemicals would either.

"Okay, next stop my parents' house." Rachael said to Tristan as they climbed into her car. She was happy to be behind the wheel of her own vehicle again, a blue Nissan Murano.

The drive from the apartment in San Diego to her parents' home in Coronado didn't take long. She'd called ahead to let them know she was on her way and when she and Tristan arrived both her parents and her twin sisters, Emma and Cara, were sitting on the front porch ready to greet them.

Naturally, the subject of Rachael's hair was a primary topic with her sisters and her mother. Her dad just rolled his eyes.

"I don't care what color your hair is," he whispered to her. "I'm just so very happy to have you back."

Their visit went well and Rachael was pleased that Tristan conversed with her dad quite easily, joked around with her sisters and was very polite to her mother. They stayed for dinner and it was 8pm when Rachael pulled into her parking space at the apartment complex.

"Long day," she said as she and Tristan walked along the sidewalk back to her apartment. "I hope you weren't too bored."

"Bored? No, not at all. It was really nice to have an ordinary day and not be thinking constantly about life and death matters and what might be around the next corner or swoop down from the sky to kill me."

They entered the apartment and Rachael was surprised to find Skye, Mr. Preston, Aidan and Megan waiting for them. Megan immediately got up from her chair and ran over to Rachael to give her a hug.

"I'm so glad you're back and you're okay!" Megan said. Her wildly curling brown hair was loose and looked a bit like a lion's mane. She wore black tights, black Doc Marten Mary Jane shoes, a red skirt that fell just above her knees and a knit pullover top that a black and red bunny print on it.

Rachael smiled at her. "Hi, Megan! This is my friend, Tristan." Rachael looked at Tristan. "Megan works for the bureau in research."

Megan grinned. "Hello Tristan. Welcome to the Bureau of the Extraordinary."

"Hello. And…thanks," he replied.

"Welcome back, Rachael," Aidan's smile was as warm as his familiar Irish brogue, and his green eyes seemed to sparkle. His chocolate brown hair hung to his shoulders, and in that way, he resembled Tristan.

"Thank you. It's great to be back. And this is Tristan." She again looked up at Tristan. "Aidan is Skye's boyfriend and he's a sort of part-time Assassin for the Bureau." She left off the part about him being a Blood-Hunter and figured she'd explain all of that later. Maybe tomorrow. "So, what's everybody doing here?" she asked.

John Preston gave her his serious face; the one where his gaze was steady and he had no trace of a smile. "I got a call today from the Bureau office up in Portland."

Rachael didn't like the sound of that. "Uh oh."

"It seems there's a rather huge, vicious creature up there. It suddenly appeared yesterday and nobody has ever seen anything like it before so the research department is reaching out to every division both domestic and abroad to find out if there are more of these things and just exactly what they are."

"What does this thing look like?" Tristan asked.

"Roughly ten feet tall, black hair over most of its body, prominent brow, heavily muscled, yellow eyes, wearing tattered clothing. Carries a weapon with a blade at one end and a claw at the other."

"Hell-Spawn!" Both Tristan and Rachael said at the same time.

"Oh no! One of them must've gotten through the portal after all," Rachael said.

"Crap," Tristan muttered. "We'll have to go back up there."

"Aidan and I can handle it," Skye said.

But Preston shook his head. "This is a creature unknown to us. We can't just go flying off to Portland without proper preparation. There are Assassins up there who have already died trying to kill this thing. It's very proficient with the weapon it carries and the clawed end seems to have some sort of venom."

Tristan nodded. "I know this type of beast. We've had the best luck when multiple Slayers attacked from the front and sides while one snuck up behind and delivered the killing blow, or at least did enough damage to disable the thing so it could be killed."

"And you're right about the venom," Rachael added. "I've seen more than one person die from being clawed by that thing. It's pretty fast acting too."

"We'll fly back to Portland tomorrow," Preston said. "Tonight, and on the way there you can work on strategy."

"I'm going with you tomorrow," Tristan said. "This monster came here from my world and I'd like to see this finished."

Rachael looked over at Preston. "I want to come too."

"Are you sure you want to do that?" Skye asked.

"Yeah, you just got home and you've already been through so much," Megan added. "Why don't you stay here? We can hang out tomorrow and…"

Megan's voice trailed off as Rachael shook her head. "No. I want to go. I want to use Fire-Starter and I want to fight."

John Preston tipped his head and studied her. "Alright. If you're sure." "I am."

He nodded. "Then Skye, Aidan, Tristan and Rachael will go back to Portland tomorrow. I'll travel with you and liaise with the local Handler."

Megan got up to leave. "Well, I guess I don't really have anything to contribute to this since I don't know about Hell-Spawn beasts and how to fight them, but I wanted to come anyway and see you and welcome you back," she said to Rachael. "And I like your new hair color too, by the way."

"Thanks Megan," Rachael said and walked the other girl to the door. When she returned, she found Tristan huddled with Mr. Preston, Skye and Aidan like they'd worked together for years, already discussing strategy. She smiled. Tristan was going to fit in very well here.

The next day the five of them boarded the plane and set off for Portland. Rachael had phoned her parents to let them know what she was doing and they weren't too happy about it. In fact, they'd pleaded with her to stay home and let those more equipped do the fighting. She'd pointed out that once she had Fire-Starter in her hand she was just as capable as the others to fight the Hell-Spawn beast. They weren't convinced.

Rachael had been with Tristan when he'd requested to use the Life-Giver sword since it had bonded to him. He believed, and Rachael agreed, that it would give him an advantage over using a regular sword and the fact this particular sword had life giving benefits wasn't lost on any of them. Mr. Preston had readily agreed to let Tristan use the sword.

The plane touched down mid-afternoon. A Handler named Joel Hoskins met them at the airport and drove them to the Portland Bureau office.

"We lost three Assassins over the last two days," he said. "Some humans have perished as well. The thing seems to find human flesh to be to its liking. This is going to be damn hard to cover up."

Preston nodded. "Yes, this will be difficult to cover up. Sometimes I wish the human population was aware of the other species among us, the dangers, but it would create mass panic. Besides, the Shape-Shifters and

Elfae have a right to their privacy. The Blood-Hunters not so much." He turned to Aidan. "Sorry, Aidan."

He shrugged. "I know perfectly well what most Blood-Hunters are capable of. Very few have any concern for humanity beyond the next meal."

"I have people watching that monster," Joel continued. "But they've been instructed not to interact with it in any way. Luckily, it's been asleep in an abandoned warehouse not far from here. Once it wakes up there's no telling how many more people this thing might kill."

"Let's go now then, while it's sleeping," Tristan suggested. "At least that will give us a little bit of an advantage. It'll be lying down, unconscious, and will possibly awaken disoriented."

"And we'll be able to get close without risk," Skye added.

"There will still be risk," Aidan pointed out.

She gave him a look. "Oh yeah, I'm fully aware of that."

"Depending on where the Hell-Spawn's weapon is, we might be able to take it away," Rachael said. "That would increase our odds considerably."

Tristan nodded. "Rachael's idea is a good one. Let's further evaluate when we get there but if one of us can snatch the weapon before the Hell-Spawn wakes up that would be fantastic."

It had been decided the night before that Aidan would be the main one to draw the Hell-Spawn's attention away from the others. Because he was a Blood-Hunter he was faster than the others and would be less likely to be hit or slashed by the monster's fists or weapon. Plus, his chances of recovering from being clawed was actually pretty good since he was almost immortal and healed very quickly from anything short of a beheading.

Rachael thought Tristan had taken the news that Aidan was a Blood-Hunter pretty well. Aidan himself had explained what a Blood-Hunter was and how he was different from most and Tristan seemed very accepting

"Let's go over this again," Preston said. "Skye and Rachael will come up from behind and hamstring the Hell-Spawn. That will leave Tristan to deliver the final deathblow by slashing the beast's throat. Rachael has her fire magic for back up and you also have the bow and arrows in case you can't get close enough initially to bring the monster to the ground or at least to its knees."

They all nodded in understanding.

"Sounds like an excellent plan," Joel nodded. "I'm impressed."

Preston gave credit where credit was due. "It wasn't my plan. They worked together to come up with it. The four of them deserve the credit."

"I imagine this team of yours has been together for quite a while then to be so able to work together and be in sync like that," Joel said.

Preston smiled. "Actually, Skye is the only one who is technically my Assassin. Aidan and Rachael are on an as-needed basis and Tristan has only recently joined us. This will be the first time the four of them have worked together."

Joel nodded. "Well, then I'm even more impressed." He looked at the group of them. "If you're ready I'll take you over to the warehouse now."

They piled into Joel's Chevy Suburban and Rachael hardly even paid attention to where they were going. All she could think about was that in a few minutes she'd come face to face with a monster she'd hoped never to see again in her life.

Joel stopped the car and Rachael, Tristan, Skye and Aidan got out of the vehicle, toting their weapons along with them.

"Call or text," Preston said. "And we'll come pick you up immediately. We won't be far away."

Skye turned to Rachael as Preston and Hoskins drove away. "You're sure you want to do this?"

Rachael rolled her eyes. "Yes, mom. I'm sure."

They'd all agreed to let Tristan take the lead on this operation. He gestured for them to remain silent and split up to look in the various semi-blacked out windows to get a location on the Hell-Spawn. When they reunited minutes later, they knew where the monster was located and they were ready to proceed.

The Hell-Spawn slept, sprawled on the floor, its back against a pillar for support. The monster's two-headed weapon, blade on one end poison claw on the other, lay a few feet away but still within reach of the monster. It was agreed that Aidan would snatch the weapon.

Rachael and the others watched as Aidan squeezed through an open window and landed cat-like on his feet. The Hell-Spawn didn't move. He approached cautiously at first, then in an instant he was gone, a blur of dark clothing. Seconds later he was back with the weapon.

"Wow," Tristan whispered to Rachael. "I had a hard time believing he could do stuff like that but now I'm a believer."

Aidan tossed the two-headed staff out the window after the others backed far away so as not to be accidentally wounded by either blade or claw.

"That was easy," he said, his voice low, once he'd joined them outside.

"Now for the trickier part," Tristan whispered.

Rachael and Skye scouted around a bit more and discovered another way in, so that they could come up behind the Hell-Spawn once Tristan and Aidan had its attention.

Rachael watched as something caused the Hell-Spawn to stir and awaken. Perhaps it was the sound of four people entering the warehouse, even though they were all as quiet as they could be.

The giant was on its feet quickly, more quickly than something that big should be able to move, in Rachael's opinion. It reached for its weapon but of course it was gone. It growled and Rachael felt the vibration in her bones.

"Ready?" Skye whispered. She tightly gripped the sword now in her hand.

Rachael drew Fire-Starter and felt the now familiar rush of power travel up her arm and through her body.

"Ready," she whispered back.

And then their whole plan fell apart.

CHAPTER THIRTY

A SECOND HELL-SPAWN REVEALED ITSELF. IT rose up behind Tristan and with a sweep of its meaty arm, sent him flying across the empty warehouse.

Rachael shouted Tristan's name. It just burst from her lips and she clamped a hand over her mouth upon realizing what she'd done because now the first Hell-Spawn was aware of her presence as well as Skye's. The beast whipped around and roared at them.

Aidan quickly sped between the Hell-Spawn and the girls, redirecting the two monsters' attention and giving the girls a chance to get it together. Both Hell-Spawn went after Aidan but couldn't lay a hand on him. He was too fast for them but there wasn't much room to maneuver, which would eventually create its own problems.

Rachael saw that Tristan had recovered and was on his feet. He positioned himself as best he could behind the first of the Hell-Spawn and Rachael and Skye did the same to the second giant. Tristan managed to cut the leg of the horrible creature. It bellowed in pain and crashed to the ground, no longer able to stand on that leg.

Rachael saw the beast go down but she was too busy with her own troubles now to keep an eye on Tristan. The other Hell-Spawn, the one Skye and Rachael were after, still had its two headed weapon which it swung at them in spite of Aidan's best efforts to distract the creature away from the girls.

Around and around they went, Rachael, Skye and the Hell-Spawn each trying to find a vulnerable spot. Rachael would've thought three people circling it would confuse the beast but it was surprisingly agile and managed to somehow keep the three of them in its sights.

Then Rachael stepped forward to throw fire. She noticed Tristan was nearby, ready to join the battle to bring down the brute in front of her. A quick glance told her the other giant was dead. Tristan had succeeded in killing it.

Rachael's fire finally offered the distraction they needed. Skye lunged forward to slash at the Hell-Spawn, as did Rachael. Her sword cut into the beast's arm and she pushed fire through the blade as well. The Hell-Spawn roared and swiped at her, in spite of its clothing being on fire and its flesh badly burned. Rachael jumped back quickly but not before the clawed end of the Hell-Spawn's weapon hit her arm.

With a cry Rachael fell, Fire-Starter dropping from her hand. She tried to reach out to have the sword fly into her palm once again but her arm had gone numb and she couldn't move it. As the giant loomed over her Rachael saw both Skye and Tristan pierce the beast with their swords, one on either side. Aidan leapt on the Hell-Spawn's back and twisted its head around, more and more until there was a dull snap. Aidan had broken the beast's neck. The huge creature crashed to the ground and lay still just a couple of feet away from her. Only someone with Aidan's superior strength could've done something like that and Rachael would've been eternally grateful except that she knew, without a doubt, that she was dying.

Tristan, Skye and Aidan hurried to Rachael's side.

"Call Preston," Aidan said quietly and Skye immediately dug out her phone and made the call.

Rachael lay on her back and looked up at Tristan. "I'm dying."

"No," Tristan said. "You're going to be okay." But Rachael heard the panic in his voice.

"Tristan, I'm so sorry. You just lost your brother and your mom and you come to a new world and now I'm going to be gone too. You shouldn't have come here. You should've stayed with the people you knew." She was beginning to feel light-headed and her mouth felt dry. Tears slipped from her eyes. She would never see her parents or sisters again. Her mom and dad had been right, she never should've come here today.

Skye was back and she was crying. "Rachael, you can't do this. You can't die."

"No choice," Rachael whispered. Her eyes fluttered closed and her body tensed as pain advanced up her arm to her neck and then went numb again. There was a roaring in her ears. Her mind started to drift away but she was jerked back to the warehouse when she felt something long and sort of heavy pressing against her stomach and along the entire length of the front of her body.

Tristan stood over her and she could feel magic, his healing magic, swirling in the air above her. Why was he doing this, she wondered. He and several others had used healing magic to try and save Alina but it hadn't worked. How could he, by himself, be successful?

She felt warmth increase along her body and then she could see that Tristan hand his hand pressed against her stomach. But no, his hand wasn't directly on her stomach, it was on the hilt of a sword. He'd placed the Life-Giver sword on her and was pushing his healing magic though his connection with the sword, right into her. The sword would magnify his magic just like the Fire-Starter sword magnified her fire magic. Was it possible that maybe, just maybe there was the tiniest chance she could live?

Rachael heard running feet and then Mr. Preston and Joel Hoskins came into view and crouched at Rachael's feet. Aidan and Skye were already there, kneeling while Tristan continued to try and heal her. And then she realized her vision had cleared and the ringing in her ears had gone away. Her mind was sharper too. It no longer wandered toward the afterlife but was firmly planted in the here and now.

"Tristan," she whispered and her mouth no longer felt quite so dry. "Tristan," she said a little louder.

"Tristan," Skye said as she put a hand on his shoulder. "Look! Whatever you're doing it's working!"

Aidan smiled. "Skye's right. Look, Tristan."

Tristan opened his eyes but didn't remove his hands from the sword or the sword from her body.

Rachael smiled up at him. "I think it's working," her voice was barely above a whisper but she did feel stronger and the numbness was definitely receding.

Tristan smiled down at her but kept up his magic, obviously unwilling to take any chances. Rachael was fine with that. She glanced at the others. Skye smiled, although tears still fell. Aidan grinned and nodded encouragement. Mr. Preston ran a hand over his face and through his hair and his posture relaxed considerably. Joel Hoskins sighed and slumped against the post at his back.

A few minutes later Tristan sat back and lifted the sword from her body. He and Skye got on either side of her and lifted Rachael to a sitting position. From there it only took Rachael only a couple more minutes to feel ready to stand. She found that she could walk with a bit of assistance. Tristan encouraged her to lean on him and kept his arm around her all the way to the car. He even kept it there once they were inside the vehicle.

"I've notified a team to come remove the bodies," Joel said. He looked around the warehouse. "Where are the bodies?"

"No need," Tristan replied. "These creatures burst into magical flame and disintegrate."

Joel looked impressed. "Oh, well that's handy."

The drive back to the Portland Bureau office was one of subdued jubilance. Rachael was excited to have completed their mission successfully but exhausted and also sobered by the fact that she almost died. What if Tristan hadn't had the sword...if he hadn't bonded with it in the first place...if he hadn't crossed the portal with Rachael and come into this world...she would be dead.

On the plane back to San Diego Rachael slept. The next thing she knew Tristan was gently shaking her shoulder to get her to wake up.

"The plane is landing. We're almost there."

Rachael pushed the button to bring her chair to an upright position.

"How do you feel?" Tristan gave her a worried look.

She smiled. "I'm fine. Really, I am. Especially now that I had a nap."

The landing was smooth and soon the five of them were on their way to the car. Mr. Preston dropped the four of them at Rachael and Skye's apartment and then sped off into the night.

"Aidan and I are going to get something to eat. Do you guys want to come?" Skye asked.

Rachael glanced at Tristan.

"Whatever you want," he said.

Rachael looked back at Skye. "I think I'd like to stay here."

Skye nodded. "Okay. We'll see you later then."

After she and Aidan were gone Rachael went to sit on the sofa and pulled Tristan down next to her.

She took his hands in hers and looked him in the eyes. "I would've died today. You saved my life."

He drew in a shaky breath. "It wasn't me. It was the sword. I'm just glad I had it with me today."

"Well, yes, the sword played a big part but it was you who thought to bring it and it was you who used it. The sword by itself would've done nothing for me. It was your healing magic, magnified by the sword that did the trick."

He nodded. "Yeah, well." His eyes had been focused on their joined hands but they snapped up to look into hers. "I couldn't lose you, Rachael. You mean a lot to me."

Rachael's heart warmed and she smiled at him. "I feel the same way, about you. I mean, at first, I thought you were kind of a jerk but..."

He laughed and she did too.

"But now...now everything is different. You mean a lot to me too."

He sobered a bit. "Because I saved your life."

"No." She shook her head. "I mean, that's a big thing but...no, things started to change for me after you let me come stay at your apartment. I got to know you better, see you differently."

"I admit in the beginning I thought you were keeping things from us and that you were a part of what was going on with the portals."

"I know. And I was keeping some stuff from you but it had nothing to do with the portals. It was because I wasn't human and I didn't know how you all would react to that."

"Yeah, I understood that after it all came out and I realized Elementals and Elfae were pretty similar. And then there's the fact that I liked you. I couldn't help but like you." He smiled. "You're pretty, you're nice, you're resourceful and you cared about people even though you didn't really even know them."

Rachael smiled at him.

"We've been through a lot, haven't we?"

She nodded. "And it isn't over...I mean, the part about the portals and Sebastian and Hell-Spawn is over but..." Rachael figured she might as well go for it. "I like you, Tristan. I like you a lot and I don't want those feelings to fade. I mean, maybe we just liked each other because of the danger and the adventure and all that. What if—"

"I don't think so. I know how I feel about you. And even if things calm down…way, way down…I'm still going to want to be with you and be a part of your life."

Rachael was happy but suddenly got a little scared and needed clarification. "You mean as friends or…?"

"Well, I'd hoped for more than that but—"

Rachael threw her arms around him in a big hug. "Yes! I hoped you would say that!"

His arms went around her too and for a moment they stayed that way, then Rachael sat back.

"I do want to talk to you about something though."

"Oh, what's that?" he looked worried.

"I think I'm going to give Fire-Starter back to the Bureau and not use it anymore."

Now he looked more puzzled than worried. "Why?"

"Well, that experience, bonding with the sword was amazing but it's not really me. I'm not a fighter type like you and Aidan and Skye."

He cocked his head and gave her a lopsided smile. "With that sword in your hand you sure are."

"Yeah, that's true but…it's not really who I want to be. I'll be happier being on the sidelines, offering assistance when it's needed with my fire magic, and helping Megan do research."

"Are you sure?"

She nodded. "Yeah, definitely. And maybe after a while the connection between the sword and me will fade and my natural hair color will come back!" She grinned. "Or maybe I can retest it for someone else to have the chance to bond with it and then that will sever the connection for good and I'll still have this crazy hair but either way I'm ready to give it up."

"Okay, well whatever you want to do will probably be okay with Mr. Preston. He seems like a good guy and he seems to genuinely care about the people he works with."

"He is and he does," Rachael replied.

"So then…you're really, really sure that you don't want to fight anymore?"

"Yeah, I really am. This whole adventure made me realize some things about myself and what I need, what I want and what I'm capable of in stressful and weird situations. I know myself better than I did before I crossed that portal into your world. And what I want is to be a regular girl." She grinned. "Of course, what's regular for an Elfaen girl who works part-time for the Bureau of the Extraordinary is still pretty unusual! So, what about you? Are you going to join the Bureau? I'm sure Preston has talked to you about it more than once."

"He has." Tristan nodded. "And yeah, I think I'm going to go ahead and be a part of the team. You know, I learned something about myself too this last week or so."

Rachael nodded. "Okay. And...?"

"Well, I've always sort of resented being a Slayer." He pushed up his sleeve and showed her the mark on his arm. "This appears on all the Slayers and there's no getting out of it."

"Yeah, I remember about that."

"So, when it appeared on me, I was annoyed because I wasn't going to be able to figure out what I wanted to do with my life or who I wanted to be. That choice was taken away from me." He pushed down his sleeve and looked at Rachael. "Now I have the chance to leave it all behind with no guilt." He shrugged. "But the funny thing is I realize now that I actually do have a choice, and I do want to fight against evil and help protect the world I live in." He chuckled. "So here I am, choosing to be a Slayer for a new organization but since it's my choice I'm happy with it. I feel like this is my destiny...to fight on the side of good wherever that takes me. And it's taken me to a place where I can be an Assassin for the Bureau of the Extraordinary and hopefully have you by my side." He cocked his head and grinned at her. "Well, not literally by my side, since you've decided not to fight anymore but...you know what I mean."

Rachael smiled back at him. "I'm happy for you Tristan; that you now really know what you want to do and that you finally have a chance to make the choice. And as for that last part about you and me," Rachael threw her arms around his neck. "Most definitely!"

And then she kissed him.

EPILOGUE

Six Months Later

"**O**NE DOOR HAS CLOSED AND ANOTHER HAS *opened.*"

He read the words in his co-worker's romance novel, which rested on the break-table face down, creased spine, worn edges, and he'd thought the cover looked ridiculous.

"Too true and quite literally," he muttered. He hoped to never see another portal, leading to a different world, ever again. He glanced at the clock on the wall. Break time was over.

He slid through the double swinging doors while retying his royal blue apron. The front read, ***Apollo Café: Coffee, Pastries, Sandwiches*** in bold white letters.

"Take over cashiering for me, huh?" asked Stephanie. The petite freckle-faced brunette brushed by him on the way to take her break and to no doubt continue reading that ridiculous book.

He stepped up to the register where a tall slender girl with glasses and long, wild curly brown hair stood ready to order. Her glasses were bright red and she wore a turquoise blue t-shirt with black leggings.

"I'd like to get a medium cinnamon latte, decaf, with coconut milk and a bagel; the one with the raisins."

"What's your name?"

Her eyes widened. "Huh?"

"For the cup," he clarified. "What name should I put on the cup?"

"Oh!" Her skin flushed pink. "It's Megan. M-E-G-A-N."

"Right," he said and finished scrawling her name on the cup. "Hold on, I'll get your bagel."

After he handed her the bagel, she moved to the end of the counter. He watched her go, then refocused his attention to the front of the store just as the door opened and two girls walked in; one with dark auburn hair pulled back in a ponytail and the other with long pale blonde hair which had fading streaks of red, yellow and orange. The two were deep in conversation and didn't look his way at first which gave him time to panic, recover and paste a sly smile on his face. When the two girls finally turned his way, he was ready.

"Rachael," he said with a nod. "What can I get you?"

The girl's green eyes widened and she stopped dead in her tracks. "Lairen!"

The other girl's eyes narrowed as she studied him.

"Yes. It's me," he said. "What do you want?"

"Well...we came in for coffee," Rachael stammered.

"Of course, you did," he replied. "What do you want?"

"Uh...a mocha. Iced. Medium. What are you doing here?"

"I work here." He turned to the other girl. "And you?"

The other girl's scowl deepened.

Rachael seemed to regain her composure and deliberately lowered her voice. "I mean, I figured after you went through the portal, I'd probably never see you again."

"And yet, here I am," he replied with another smirk. He turned back to the auburn-haired girl. "Are you going to order?"

"No," she snapped.

"Alrighty then. Could you two head on down to the end of the counter so I can help the next customer?"

The two girls moved away, but Lairen noticed the girl with the dark auburn ponytail still glowered at him.

A couple of minutes later Stephanie returned from her break and took over cashiering so Lairen began to restock product that had gotten low in the pastry case. He kept an eye on the two girls and noticed they'd joined the girl named, Megan, at one of the tables.

A short time later the three of them left together. Lairen saw Rachael cast a last look over her shoulder at him, but she didn't look angry like her friend. Instead, she looked sort of sad, and then she was out the door. Lairen was surprised at that. After all, the last time he'd seen Rachael, he'd threatened her and he'd expected her to be as angry with him as her friend seemed to be. His eyes widened when, a minute later, she was back.

Rachael strode up to the counter and took a breath, as though to give herself courage.

"Lairen, come to lunch with me and my dad…our dad," she corrected. "Or dinner, if that's better for you. He'd like to see you. Will you do it?"

Lairen was taken aback. He hadn't expected to be invited to a family reunion of sorts.

"Ah, I don't know if that's a good—"

"Yes, it is. It's a good idea. Please. Tonight, tomorrow, you choose."

"Ok? I guess tonight. Where?"

"At the Enchanted Dragon. Do you know where it is?"

"No, but—"

"It's not far from here. It's Chinese food. Is that okay with you?"

"Sure."

Rachael smiled for the first time. "Okay. 6pm?"

"Ah, yeah, okay."

"Alright! See you there."

Rachael turned, after giving him a dazzling smile, and left the café, the bell on the door jingling for several seconds even after she was gone.

Lairen was in a bit of a daze. What had just happened? His whole life was based on his not having family connections and not caring about anyone or anything particularly much; and he was making his way through life perfectly well, right? Wasn't he? What did this mean; this dinner with his half-sister and his father?

As his shift wore on, he thought about cancelling, but he had no way of contacting Rachael. Of course, he could just not show up, but he shrugged off that idea. Why? Because a part of him really did want to go. And so, he would. He would go and see the man who had fathered him and had been a positive presence in his life for a short time.

At exactly 6pm, Lairen strolled through the doors of the Enchanted Dragon. Rachael had been right; the restaurant wasn't too far from where he worked and the GPS on his phone had taken him right to the parking lot.

The girl at the hostess podium greeted him and asked him a question, but before he had a chance to say anything he saw Rachael waving at him from across the dining area. He nodded at her in acknowledgement and approached the table.

Gabriel Perry, Lairen's and Rachael's father, rose to his feet, as did Rachael.

"Thanks for coming, Lairen," Mr. Perry extended his hand and Lairen shook it.

They all sat down and Lairen hoped this meal wasn't going to be too awkward, although he was almost certain it would be.

"So where have you been since you came though the portal?" Rachael asked after they'd ordered. "What have you been doing?"

Lairen shrugged. "Well, as you know, I work at Apollo Café and I've been around here and there. What have you been doing?" Not that he really cared. Or did he?

"Oh, well I—"

"Lairen," Mr. Perry interrupted. "I'm so sorry that we lost contact over all these years. I want you to know that wasn't my idea. Your mother had her own ideas about what was best and I—"

Lairen cut him off. "She's dead now, you know."

Gabriel Perry's eyes widened. He glanced at Rachael and back to Lairen. "No, I didn't know that. I'm...I'm sorry to hear that."

Again, Lairen shrugged. "Don't be. She was an awful person."

"Ah, yes," Gabriel agreed. "Unfortunately, she was."

The waiter came with their food and everyone dug in.

After his first bite, Lairen's demeaner thawed a bit. He looked over at Rachael. "Good choice of restaurant, little sister. This is the best Chinese food I've eaten in...well, ever."

Rachael smiled. "Thanks, I'm glad you like it!"

The three of them went back to eating for a bit, then Gabriel spoke up.

"Do you remember anything of your childhood when I was still a part of it?"

Lairen nodded. "Yeah, actually. I remember playing in a park with my mother glowering at us while you pushed me on a swing, but that's about it."

Gabriel nodded. "Yes. She wasn't happy that we were in a public place in case you exhibited some sort of magic and freaked out the humans

446

nearby. But there was no danger of that. You were still much too young for magic to have developed."

"And," he looked over at Rachael with a smirk, "I remember the cupcake incident."

She smiled. "Yeah, you told me before."

"Cupcake incident?" Gabriel asked, a confused look on his face.

"You have two more sisters," Rachael said in an abrupt change of topic. "Emma and Cara. They're twins."

At that last comment, Lairen perked up. "Twins! Now that's interesting." He looked at Gabriel. "Do twins run in your family? They're certainly not very common among the Elfae."

"No, not on my side. They run in my wife, Amelia's family, but not for a few generations. I think the last twins were her great, great uncles," Gabriel replied.

"You should meet them; Emma and Cara, I mean, not the great, great uncles. They'd like you," Rachael said.

Lairen tilted his head and gave her a look. "I'm not the most likeable or sociable guy, as you well know."

Rachael shrugged. "We didn't get acquainted in the best of circumstances. We could try it again. And I know Cara and Emma and Mom would love to have you come over for a dinner. Or we could meet up somewhere if—"

"Slow down, sweetheart," her father admonished. "You're getting excited and tripping all over yourself." He laughed. "You remind me of Megan."

Lairen grinned. "I know her. The girl from the café this morning, right?"

Rachael nodded. "Yes. Megan works with us."

"And by us you mean you and that girl with the dark red hair."

"Skye. Her name is Skye."

"Yeah, well, she doesn't like me very much. The look on her face this morning was daggers."

"Well, she is an Assassin," Rachael laughed. "But she'll give you a second chance."

"Gee, thanks. I'm honored." Lairen rolled his eyes.

"So," Gabriel interjected. "Will you come for dinner one night?"

"Yeah," Lairen replied, surprising himself. "I will."

"Great!" Rachael grinned. "And eventually you'll have to meet Tristan again, this time on better terms, and Aidan and Mr. Preston and—"

"Wait, wait!" Lairen held up a hand and laughed at her enthusiasm. "One thing at a time. I've barely agreed to meeting your sisters."

"YOUR sisters," Rachael corrected him.

"Yeah, okay. My sisters."

By the end of their meal and conversation, Lairen was surprised to find that two hours had flown by. The conversation had grown more and more fluid and easy and by the end of their time together he was surprised at the lightness in his step and his mood. Perhaps this was an opportunity. Perhaps he could allow these people, his family, to become an actual part of his life. He didn't fool himself though, it wouldn't be entirely easy. He had many years of going it alone, but he was willing to give it a try. In fact. He was looking forward to it.

About the Author

SUZANN FORTUNATO GREW UP IN THE SOUTH-west; riding horses, taking dance classes and reading books. Horses were her first love, but eventually horses took a backseat to ballet. Suzann danced for many years with a local ballet company, but has since hung up her pointe shoes and moved on to writing as her creative expression of choice. She currently lives in Arizona with her husband and two adorable but noisy beagles.